Hidden Talents

Book 1 of the Bayou Talents Series

Edward Branley

COPYRIGHT

Cover art by Wendy Warrelmann

ISBN: 978-0-9967640-2-5

Second Paperback Edition

To the reader:

As much as the author would like to believe Magic and the Talents are real, this is a work of fiction. Names, characters, businesses, places, events and incidents are either the products of the author's imagination or used in a fictitious manner. Any resemblance to actual persons, living or dead, or actual events is purely coincidental.

For Helen...

Prologue

Five minutes to air is always hectic at Jay Hadley Ministries. Cecilia McIntyre, producer of the radio show, *Talk Now! With Jay Hadley*, settled into her chair adjacent to the studio. Cecilia's engineer and right-hand-woman, Annie, was already in position, manipulating the dials and switches on the control board. Cecilia hooked up the telephone headset and double-checked her computer. While her boss was on the air, she would screen the calls, Tweets, and Facebook comments, while pulling up sound files of past shows needed today. All hooked in now, Cecilia turned and smiled at Annie, who gave her a thumbs-up and continued her pre-show checklist.

Two minutes to air. The star of the show hurries from his office at one end of the suite to the studio at the other, all but ignoring the beautiful view of Lake Pontchartrain his suburban New Orleans location offered. The rent had to be paid, and that didn't happen if Hadley didn't get on the radio and ask for it. With a quick wave for the women preparing in the control room, Hadley took his place in the studio behind the microphone. Even though Hadley had a strong, radio-preacher's voice, he did not cut an imposing figure in person. At 5'7" and 160 pounds, he might still be able to run five miles a day at the age of 47, but he'd never be mistaken for the corporate CEO he was. This bothered Hadley during the few times he spent in quiet reflection, but not now. He was in his domain, in control, and ready for the world.

One minute to air. Hadley reviewed the various bullet

points Cecilia left on his desk. These outlines covered the topics he should use when doing the many off-the-cuff requests for donations he would make during the two-hour show. Chuckling at one particular line of attack listed, he looked up and waved at his producer and chief-of-staff, who beamed.

3:00pm CST. The satellite links are all on-line and the red "On Air" light above the door in Hadley's studio goes on. As the theme music and voice-over finish, the star begins his opening monologue.

"Good afternoon and welcome to '*Talk Now!*' I'm Jay Hadley, and I'll be here for the next two hours to say what I have to say and listen to what you have to say. My topic for today is 'Sharpshooting Sub-teens.' What's going on in our schools? We've got kids as young as eleven years old bringing guns to class and shooting down other students. The breakdown of the moral fiber of this nation is happening at an accelerated rate in these last days. I've got a lot to say about this, and I'm sure you do as well..."

As Hadley dug into the topic du jour, things got more active in the control room. Annie busied herself with level adjustments and verifying the links to the outside world. Cecilia's phone lines were already ringing off the hook, with both supporters and detractors alike trying to get through to Hadley. She received regular activity updates from the telemarketing center down the hall, letting her know phone activity and the dollar amount of pledges to the Ministry. She then passed this information to her boss' computer in the studio when she felt it appropriate. Grabbing a quick sip of her Diet Pepsi, she flipped the switch for an outside line.

"*Talk Now! With Jay Hadley.*"

"Yeah, I want to talk to the holy man!" The voice was male, late teens, and trying to growl like his favorite heavy-metal lead singer.

Cecilia sighed. She knew this one well. "Hi, Lonny. I thought I told you I wasn't going to let you on more than once every couple of weeks. You're calling back waayyy too early."

"Lonny is no longer. Only Destructor exists."

"Oh, sorry, that's right. I forgot that you only use your stage name these days. Still, "Destructor", I'm not ready for you today."

"I want to talk to the holy man today! Kids who kill is perfect for Deeee-struc-tttttor!!!" The young man's attempts to sound demonic were truly amusing Cecilia.

"OK, Lonny, stay on the line and I'll see what I can do." She hit the hold button on the console and looked up into the studio. The kid was entertaining and usually generated good donor response. A quick review of her "regular callers" file indicated that Lonny/Destructor not only generated response, but the response was of the immediate impact kind—credit card donations. Smiling inwardly, she turned up Hadley in her earphones to see where to work in the caller.

"...nothing but dope-smoking death-dealing Democrats poisoning the minds of our youth and leading us to situations like we saw on CNN yesterday. We're taking back the country, brothers and sisters, but it's not happening fast enough! I need your help, friends, to keep this Ministry on the air, fighting the fight for our youth!" Jay was on a roll today, Cecilia thought. She watched as he flipped the switch to run the theme music for the bottom half of the first hour, then keyed her intercom.

"Boss, do you want Lonny today?"

Hadley looked up from his notes. "Wasn't he just on day before yesterday?"

Cecilia frowned a bit through the glass. "Yeah, but he's got the right shtick for this topic, and he's hot to trot on line six."

"Hold him for just about the end of the show. If he's still there around 4:45, we'll do it. That'll be a great follow-through to the daily offer summary. If he hangs up, he loses his chance at fame. This show is a path to better things, even for the wannabe devil-worshipers who harass us." He smiled.

"OK, then, 4:45 it is." She killed the intercom and went back to the phone. "Lonny, sit tight for a while and we'll work you in."

"Very well. Destructor will consent to wait for the holy man..."

"Sure thing." She put him back on hold, gave Hadley a thumbs-up and went to the phones again. The callers were the usual mix of true believers, kids who objected to Hadley's opposition to heavy-metal music, non-Christians who felt the

Ministry preached intolerance, and just plain crazies. The calls usually worked themselves out—put on an "anti" call, fire up the phone lines, then a few true believer calls to get Hadley psyched up for the next crazy on the line.

The cycle ran true through the first hour, and into the second. There was no guest today, either in-studio or on the phone. Hadley continued on-message, and the phones were lighting up.

4:30 PM CST: Hadley clicks the intercom switch.

"Is Lonny still on hold?"

"Yup, he's on line six."

"OK, let's shift the live solicitation up, then I'll take him right after that."

"OK, boss." Cecilia popped the phone button, double-checked on Lonny, and then went back to the other phone lines. She needed to get some solid true believers on right after Lonny to keep the faithful pulling out their wallets. After she got a third caller on hold, she took a deep breath and listened as Hadley wound up the donation pitch.

"Brothers and Sisters, I must have your help for this Ministry to survive. I need you to give that $20 a month, or better yet, be that $1000 soldier for Christ we need to underwrite today's broadcast. If that's just something you can't do, then let's have two of you giving $500. I need to know you're backing me. These kids need to know you are there. We have to get the message of the Lord out before we have more children killing children!

"OK, speaking of out of control teenagers, we've got Destructor on the phone. Hello, Destructor, are you still there?"

"Hooollllyyyy Maaannnn." Lonny was pretty good at the evil voice bit. Hadley wasn't all that impressed, though.

"I'm not a 'holy man,' just a man doing Jesus' work on the radio."

"Hooollllyyyy Maaannnn, you do not know us. We will defeat your so-called 'God' and crush your religion!"

"Not a chance, Destructor. The only thing that's going to 'destruct' is your belief that you will succeed. I have the authority of the blood of Jesus Christ, and that gives me and all who believe in Him the power to bind you and yours and condemn your masters to the eternal pit!" Hadley's finger was poised right next to the 'panic button,' the switch that shuts off the signal in case a caller gets obscene. Lonny's file indicated that he never used improper radio language, but you never know with kids.

"Hooollllyyyy Maaaaannnnn, your God is worthless. Your life is worthless. You will be crushed like the sheep that you are. My master will be victorious. My master will come for you and destroy all you love and hold precious. My master will put bullets in the brains of your followers. My master..."

Hadley cut off the litany: "Destructor, I bind your threats and wash them away with the Blood of Jesus Christ. You and your master have no power here. The Risen Lord is forever!"

Almost as if it was rehearsed, Destructor began coughing when Hadley cut him off and began his counter-claims. Lonny regained his composure and snarled into the phone. "I would like to ask a question of the Holy Man."

"Ask away."

The question came, not in the "Destructor" voice, but Lonny's post-adolescent whine. "Why is it that you like to take vacations with married women who work for you???"

Hadley slammed his hand down on the "panic button" that controlled the seven-second-delay system. The public did not hear anything Lonny said past the word "vacations." Red-faced with rage, he turned and glared at Cecilia.

Cecilia was stunned. Lonny's profile had no record of being a Challenger to the Ministry. He never would have made it on the air in that case. No, something went terribly wrong just now. She was set up, and Hadley was furious. Ministry statistics showed that contributions regularly drop 20%-30% for half an hour after someone questions the Rev. Hadley's personal lifestyle or the way he handles Ministry money. Sure, some of the callers get through, but that's why Cecilia developed the caller profile database. The more "safe" calls she let flow through, the less the chances of something uncontrolled happening. Something like Lonny's question, generated ten seconds of dead air, and that was something that could not happen regularly.

Hadley recovered quickly, and began damage control.

"Destructor, you are history. You just can't use language like that on the radio. This is a family program with a family audience, and we just can't have that here." He glanced over at the computer monitor and hit a button.

"Joanne is on the line from Dallas. Go ahead, Joanne!"

A positive call from a true believer would pick things up, but Cecilia still saw the smoldering anger in Hadley's eyes. It was going to be a tough twenty minutes, but she had to keep the callers moving. She could figure out what went wrong later.

CHAPTER ONE

Beer on the Lakefront

Janet frowned as her friend pulled only one of the earbuds from his ears. "You're listening to that kook on the radio while we were hanging out, instead of me. Is his ass cuter than mine?"

Renard Alciatore smiled, leaned over, and grabbed two fresh beers from the cooler. Tossing one to his friend, he sat back on the sea wall and gazed out over Lake Pontchartrain. At a quarter-to-five, the New Orleans air was crisp and cool this sunny April afternoon. Renard (Ren to his friends) had been listening to *Talk Now! With Jay Hadley* in the car on the way to his bi-weekly stress break along the lake with his best friend Janet Julianne Garrison, whom he affectionately called "JJ". She frowned at him again. Having heard all he needed to, he took out the other earbud and turned off his MP3 player.

"I'm sorry JJ, I know I said I wouldn't listen to Hadley when we're here, but this is was something I just had to hear live. We knew a regular visitor to my website would get past the call-screener. And boy, did he get through. Made ol' Hadley hit the panic button big-time!"

Ren knocked back the rest of his beer and his ebony eyes glowed as the sun dipped to the horizon. He stood up and stretched his six-foot frame before reaching for another beer.

Janet frowned a third time. "I still don't get your obsession with a radio preacher. You're thirty-four years old. You're Catholic, you went to a Catholic school. You still go to a Catholic church. So the guy is a good target and he's probably fun to mess with. But you're taking this way too seriously these days. It's gone so far past simply being a guilty pleasure that it's not funny anymore, Ren."

JJ was a petroleum engineer and a practical sort of woman. She and Ren first met in graduate school at the University of New Orleans, both working on MBA degrees. Even thought she was married and seven years his senior, the two had bonded quickly and had become fast friends.

"JJ, this guy isn't really a radio preacher, he's a crook. He doesn't have a church, he's never been ordained by a respectable denomination, and he spends over a third of his two-hour show begging for money. Guess where that money goes? Straight into his own pocket, that's where! He's even got his own fan-page on Facebook!"

He paused while his eyes followed a sailing dinghy about a mile offshore on the lake. Then he finished expressing his thought: "Look, it's not really a religion thing; it's an honesty thing. This guy is taking money from old folks and lower middle-class families who buy into his line. If he was selling some product or legitimate service, that would be one thing. All he tells people is that they'll get blessed if they donate to him. That's as bad as the indulgence-sellers from Martin Luther's time. I like to think I'm making a small contribution to ridding the world of con men like this guy. That's all."

Janet was not all that impressed. "OK, that's all fine and dandy, Ren. But some of these fundie types aren't stable. You go messing with the wrong person and you're asking for trouble! Consider that, before getting too involved with bringing down kings."

Ren smiled sheepishly. "OK, point taken. I'll remember that. Wanna get something to eat?"

"Nah, I'd better get home. The boys have soccer tonight so Joe will want me home at a reasonable hour."

Ren smiled. Janet's husband Joe was as much his friend as JJ was. "OK, far be it for me to get in the way of marital and maternal bliss. Get on with yourself then."

“Yeah—seriously, Ren, I really want you to think about what I'm saying about this Hadley thing."

Ren grabbed her shoulder and pushed himself up. "Fine, I'll give it some thought. Really, I will."

She kissed him lightly on the cheek and touched his shoulder.

"See ya."

"Later."

Ren gathered up the cooler and headed back to his car—a 1970 Mustang Mach One. The car used to be his brother's, but he sold it to Ren about a year ago when he and his wife had their third child. It had been worth the trip to Seattle and back to get it. Ren's house on Moss Street, along Bayou St. John, was only five minutes away from his rendezvous at the lakeshore. He parked the car in front of the house and bounded up the walkway.

Ren's house was his home, office, and photography studio. Most of his work as a photographer had been on location, but he had converted his master bedroom on the first floor into a small professional studio for indoor work. He slid the cooler down the hall towards the kitchen and entered his office. People who did not know Ren would swear they had just walked into a computer company rather than the office of a photographer. Five computer systems were running: Ren's desktop workstation, a system dedicated to photo-scanning, editing, and composition; and three servers, for Ren's business and websites. While Ren had met many photographers who tended to shy away from computers, he fully embraced the technology. A substantial portion of his business was now derived from web design and development.

It had been a busy day for Ren before he had met up with Janet. The sigh he let out when he fell into his desk chair reflected his weariness. Skillfully spinning the trackball on his desktop system, he checked his email.

In addition to several messages related to soccer refereeing, a passion of Ren's second only to photography, there were a half-dozen messages from those in the know about Lonny's on-air antics with Jay Hadley that afternoon, as well as some business-related inquiries and a note from his brother.

He had no sooner settled in and begun to read through the day's correspondence than his phone flashed, indicating that someone was paging him with a new message on Kik. Since most Kik users are anonymous, his curiosity was piqued:

"Hi, I have information you might find useful. Information about Jay Hadley."

Interesting! In spite of no simple way to identify the sender, he replied anyway.

"Oh yeah. And what sort of info would that be? :-)"

Ren usually ended messages with a "smiley-face" icon because it tended to put at ease whoever he was to talking with.

"Lonny was right, you know. Hadley paid to fly his copy-editor and her kids to Dallas at the same time as he was doing a public appearance in Fort Worth about two months ago. Had a teenager take the kids to Six Flags all day that Saturday and they spent the day going at it like rabbits."

The mystery messenger had Ren's full attention now:

"Ok, I can confirm the travel arrangements for this woman and her kids, but how do I confirm your allegations of sexual impropriety?"

There was a pause. Just enough to make Ren wonder about the truthfulness of the person at the other end.

"Hadley likes to play with SnapChat."

That statement took Ren aback. SnapChat was a photo-sharing app for mobile devices most popular with teens. The idea is to send photos that only stay on the recipient's phone for a few seconds.

"Are you saying you have pics of ol' Jay with this woman?"

"Yes."

Trying to remain calm, Ren continued:

"Great, when can I get these files from you?"

"Not yet. Remember Woodward and Bernstein during Watergate? It's the same deal here. You have to build up to it, follow the trail. I can guide you but you have to do the work yourself."

Trying not to get annoyed, Ren pressed forward:

"Are you saying you're too close to the situation to become directly involved?"

Another pause.

"In a way, yes."

Ren could feel the tension of the person at the other end almost oozing through the phone. One of the reasons he enjoyed chatting on these programs so much was that he had a gift for "feeling" emotions online, even if the party was in another country. His next question would confirm his instinct to be right.

"Can we meet?"

"Eventually, not yet though."

"How do I know you're not just jerking me around or, worse still, setting me up?"

Ren was satisfied that his instincts were correct, but it didn't hurt to ask.

"Check your email in a little while. You'll find some interesting reading that will establish my credentials with you."

There was no further response from the mystery messenger. Ren leaned back in his chair, closed his eyes, and tried to use his intuition to sense whether he was on to something here. Or whether he was walking into a trap.

Had Ren been able to see the face of the person on the other side of the connection he would have known immediately that this was legit.

***

Cecilia McIntyre had worked for Jay Hadley Ministries for five years, but she had never seen Hadley as angry or as upset as he had been after this afternoon's show. She had spent 15 minutes in Hadley's plush office being screamed at for allowing Lonny to get through to the show and embarrass him. Worse still, he did his screaming in the presence of a representative of the publisher of all his books.

Feeling thoroughly humiliated, Cecilia hurried out of the office and headed for the little pub she and her friends frequented regularly on Thursday nights. Even though this was a Tuesday evening, she was still welcomed as a regular and she proceeded to gulp down several glasses of Chardonnay.

The wine had kicked-in by the time she arrived at her apartment in Old Metairie and her feelings of humiliation had turned to anger. She activated her computer and quickly accessed the personal web page of Renard Alciatore, whom she knew was the webmaster of the most active anti-Hadley site on the Internet.

She made note of Alciatore's account on "Kik", the service offering the closest thing to "total anonymity" and messaged Alciatore, dropped some teaser information on him, then emailed him some interesting inter-office memos from the Ministry via an anonymous email server. She was more than a bit good with computers; covering her tracks was no problem at all. Neither Hadley nor Alciatore would know this information would have come from her unless she decided she would want them to know. She wasn't ready to risk her job by identifying herself to Alciatore.

She chuckled inside then shut her system down before

curling up on her couch to watch TV. Alciatore and his buddies had been playing small-time faith-busters up until now. She had just moved them into the big leagues.

Ren was on his second reading of the information emailed from his mysterious chatter. None of the memos' contents was what anyone could call "earth-shattering", but it was all juicy enough to be considered annoying by Hadley and his staff. If this were not merely an isolated acquisition by his newfound chat source, this individual could become very useful as a conduit of data about the Ministry.

Using a little cut-and-paste wizardry, Ren integrated components of the email memos he had received into the "What's new" section of his blog. This was a big step for Ren: prior to this point the entire contents of the site had been compiled from things Hadley had said on the air. Various rumors and innuendo regarding Hadley's personal life were always reported as third-party hearsay, repeating what managed to get out on the show before Hadley cut them off. Now, by publishing the contents of these memos, even in the paraphrased format Ren was using, he was entering directly into an effort to bring down Jay Hadley Ministries.

Ren took a deep breath, got up from his desk, and walked quietly through the house to the front door. The hot humid night air seemed to hit him in the face as he descended the front steps and headed towards the bank of the bayou across the street. The waxing moon was a fingernail crescent, only barely illuminating the surface of the water. Ren sat down at the water's edge and sighed, deeply. He had always thought that the content of his website was aggressive and productive. But now all he could hear was JJ's voice in the back of his mind, warning him that going after Hadley might be more than he could handle.

Still, if he did not publish this information, he was all but assured that his source would not provide him with any further goodies. It was clear now that there was someone inside the Ministry who shared his sentiments. How could he not press forward with this data?

He tossed a twig into the water and listened for the splash before turning back to the house. Back inside, he leaned over his desk chair, Ren moved the trackball and clicked the keyboard to send the new Hadley information into publication via the server. He had not even sat down. He closed his work computer and headed for the shower. And it was time for a beer or two.

The next morning Ren awoke with a start. Even though he had no early appointments that day, his alarm was still set for its usual wake-up time and he could hear his alarm clock chiming. As he rolled over to switch the alarm off, he realized that the chimes were not from his clock but from his web server system. He climbed out of bed and stumbled sleepily into his study. The chiming became louder as he approached the server and a quick glance of the system's activity report from the time since he had published the new Hadley information showed that not only had the number of visitors to the website increased, but now someone was trying to make a crude attempt to shut down the server by repeatedly issuing the same request immediately one after another from multiple locations on the Internet. Ren made a few quick modifications to the server's configuration to deal with the problem and the chiming ceased. Ren could now turn his attention to his workstation computer to check his emails and, hopefully, find out what had been going on while he had been resting.

His server's email filters had been doing their job by removing the usual annoyance emails sent to him by Hadley's supporters. His inbox was thus left with merely a few notes from friends. Among them, one from his niece in Seattle and another from one of his fellow Hadley-bashers from Abita Springs, on Lake Pontchartrain's north shore.

This last email congratulated Ren on publishing confirmation that Jay Hadley Ministries had withdrawn its application for full membership of the Association for Broadcast Ministries (ABM), a watchdog organization formed after the Rev. Jim Bakker had been imprisoned for his Praise the Lord (PTL) network dealings. When he had published this the evening before, Ren had regarded this fact as only a small item of news. But his north-shore acquaintance, who went by the moniker "Professor Apocalypse", went into some detail to explain that ABM certification was becoming increasingly important to a TV- or radio-based ministry and that Hadley's reticence to become a full member could only indicate that his financial dealings and records might not stand up to independent scrutiny.

While this revelation might not be considered enough to deal a major blow to Hadley's fund-raising efforts, he considered it to be a setback that would keep him from joining the ranks of the well-respected media ministries, such as Dr. James Dobson's *Focus on the Family* program. As "Professor Apocalypse" pointed out, anything that held back JHM from moving into that top echelon of ministries would serve only to incense the Rev. Hadley.

Ren didn't know whether to laugh or cry while reading his colleague's explanation of why his web server had been "under attack" for the previous couple of hours. Professor Apocalypse's knowledge of what this ABM situation was about made him feel better in that Hadley would probably figure he had been Ren's source of information. Today's *Talk Now!* show might just be the most entertaining one of the month.

***

The staff of Jay Hadley Ministries was having a most uncomfortable morning, especially Cecilia McIntyre, who sat in her boss's office while listening to him carry on about the impact of Ren Alciatore's newly published information on the Ministry's financial position.

"OK. I need a major diversion today, Cee." Hadley was pacing behind his desk, stopping occasionally to look out over the lake as he spoke. The view was spectacular, with cars darting in both directions along Lake Pontchartrain Causeway. Cecilia could almost see a shiver go up Hadley's spine as he contemplated the possibility that the day might come when he would not be able to meet the expenses on this plush office suite and they would be forced to find a less opulent home for the Ministry.

"We haven't had a full-blown exorcism in, what, six or seven weeks, right? See what you can line up for me."

Cecilia cringed inwardly. Of all the things she did "for the good of the Ministry", this was one of those things that really turned her stomach. What Hadley wanted to "line up" was someone who was "possessed" with demons that Hadley could cast out. Cecilia would arrange for aspiring actors to play the role of the "possessed" and Hadley would play the person along before eventually bringing them to the Lord, live, for all the True Believers to hear and, hopefully, for them to pay for.

She nodded to him. "Yeah, I was planning to do one next week, so I've got a few people already briefed. Let me track one of them down and see what we can do. Would you prefer a male or a female?"

Hadley grinned. "Oh, female. Definitely. I want a real gut-twister of an exorcism, with a total focus on the positive. An exorcism gives us a great excuse not to take negative calls without appearing to be hiding from the issues."

He stood, reached for the phone, and gave her a stern look. "Let's have no nightmares this afternoon, OK, Cee?"

Cecilia nodded again, stood up, and returned to her office down the hall from Hadley's. She was still reeling from the dressing-down she had received from Hadley the day before. She flopped down in her chair, reached for the phone, and punched in the number of a dinner-theater actress who was about to endure a sudden case of demonic possession.

Forty-five minutes later, the feature event for that afternoon's show was all planned. The best exorcisms they had staged on the radio had been those in which the "victim" had a concise script and a background story worked out beforehand with Cecilia. She kept Hadley in the dark about the specifics. That way, he was forced to pull the facts out, little by little. Any prior knowledge of the facts would risk blowing the apparent spontaneity of the call. Hadley was good at this, and if the "victim" could keep up with him the whole experience could be a significant revenue-generator for the Ministry.

Of course, there were occasional real exorcisms on the show, too: people who just called in genuinely looking for help. But those made Cecilia very nervous as there was no way to control the flow of the call, making it difficult to get scheduled breaks in. Sometimes the real calls worked out well. But more often they fizzled out as the caller grew silent or simply hung up.

Annie knocked on Cecilia's open door, smiling at her.

"You OK?" She asked.

"Yeah. For the moment." Cecilia sighed. "We're 'exorcising' today."

"Well, at least the 'simulations' show the public what's at stake in fighting the forces of evil in this world," Annie said with a wry smirk.

"Yeah, but all you handle is the tech," responded Cecilia, mockingly tossing a pencil at Annie.

"You're good at this Cecilia. You'll do just fine!" Annie waved, turned and continued down the hall.

Even though Hadley was just a few feet down the hall, Cecilia sent an email to him to let him know that everything was set up for the show. She was not interested in being reminded again about yesterday, so she shut her door and used email to control her communication with the outside world. A quick check of Twitter and Facebook showed that Ren Alciatore had been a busy bee the previous night, which more than explained Hadley's desire for a big-time diversion this afternoon. Using her word-processor program, Cecilia began to compile "talking points" for Hadley's unscripted pledge-breaks that focused on defending the ministry from outside attack. These were always presented in general terms, avoiding the recognition of specific attacks but acknowledging that there were people who were trying to bring down the Ministry.

After an hour of typing and revising, Cecilia sat back, rubbed her eyes, and smiled a satisfied smile as she reviewed her handiwork.

She was just about to email Jay the file she had completed, but decided to print it out and deliver it by hand. As much as she didn't want to face further criticism today, she also did not want Hadley or anyone in the office to perceive her as a wimp. The document she was pulling from the printer was good stuff. She had nothing to be ashamed of. Things had gone awry yesterday and she was now taking steps to put everything back on track.

Cecilia stood up from her desk and walked the short distance down the hall to Hadley's office. Seeing his door open she went in unannounced to find Hadley on the phone. The twang of the voice emanating from the speaker-phone made the caller immediately recognizable to her. It was Anita Delatorre of Marcus-Kayson, one of the world's largest publishers of Christian books. Cecilia slid her document onto Hadley's desk as she listened-on on the caller.

"...Okay then, Jay, I'm on my way to Love Field in a few minutes. I'll make sure to stop by your office as soon as my other business is finished. Y'all have a good afternoon and hope the show goes well today!"

Hadley was smiling his "charm-the-ladies" smile, even though the conversation was on the phone. "Great, Anita. Call me on my cell when you get done. Maybe we can grab a bite to eat tonight."

"Wonderful Jay. Ciao!" Cecilia smiled inwardly as she visualized the big-haired blonde Dallas débutante on the other end of the connection as she turned and walked out the door. Hadley called after her.

"Hey, Cee. Make reservations for me at *August* tonight, willya? Thanks babe." She decided not to turn around but instead gave him a thumbs-up and headed back to her office to grab her purse before going out to get some lunch.

CHAPTER TWO
Coffee and Donuts

"I don't like doing business in such a public place, any casual observer of this conversation would conclude that you're from out of town. Locals don't wear dark clothes when they eat beignets at Café du Monde. Most ladies don't like powdered sugar all over an expensive suit," sniffed the twenty-something man to the woman seated across from him.

William Ryan was talking to Anita Delatorre, who had arrived in New Orleans the night before.

"I seriously doubt you have to worry about being seen in public with me at a coffee stand. Besides, my reputation would be in greater jeopardy if I were to be seen in your usual haunts in this city." Her blonde hair was pulled back severely and her navy-blue business suit was conservative even by old New Orleans' standards.

"Hmm...I dare say, under those outrageously simple clothes you have on, that there is a body which would fit right in with my preferred sort of establishment."

Even though he had lived in America for the past ten years, Ryan's voice still maintained a hint of his Belfast origins. "So, what is important enough to draw you away from Dallas?"

"We've come across some obstacles in our long-range marketing plan for a Christian preacher, right here in town, out by the lake. The guy's written some trade books for us and his show does well in Christian outlets, but we see him moving to a more mainstream market. He's great on the end-times stuff, and we want to move him into the homeschooling resources. There's a solid base for homeschooling resources here in Louisiana, and we can build on that nationally."

Her features took on a harsh expression, yet one totally in keeping with her demeanor. "The problem is, his divorce from his first wife was messy. The records were sealed but an Internet-based skeptic group has acquired them. He also has a challenge keeping his dick in his pants."

"And you need this group handled?" The young man sipped his strong café-au-lait with an eerie calmness. "Internet, huh? Sounds like you need a 15-year-old hacker, not me."

Anita smiled inwardly. Ryan was 22 and looked like he could pass for 15. "No, we've got that angle covered. I need to get down to the root of the problem. Can we do business?" Her smile was so sweet that the couple in the next table might have thought she had just propositioned the young man.

"How many?"

"Five definite. Possibly three others." Anita wiped the sugar from her fingers and pulled a small envelope from her jacket. "They are to be handled in order. It's possible that the activist group will ease up after the first one or two. Your fee is for all five in any case."

Ryan looked concerned. "I don't like contact with a client in the middle of a job."

"I'll get word to you indirectly. The details are on the second note. You will proceed after the first two depending on the photo placed on the website listed here. You stop when the 'no-go' photo is displayed. I have total control of that site, so there will be no possibility of miscommunication."

Ryan nodded. "I'll let you know tomorrow. Are you going back to Dallas immediately or can I tempt you into coming out with me later?"

Anita smiled. "I'd love to go dancing but if I was spotted at The Bourbon Pub, it would be my ass at work. Maybe if I ever switch to a mainstream publisher."

"If you do, then you won't be doing business with me, that's for sure. Mainstream publishers don't have the need for damage control that you Christian types do." Ryan's grin was totally mirthless.

Anita maintained her sugar-sweet grin. "This is quite true. But the pay is darned good. For both of us."

Ryan's gaze turned serious.

"Doesn't it bother you to work for people who so completely hate what you are?"

She smiled.

"Well dear, I could ask you the same question, since you are taking their money. But I'll answer you. These people pay well, and the best way to keep tabs on your enemies is to keep them within arm's length."

"What are these people to you personally? You could use your Talents for so many other purposes than this. Your interest in these people just doesn't make any sense."

Anita's smile turned serious again. "You see, sugar, it isn't merely my own personal interest. I have acquaintances that take an interest in these people and I report their movements to those acquaintances."

Ryan became startled: "You mean someone with Talents has some kind of authority over you?"

"Yes."

"I've heard of such things, of course. But I have never encountered them before." His eyes had widened during this last exchange. Anita put her hand on his for a few seconds, and then looked directly in his eyes.

"Will, you are good at what you do. You are well-trained in the use of your Talents. But you're young and there are many things you have yet to learn about those Talents. Always remember that, as you go about your business."

Ryan nodded, as one would expect from a young man aware of his immortality. Anita smiled backed at him and patted his hand as she stood to leave.

"There's a phone number in there that goes to a voicemail which will page me when a message is left. I know your rules, but this is a just-in-case thing." She left and continued on her way without looking back.

Ryan sat silent for some time. Eventually, he opened the packet Anita had left for him. Inside, was a set of bio-sheets, one for each of his targets: Three on the north shore, one in the city, and one over on the Gulf Coast. His instincts told him to do two of the north shore targets first, head over to Bay St. Louis for the one on the coast, back to Mandeville for the third north shore guy, finally heading back to the city to finish the job. Anita's instructions were specific as to their order, however; he would have to do the targets on the north shore first, then back to the city for the third, and out to the coast and then finishing in Mandeville.

Will sighed. New Orleans is a city full of possibilities for a young man who likes other men, but Anita's job meant he'd be going into the suburbs. As much as New Orleans the city lived by the motto of "let the good times roll", its suburbs were extremely conservative. There was no way he could drive the thirty miles back to the French Quarter and back, while maintaining the low profile required to complete the job. Ah well, the sacrifices we make for our careers. He waved to the waiter for another coffee, then he went back to studying the bio-sheets.

***

Ren did not care for driving on the Causeway. Twenty-four miles of nothing but flat water and the thump-thump, thump-thump of the tires as they hit the expansion joints on the bridge. It was enough to drive a sane man to distraction. Still, there were tons of opportunities for photography jobs in Mandeville and Covington, given the suburban migration that took place in the 80s and early 90s from the city and the south shore suburbs. Besides, two of his best resources for the JHM website lived across the lake, so he could easily dovetail business with a little Internet fun.

Well, he thought, it used to be two of his best resources. Nick Thibodeaux was a former Coast Guardsman who listened to *Talk Live!* every day like clockwork. He was a smoker, and Nick and Ren certainly shared more than one pitcher of beer on Ren's adventures across Lake Pontchartrain. Still, the news that Nick had dropped dead from a heart attack in the middle of lunch the previous day had come as a shock to Ren. He decided to go to the Thibodeaux house after the photo shoot to give Margie a hug and what little comfort he could offer. Ren had not planned on seeing Nick's grave this trip over, however; his first stop when he finally got off the Causeway would be a coffee shop in Covington to see his other blogging resource.

"Annie's Attic" was no name for a coffee house, thought Ren. Its Highway-190 location made it a busy place every morning, though, so the name didn't hurt. Commuters heading towards the city stopped-by in droves for their premium coffees, which is why Ren usually tried to schedule his meetings with his north shore buddies for a little after the morning rush.

Anybody still on the north shore after nine o'clock would not be getting into the city until lunchtime anyway, so Covington traffic was a little lighter by then. Ren pulled his car into the parking lot, locked it, and headed into Annie's with a spring in his step.

James Michael Kahn III, "Trip" to his friends, waved Ren straight to the table. "I got yours right here. You are so predictable on Wednesday mornings that I can even have your coffee waiting for you, still steaming." Kahn's smile was infectious, and he was good at charming anyone from the most obnoxious police juror to the most conservative Rabbi back on St. Charles Avenue.

Trip was just a year older than Ren and was the cultural opposite of his late north shore partner, Nick Thibodeaux, in Internet religious mayhem. A lawyer by profession, Trip Kahn had given up most of his active practice several years earlier to join his father's real estate development business. The rapid growth of St. Tammany Parish meant that more north shore residents need fast-food restaurants and drug stores, and Trip's father was the man to see when you wanted either in your neighborhood. The elder Kahn no longer ventured out of uptown New Orleans, leaving Trip to supervise operations on the north shore. Trip was not one for a coat, a tie, and an office; he preferred to do his mornings' business from Annie's, stop by his house to change batteries on his cell-phone, then head to a coffee-shop in Mandeville for his afternoons.

"Well, Trip, you seem to have managed to make the transition to a Mandeville country gentleman, but I don't know if I'll ever be able to cope with living anywhere but within the city. Even when I come up here for a shoot or to see you guys, I feel like I've left a piece of me behind. I just don't feel right."

Trip laughed at his friend. "It's just you artsy-fartsy types.

Harder for you to leave what you're used to." His expression turned serious: "I'm going over to see Margie this afternoon. It's still hard to believe, Ren."

"Yeah, I'm still numb about it."

Trip's face brightened immediately. "Well. I'm not Irish, but I do know it's our time to celebrate his memory by going forward. What's our next fun project on the blog?"

"As usual, you have managed to say just the right thing at the right time." The spark in Ren's eyes had returned.

"I've got a line inside the ministry, Trip." Ren handed over hard copies of the messages from his mystery contact.

Trip read through the manuscript, reviewed the documents, and then repeated the process. After the second reading, he looked up at Ren and asked, "Have you considered the possibility that this is disinformation? Or, at worse, a set-up?"

"Yeah, I have. But I'm inclined to believe it's genuine. It's just instinct though, so I wanted you to have a look. Us artsy-fartsy types aren't as suspicious as you lawyer types," said Ren, grinning.

Trip laughed as he stood up to order another coffee.

"Well, my initial instinct is that they're genuine, too. Is she serious about pictures?"

"I think so. Remember Jimmy Swaggart? Some of these guys are pretty kinky."

"OK then. Well, you did a good job of sanitizing the first installment of this, so you should work the rest of this material into the blog on a staggered basis. You obviously shook the shit out of Hadley with that first bit, since he did an exorcism the next day."

"You think the two were related?" Ren was puzzled.

"You bet! Either God really is on his side or he's got a helluva system for putting those together quickly. Think about it Ren. There's no better way to deflect all criticism of the Ministry in general or Hadley in particular than by a troubled soul in need of Jay's specific brand of assistance. And that makes for awesome radio. One of these days we are going to find out how he pulls those off. It's got to be paid actors, but the system is what I'm interested in. It's not rehearsed--not with Hadley at least. I'm sure of that. His reactions, his on-air confusion, that sort of thing. It's not forced; he really doesn't seem to know what's coming next. Thing is, the rest of the show is too controlled, which means someone there knows what's coming next, and keeps the lid on it."

Ren was just nodding as he absorbed his friend's comments. "Well, perhaps my mystery friend can help us in that department."

"She just might be able to."

"How do you know it's a she?"

"Think about what we know of the staff, Ren. The only men there are Jay and his CFO."

"That's true."

"Besides, you were contacted initially via a mobile chat program. You know as well as I do that guys don't message guys using those things."

"Well, no, not usually. At least not straight guys." Ren was smiling broadly.

"You got it sport. I take it you tried to back-track the source of the messages?"

"Yes, but she's good at anonymity."

"Well you're more of a computer geek than I'll ever be, Ren. I do have a guy that comes to work on the office computers that might know something you and I don't. Lives in Metairie, so maybe we can involve him if we want to pursue that."

Ren looked thoughtful as he nodded again.

"No, let's keep this one close. If this is genuine, which I believe it is, we're going to want to keep a tight lid on the source. Even to the extent of people who have no interest in JHM. After all, the best way to keep a secret is not to tell anyone."

"Definitely." Trip raised his hand momentarily as his cell-phone chimed.

"Let me take this one, OK?"

Ren got up to order a regular coffee as his friend listened intently to the voice on his phone. He took the long way back to the table, stopping to check out some of the photography on the walls.

"That's a new photo of the Cathedral," he thought.

Looking at the little card attached to it, he noticed that a

Mandeville lady he had heard of had shot the photo. She was your basic empty-nest housewife who was trying her hand at a new career. Judging by the quality of the composition, she was on her way to at least having fun with it.

Ren's leisurely stroll around Annie's wound him back to their table just as Trip hit the "end" button on his phone.

"Ren, I've got to run. All hell is breaking loose with a Slidell project. That was a friend of mine who works at a church over there. It's amazing what she picks up just by keeping her door open as parishioners come in and out of the office." Trip grinned, and then stood and gathered up his coffee with his phone.

"Let's take a steady pace on this stuff, Ren, and see where it leads you. What you've shown me could be a significant break; you should start writing a journal of what happens from now on. If this gal comes through with some good information you could write a book about the experience of how you brought down a ministry! Take care, my friend. Email me later, when you have worked up the next installment."

Trip Kahn strolled out of Annie's without looking back, as was his style. He walked over to his luxury SUV and climbed in, not noticing the young man sitting in the rented sedan on the other side of the parking lot.

***

Not that he would have seen him anyway. William Ryan had taken a number of precautions well above and beyond those things a good cop does during a stake-out. Ryan had all but made himself invisible to those around him from the moment his car had left the Causeway that morning and had made its way a few houses down the street from Kahn's home. Ryan's success as an assassin was based on his ability to use his Talents two-fold: first was his ability to conceal his presence in the area almost completely; and second was his expertise in creating "accidents" so that his victims apparently suffered some tragic fluke of nature. No bullets, knives, or poisons from this hit man. His stock-in-trade was to create heart attacks, slip-and-falls, choking deaths and auto accidents. Ryan thought of himself rather as an artist in the composition of the perfect automobile accident. His last foster-father was a cop, and often the young man would proofread his auto-accident reports.

"Yes, accidents are an art form," thought Ryan.

They were an art form he loved to develop and to perfect. As he watched Kahn pull his SUV out of the parking lot, Ryan's mind moved quickly, taking in the surrounding traffic flow, road conditions, and the position of Kahn's vehicle. He knew it would take a large vehicle at high speed to wreak significant damage to the navy-blue luxury SUV. And here came an 18-wheeler from the north to oblige him. Focusing his vision, both inner and peripheral, on the driver of the rig, he gave a mental shrug and the driver's heart stopped beating. Another mental shrug and the rig accelerated, swerving across the two southbound lanes before sideswiping a car heading straight for the side of Kahn's vehicle. The rig collided like a T-bone with the SUV and continued to plow forward, pushing the SUV in front of it. Ryan skillfully guided the rig mentally into a light pole on the other side of the street, crumpling the SUV like a tin can, with Kahn inside.

The sound of the impact startled everyone in every store in the little strip mall nearby. Ren and the barista in the coffee shop dashed outside to see what had happened. Ren was horrified to see his friend's SUV pinned and crushed by the massive rig. He yelled out at the girl to call 911, and he darted over to the wreck to see if he could assist Trip. There was no hope; Trip's head rolled sideways, his neck snapped by the impact. Ren checked on the truck driver but it was obvious he was dead also, but not from the force of the accident. He was slumped over the steering wheel, bleeding slightly, but the truck had not suffered enough physical damage to cause the driver's death.

Emergency crews were on the scene within moments, but there was nothing for them to do but to clean up. Ren sat on the curb, trembling. The girl from Annie's brought him a glass of iced water and occasionally walked out from the shop to make sure Ren was all right. The police spoke with them both, but neither he nor the girl could contribute anything to explain why the morning had gone so terribly wrong.

The one person who could explain things continued to sit all but motionless in the parking lot as everyone hustled and bustled around him. Ryan was stretched out low in his seat, not so much to hide from anyone, but for his need to release tension and relax after such an extensive and intense use of his Talents. He had not eaten anything since the previous night, so he could keep his mind sharp and focused on the task to come. His throat was parched; the last drink he had had was a cup of tea before driving over from the city early that morning. He had not wanted to cause a full bladder to distract him, either, so he had abstained from drinking anything else. Reaching over to the passenger seat he grabbed a bottle of spring water and guzzled it rapidly. He scanned the scene of the wreck and noticed a familiar face on the curb. Yes, that was indeed Renard Alciatore! His mind began racing with the possibilities but he checked himself mentally, remembering his instructions to wait until after the first two for a go-ahead signal.

"Damn it, I could cut down the timing of this job dramatically with this opportunity," thought Will. He sighed, opened another bottle of water, and sipped slowly on this one while he waited for the emergency services to finishing clearing the carnage he had created.

Ren had to call his client and cancel the photo-shoot; he was entirely too shaken-up to be productive and there was no way he could face Rachel Kahn today, his horror of what he had seen earlier would be too obvious to her.

He considered checking into a motel on this side of the lake so he could avoid having to dwell on the accident all the way back to the city. But he decided just to jump into his car and get home. The 45-minute drive was terribly difficult for him, but he managed eventually to pull into his driveway, make his way to the kitchen, and knock back two large shots of whiskey before lying down on his bed until sleep finally overtook him.

Ryan decided to follow him back to his home in Faubourg St. John. Even though he had not checked-in to determine the future status of his current assignment, he decided to capitalize on knowing Alciatore's whereabouts to begin formulating a plan. A photographer was likely to be more of a challenge in some ways, because a target of that profession has no set daily routine.

"But the lack of any routine was an opportunity in itself," thought Will, as it would be easy to find just the right set of circumstances to chalk up another success.

When it was clear that Alciatore was not about to leave home anytime soon, Ryan returned to his suite at the Bourbon Orleans Hotel. He went over to the expensive notebook computer on his desk, and connected it to the hotel's Wi-Fi to check the site that Anita had given him as their main contact point. He found the Evangelical Christian theme of the site a little repugnant, but he clicked his way to the specific page that contained the message for him. According to his instructions there would be either one of two photographs on the page: an illustration of a cross encircled by clouds would be the signal to stop and await further instructions; while an aerial photo of Old Jerusalem would be the signal to proceed to the next target.

The sight of the gleaming dome of the Al-Aqsa Mosque in Jerusalem staring back at him from the computer screen caused Will's pulse to race. Sure, he was being paid handsomely for the job no matter whether or not he continued. The fun was in the game, not the money.

CHAPTER THREE

Mortality Reminders

"I'm sorry to hear about your friends. Are you OK?"

The message on "Kik" was from someone named Isis and the last time that name had flashed on his phone, he had received some very interesting information about Jay Hadley Ministries.

"I'm better, thanks. It's a shock, but I came straight home and slept through this afternoon. The funeral will be tomorrow so I'll see his family then. There's no way I could face his wife today after seeing him trapped in the car like that."

"I've never lost someone like that before. I can't even begin to imagine how terrible that must be. Well, to change the subject, did you get those files I sent?"

"Yes, I did. In fact it's what Trip and I were discussing just before the accident. I wanted him to look over the material before I went forward with it on the site."

"What? You don't trust me?"

"Well, I was never a big fan of Ronald Reagan, but he was quite right when he said 'Trust but verify' :-)"

"I agree. That's what I would do in your position. And what was your friend's reaction?"

"His instincts were the same as mine. We both feel – well, we both felt – that you are telling the truth and that the documents are legitimate."

"Oh they are... you can count on that."

"My intuition is usually pretty good, but this is potentially very embarrassing to the Rev., and Trip felt that Hadley went into damage-control after that last memo you gave me. He said there was a direct connection between that exorcism the next day and the website."

"Oh, there was. Your friend was right on the money."

"How are you so certain of this?"

":-)"

Ren tried to follow-up, but there was no further response. He shook his head and went into the kitchen to fix something to eat. A light dish of pasta was just what he needed to re-charge after the trauma of the day. He was feeling far from a hundred percent but at least he had stopped trembling. He settled back down at the computer and began to compose the next update to the blog. His email and his Facebook page were flooded with messages expressing sympathy for the loss of his friend. At least one television channel had run extensive coverage of the accident on their noon, 5pm, and 6pm newscasts; the reasons being both the severity of the accident and the status of one of the victims, who was from one of the wealthiest families in the New Orleans metro area.

Ren tossed all the sympathy email into a special folder he created in his account. He would compile a list of everyone in that folder and send a generic reply to acknowledge their kind words.

He did, however, answer just one email immediately:

To: JanJuNOLA@gmail.com

'Allo love. Thanks for worrying about me. Am OK at the moment, will go to Gentilly tomorrow for the graveside service, then going out with some of Trip's friends. Intend on getting very, very drunk. XOXO.

He clicked Send and went back to work.

While Ren was working at the computer and was pacing around his house, Will Ryan was sitting back on his sofa in the downstairs sitting room of his French Quarter suite and was studying the data on Renard Joseph Alciatore. The third son of a well-established New Orleans caterer, Renard – Ren to his friends – had attended Brother Martin High School, where he had graduated with Honors. After high school he had spent a year in Europe, particularly in London and Edinburgh, Scotland. Upon his return home, he had attended Loyola University New Orleans, where he earned a degree in History.

His passion for photography had been nurtured and encouraged by his mother from the time he had been in high school, while his father had given him a good bit of financial support to set up a studio and turn his creativity into a profitable business.

Ryan put the bio down and looked over the picture included, alongside a few photographs he had shot with his digital camera earlier in the day. Yeah, I'd do him, Will thought, in a heartbeat. Shame he's straight. Ryan chuckled and continued to study the bio. A soccer player since high school, Alciatore was now one of the most competent soccer referees in the state. He usually ran daily in the early mornings along either Bayou St. John or the Lakefront.

Will paused to adjust the volume on his iPhone, pulled his earbuds in, and let the bio data fall to the floor. Mr. Alciatore was going to be a bit more of a challenge than the previous two targets had been but there was no way Ryan was going to concern himself about dealing with a man who didn't even know what he was. Ryan's only regret was that Alciatore would not discover his Talents until the very last moments of his life.

Ryan closed his eyes and relaxed. He did not want to start thinking too far ahead by considering his target after Alciatore, in Biloxi.

The following morning dawned cloudy and heavy. The humid air clung to everything. Family and friends were making their way back to their vehicles from the Hebrew Rest Cemetery in Gentilly after saying their final farewells to Trip Kahn. Ren remained melted into the crowd as he did not know many of the Kahn family other than Trip's wife Rachel and their children. It was difficult to understand the reason for such a quick burial. Was it the Jewish tradition of burying their dead within 24 hours, a desire to minimize the trauma to the family, or their desire for privacy? Ren waited for the right moment to go over to Rachel and give her a hug, then over to Trip's parents to express his condolences. Removing his coat and tie, he got into his car and drove away from the cemetery, lost in memories of his friend.

Ren toyed for a moment with the thought of stopping by at his old high school, since it was just across the street from the cemetery. He decided he would not be very interesting company to anyone at that moment and instead drove up Elysian Fields as he reveled for a few moments in memories of his high school days: hanging out in the various haunts of Gentilly – Po-Boy Bakery, Bud's Broiler, the comic-book store, and, yes, several quiet little corner bars in the area. As kids at that time, they may have been under-age, but thank goodness for New Orleans, he thought. Many bar owners preferred to let the kids come by because at least they knew where they were, rather than being elsewhere doing something dangerous.

Most of these places were now gone; drowned by the floodwaters loosed on Gentilly by Hurricane Katrina. The locations were now empty lots, buildings demolished after the 10-12 feet of water which had rolled through the neighborhood had subsided.

There's nothing like a funeral to remind you of your mortality, Ren mused as the car reached the traffic circle where Elysian Fields Avenue met Lakeshore Drive. As he turned west along the shore of the lake, his car seemed to be on autopilot as he made his way to Marconi Drive, where he could sit and think. Ren had never been one to pay much attention to other drivers around him, and he had failed to notice the blue car that continued to dog his movements.

Sit and think, was exactly what Renard Alciatore did. He got to the Lakefront at just around noon, stopping only once en route to pick up a bottle of water at the new Gentilly grocery store that had opened after the storm. The cloudy sky kept the temperature down, and the humidity was typical of New Orleans at near 100 percent. A light breeze was enabling seagulls to soar up and down just off the seawall, and this breeze was serving also to make the stickiness of the afternoon a little more bearable.

As he sat, Ren noticed his phone flash several times but he chose to ignore it, knowing that the call would transfer automatically to voice-mail; he would catch anything important later. Besides, Nadine was at the house today working on the books for his business, so she would track him down later if anything essential arose.

Yup, funerals really do suck, he thought during one of his brief stretch-break walks from his position on the seawall at the canal along the lake to a shelter a couple of yards down, then across the street and back.

Ren started to think about who would have shown up had today's service had been his own and not Trip's. Well, at least nobody would have had to tell a child that she no longer has a daddy, he pondered wryly. Ren had never married. It had been five years since he had been in a relationship that had lasted more than six weeks; much less had a serious girlfriend. Sure, he had female friends and he dated regularly; going out with women who lived locally as well as the occasional liaison with friends from online from other parts of the country – and the world – which visited New Orleans. Some of these encounters had even been steamy, Ren recalled, to the point where he felt he should write them into the plot of a book someday. Great, a novel detailing my life as a computer geek: that's a helluva legacy. I need to get off my ass and get a real life, he mused. But not today, I have to grieve first. He lifted his water bottle the heavens and toasted his late friend. Don't worry, Trip, he mused. I'll toast you properly later. With that thought he lapsed back into the mind-blanking free-form meditation that was his usual Lakefront style.

Ren's thoughts had become so deep that he did not hear the car pull up in the parking bay, nor the footsteps behind him. It was not until he felt something cold and wet against the back of his neck that he jumped, startled, and looked up to see a very good friend standing over him with two cold beers. Ren smiled and leaned back in an effort to look up the short skirt of his friend, earning him a smack across the back of his head.

"You're in mourning, you pervert," she said. "And I have panties on anyway, so knock it off." Janet Juliane Garrison laughed and handed him one of the beers she had brought from her car. "I tried calling you twice to see if you were OK but I kept getting that bloody voice-mail of yours. I figured you'd be here, though, so I didn't leave my usual obscene torrent to be recorded for posterity."

"Oh I love when you talk dirty to me," teased Ren as he took a long pull on the cold beer, its refreshing tingle feeling most welcome at the back of his throat.

"Yeah. Well, I decided to come and check up on you. I know how you can get when you start to feel sorry for yourself. And that, my dear, is simply not permitted. You lost a friend, but you do have others who will take care of your sorry ass; so you are not allowed to wallow in your own thoughts for more than half a day. Now you get mine as well. I'm probably the only person on this planet who knows your thoughts, hopes, and dreams better than anyone else. I didn't know your Mr. Kahn in any other way than from your tales, Ren, but I figure he must have been a good guy. It sucks when a good guy is lost, but shit happens."

She was sitting on the bench next to him by the end of her speech. Her sandals were kicked off and she had her arm around Ren's shoulders. "I'd take you home and molest you, but I don't think Joe would want a threesome tonight." The reference to her husband caused Ren almost to choke on his beer as he burst into a fit of almost uncontrollable laughter.

"Yeah right! Like that's going to happen in my lifetime – you in a sandwich between me and Joe!"

"That's true. If you want a threesome with me, it had better be with me and one of my girlfriends then." She laughed back at him smiling that infectious smile that had attracted him to her as a friend when they were classmates. Her smile then turned deadly serious in an instant, though, as she took his hand and looked him in the eyes. "Ren, I'm really worried about you."

"Oh, I'll be fine love. You know me. I don't dwell upon death very long."

"Yes, and that's the problem. You don't dwell on it at all sometimes. Hasn't it occurred to you that there may be a connection between the losses of two friends of yours in such a short time?"

"What connection? The only thing bringing Nick's and Trip's paths together was their work with me on the JHM website." Ren was a little confused at this point.

"That's exactly what I'm talking about, Ren. Doesn't it seem strange to you that the two people working on this project with you have died within days of each other?"

Ren broke eye contact with her and stared out into the lake. "C'mon JJ, that's ridiculous. You're starting to sound like a conspiracy theorist. Besides, one of them died of a heart attack and the other in a traffic accident. Those weren't murders, sweetie."

She pulled on his shoulder so he was facing her again. "Oh, they aren't? Says who?"

Ren shook his head. "Listen to you! This is one of the loopiest things you've come up with for ages. Hadley may be a complete asshole, but he isn't a murderer. Honestly, love. He just doesn't have the stomach for what you're pinning on him."

She was undeterred. "Ren, perhaps someone around him does have the stomach for it. What I see is that your blog has lost two-thirds of its creative team and the major beneficiary of this is one Jay Hadley."

"You're just nuts, JJ."

"Nuts I may be. But I want you to call Bubba and run this past him."

Now Ren was really confused. "Bubba? JJ, Bubba works for the Kenner cops. He wouldn't be involved in investigating these deaths even if anyone besides you suspected foul play."

"I know that, you goof. But Bubba's a cop. And he's your friend. He's the perfect sounding board for all this. If Bubba tells me I'm nuts, I'll gladly back off and let it go. In the meantime, though, I want you to talk to him." She was sitting up straight by now, and that meant she was most serious about what she was saying.

Ren sighed. "OK, I'll call him."

She looked sternly at him. "Now."

Ren knew there was no arguing with his friend when she got like this. She was a career woman and a mother and she was not to be denied once she had made her mind up. He shook his head, pulled his phone from his pocket, and pushed the numbers for the City of Kenner Police Department. The New Orleans suburb of Kenner, about 15 miles west of New Orleans, had a police department with a force of around 250 officers, and Bubba was a squad Lieutenant there. He was first and foremost a patrol cop, but he also handled the occasional special investigation.

Ren frowned for a moment to indicate to JJ that he was listening to a voice-mail system. "Hey Bubba, this is Ren. I've got some questions about an interesting set of events over the past couple of days. Nothing earth shattering, but I wanted to run it past you and see what you think from a professional viewpoint. Anyway, give me a call when you've got time, or maybe I can come out some day and we can have lunch." Ren was about to say "goodbye" when the phone was snatched from his hand.

"Bubba, this is JJ. The questions this idiot has for you are actually from me. So I don't want you taking your sweet time about getting together on this. I know how you guys work. You'll fart around for a few days before returning this call, then Ren will fart around for another day or two, and you guys will have lunch sometime next year. Now that you know I am waiting for your answer, dear, I'm sure I'll get the info I'm looking for in a timelier manner, right? Sure I will. Bye love!" She was smiling as she thumbed the "end" button, passed the phone back to Ren, and kissed him on the cheek.

"Jeez JJ. Now I'm definitely going to buy you that bumper-sticker I saw the other day that said Beyond Bitch," Ren laughed.

"Oh, I WANT that one!" JJ laughed as she tossed her hair back and reached for her sandals. "Or the one that says, Zero to Bitch in Sixty Seconds."

Ren stood up from their bench in the shelter and helped JJ to her feet. "I'll get both of them for you tonight, from one of those t-shirt shops on Bourbon Street. I'm going to run home and shower, then I think I'll walk around the Quarter for a while and have a drink or two at Tujague's later."

"You sure you're OK, Ren?"

Ren smiled and kissed JJ on the cheek. "Yeah babe, I'm fine. I think you're nuts but I'll ponder that a bit as I walk the Quarter. Wanna come with me?"

"Love to. But the obligations of wifedom and motherhood beckon. Much as I would love to walk around and soak up real life for an evening, I also don't want to hear it from the kids because Daddy's cooking dinner." She leaned on him as they walked arm-in-arm back to their cars.

"OK, that I understand. But come with me soon; it's been too long since we've just hung out in the Quarter together." He was running his hand lightly up and down her back.

"Deal." She kissed him again, climbed into her car, and drove off. Ren watched her disappear then jumped into his own car and headed for home.

Nadine was still working quietly as he walked into his house. He checked in, took her update on the day's business dealings, and sent her home. He showered and changed then hopped back into his car to head for the Vieux Carré, the Old Square, the French Quarter.

***

There was no other neighborhood in New Orleans that had experienced ups and downs more than the Quarter. In spite of the increase in tourist-based places and activities close to the river, the Quarter still remained a viable neighborhood. It had been spared the horrible flooding and resultant damage that other areas had received during Katrina. People lived, worked, played, and loved around the clock there. Ren was fascinated by the Quarter; he would often take a camera or two along with him and photograph just about anything that struck him. At other times, like today, he would just wander around taking in the sights and letting things hit him for later inspiration. This evening would be one of those soak-in occasions. Far better just to pick up on the vibes of the neighborhood than to try shooting them on such a strange day for him, he thought. He pulled his car into the French Market parking lot, totally unaware that he was still under surveillance.

Ren waited for the red Riverfront streetcar to pass by before walking up the steps by Washington Artillery Park, directly across the street from Jackson Square. As he landed at the top of the overlook a young black man confronted him.

"Bet I know where ya got dem shoes!" While the question seemed innocent enough, there was something of an intimidating look in the young man's eyes as he made his statement.

Ren looked him straight in the eyes. This startled the young man, since most tourists were too surprised by the approach to be confrontational in return. "They're on my feet. On Decatur Street. In New Orleans." Ren said this loud enough that a couple who had been confronted in similar manner by a black man on the other side of the overlook heard it and turned to listen to him, much to the consternation of both young men. "In other words, I'm local. So leave me be."

The young man was initially quite angry at Ren's response, but one look from Ren disarmed him totally. Ren had that effect on many people – something about his disposition either put them at ease or communicated the impression that he was not someone to be messed with. His look to the young man must have conveyed both impressions at once, because he immediately averted his gaze and stepped aside to allow Ren to pass by.

Satisfied that he had saved those tourists the cost of a shoe shine, Ren bounded down the steps on the Decatur Street side of the overlook and headed directly across the street to enter Jackson Square from the gate on Decatur. The Square was still open for another hour or so, when they would close the gates at 6pm to keep the homeless from sleeping there. Ren stepped into the Square slowly and turned immediately at the first ring of pathway around Ol' Hickory's statue, and walking clockwise around it while taking in the sight of both the denizens of the square and the tourists who were still milling around.

Ren stopped by the gate on the St. Ann side of Jackson Square. This was the "downtown" or downriver side of the Square, which was bounded by Decatur by the River, then St. Ann Street, Chartres in front of St. Louis Cathedral, and St. Peter on the "uptown" or upriver side. He turned full-circle in front of the gate, and kept hearing Trip's voice in his head, talking about him being attached to the city. Trip was teasing him about it, calling him artsy-fartsy, but the more he considered it, especially while standing in the emotional heart of his town, the more he believed Trip was on to something. Ren shook his head slowly and turned again towards the Chartres Street gate, while admiring the trim green grass and the bright flowers in the gardens of the Square until he stepped into the street. He stood directly in in front of St. Louis Cathedral, then turned right, and headed down Pere Antoine Alley rather than the more famous Pirate's Alley – one of his regular habits. Most historians believed Jean Lafitte and his brother rarely came near the Cabildo, which was the seat of government, yet the alley still honors them. The surge of energy was always more noticeable on the Presbytere side than the Cabildo side of the cathedral, perhaps because the Presbytere was (and still is) the rectory for the church parish. Peering into St. Anthony's Garden (so named to honor the saint that was Pere Antoine's namesake). The garden, which was behind the church as he walked past it, always looked calm and inviting. He came out of the alley onto Royal Street and turned to walk down Orleans Avenue. After another block he was crossing Bourbon Street, already getting noisy as tourists began to explore the decadent side of the city. Ren stopped at the corner and toyed with the idea of walking along Bourbon for a couple of blocks but a shiver went up his spine while passing the Bourbon Orleans Hotel.

Something was wrong there, but now was not the time to figure out the cause of that feeling. The source of his sensation was not the tourist Voodoo shop across the street. No, it was definitely the hotel. He shivered again but quickly shook it off and crossed the street. The smell from the hot-dog wagon was tempting – there's something about a hot-dog that awakens a primal hunger in the human animal. Ren chuckled to himself as he pondered that thought.

Bourbon Street is like an invisible dividing-line between the "tourist" part of the Quarter and the "neighborhood" section. As soon as Ren had walked past the corner and into the adjacent block the atmosphere changed dramatically. Tourists rarely just wander around in the Quarter north of Bourbon Street. They seem to remain content with the shops and the restaurants on Chartres, Royal Street, and Decatur, as well as with the historical attractions near the river. When it came to photographic inspiration, however, nothing could beat the upper section of the Quarter, Ren thought.

As he crossed Dauphine he slowed his pace a little. This is where real people live, not tourists who simply hang out. Crossing Dauphine Street – Rue Dauphine, named after the heir to the French throne – he turned east, heading towards Esplanade Avenue. Dauphine was quiet compared with Bourbon Street, with just a few people coming and going. Ren passed one old guy sitting on his front steps, and they each exchanged the traditional New Orleans' greeting, "awrite". That says it all for a local: you nod and say "awrite" as you walk by.

Ren took in the sight of the balconies with their lush hanging plants as he walked down a few blocks towards Ursulines Street. He then turned back towards the river, passed the old convent, and looked down Chartres at St. Mary's Italian Church. The whole block gave him a sensation exactly the opposite of the one he had felt while standing on Bourbon Street, and this puzzled him. He cleared his head again and walked around the corner of Ursulines and Chartres several times, looking first down Chartres to Esplanade, then back to Canal Street, then down Ursulines to the river, finally to turn back around to study the scene going north. He pulled out a small digital camera he usually carried with him, and shot all four perspectives while enjoying the relaxing feeling this location was giving him.

After shooting several frames from each point of view,

Ren walked along Ursulines towards the river, turning on to Decatur again, before heading back towards Canal Street. Absorbing the sights and sounds of Decatur Street and the French Market, he walked back towards Jackson Square, stopping at the open door that invited passers-by into the bar at Tujague's Restaurant. Even though he still had to admit that his family's restaurant – Antoine's over on St. Louis Street – was still his favorite place to eat in the Quarter, the bar at Tujague's had become special to him as a place to hang out. Jerry the bartender poured Ren an Abita Amber from the tap and set it in front of him without Ren even ordering. Most of the regulars had known Trip as well as Ren, and everyone was expressing their regrets to him.

Ren thanked everyone and stood in the middle of the bar to propose a toast. "To my friend and yours, Trip Kahn. L'chaim, Trip!" He knocked back his beer, as did everyone else in the room, then put the glass down for another. After casually finishing his second beer he paid his tab, said good-night, and headed back to the parking lot. He drove down to the end of long narrow lot along the river, paid the attendant, and turned to drive along Esplanade towards the bayou and home.

CHAPTER FOUR

Under Protection

Will Ryan waited for his prey, in the shadows of Ren Alciatore's front lawn. He heard Alciatore close the door to his car, and the beep acknowledging that it locked. The low gate at the sidewalk opened quietly, and he stepped inside the fence surrounding the house. Closing the gate triggered Alciatore's inner senses. He knew something wasn't right.

He doesn't know it's the end of his life, thought Will.

Ryan knew exactly what Ren was experiencing. He paused for a moment, recalling when it happened to him. Even though he wasn't an orphan, at the age of two, his father was dead, shot in the course of a robbery he and two friends staged, while his mother was sent to prison for her involvement in the same crime. The government took her baby, and Will began his life as a ward of the state. Ryan's evaluations by the social services agencies of Belfast, Northern Ireland, used words such as "disruptive", "combative", and "lashes out easily". Those same evaluations also described him as "creative" and "highly intelligent". Because he was a problem placement, Ryan bounced from one foster home to another. As he moved through those homes, he came to realize he was different. He couldn't explain it, but he just *knew* whether or not people were telling the truth. When older kids in a group home tried to bully him, he could "think" nightmares in their minds, and they left him alone. As he discovered that the mind-games he could play weren't random, he settled down. Instead of being "combative", he turned inward. He wanted to be left alone.

They left him alone. Alone to the point where Will grew

more and more isolated, even when placed with a family. He learned there was a “wall” of some kind of around him. If he didn’t want people to get inside that “wall”, they didn’t get in. And he didn’t want anyone in. At all. Ever. Foster parents, used to children who acted out, found Will’s quiet, solitary existence a relief. They let him read books from the library, search the Internet, and play video games, as his behavior improved. The only times the “old Will” reappeared was when circumstances forced him to move to another foster family. Disruption was not good for the boy and he would act out for a few days. Once he re-established his boundaries, he settled down.

At the age of eleven, Will landed in the home of a police sergeant and his wife. The policeman’s wife gave him a few days to adjust to their home. She felt his “wall” going up. When he was settled, she came to him.

“I can feel your shields,” she told him.

“My shields?”

“Yes, that thing where you lock everyone out and push them away from you.” Mary Rose Smyth smiled at Will.

“I call it my ‘wall’. It makes people leave me alone,” Will explained.

“I know, it keeps people out. But you don’t want to do that forever. Let’s see what we can do about your control of this,” she said, encouraging him to open up.

Will smiled back, nodded, and listened to her instructions.

Mary Rose recognized Will’s special abilities, and helped him develop his Talents. She showed him how to control his anger, focus his thoughts, and make his Talents do his bidding.

After his first year in what would be his final foster home, Will stopped alternating between fighting everything and anything and shutting it all out. His school performance improved dramatically, as he merged what he learned in the classroom with his foster mother’s lessons. By the time he was sixteen, Ryan decided there was nothing more that either school or his foster home could offer him. He left Belfast for Manchester, UK. Able to recognize others of his kind, he quickly connected with others who possessed Talents. Living on the fringe of Manchester, he played soccer and developed contacts among the city's criminal elements. He quickly acquired a reputation as a skilled burglar, quiet, in-and-out, leaving no trace. In less than a year, Ryan was one of the top individual "specialists" in Manchester, able to pick and choose the jobs he'd do and the crews he would work with. Approached by one of the city's organized crime leaders, his career took a turn when he was offered a contract to eliminate the crime boss' competition. Ryan's targets fell victim to a series of "accidents", while he collected lucrative fees for his services. By the time he was eighteen, Ryan was not only in control of his Talents, he had developed a solid clientèle as an assassin.

Ryan's contracts began to take him outside Greater Manchester: first, train rides over to Liverpool, then longer ones down to London. He used trips to London to broaden his circle of contacts, and soon was regularly flying first class to New York from the UK. His jobs went unnoticed by the authorities, but his successes were touted in the private dining rooms, gentleman's clubs, and nightclubs where dark and deadly decisions were regularly made. Ryan would spend half the year in the UK, the other half in the United States. He lived in different cities on either side of the ocean, so as not to draw attention to himself. After spending time in New York City, he branched out, learning San Francisco, Los Angeles, and Chicago well enough to "work" in those metropolitan areas.

His attraction to other men led him to spend more and more time in gay-friendly cities. On one trip to New Orleans, Ryan met a woman in her early thirties who also possessed Talents. Anita Delatorre had been seduced by the club scene of New Orleans' French Quarter, just like Will. They became the sort of acquaintances that made others believe they were old friends, even though they'd only run into each other a handful of times. On one of those occasions, while dining at one of the city's top-flight restaurants, Anita lowered her shields, revealing her tightly-controlled aura to Will. He gasped, stunned that he'd never realized she was Talented. That evening ended with Will in Anita's bed, beginning a friendship that grew into a professional relationship, as she realized just how useful Will's special skills could be to her and her employers.

Will sighed and drew his thoughts back to the moment.

He would end this evening at one of the clubs he was just recalling, but the man who'd just closed that gate was about to die.

***

The waters of Bayou St. John were as smooth as glass as Ren parked the car in front of his Moss Street home. He would normally go around the side of the house to the kitchen door but he decided tonight to go up the front walkway. He opened the gate set into the black wrought-iron fence running along the sidewalk and stopped short. Something clung to him, thicker than the night air. The sensation of dread was similar to the point where he could almost see a black cloud blocking the way from the sidewalk to his front door. As he was ready to turn and head back out to his car, the gate closed shut behind him with a soft clang, startling him and further increasing his feeling of danger.

The more Ren felt nervous about his current predicament, the more the cloud in front of him became a visible, almost-living entity; a gray-black haze which was making it gradually more difficult to see the front door. Its surroundings seemed to be growing brighter, almost as if Ren had donned a pair of night-vision goggles. From out of the shadows at the side of the house, a calm voice entered Ren's consciousness.

"Ahh, you're feeling it aren't you? Yes, we all feel it when our Talents surface in some way. It's a pity you'll never fully understand that. But, business is business." Ryan stepped into full view, the brightness of Ren's eyes dimming dramatically as a dark violet aura began to emanate from the stranger and wrap itself around him as if it were a suit of armor. Armor made of light.

"Who are you? What are you?" Ren's question was barely audible but the words rang loudly in both his and William Ryan's minds.

"I am the end of your life," the stranger said to Ren's mind. "Art thou ready to defend thyself, Sir?" Ryan was standing at attention and then bowed after the question.

"I-I don't understand." The formality of the stranger's tone, combined with his own heightened senses, took Ren aback. As soon as he completed the bow, the man in front of him raised his hands. A sweeping arc of violet light streamed from Ryan's fingertips. The stream went out about three feet from his fingers and formed a semi-circle from Ryan's waist to over his head. The stranger moved from a stiff, erect posture to that of a karate fighter about to execute some sort of martial arts move.

Even though he had had no training in hand-to-hand combat, Ren had dodged enough kicks and balls on the soccer field to know when something dangerous was coming. He instinctively swept his own hands upwards when he saw the violet-red bolt of lightning surge from the stranger's hands and come flying out towards him. As his hands went above his head Ren found himself enveloped in a golden aura similar to the violet one of the stranger. The violet bolt of light bounced harmlessly off his golden-light armor, sending a thousand orange sparks high into the night. Not that everyone could see those sparks, of course. But anyone with Talents would have noticed a small explosion.

William Ryan was startled by this turn of events. He was more than aware that Protocols had to be observed, in that Alciatore could not be dispatched in a manner similar to his other targets. Still, this was a man totally untrained. That bolt of energy should have been sufficient to overload his entire nervous system and generate either a stroke or a cerebral hemorrhage. Instead, he was standing in front of an adversary with fully-armored shields. This was going to be much more difficult than he had bargained for. But he was determined to prevail.

"So, my pretty, you are more than you appear to be. Fine, then. Let us see just how much more!" Ryan began to wave his hands before him, weaving the next spell in his attack. His lips were mumbling words Ren could not make out, as the dark mist that had descended on his front lawn began to coalesce between the two men and take on a definite shape of its own. First, thick legs, then a cylindrical body. Finally, a hideous snarling head that bared a misty set of fangs dripping with blood. Ryan completed the spell and made a two-handed gesture towards the creature, pushing it nearer to Ren.

The feelings of confusion and fear Ren had been experiencing were now turning into full-blown panic. His feet remained riveted to the ground; his eyes focused on the mist-creature moving towards him. Ren's brain was racing but no options presented themselves. For the first time in his life Ren truly thought he was about to die. There was no logic to the entire situation but he knew that what was slowly moving towards him was more than a cloud of mist. Fear gripped him, and that fear manifested itself as a plume of psychic light shooting into the sky. The stranger grinned as the light-show continued; smug with the satisfaction of knowing his approach had been correct. His target had shown strong natural defenses against a raw psychic energy but had no practical experience with things arcane. Renard Alciatore had no clue what was coming towards him and, therefore, could muster no defense.

The creature was half-way between the two men. The distance was short, but the thing was moving at a snail's pace. A pace deliberately set by its conjurer. Ryan wanted to ensure that his target's fear would continue to grow, leaving him totally helpless when the fangs of the creature would begin to separate Ren's soul from his body.

Those dripping fangs came to within a few feet from Ren, and the cries for help he tried to make were stuck in his throat. Terror had overwhelmed him to the point that he could not even imitate the initial warding gesture his attacker had done when this had begun. All the prayers he had learned as a boy in Catholic school were coming back to him. All but the one he wanted: The Act of Contrition. The prayer you said when you begged to God for absolution. He wanted that absolution now, since he was soon to be a dead man.

The mist was beginning to wrap itself around his feet. Ren imagined he could smell the foul stench of the creature as it approached. He closed his eyes and braced himself for his own death. As his eyes shut, he felt a swooshing sensation at his feet as the dark mist pulled away from them and retreated. He opened his eyes and saw that the creature had stopped moving, inches in front of him, and the mist from which the creature had been created was rapidly dissipating.

"Stay this duel...!" A third voice shouted from behind Ren on the sidewalk. Ren turned to see a man climbing over the short fence and walking swiftly between himself and his attacker. The newcomer also appeared to be wrapped in light; but not the tight, armor-like aura he and his attacker sported. Instead, it appeared like a mantle that was wrapped around him like a judge's robe. Its color was bright white and a symbol or badge appeared to be glowing on his right shoulder. It was glowing so brightly that Ren could not make out any of its detail.

"And why must I do this, worthy teacher? The Forms and Protocols have been followed." His attacker was visibly annoyed by the intervention of the new apparition, but was obviously concerned, as his voice took on a deferential tone.

"Yes, Master Assassin. You have followed the Protocols, but so must I. I cannot allow you to take the life of one with Talents while that one is so totally unaware of what you are doing. Ply your trade on the mortals, sir, or enjoin those who are trained in all the combats you wish. But you will not kill this way, with such flagrant disregard for our traditions. I place this man under my Protection and you continue this duel at your peril!" The newcomer may have looked like a supernatural college professor, but his demeanor indicated that he was more than capable of backing up his words with the same extent of magic his attacker possessed.

William Ryan lowered his hands and bowed. "I yield to you, my Lord. I do not fully understand your jurisdiction here, but nonetheless I yield and release this man to your Protection."

"Thank you, young Sir. In time you will understand the wisdom of your decision, not only because you will learn more of our ways, but because you will live beyond this evening to discover those ways." The newcomer smiled with a mirthless grin, giving a look that chilled even Ryan's cold, hard composure.

Ryan once again bowed and waved his hands. His armor of violet light seemed to vanish, absorbed into his body. Another wave of his hand caused the remaining dark cloud of mist around Ren's front yard to sink into the ground and a third wave caused the small front gate to open. He walked out through the gate and nodded as he passed the newcomer, then crossed the street and walked to the edge of the bayou and away from the scene.

As soon as Ryan was out of sight, Ren closed his eyes and tried to walk. He got as far as a live-oak tree in his front yard and leaned against it. His entire body shook as he released the tension built up over the previous few minutes. By the time he opened his eyes, Ren's senses had returned to normal and before him in the darkness a could see a short stocky man, standing in front of him dressed in blue jeans, t-shirt, and sneakers. The man placed his hand on Ren's shoulder and smiled.

"You know, I was on my way to Port of Call. I've had this major-ass craving for a cheeseburger all afternoon and decided I deserve one. You look like you could use something to eat yourself. Care to join me?"

CHAPTER FIVE

Burgers and Beer

They rode down Esplanade Avenue, heading towards the river. The Porsche 914 his rescuer drove was old but well-maintained, and the fresh air went a long way in terms of helping Ren clear his head and compose his thoughts.

As they pulled up to the light at Esplanade and North Rampart Street, the driver pointed to the complex of condominiums on the corner.

"I liked it better as an empty lot. You know, we've a bit of common heritage. St. Aloysius, that is. I graduated from Brother Martin as well. The name's O'Donnell. Michael Aloysius O'Donnell, at your service, sir." The man's smile immediately put Ren at ease.

Pointing to the driver's University of New Orleans t-shirt, Ren finally was able to speak coherently.

"Do we have UNO in common as well?"

"Sort of. I work over at UNO, as a teacher, and I help out at the school's Newman Center." The light turned green and they continued towards the Quarter.

"The Newman Center? You're a priest?" Ren hadn't been a church-going Catholic in years, but he still knew that the man was referring to the Catholic Student Center on campus.

"Yup, that I am. I teach History, actually, so I live at and lend a hand at the Center. It frees up the guy who is the Director to get out and about on campus and in the neighborhood." Again he was smiling, as if nothing more serious had happened this evening than maybe someone cutting him off while driving.

O'Donnell's relaxed demeanor had its desired effect on

Ren; he was coming out of the shock of what had happened in front of his house just a few minutes earlier. He turned to the driver for more on what he'd seen.

"Back at the house, who was that? Just what hap..."

Putting up his hand, O'Donnell cut him off.

"Not just yet. Let's wait till we get settled down and order our food. I promise you'll get your answers, but let's wait till we are hiding in plain sight." He smiled again.

Ren smiled back, for the first time. "Thanks, Father."

O'Donnell looked at him with mock sternness.

"What, I look like your daddy? It's Mike, fella. If I've got the uniform on, or if we're in a group of kids, then 'Father' is appropriate. Otherwise, please, call me Mike."

"OK, Mike," Ren grinned sheepishly. "Besides, it's not like I have to wait long, given that we're almost here. Providing we can get a parking place."

"Oh, that's why I've always hung on to this car. Back in in the day, I helped the original owner and two other guys pick it up and parallel park it down on Royal Street one evening. I swore to myself that I'd buy it or another one some day. And I did, right after the storm flooded my very-boring Taurus. Have no fear, young sir, we will stable this steed while we seek out our nourishment!" He laughed at himself as he lapsed into speech one only usually encountered at Renaissance festivals these days.

Ren's basic instincts about people were usually pretty good, and his feelings about this man next to him were extremely positive.

"Maybe because he just saved my life, my judgement is clouded right now," he thought wryly, as O'Donnell turned the car off of Esplanade into the Quarter, seeking a parking space close to the restaurant.

"Well, it's a Thursday night, and it's early, so we got lucky," Mike said as they exited the little car about a block away from the restaurant. "C'mon, I wasn't kidding about being hungry before, and all this activity hasn't done anything to dampen my appetite!"

Port of Call is one of those places natives don't often bring visitors to New Orleans on their first trip unless the visitor has specifically requested to eat in a hole-in-the wall. Like any local who grew up and went to college in New Orleans, Ren knew the place well. Walking up the three front steps to the front door, he smiled at how little the place had changed.

"I'll bet they've still even got Frank Zappa's *Zoot Allures* on the jukebox," Ren observed.

The shrimp nets hanging from the ceiling looked as if they hadn't been changed or repaired since the place opened, the walls were still filled with things nautical, and the customers were still a mix of Quarter denizens, yuppies, and college kids. It was a bit crowded inside, and it appeared that they'd have to wait a few minutes for a table. He watched as Mike went up to the hostess, smiled, winked and then motioned for Ren to follow along to their table around the corner in the back room.

"I don't usually use any additional persuasion when trying to get a table in a restaurant," Mike said, winking. "But you're probably gonna explode if we don't sit down and discuss things soon."

Ren nodded, thinking he understood what Mike meant by "persuasion," but all of a sudden he was not so sure. They sat down, and Mike held his hands outstretched, indicating that it was now OK for Ren to begin.

Sighing deeply, Ren was almost at a loss for where to start.

"Who was that guy back there? What was he doing to me? How did you know what was going on?"

Mike nodded, indicating in a subtle way he fully intended to answer all of his questions.

"The man waiting for you on your front lawn was an assassin. Someone wants you dead, and was willing to hire a very good hit man to do the job. What he had done was to engage you in what we refer to as the 'Combat Protocol,' which specifies very strict rules for a duel between two individuals who have magical Talents."

Still a bit confused, Ren shook his head.

"What do you mean 'we?' You make it sound like this happens all the time."

"Not all the time, but duels such as the one you were just involved in have taken place for the better part of a millennium.

There are very specific rules to how those duels are to be conducted, however, and one of them is that those individuals with Talents who are in training or are not aware of who or what they are must not be Challenged. Our young friend in black back there has received some excellent training in the mechanics of using his Talents, but he is obviously lacking in training in the traditions behind their use." Mike paused for a moment as the waitress came up to take their order. She was attractive; in her late-twenties, on the short side, wearing a long plaid skirt and a Grateful Dead tank top. She had a very pretty red rose tattooed on her left shoulder.

Mike ordered a cheeseburger; Ren ordered a mushroom burger.

"When I got in your car, I wasn't hungry at all. I came along to talk more than eat. Now that I'm here and my heart rate is going back to normal, I'm very hungry!" He said to the priest.

"Well, Port of Call's half-pound burger and stuffed potato is just what the doctor ordered to fix that! Feed my friend, please, pretty lady!" Mike said, directing the last to the waitress.

The waitress smiled and swayed away with their orders, glancing back just before turning the corner to confirm that both men were staring at her rear end. Mike chuckled and Ren smiled back at her. Alone in the corner of the room again, Ren continued. "I'm still confused here. You keep saying 'Talent,' as if it would have a capital 'T' if written down. What 'Talents' are you referring to here?"

Mike pointed to his temple with his right index finger. "These are Talents that begin up here, Ren. The scientists call them ESP—extrasensory perception. The superstitious call them 'magic'."

"Which is the right answer?"

Mike chuckled. "Both. Neither. You see, that's the thing, even those of us who possess these Talents still are not quite sure about what they are. Formal study of who and what we are began almost fourteen hundred years ago. In some ways we know a lot about the Talents, and in other ways, we have forgotten much. But you'll learn more about that as we go along here. What is important for now is that you realize that you have one or more of the Talents, and that we should explore what you are in detail to determine just which ones you do well at."

Part of Ren was still confused, part was overwhelmed, but something deep inside him understood what Mike was saying. He nodded. "I still don't understand what I have that would be worth someone hiring a hit man over."

"Well, I don't know enough about you yet to answer that, Ren, but I suspect that the reason you were targeted has to do with the life you were living before this evening, not the Talents that have been awakened in you." Mike frowned, unable to help shed any more light on the mystery.

Ren sighed. "So, someone wants me dead. Wonderful."

Mike's eyes twinkled. "Well, I think it's safe to assume you've won a bit of a reprieve. That young man is not going to come after you again. He knew I meant business on that subject. No doubt he is reporting to his employer now what happened. If his employer knows what we are, they also know what being under Protection means. If they don't know about all this, you can still be sure that your attacker will find some way to convince them that killing you is a bad idea, because he doesn't want me coming after his ass should something happen to you now. And rest assured, I would."

All the reassuring looks and infectious charm that Michael O'Donnell possessed vanished in an instant. In one way that shocked Ren, but in another way it put him quite at ease as he became well aware that his life was very safe at the moment.

The waitress had returned with the beers they had ordered with their burgers. Ren made tight eye contact with her, his thoughts turning to what it would be like to run his hands up under her shirt and get at those bare breasts waiting there for him. Even though he had not said a word or lifted a finger, she gasped, as if he had indeed slid his hands up under her shirt and began to rub circles around her now-hardening nipples. Mike noticed the exchange and the level of arousal in the waitress and shook his head as she walked back towards the bar.

"You're going to have to be careful what you think about, Ren. I think you just gave that gal an orgasm."

Ren snapped back and blushed. "What do you mean?"

"Your emotions are projecting big-time, right now. When you took one look at her tits, your mind told her in no uncertain terms what you wanted to do to her. Under normal circumstances this would be no big deal, but tonight has opened up all the channels your Talents use to project. Whatever you just thought, you sent straight into her mind. Relax, though, she liked it." Mike laughed loudly at that, and Ren blushed even deeper.

"Oh sweet Jesus," Ren mumbled.

"Oh, don't worry, m'boy, He doesn't mind," chuckled Mike. "But we will work on this for the future—you will learn how to shield your thoughts and not to project your hands onto a gal's tits or up her skirt unless you want them to be there."

Ren took a long pull on his beer and regained his composure. "I'm not sure I quite understand all this," he said, "But I do want to learn."

"Excellent, then! Do you have any appointments tomorrow?" Seeing Ren's negative nod, he continued. "Better still. We'll begin in the morning to bring you up to speed on just what you are."

Their dinner conversation from there on consisted of get-acquainted talk, as they chatted about a number of subjects ranging from teachers they both had in high school to Clausewitz's theories of siege warfare. Just before the waitress delivered their burgers, Mike threw a simple shield over Ren so that his thoughts did not manifest themselves in some other way on her body. That first encounter obviously pleased her, though, and she sat with them for a few minutes chatting at the end of the meal as she totaled up their check and Ren fumbled for a credit card to pay the tab. Mike was a step faster, however, as he handed the waitress a crisp new hundred-dollar bill.

"I feel guilty letting a priest pay for dinner," Ren mused.

"Ah, don't sweat it, I'll get it back from you one day. I'm notorious for showing up and not having any cash in my pockets. Enjoy the fact that I've got some this time."

The waitress was back with their change, and she walked with them to the front door. The chemistry between she and Ren was still very strong. It was early for Port of Call, though, and she had to get back to work, so she waved at them from the doorway and they headed to the car.

The drive back to Ren's house was uneventful and quiet

as both men sat back in their seats and allowed their dinner to digest. Ren invited Mike in for a nightcap or a cup of coffee, but he politely refused.

"No, thanks, Ren, because you're going to find yourself very tired in no time flat. Go get yourself a good night's sleep, because we're going to get started early tomorrow. I'll meet you here around 8am, but don't have anything more for breakfast than a cup of black coffee or tea, OK? Working with the Talents is best done on an empty stomach. I'll explain this more fully as we go along, don't worry." He turned from the doorstep and headed back to the street.

Ren was already beginning to yawn, wondering all of a sudden if Mike hadn't planted some sort of sleep suggestion in his mind. "OK, see you in the morning. And thanks again…for tonight…"

"Don't mention it. And here I was this afternoon, ruminating about how uninteresting this summer was shaping up to be!" Laughing, he jumped back in the little car and drove off with a wave.

***

Mike O'Donnell and Renard Alciatore were not the only two who were exhausted from the evening's activities, but William Ryan didn't have the luxury of a leisurely dinner and a comfortable bed. The stranger who interrupted his attack on Ren Alciatore shook his composure in a big way, and he knew there would be a great deal of explaining to do. After recovering the rental car he parked two blocks down from Alciatore's house, he drove over by the cemeteries at Canal Street and City Park Avenue, got on his phone, and began making calls. First was to United Airlines, booking himself a first class seat on the last flight of the evening to Houston. He would transfer there to another flight to Dallas. With a ride out of town secured, he continued to drive out to the airport, contacting the hotel and instructing them that an emergency called him away at literally a moment's notice and requesting that they ship his luggage to Dallas. Being a very regular guest at the Bourbon Orleans, they gladly agreed to perform this service. Will then made a third call, to the answering service number given to him by Anita Delatorre during their meeting to discuss the particulars of this job. He suggested that they meet for an early lunch the next day because complications with the assignment had developed. He didn't usually sleep on airplanes, but Will knew he'd get some on the short flights.

***

Ren woke up around 7am the next morning, feeling surprisingly refreshed. Remembering Mike's instructions about breakfast, he put the kettle on to make a pot of green tea. Heading over to his office/study, he sat down to check the overnight e-mail. Most of the messages were still notes of condolence from regular readers of the blog who had learned of the deaths of his friends. One message caught his eye, though; addressed from a web-based e-mail account named "revelation." There was a file attached; an image of some kind. Ren activated his virus-checking software (one can't be too careful in that regard), headed back to work on the tea, and then opened it when he returned.

At first Ren thought it was just another nudie pic, the kind he received regularly in unsolicited e-mail advertising, but the image in the corner told him this was different. The foreground was a naked young blonde in her mid-twenties. What made this image interesting was the reflection of the photographer in the mirror. Saving the file, he closed down the e-mail and opened up an image-enhancing program.

Zooming in on the reflection was truly a "revelation," namely the image of the Rev. Jay Hadley, nude from at least the waist up, photographing a girl young enough to be his daughter. Further study of the image confirmed to Ren that it was not faked; inserting an image into a mirror is difficult to conceal. Sliding his chair back a moment, Ren didn't know how to handle this information. His anonymous source told him early on that Hadley liked to play with cameras, but she also said that he would have to find out more on his own. Now he's getting pictures of Hadley. This made little sense.

Ren's attempts to trace back the "revelation" e-mail

account ran into dead ends as the doorbell rang. His watch chimed the hour as he opened the door to greet his new mentor.

"Morning!" Mike said as he stepped into the house. "Hope you got some rest, because you've got a lot of catching up to do if we're going to make this work."

Ren led the way into the kitchen, offering his guest coffee or tea. "What do you mean, 'catching up'?"

"Well, we usually like to identify those with Talents as young as possible, beginning their training as young as three. We can do this when we know the lineage of the parents. We have a lot of work to do with you, but don't worry, in some ways it's easier to train an adult than it is to train a child. When you're ready, we'll get rolling on this." Mike had all but drained his cup of tea while talking.

Smiling, Ren held his hands open, indicating that he was in Mike's hands. "Let's go for it. Where do we start?"

"We start with the most basic concepts: grounding, centering, and shielding. We have to make you aware of what you are, and get you some defenses. Then we can look at your specific Talents and plan to develop them." Mike proceeded to walk Ren through some basic grounding exercises, giving him specific visualizations for making a connection with the earth. After an hour of this, they were ready for another break.

"I feel like I'm floating just before I ground," Ren observed, pouring them both another cup of tea.

"That's good. It's also why you haven't had anything to eat yet. Food and drink naturally ground you. They shift your body's inner workings to what you want to be concentrating on to the natural process of digestion. This way, your stomach may growl occasionally, but your mind is free to think."

Ren slurped his tea. "Gotcha. What next?"

"Let's jump to some basic defensive techniques, starting with your shields. Do you remember the light that surrounded each of us at the height of the confrontation last night?"

"Yes. His was purplish, mine a gold shade, and yours was bright white."

"Right. All of us, those with Talents, and those without, have an aura. Those auras are usually visible to others with Talents. Still with me? Good. When we feel threatened, all of us have natural defenses that kick in, such as adrenaline and other hormones. In addition to these natural defenses, you have the ability to create a defensive 'shield' around you, like a psychic force field. This force field, your 'shield' will block psychic energy, just like it did that energy bolt I'm assuming our friend threw at you last night." Mike winked at that last part.

"How did you know that? You weren't there when he did that!"

"Ren, that's what led me to you in the first place. When that bolt of energy hit your shield, it was like shooting off a hundred flares in the sky. It didn't take much for me to double-back on Esplanade and nail down the exact location of your little altercation. That's something to keep in mind for the future—to the untrained eye, a psychic duel looks like two people standing still for an extended period of time. To someone with Talents, it looks like a Pink Floyd light show. There's no covering that light show up unless you expend an incredible amount of energy to shield the combat area. Now, let's start some basic exercises for controlling your shields."

They worked at this for almost two more hours. It was now after 11am, and Ren was developing a major headache. Mike noticed that Ren was having to stop and rub his eyes over and over before he could repeat the series of exercises. Reaching out, he touched Ren's left temple with the first two fingers of his right hand, mumbling what Ren thought to be a prayer.

"I don't possess any specific Healing Talents, but there are a few spells we all learn that are helpful when we're tired, or when psychic exertion manifests itself as a headache. What's that look? You don't like the word 'spell?' Don't sweat it, me boyo, I could have just as easily substituted 'technique' or similar word for 'spell.' In this particular case 'treatment' would also be appropriate. Jeez, Ren you'd think you were raised Irish Catholic, you're so superstitious." Mike chuckled, shifting from Ren's left temple to the right.

Exhaling deeply, Ren smiled thanks to Mike for the "treatment." His head did indeed feel much better, which reminded him that his stomach was also aching for some attention. "You know," he said, "My momma went to Redemptorist High, in the Irish Channel, so I do have a little of that Irish Catholic in me you're talking about."

"Did she indeed? Wow, what a small world. I was assigned up at St. Mary's there, across the street from Redemptorist for a year, but I didn't last long. Between teaching and some...errrr...disagreements with the pastor, I decided it might be better to find a different place to hang my hat. Hey, if you know the Channel, then you know where we just have to eat today, right?" Mike's eyes twinkled at the thought of good food.

Ren immediately picked up on what he was saying, and the result was a scene from a movie.

"Parasol's!" They both said simultaneously, and off they went, heading across town to the old Irish Channel neighborhood.

After a very filling meal of roast beef and shrimp po boys, the men climbed back into Ren's jeep and headed back to the old Creole side of town where Ren lived. While still in the Irish Channel, Mike had Ren drive a couple of blocks out of the way so he could point out a neighborhood bar to Ren for future reference. The "Dixie 45" beer sign out front proclaimed the place to be the "Triple-7" bar.

"Yeah, that's the Triple-7. I know you've got a lot of new information swimming through your head, Ren, but do try to remember the Triple-7. If you ever get into any kind of jam, or you develop any sort of problem related to your Talents that you can't sort out on your own, obviously call me immediately. If you can't do that, or if something were to happen to me at some point, I want you to go over to the Triple-7 as soon as you can get there. Ask for Jake, the owner. If he's not there, lower your shields a bit and flare your aura, like we worked on earlier. No, don't worry, it's a safe place. You unzip your fly, psychically speaking, and someone will step in and lend a hand." Mike had his serious expression on again, which worried Ren a bit.

"You get this look sometimes that makes it very clear that this isn't a game, you know," he said.

Mike nodded slowly. "No, this certainly isn't a game. You've discovered that already, I'm sure. A legacy of your birthright as one of those with Talents is that you've inherited a number of enemies, in addition to the ones you've already picked up in your life. Still, I think you should give serious thought to those folks that didn't care much for you before last night, Ren. That assassin didn't appear out of thin air, so you still might be in danger, as well as those around you."

"Mike, I can't just go to the police with what happened last night, can I?"

"No, that's for sure, but there are some things you can do. We now know there is a direct connection between the deaths of your two friends, so you should pass this on to the authorities."

"Yeah, I plan on doing that in the next few days. I've got a call into a friend of mine who is a cop so I can see what the best way to approach passing this information on is. Hopefully this can be sorted out. I still don't think Hadley's got the balls to kill us over the blog, though."

Mike nodded agreement with the last statement. "Neither do I. Still, the connection with your website is staring us in the face. Besides, history is rife with outrageous things people of all races have done in the name of God. And every one of these radio preachers has some kind of financial backing or investment behind them. Find out who stands to gain by Hadley's success, and you'll find the person who stands to lose most by his failure."

Ren shook his head as he pulled into the driveway of his home. "Yup, I do believe you've got a point, kind sir. What's next for my Talents?"

Mike smiled a happy grin again, the cloud of the last few minutes passing over and his sunny disposition returning. "Work on the ground/center/shield exercises for a few days, say a week. Let's get back together next Thursday and see what kind of mischief we can get into then!"

They both laughed.

CHAPTER SIX
Lunch Meetings

A much more somber luncheon was taking place in the Dallas area that day. Anita Delatorre never did relish the prospect of driving to the suburb of Arlington for lunch, but it made more sense to conduct this kind of business in part of the Metroplex where she would not be likely to run into others from the Christian publishing industry.

Of course there was no way she could avoid the meeting. Will Ryan's message on her voice-mail made it clear that a serious problem had developed. And Anita was paid well to deal with these kinds of situations. Most of them went smoothly, so there was no point in bitching about those that didn't.

She pulled off I-30 just past the amusement park and the stadiums and pulled into the parking lot of La Lune, a chain restaurant with a French country bistro theme. She ordered Caesar salad and an iced tea, sat down with her food, and waited for Ryan. She was just sending a short mind-call to him when he walked through the front door. He turned and nodded to her, ordered grilled chicken and sat down with her at the table.

"I appreciate you joining me. You know I wouldn't have called if the situation wasn't serious." William Ryan was still visibly shaken.

Anita sighed. "Yes, Will. Now please tell me what is going on."

Ryan began by describing the events of the previous evening. Anita was startled to learn that Renard Alciatore possessed Talents; and even more startled when Will began to tell her of the intervention of the stranger robed in the white aura of a Teacher. She cut him off in mid-sentence, too impatient to continue listening.

"Give me your memories, Will. I want to see this as you did." She held her hand out, inviting him to join hands with her to form a mind-link.

Will grasped her hand lightly, closed his eyes, and began to transmit his memories of the aborted duel from the previous evening. His shock at seeing the creature he had conjured to finish-off Alciatore being dissolved by the intervening stranger was still so powerful that Anita was almost forced out of their link. She opened her eyes and locked-on to Will's to settle him down again, wordlessly encouraging him to continue transmitting his memories to her.

She sat for a moment, sinking back into her chair, and then took a bite of her salad. Sipping her iced tea she looked back at Ryan. "Yes Will, you were right to come. This is an interesting turn of events. We will have to consider this job concluded. I was very specific about the order the targets should be dealt with and the two successes you have had will, for the time being, be effective in dealing with the situation I am trying to handle. Alciatore will be busy for a while now, trying to do the same thing I must do: figure out what the fuck has happened here. In any case, your part in this little play is concluded."

"I'm not comfortable leaving something I have started unfinished. For one thing, that guy can identify me. I don't like that Anita."

"You may not like it but you'd better take the admonishment of that Teacher seriously, Will," she said as she leaned forward. "It's more than a little obvious that this man has the resources to hunt you down if need be." Anita's expression was unchanged as she picked at her salad, but the serious tone in her voice was clear.

"Nothing is obvious about what has happened here, Anita! What is it you aren't telling me?" Will's eyes betrayed his pleading.

"Listen Will. There are things I simply can't discuss with you. I am bound by certain obligations not to go into these matters. Trust me on this: if you leave Renard Alciatore alone, he and those associated with him will leave you alone. You can also be sure that the traditional authorities will not be involved in this matter. These people won't call the cops."

Will sighed. "I've lived most of my adult life totally confident that I could handle any situation I got myself into. I'm having a very hard time dealing with this."

Anita locked her eyes into his again to re-establish the mind-link and sent soothing, relaxing thoughts to Ryan. "Will, you've done well and you will continue to do well. I will make some enquiries about you with people who have followed your career with great interest. Try to relax, my friend. You will be fine. Don't consider this contract to be a failure; what has happened here is bigger than you and frankly been getting out of my league too."

Will nodded as he dug into his lunch. Whatever was going on was not affecting his appetite. He had not eaten since breakfast the previous day and, after devouring half of his meal, he resumed the conversation.

"So how will you deal with this situation if you can't follow your original plan?"

Anita smiled.

"Well, my preferred method of dealing with this would have been to keep myself totally out of the picture, but there were alternatives suggested before I even contacted you. We'll just have to use one of those instead. I'm not a fan of loose ends because they tend to become unraveled. Still, they might achieve the desired purpose."

She finished her salad and wiped her mouth with her napkin.

"Go and rest, Will. You're going to need a week or two to get back into full condition. Why not go and find some mischief out west in San Francisco?"

Will Ryan grinned for the first time during the lunch meeting.

"That sounds a great idea, Anita. I might just do that."

She returned the smile with more sincerity than previous.

"Good, I'll have my girl book you onto a flight for this afternoon. Give me the number of that phone you're using, so she can call you later." Anita was quite fond of Will, even though his taste in lovers was rather more masculine than she was. Part of her was disappointed that she would not be able to 'console' him in that particular way today. Finding lovers who had Talents and a body like Ryan's was next to impossible.

Ryan pushed his plate aside and reached over the table for her hand.

"Thanks Anita. I really appreciate this. I hope I may be as much help to you one day as you have been to me today." He arose from the table and left the restaurant.

"Oh I'll see you will, you can count on that," she thought.

Being discreet, Anita waited for ten minutes before leaving the restaurant herself. She climbed gracefully into her Cadillac SRX for the drive back downtown and, as usual, she was on the phone within a matter of seconds to check in with her secretary and then with her assistant. Once satisfied that everything was OK, she pulled into the middle lane of I-30 and prepared herself mentally for a phone call she really did not want to make.

Anita adjusted the headset, and used the voice-command system to call a number. She took a deep breath, and exhaled as the phone rang. The party at the other end answered on the second ring.

"Yes Anita." It was a male voice.

"Sir, some complications have arisen with my first option on our latest project. I would like to suggest that we begin the first alternative option with the third level." Even though she knew this was a secure line she did not want to discuss details such as these openly.

"Have the preliminary preparations been put in place for that option?"

"Yes sir. This morning, before I left the office."

"OK. I'll handle the arrangements. Do you want a light treatment or should this be the full heavy-handed kind?" The man's voice was monotone which made it difficult for Anita to sense his mood.

"Just light, for the moment," she replied. "There are circumstances I have just learned that indicate a gentle handling from here on would be prudent. I'll be able to make a full report to you in about 20 minutes." The discipline of her breathing pattern was all that kept her voice from trembling.

"Very well. I can't say I am happy with this, Anita. I am looking forward to your report, as I am sure there is a reasonable explanation why you have me involved at this point."

"I'm sure you will find my report interesting, sir."

"Keep control hun," she thought.

"Yes. Goodbye Anita."

"Thank you, sir. Goodbye." She ended the call. Then the shakes began.

***

Practicing the techniques Mike had taught him was not as difficult as Ren thought it would be. It had helped that it was a light week for him and he could spend some additional time working at them. By the following Wednesday he was able to ground himself completely, then center, and physically 'float' for around 45 minutes to an hour without getting a headache. After that float time he was able to ground again and become in very good spirits about what was next on his agenda.

He had made an early start on Thursday as he had to get up before dawn for a sunrise photo-shoot at City Park. He arrived home at around eleven and was able to float for a half-hour or so before the doorbell rang. Ren was a little startled by the bell. He was supposed to have lunch with his friend Bubba that day but he wasn't expecting Bubba until noon, and Bubba had never been on time once in the five years Ren had known him.

Ren opened the door to reveal two men in business suits. One was in his early forties; the other in his late twenties. The older one produced an ID wallet, the kind policemen carry. As he showed Ren his badge and ID he began to speak: "Mr. Alciatore? Sergeant Donald Jeanfreau, Louisiana State Police, sir. This is my partner, Trooper John Hendrick. We'd like to speak with you for a moment concerning your Internet server, sir."

"Sure, come in, please." Ren opened the door fully and showed the two men into the living-room. "Can I get you a cup of coffee or a Coke or something?"

"No thank you, sir. We'll only be a moment." His partner

produced a small pad and prepared to take notes. "We're working on several cases involving child pornography on the Internet and your email address came up on one of the computers we seized from a suspect last week."

"Did it now? And where is the problem with that? I get a lot of email from various sources, solicited and unsolicited."

"Well, sir, the 'send' log on that computer indicated that an image was transmitted with the email. Given some of the images on that computer we are looking into all possibilities. We would like to have a look at your equipment, sir." Sergeant Jeanfreau's expression remained throughout as the all-business look of an experienced cop.

"Sergeant, while I believe in cooperating with law enforcement, some of the materials I have on my server are for clients of mine. As such, they are confidential. I would have to secure the permission of my clients to allow that. Or you will need a search warrant to compel me to make the server available to you." Ren was not a good poker player but it was clear to the troopers that he was most serious.

"Well, Mr. Alciatore, as I said, this is a preliminary investigation and we're trying to run down some leads. I'm disappointed that you won't cooperate with us, but I understand your situation."

"Thanks Sergeant. I find child porn to be disgusting and exploitive. I hope you can shut down what's going on there. Was there anything else, gentlemen?"

"No sir. Not at this time." The policemen stood up to leave.

"Well, good luck in your investigation." Ren led them back to the front door.

Trooper Hendrick spoke for the first time: "Sir. Just so you know, we're far from being done with you. Good day."

The two policemen turned and headed towards their car, passing an Asian man in shirtsleeves on Ren's front walk. They didn't recognize him, and the older man tried to mask his look of distaste at being so close to a Japanese man. For his part, the newcomer smiled and nodded at the two men in a sort of non-verbal version of the traditional New Orleans greeting, "awrite". He waved at Ren to hold the door open but he did not say anything until the policemen were inside their car.

Ren greeted his guest first. “Bubba! How the hell are you?”

The Japanese man smiled and held out his hand to shake Ren’s. Toshihiro Watanabe got the nickname ‘Bubba’ when he had entered law enforcement. He was born in Osaka, Japan, and the 35 year-old’s parents had moved to California when he was a child. His wife was a geophysicist and had been transferred to New Orleans ten years previously. She made good money so Bubba had no problems letting her career take the lead. After signing-on with the City of Kenner Police Department he had risen through the ranks and was now a lieutenant of a street patrol platoon. After taking a graduate course in finance with Ren and JJ Garrison, the three had become fast friends.

Bubba’s smile faded as he withdrew his hand from their handshake. “I saw your company, Ren. Who did you piss off on the Governor’s staff to rate a visit from those two?”

“Huh? What are you talking about, Bubba? They said they were working on an Internet case. Kiddie porn or something. They wanted to take a look at my server and hardware. I suggested they go get a warrant.”

“Well I don’t know about the young one but the older one is Donny Jeanfreau. He’s on the detail personally assigned to the Governor. He used to be part of the bodyguard team but I’m told he now handles ‘special projects’. What makes you a special project, Ren?”

Ren smiled inwardly. He really should have been taken aback by this discovery but, after the events of the past week, this was just a mild tremor. “How come you know this guy, and he doesn’t know you, Bubba?”

“If you knew me only as ‘Bubba’ and never spoke to me, you’d walk right by me in the street, too.” Bubba grinned. “Let’s get something to eat. I’ve got to be in Federal Court for 2pm.”

Ren grabbed his keys and phone and followed his friend to the sidewalk. “Yeah and since you are not driving that POS the chief assigned you as a vehicle, I can see why he wouldn’t think you were a cop. I can’t believe you took Didi’s Jag today!”

“Well, I drove her in and I’ll pick her up later. She’s going for happy hour with her friends from work. This way, she can get blasted and I get her home safely."

"Cool! Well I have no problem with not riding in a cop car!" Ren laughed.

The pair enjoyed a light lunch at a little place on Esplanade Avenue, just down from the bayou. During the meal Ren laid out for his friend the circumstances of both of the deaths of his blogging colleagues. He left out the part about him being attacked. Ren really didn't know how he would explain that, even to his close friend. Bubba listened intently, took a few notes, and read through some of the Jay Hadley material Ren had brought along. When Ren had finished his story, Bubba looked up from the material and stared out as if into space for a moment, before responding.

"I'm not big on conspiracy theories, Ren. Ordinarily, I would look at the incident reports of these two deaths and would conclude that they are unrelated. However, the fact that there were three of you working on this web project and now two of you are dead makes my cop's intuition stand on its head. Now, having seen a couple of goons-with-badges from Baton Rouge on your doorstep, alarm bells are going off in my head like you wouldn't believe." Bubba was still making notes as he was speaking.

"Yeah. It seems you and JJ have the same intuition going on here," said Ren as he smiled.

"She's a smart lady, Ren. No arguing that. Tell you what, do this. Lie low with the blog for a week or two. Don't deliberately escalate whatever is going on while I make some deep background inquiries about what is happening here. At the same time, why don't you call that cousin of yours who is a state representative and see if he can get these troopers off your back."

"Jeez, Bubba. I don't know about that. They said they've got an investigation in progress. I don't want to get into trouble for messing with that." Ren looked concerned.

"The only thing being messed with here is you, my friend. Those two are attached to the Governor's staff, so you can be sure they aren't working a regular case. Their visit was an off-the-books appointment, if you get my meaning. I'd give this relative of yours a call and see if he can get these guys to back the fuck off."

Ren nodded. "Yeah, I'll call Ted and see what he can do."

"That would be helpful on my end. I don't want cops taking an interest in your affairs before I can get a handle on things. Now, you try to stay out of trouble for a while, OK?"

Laughing, Ren agreed. "Deal. Now tell me about what Didi and the girls are up to."

Bubba dropped Ren off at his house with more than enough time for him to get down to Camp Street and his court obligation. Ren returned a couple of phone calls then rang his cousin's law office. His cousin was in Baton Rouge, of course, since the legislature was in session. Ren left his name and number on the voicemail and was confident of a return call. Family was important in New Orleans, particularly among the Alciatore family.

With his phone calls out of the way, Ren went back to his computer monitor and to the graphic design he had been working on over the course of the previous few days.

His phone rang about an hour later. Ren's pulse quickened in anticipation. "Hello," he answered.

"Hey there, Ren. How is your grounding going?" The voice was the one he had hoped for, Father Michael Aloysius O'Donnell.

"Yeah, it's going just fine, thanks. I'm feeling very good about it."

"Think you're ready for more?"

"F'sure."

"Great then. Why don't you meet me at The Fly in half an hour. The next bit of work is best-suited for the outdoors."

"No problem, Mike. See you then!" Ren ended the call and went back to working for a while. It would take him only about fifteen minutes to get to The Fly, so he had time to check his email.

In spite of several enquiries to various people he knew who were adept at unraveling Internet mysteries, none of his contacts could shed any light on the source of the "revelation" email he had received. However, while reading the latest reply from a friend in the Boston area, it had occurred to Ren that perhaps his visit from the State Police that morning had been precipitated by other events. Namely, his receipt of an unsolicited photograph of a nude woman.

He opened the computer file and looked again at the image, this time in some detail.

"Yes, this girl could be underage," he thought.

He was aware that there was a lot of that on the Internet; pictures from magazines that are legal in Europe that make their way onto scanners and then into the US.

"Damn," he thought, *"If this is a fake of Hadley, it sure had me fooled. What better way to be discredited than to be arrested for having child pornography. Still, the cops didn't arrest me."*

So, why the visit? Perhaps a warning, he thought. These and other thoughts swirled around Ren's head as he went out to the Mach One so he could get uptown.

Some people call it The Fly and others call it Riverview, referring to the area of park alongside the Mississippi River just behind Audubon Zoo. Ren knew this area well because of the complex of soccer fields nearby where he had often refereed games. On weekdays, like today, the area was quiet and peaceful with just a few sunbathers. Ren pulled his vehicle into the parking stall next to a now-familiar Porsche 914, got out, and looked for his mentor.

Mike looked him up and down as they shook hands. "Yeah, you look a lot better than when I first met you!" Mike chuckled and led Ren down to the edge of the river. "I wanted to come down here because there's something primal about being this close to such a large flowing body of water. There's lots of energy here; a good place to recharge the batteries. Or, in our case today, to plug directly into a power source so you don't drain yourself."

Mike was quiet for a few moments before continuing: "OK, now that you have no problem grounding and manipulating your shields, we're going to work on more proactive tasks. The first one will be a bit of mind-reading. Don't look at me like that, it's exactly what it sounds like! The idea is to be able to enter the mind of another person and exchange thoughts. It's a wonderful way for two people with Talents to communicate because you don't have to worry about words. You simply form images in your mind and transmit them; similar to the way you upload and download images on the Internet. Ready to give it a try?"

Ren was a little nervous. But he was ready. "Let's go for it."

"OK, look at the river. Feel the force of the current. Open your mind to it and let its energy in."

The Mississippi River in New Orleans is big, wide, and majestic. Ren looked over the fast-moving water as he took a deep breath and lowered his shields. A large oil tanker was heading down-river leaving a massive wake behind it. Ren's gaze followed the waves to the river bank and he allowed the force from the water to enter him, filling him with its energy. Satisfied that he was completely "charged up", he closed his eyes, centered his thoughts, then opened them and turned to Mike with a look of "what's next" in his expression.

"Right, I want you to look across the river at that barge coming towards us. Look at the tug-boat pushing that barge and try to capture the image in your mind as if you were taking a photograph. Good. OK. Now visualize that image as a file in the memory of the computer that is your mind. Got it? Great. Now I want you to search out my mind as if it were another computer connect to the Internet. You don't have far to travel since I'm right here." Mike grinned as he made that last comment.

Ren closed his eyes and began to initiate the floating sensation he had been working on all week. Once that feeling had kicked in, he sought out Mike and immediately found him. Sensing the link had been established he "opened" the "image file" in his brain and "uploaded" it to Mike. In a flash he recognized that he had successfully transmitted the image to him.

"Excellent!" Mike was very pleased. "You see, this is the advantage of working with an adult as opposed to a child. The Talents are strong in children but they don't have the life experiences adults have to be able to do what you have just achieved. We first have to teach them much of the basics of observation and other human concepts before we can teach them to send those experiences mentally. I suspect your dormant Talents have helped you to become the excellent photographer you are, Ren."

"Thanks Mike." Ren too, was very pleased and excited that he was achieving this so quickly.

"Now that you are able to 'upload' an image, let's see if you can 'download' mine too. Close your eyes and wait for it."

Ren did as he had been instructed, eagerly anticipating an image. He felt a tingle in his mind as a picture began to form in his mind. Green grass. Vivid color. It was as if he had his eyes open and he was looking down at his feet. Then, the color of the grass turned into glistening beige, then to a stripe of neon blue. He mentally adjusted his focus on the image as though he were looking through the lens of a camera and realized he was seeing a well-tanned woman wearing a bright blue bikini bottom. He looked closer and saw that she was laying face-down on a blanket. Her top was untied and beneath her breasts. It was clear that she was absorbed in her worship of the sunshine. The intensity of the image startled Ren, especially when he considered the source of the transmission.

"Mike. Jeez, you're a priest. That was a pretty graphic image!"

Mike laughed loudly and took a few seconds to regain his composure.

"Ren, just because I am not ordering does not mean I can't look at the menu. Especially when the items on the menu look as tasty as that one!"

He pointed discreetly at a spot about a hundred feet away where the woman from his image was laying on the ground.

Over the next couple of hours, Ren and Mike passed images and thoughts back and forth to each other to the point where they were able to engage in conversations without actually speaking. Ren was amazed at how much progress he had made in such a short time.

"Does it always work this well? Somehow, I sense that this may be an exception."

Mike smiled and nodded in agreement.

"Yes, this is definitely an exception, Ren. You will find that mind-links like we have just generated are not difficult to establish. But you will probably need to have contact with the person you're linking with. Once you adjust to the way an individual 'connects' with you, you'll be able to get away without the touch but it is almost a prerequisite when connecting with strangers."

"OK. But you and I don't know each other all that well. Why does it work for us?"

"As my students would say, Dude! I'm good at this, OK?" Mike laughed. "That's where the river comes into play, we're both tapping into some serious energy right now, keeping ourselves topped off. You're not going to find that such a regular thing."

"Oh, OK," Ren replied, beginning to understand.

"Speaking of energy, it's time to release some of that right now. Another important aspect of grounding is that we want to make sure we channel back out of us some of the energy we have absorbed. Too much of a build-up of psychic energy is guaranteed to give you one heck of a headache by the end of the day, just as over-use of your Talents will."

He motioned to Ren to stand up, just as he stood up and brushed off his running shorts. "Close your eyes again and visualize a tap opening right at the ball of your foot. Now let the energy you've pulled in from the river flow out from that tap and into the ground. When you feel like the level of energy inside of you is right, close the tap again."

"How will I know what level to stop at?"

"You'll just know. Try it."

Ren did as he had been instructed and visualized the tap opening, at the ball of his foot. He could feel immediately the energy flowing out of him. Somehow, he sensed that his energy level was reaching down to his waist, so he closed the tap and the release stopped.

Mike was right, he thought. It feels just right. He could see that Mike was doing the same process so he waited before he said anything.

When Mike opened his eyes, Ren looked at him and said, "Yeah. That feels just right. Feels good. I'm ready for a beer. Care to join me?"

The priest laughed. "A man after my own heart!"

CHAPTER SEVEN

Talents on the Bayou

The Monday morning meeting of the senior staff at Jay Hadley Ministries was the most upbeat it had been for weeks. The radio shows had gone exceedingly well over the previous two weeks, donations were at a 15-month high, and the latest two-DVD package on *Bible Prophecy* was selling like hot cakes. They were ready to release the Christian homeschooling materials that accompanied the DVDs the following week.

Attacks on the ministry had tapered off and no new startling items had appeared on the Internet. The project heads were happy, mainly because they were able to report good things to their boss; Jay Hadley was the kind of boss who did not like to hear bad news.

Anita Delatorre smiled at that thought. She was sitting-in on the staff meeting that morning. Jay Hadley was ninety-nine percent responsible for the trouble that had developed; while he was, of course, responsible for the majority of the ministry's successes also.

Well, at least until Hadley had met Anita. Jay may be the voice on the radio, but Anita was the brains behind most of the marketing moves and development techniques implemented by the business. She had placed Hadley on the national map when it came to Christian Radio Ministries. It angered her that he could not control his hormones now that it was finally pay-off time.

For Anita, New Orleans was a nice place to visit, but her heart was still in Dallas. Hadley's behavior of late had made it prudent for her to be here. The good Reverend Hadley had always been discreet when he was married. His wife, Suzanne Collins Hadley was the only daughter of a New Orleans businessman who donated heavily to the New Orleans Baptist Theological Seminary. Her personal wealth enabled Hadley to pursue his vocation. Involvement in scandal would have cut off his means of support. As his ministry grew, however, his need to bow to his wife's wishes shrunk, to the point where Suzanne decided to take her life in a "new direction". Now that his divorce was final, Hadley was becoming increasingly brazen in his personal life. As long as she was here for him, though, she figured she could keep him under control.

"The guy has no clue," she thought. *"It really is true that some guys think with the wrong head."*

She returned her attentions back to the discussions of the staff, and heard Cecilia McIntyre presenting the pros and cons of increasing the number of on-air exorcisms.

"As everyone knows, exorcisms perform two functions for us: they stimulate donations in a big way and they eliminate the need for us to have to field calls from outside. The downside is that they don't just pop up on schedule and many of the callers just plain don't work out. Still, we could increase the number of 'possessed' callers that actually make it onto the air. The more we take, the more chances we'll get of nailing a live one."

Hadley was taking notes. He looked around the room then turned to Cecilia. "Cee, what about taping callers off-air and playing-back the exorcisms later?"

"We could do some of those," Cecilia replied, "but fundraising activity on those days is not as good as on truly live days. Focus-group polling indicates that people are concerned that taped shows aren't truly genuine, that we're doing something to fix the outcome. They believe it's all too easy to edit, tape, or rig the show in some way. Given all the attention our finances have received over the last twelve months, we need to be careful about credibility." Cecilia was one of the more outspoken members of staff when it came to financial impropriety. While most of the staff was loath to criticize the boss for the way the books were handled, Cecilia did not pull any punches.

Hadley winced, inwardly, at Cecilia's comments but went

forward. “Is there a middle ground?”

Cecilia looked thoughtful. “One thing that has worked is to begin an exorcism late into the show, then continue the process off-air and play the tape the next day. Donations are still off when we do this, though. What it boils down to is that the real thing, on-air, is still the best way.”

Joelle Guidry, Hadley’s lead copy and developmental editor, spoke up. “Cee, let’s talk about shows other than exorcisms. We’ve got the Bible Prophecy book coming out next month and the New-Age book in August. Can we get some shows planned with tie-ins to these?”

“Well, the New-Age stuff is easy to plan for, since there’s always something we can use there. We can line up some guests on anti-pagan topics and go from there. Bear in mind though, that our best exorcism cases come up out of our attack shows on Wicca in particular. So we would run the risk of messing-up a good book promotion week with an exorcism.”

Cecilia cocked her head to one side. “Still, if we prepare the appeal spots and promotional pieces in advance we should be able to work that through. The trick is to have our donation break pieces ready to run. Statistics show that there’s little difference in donations on days when breaks are done live and when they’re canned. We just need to get Jay recorded.”

“Ha!” Anita thought. *‘You mean while I’m on my knees doing what has to be done to keep you from calling any more call-girls.”*

She was not interested in letting that tidbit go public though, so she got her thoughts back to business fast.

“M-K can help with some of the promotion spots,” Anita said. “We’re going to be putting together some spots for Evangelical TV. If we do those EvTV spots carefully you should be able to use the audio tracks from them on the show. I know y’all prefer to record stuff on shorter notice, to make the spots timelier, but these could work as a good back-up.” Anita smiled sweetly at Cecilia. She did not think Cee had any romantic interest in Hadley, but she sometimes wondered why the girl was so hostile towards her. She had tried on several occasions to mind-link Cecilia to see if she could find anything out, but her surface shielding had made this difficult to achieve. The girl didn't possess Talents, but Cecilia's basic intuition was strong enough to make the process more difficult than Anita wanted to attempt.

"I guess that's why she's not married, the girl is all balled-up in there and won't open up to a man," thought Anita.

Cecilia returned the smile with one equally insincere and the meeting continued on to other topics. It broke up half an hour later and the staff went back to their offices. Since Jay and Anita had just walked out of the office together, Cecilia decided to run home for lunch. Since she often took work home with her, nobody who saw her leave really paid any attention to the stack of files she was carrying. Once home, she moved quickly to scan a dozen or so documents contained in those files and return them to their original folders. While wolfing-down a blueberry yogurt, she packed up once again and zipped back to the office. She settled her purse and her briefcase back in her office and took several of the files from her briefcase and replaced them in the file cabinet next to Jay's desk in his office.

Anita and Hadley headed down to the parking garage and to her rented Mercedes. It wasn't until they were approaching the interstate leading into town that Hadley began to speak.

"I don't like this one bit, Anita. They're just too goddamn quiet. Nothing new on that damn website for two weeks." The look on Hadley's eyes was almost one of fear. "Not even anyone trying to sneak onto the air. It's uncanny."

Had she not been so directly involved with the recent unfolding events, Anita might have found Hadley's attitude amusing. She drove the car off the interstate at the Metairie Road exit and turned into the entrance of Metairie Cemetery without saying a word. Hadley was incredulous.

"Anita, we really don't have time for sightseeing. If you want to look at gravestones I wish you'd do it some other time. We have serious issues to deal with here. This is ridiculous. Now, are we going to review the plans for the book signings or not?" Hadley was getting angry now.

Still without saying anything, Anita pulled the car into the back end of the older section of the cemetery. There was no one coming in or out of this area. She pulled the car between two large double-capacity tombs so it would not be noticed.

Hadley was beside himself by now and was ready to begin a new tirade when she put a finger to his lips to stifle him.

She leaned towards him and kissed him lightly on the lips. She removed her suit jacket and sensed that Hadley would need a bit more encouragement before he would relax enough for her to relieve him as she had planned. Leaning back a little, she began to rub her nipples through her chemise, slowly at first, teasing them through the fabric to grow and become hard. Hadley watched her intently and leaned back in his seat, eventually realizing just why she had brought him to the cemetery. Anita continued to tease her nipples with her left hand as she reached over to Hadley and began to run her hand up and down Hadley's thigh and across his crotch.

He was more than responsive to her touch and emitted a slight moan as she stroked his manhood to full erection through his pants. Reaching over with both hands now, she unbuckled his trousers while continuing to rub him. She unzipped him and slid his pants to his ankles, making sure to maintain contact with his erection as she readied him. She tugged his boxers down too, and freed his manhood from its constraints as it sprung to full attention.

Anita moved up now to kiss him and her tongue explored his mouth deeply. He returned her embrace as he thrust his hips gently against her. She pulled her skirt up around her waist to reveal her white thigh-high hose and white silk panties that were becoming wetter by the second. She sucked his lower lip into her mouth and dove her hand into her panties to soak her fingers with her own juices, then stroked his erection with her lubricated hand. Hadley moaned a little more loudly as she moved her mouth down from his lips to his neck, then chest, biting his nipple lightly through his dress shirt, then down to kiss the tip of his erection.

Hadley sighed again and stroked her blonde hair as she took him fully into her mouth, sucking him deeply then moving back to the tip. She ran her tongue around the head, lightly flicking the moisture forming there from the tip, then engulfing him deeply again. After she had repeated this three or four times she pulled up her chemise to reveal her milky-white breasts and deep rose-colored nipples. As she rubbed first one nipple and then the other against his manhood he thrust rapidly against her breasts. She repositioned herself to suck him again and she picked up the pace until he let out a stifled growl and flooded her mouth with his orgasm. Anita didn't miss a beat and matched him thrust for thrust, swallowing every drop he offered her.

Satisfied that he was finished, she sucked him a moment longer then licked him clean. She reached to his ankles and looked him in the eye with a look that suggested it was time for him to pull up his boxers and trousers. Once he was fully dressed she pulled down her chemise again to cover her breasts.

Anita pulled her suit jacket back on and shook out her hair. She turned to Jay and spoke to him for the first time since leaving his Metairie office suite.

"I think it's time we went to that meeting now, don't you?" She started the car and headed towards the cemetery exit.

***

"There's nothing better than a muffuletta on a summer's day," Ren commented as he sat alongside Bayou St. John, eating lunch with his friend.

"Yes there is," Mike O'Donnell said wryly. "A muffuletta on a spring or fall day when it isn't so fucking hot!"

Ren laughed self-consciously, still surprised that a priest would use the language that Mike occasionally used. Not that Ren had a problem with it. Hell, he had been to Catholic school and had picked up the same words. Still, folks raised Catholic always seemed to put priests on a higher plane and it was nice to know that there was at least one down here on earth. He bit into his sandwich again.

Having consumed the last of his sandwich, Ren lay back on the grass and stared at the clouds. He and Mike had been working some more on mind-links and mind-to-mind communication. They had taken the concept from the basics of one person with Talents sharing information with another, to the notion of actually planting thoughts and images into the mind of an average person; one who would not be aware of what was going on. Ren was still mulling-over pieces of their discussion.

"The ethical implications of this are staggering," he had said to Mike after being taught how to deliberately send emotions to another person. "You can drive a person literally crazy with these techniques."

"Yes, this is true," Mike responded. "But consider the possibilities short of that: the policeman who can disarm a violent criminal without shooting him, or the teacher who can pick up the mood and spirits of a teenage girl who has just broken up with her boyfriend. Or how about the soccer referee who wants to settle-down a coach who is really pissed with the ref's last call?" Mikes eyes twinkled as the last example hit home.

"Jeez, I never thought of those."

"I didn't think you did," said Mike as he chuckled. "How's the investigation coming along into who wants to do you in?"

"Still a mystery. Background checks on all the staff at JHM show they're all a bunch of saints. It isn't likely any of them would be involved in any murder scheme or that they would even know who to call to get a job like that done." Ren sat up, frowned, and took a sip of his drink.

Mike also picked up his drink and took a sip before replying.

"What's more of a mystery to me is how a group of Christian crazies like these managed to hire a hit-man with Talents. I suppose it could be just co-incidence; that he was hired just through a normal channel and he happens to be good at what he does because of his abilities." Mike took another bite of his sandwich and finished his musing with his mouth full.

"But nobody, including me, even knew I had Talents," Ren observed.

"Don't be so sure, Ren Just because I didn't know you had them and others I associate with didn't know, doesn't mean nobody knew."

"Who else would know, or even care? I don't get it." Ren had resumed his prone position, staring at the clouds.

"Leave those details to me for now. Just concentrate on shields and defenses. I'll take care of the big picture for the time being." Mike smiled that disarming smile of his, but Ren wasn't buying it.

"You make it sound as though there's something cloak-and-dagger going on here."

"Well maybe not the cloak, but certainly the dagger, Ren. Or at least the psychic equivalent of a dagger. We have a puzzle on our hands, to be sure. In the meantime let's see your shields and your combat defense."

Ren stood up facing the water, hoping to draw from the natural energy of the bayou. He began the mental imagery he needed to raise his shields. Mike had suggested several possibilities and Ren decided that a visualization of a brick tower encircling his mind was the one that worked best for him. He raised that tower a little at a time over the course of two or three minutes. He had developed so well that he could now raise the protective tower immediately if necessary; but that was not without cost to his energy drain. The slow upward movement was a nice natural progression that allowed him to focus on his surroundings as well as on his shields.

With his shields now fully-raised, he began to extend their protection outwards. The initial tower surrounding his head was sufficient to protect him from unwanted intrusion, both deliberate and accidental, but further shielding was needed to deal with the combat attacks he had experienced in the duel. Now, he kept his eyes closed and began to draw energy from the sun and the water as he visualized pure white energy entering the top of his head and wandering throughout his body.

That sensation of energy began to manifest itself around his heart, wrapping his heart and his chest in white light, just under his skin. Once he had generated enough energy, Ren made a mental shrug and that energy projected itself from his heart outwards, moving up and down his frame until it covered him with the gold-light armor he had seen in the duel.

Standing like this, Ren was now impervious to any surprise psychic attacks, even those which an experienced person with Talents could throw at him. He turned towards Mike and bowed to his Teacher, a formal part of the Protocol of raising armor. He was not fully-steeped in the mechanics of the Protocols yet, but Mike had made it clear that he should begin to respect the traditions of his heritage.

Mike held his arms outstretched. He nodded approval and then drew both hands together in a testing spell. He shot a quick bolt of green energy at Ren's right arm and it bounced off harmlessly. Ren grinned a cocky smile at his teacher. Mike returned his smile with a smirk and raised his hands again. This time, a red bolt of light appeared from the fingertips of his right hand. It did not shoot immediately forward like the green one had. Instead it was slowly released by its owner and it floated towards Ren, his prodigy, who was standing proudly, unaware of the threat this latest bolt posed to him.

As the red bolt of energy approached Ren's arm it jerked forward a little and a thin white needle of light appeared at the tip. As soon as that needle appeared, the bolt pierced the golden aura of Ren's armor and jabbed him in the upper right arm. Ren howled as if he had been stung by a giant bee.

"Sonofabitch!" he exclaimed as his armor blinked into nothingness in a millisecond. He realized immediately his defenses had dropped then had the presence of mind to regenerate the armor and turn towards his teacher.

"All right, Obi-Wan, what the hell did you do?"

Mike was trying hard not to laugh., but Ren's outburst made it difficult for him to maintain the serious tone this lesson required.

"What I just did was to pop your balloon. It wasn't for long, but in those seconds when your armor vanished there was enough time for a trained attacker to wreak havoc on your body."

"That's nasty! How do you counter that one?"

"Yeah, it's nasty, but it isn't hard to beat. Open your mind to me and I'll show you."

The pair spent the next half hour with Ren blocking slow bolts as well as fast. When Ren had blocked a dozen or so slow bolts mixed in with standard fast attacks, Mike lowered his hands and sat down in the grass.

"Much better. Now you've got the idea, Ren, you're aware that you can't assume that your armor is going to hold. Just like a tank commander knows that most types of bullets and shells will bounce off his vehicle's hull, he also knows that there is nasty shit out there that will indeed pierce his armor. Be that tank commander, Ren. Stay aware of your surroundings and you'll know when something is approaching."

Ren let the golden armor around him fade, and then lowered his shields to restful state. "What about sneak attack, though? What happens when someone doesn't follow the rules?"

"Well, I'd love to be able to tell you that everyone follows the rules. But, yes, sometimes that's just not the case. Even with our friendly assassin though, you saw that he followed the rules. Believe me when I tell you that anyone who doesn't will be found eventually and punished. Does that stop them? Sometimes not. But what does happen is that person is usually nervous and, unknowingly, will telegraph his nervousness all over the neighborhood. That signal will be your warning that something is wrong. Listen to your feelings at all times, Ren."

Ren sighed and shook his head. "I always thought I did. Now you've got me second-guessing myself. Oh well, I'll get over that feeling, don't worry. What does the rest of your afternoon look like?"

"Back to UNO for a while. I haven't done any Newman Center work for some days now. And you?"

"Going to see a politician. A relative of mine, Teddy Barnes. He's state rep for Lakeview.

"Lumpy? You're related to Lumpy Barnes?" Mikes expression was one of fond memories as he chuckled.

"Yeah, he's my cousin. My daddy's sister's son."

Mike was still chuckling.

"You know how he got the nickname 'Lumpy', don't you?"

"Well, he always tells a story about how he can't make a roux; that it always turns out lumpy, so they wouldn't let him work at the restaurant. But it always sounded bullshit to me." Ren smiled.

Mike's chuckles turned into outright laughter.

"No. That's not it at all. I went to high school with Lumpy. One year, at the homecoming dance, his date got very, very frisky on the dance floor. The band was playing 'Stairway to Heaven'. You know, eight minutes straight of making-out, and the Brothers don't interfere. Well, this gal moves Teddy into the middle of the dance floor and starts rubbing close up against him. By the time the song was over he had the biggest hard-on and nothing he could do was going to conceal it. This other girl sees it and says, 'Jeez, that's a serious lump you got there!' So that did it. The name stuck."

Ren was laughing along with Mike now.

"Gawd, no wonder he changed his story."

"Yeah, well he had to, because none of us could call him 'Teddy' ever again. He was always 'Lumpy' from then on. I swear, the guy might run for governor one day, but he'll still be 'Lumpy'."

"Well, I got a visit from some state troopers the other day, so I'm hoping that he can make a phone call or two and find out what's going on for me," Ren said.

Mike turned serious again and looked back at Ren.

"Is this related to the other night in some way?"

Ren shook his head.

"No, but I suspect it's related to JHM somehow. I'm gonna see if I can get Teddy to have them back off. The guys who came to my house are on the Governor's staff which, my friend from the Kenner cops says, means that whatever is going on is political not criminal."

Mike nodded.

"OK, well I may make a few back-channel inquiries myself, if it's alright with you. I don't like the sound of it." Seeing Ren's "be my guest" gesture he continued: "Yeah, a number of the staff of our current governor are what can be referred to as 'Christian crazies', so I'll do some asking around to see who likes to use cops as the hand of God."

"Gotcha." Ren hauled himself up and headed for the car.

"Let me go see what my cousin can do. I'll keep you posted."

***

Ren watched as Mike continued to lie in the sun and meditate a while longer. The Mach One roared to life underneath him and he pulled off in the direction of West End and the office of the State Representative The Honorable T.R. "Lumpy" Barnes. The "T.R." stood for Theodore Roosevelt, because his daddy was a big fan of the Rough Riders, and also because his father had served under Theodore Roosevelt, Jr. in World War II.

Ren announced himself to the secretary, but his cousin was there in a flash to greet him with a back-slapping hug. He looked Ren in the eye: "Jeez, it's good to see you. Been too damned long. C'mon in and tell me what you're up to."

Ren followed Barnes into the inner office, accepted a cup of coffee, and got comfortable. After a few minutes of small-talk Barnes cut to the chase. "OK, now we've caught up a bit, let's have why you're really here, cousin. I know you, if this was a social visit you would've told me to meet you at a restaurant or at some bar downtown." Barnes eyes gleamed. "Let's have the story."

Ren outlined his activities with the website briefly, then explained in detail about his visit from the state police. At the description of the names of the troopers in question, Barnes eyes opened wide with disbelief.

Jeanfreau? Someone sent Jeanfreau to your house? Jesus, someone up there is fucking stupid! That guy's not just an enforcer on the governor's staff, cousin; he's a fuckin' religious nut! And I'll wager that whoever is behind this is also one of those religious nutballs up there as well. Well, I will put a stop to this shit right here and now. Barnes picked up the phone and buzzed his secretary. "Get me Dave DeMatteo's office in Baton Rouge," he requested. He placed his hand over the mouthpiece so he could tell Ren: "Dave is the governor's chief of staff. I was dead-ass serious about putting a stop to this shit." He held up his hand before Ren could reply, to indicate that the other party had come on the line.

"Hey, Davey? Lumpy here. Davey, look, clear your board for a minute. We need to have a talk right now, OK? Yeah, I'll hold on a minute, but make it a 30-second minute, capiche?" Barnes put his hand over the mouthpiece again and turned to Ren. "You just don't realize how pissed off I am right now." He uncovered the mouthpiece and spoke again into the phone.

"Look Davey, I just got finished talking to a cousin of mine. His name is Renard Alciatore. Yeah, that's right. My momma's family. Yeah, the restaurant. Davey, Ren tells me that Donny Jeanfreau paid him a visit last week. No, I'm not mistaken. Look Davey, you know I'm willing to play live-and-let-live with you guys and your Christian allies when it comes to most things, but I just found out you sent one of your thugs to someone in my family. That's MY FAMILY, Davey! You understand what I'm saying? You can let your little crusaders go play all over the state if you want to. Hell, Davey, your boss isn't the first governor who has used the State Police to his own ends; I know how that works. But you also know how we feel down here about family."

Barnes was on his feet now, the volume of his voice having increased considerably. "AND I WILL NOT HAVE YOUR PEOPLE FUCKING WITH MY FAMILY!"

He sat down again.

"What? Hmmm, listen Davey, I can't begin to tell you how much I don't give a shit what you do and do not personally know about this. Davey, fuck your personal integrity right now, you are in a bigger world of shit than you think. Yeah, that's right, the special session. You get your little mod-squad off my family yesterday and I'll do what I can to put this in the back of my mind. I assure you, Davey, I'll never forget it. And you don't want me coming up there and getting into your boss's face over this. BELIEVE ME Davey, I will. OK, thanks Davey. I'm counting on you to handle this. Yeah, same here, Davey. Thanks, big guy. I'll call you about the session. Yes, I will. Talk to you soon, Davey." Barnes hung up the phone.

Ren was by now totally confused. "Teddy, what was that all about?"

"Ren, Donald Jeanfreau isn't just a state trooper. He's not just a state trooper on the governor's staff. He's a state trooper on the governor's staff who's a born-again religious fanatic. A real avenging angel. He takes orders from some of the more right-wingers up in Baton Rouge. Now, the tradition of governors using troopers for their own purposes goes back a long time, and isn't limited to Louisiana by any means. But this isn't about politics, it's about religion. And that scares the shit out of me. And that was before I found out this guy had turned his attention to my family."

Ren was a little shaken-up now. "Teddy, I hope I haven't caused you any trouble here."

"Nah, don't sweat that. I've been cooperative with that group for some time now. And I don't want you to stop messing with this radio preacher, Ren. If you feel like this guy needs to be brought into the light of day, then you go for it. You heard what I told that asshole just now. You will not be bothered by those people again, I don't care how much contribution funds from Dallas the governor loses!" Barnes slammed his hand on his desk as he finished his sentence.

"Thanks Teddy. As a matter of fact, I've got stuff for the blog that I've been putting off publishing because these guys worried me. It's way too easy to accuse someone of something like kiddy-porn and have the DA or the cops come in and seize everything I've got."

"Well you just make sure you keep that end of this straight. If someone sends you anything that you have your doubts about, you ditch it. If this guy Hadley is really doing little girls, we'll find another angle of approach. If this is just consensual sex and exposing hypocrisy then you go for it, cuz." Barnes smiled a vicious grin.

"OK. Thanks, Teddy. I really appreciate the help."

"Nuttin' to it, cuz." He shook Ren's hand and his cousin turned to go.

Ren took a very roundabout route home, cruising along the lake front all the way to UNO, then doubling back and stopping for a coffee in Gentilly. Some of what he had overheard in his cousin's office had set him thinking. Contributions to the governor from sources in Dallas. That, in itself, was no big deal. But Ren's intuition told him there was something more to this than just the usual business donations. He pulled out his notepad from his back pocket, drew a circle, and wrote "DALLAS" in the middle. He drew two more circles below that circle and then lines connecting the lower circles to the Dallas one. In the lower left circle he wrote "JHM", and in the lower right one he wrote "GOV". Ren stared at the diagram for some time. He sipped his café mocha and contemplated the possibilities. Nothing came to him but he was sure of one thing: it was time to find out what sort of connections Jay Hadley had in Dallas.

After a light supper at home, Ren sipped on a cup of tea

while downloading information about the publisher of every book Jay Hadley had ever written. Marcus-Kayson, of Dallas, Texas, appeared to be huge in the world of Christian books and media. So huge, in fact, that its nearest competitor was only 40% the size of "M-K", as insiders called the company.

He opened a new folder on his system and saved all the information had found about the company through a number of Internet search-engine sites, not just Google. His project for the evening was just about done when he heard the "new message" tone from Kik on his phone.

It was "Isis".

"Hi. How's your evening so far?"

"I've been working on publishing some of the stuff you sent me, as a matter of fact."

"I was wondering why you hadn't jumped on that. Are you satisfied the documents are genuine?"

"Oh, I was satisfied of that fairly quickly. But when you get visited by the Governor's personal 'God Squad', one tends to move a bit more cautiously."

"What are you talking about?"

"Oh, come on. If you are connected enough to get the info you've been able to get, you can't tell me that you didn't know about my visit from the state police."

"I'm serious... I really didn't know. Please tell me what happened... maybe I can help. Please tell me?"

Ren relayed the story of his visit from the cops, but did not mention anything of his meeting with Lumpy.

"The bottom line is that two guys worked on this project are now dead and I've got cops interested in

my activities. The one person who gains most by this turns of events is Jay Hadley. I have no proof that the deaths are anything but natural and accidental, and I don't know who put the cops on my butt, but things are looking less and less co-incidental."

There was a pause before a reply came back.

"Ren, I can tell you with some authority that Jay Hadley not only doesn't have a clue about how to have someone killed, but he is also too much of a coward even to consider such a thing. As for the state police, the ministry isn't very well-connected politically. I'm pretty sure Jay has never even met the governor."

Ren wanted to trust this person. His instincts said he could, even though common-sense told him this was just an anonymous chat contact on his computer.

"OK, I believe you. Still with all this stuff happening, and JHM donations go up. Can you tell me who besides JH personally gains when the ministry is doing well?"

":-)"

The "smiley" face was followed by a website address. Ren clicked on that address and his browser jumped to the home page of Marcus-Kayson, the Dallas publishing company. The page on his monitor now was the same one he had been looking at earlier. Ren shuddered. He had made notes to research Marcus-Kayson eventually, but now it looked as though it would be sooner rather than later.

Ren closed the website, double-checked his email, and switched to his Twitter account. Nothing better than talking with some anonymous Australian women to get things off his mind, he chuckled to himself.

CHAPTER EIGHT

Brides

Ren slept dreamlessly. It was a blessing, given all that had been happening in his life. He awoke early and went immediately onto his computer to dig into the various online resources made available by the state of Louisiana for researching campaign contributions made to politicians. It was a slow process; Ren found that the websites were not well-designed. After an hour of digging, his Twitter app beeped and a "direct message" from someone named "Wynterbreeze" appeared.

"Love, love me do."

Ren smiled. "Wynterbreeze" was none other than Janet Julianne Garrison. She and Ren were both huge Beatles fans, to the consternation of many of their mutual friends.

"You know I love you."

"I'll always be true."

"So pleeeeeeese."

"Love me do... :-)"

"What's up, babe?"

"Not much. I'm at work and bored. Buy me lunch? :-)"

"Anytime. When and where?"

"Hmm… when, right at noon. And where… how about you pick me up in front of the building and we'll go from there?"

"Sounds great to me!"

"OK. See you downstairs at noon. I'd better find something constructive to do till then. Ciao, sweetie!"

Ren sat back in his chair, smiling and thinking about his friend. He decided to give up on the political search for a while and resumed the update to his JHM website. After his meeting with Lumpy, Ren had decided to resume posting the data which his mystery chatter had been sending.

The latest bunch of JHM data was more personal than business.

"But what the hell, sex sells," Ren thought.

It appeared that Jay Hadley regularly instructed his staff to have the travel agency book adjoining rooms for himself and his lead copy-editor. Ren couldn't resist a wry smile. This was good stuff; some people would get bent out of shape over a minister extravagant enough to book a suite. Others might wonder why his copy-editor would need a suite, or why a married man would want to be so close to a divorced woman and her 14-year-old daughter. By the time he had finished composing the new web pages, Ren was chuckling.

While the changes to the blog were uploading, he clicked back to the Marcus-Kayson home page. The feelings of dread he had experienced the previous night while looking at this site had not gone away. He sighed, shifted focus again, confirmed that the JHM updates had gone through, and closed down his web development program. Ren got up from his computer desk, went over to his photo studio to gather up his daytime bag, and headed out.

At least I can go and take pictures and appear to be working, Ren thought. He jumped into his Jeep, left the Creole

Faubourg he called home, and wound his way across Mid-City along Carrollton Avenue. After stopping at a coffee-shop for a quick cup-to-go he followed Carrollton to the neighborhood that used to be the old city of Carrollton, now part of "Uptown".

He had to drive slowly along the two-lane street which Carrollton had become and he took in the majestic old oak trees and the romantic sight of streetcars rolling along the middle of the neutral ground. He chuckled, thinking about "neutral grounds". The rest of the world calls the space in the center of a divided street a "median". Only in New Orleans do we see that space as a "neutral zone", a boundary. Ren parked the car and walked down the street for a while, taking photos as the mood struck him. He wasn't so much looking for specific images, rather he was looking for a combination of events such as a gal on a bicycle going one way while a streetcar went another. Continuing his walk a few more blocks along Carrollton, Ren turned into Willow Street to check out the "Car Barn", the main streetcar station. The Willow Street Car Barn was the home base of all the streetcars in New Orleans, both the classic green Perley Thomas 900-series cars of the St. Charles line, the Riverfront 400-series streetcars, and the Von Dullen 2000-series streetcars that run along Canal Street. Ren was able to get a good shot of one of the Riverfront's "red ladies" next to one of her older green cousins. After shooting a few pictures around the barn, he discovered two Czech-built trolleys in red and white. The Car Barn was always a treat for fans of urban traction lines because the New Orleans Regional Transit Authority (RTA) was always buying-up old cars to experiment with and for parts.

Ren spent almost two hours walking around Willow and Oak Streets, shooting pictures of houses and businesses in the neighborhood, before heading back to the Jeep. He felt satisfied to have taken a few shots which would look good on his online photo collection of New Orleans. With ample time left to get downtown and pick up JJ for lunch, he started the car and took a roundabout way from Uptown to Downtown, which included wandering down Freret Street, back up to Claiborne, then turning towards the river to end up back on St. Charles Avenue just before Lee Circle. He noticed that the clouds were playing strangely on the statue of Robert E. Lee, so Ren double-parked the car and took a moment to grab a couple of shots of him as well.

It was right on noon when he arrived at the Poydras Street office building which was the home of the oil and gas company where JJ was employed as an engineer. JJ was standing outside the building, in a pair of tight black jeans, a long-sleeved white blouse, and a burgundy vest. She jumped into the car and threw her arms around Ren's neck before planting a kiss on his cheek.

"Hey, sexy man!" she said as she smiled. "Where have you been all my life?"

Ren smiled back and turned the car towards Poydras to the river. "Where to, m'Lady?"

"I'm in the mood for Italian. I want something full of tomatoes and cheese."

"You want Italian and you're in a white blouse?"

"Sometimes you just have to live dangerously, love." JJ smiled and nodded solemnly as she tossed her raven-colored hair.

"Cool. Let's check the places on Magazine and see who doesn't look so crowded."

"It's a plan!" She was still bubbling with energy, but turned towards him, looking serious. "So what has Bubba been able to dig up for you?"

Ren frowned. "Not much. As we expected, kid, there's nothing at all to connect the two deaths. It comes out still looking like a terrible tragedy and co-incidence."

"It's no coincidence, Ren. I feel it and you know it. You know more than you're telling me. I should be pissed about that but I also feel like you don't have all the answers yet; and it's your style not to give out incomplete information."

Ren smiled, sheepishly. "Yeah babe. Working on this Hadley website has put me into reporter mode. You know, double-check everything before you say it or print it."

JJ pinched his thigh. "Humph. Well, for all my worldly experience, love, I'm still just a Catholic girl from New Orleans who loves to gossip. And you're denying me gossip on a good friend. I should be very cross with you." Her mock-serious stare was about to elicit a response from Ren when she stifled it immediately. "Oh, don't worry dawlin'. I'm just teasing you. I realize this is more than just idle gossip, really I do. But don't you ever forget that us good little Catholic girls don't appreciate being kept in the dark for very long."

"Yeah, and you also look good in short skirts," said Ren as he patted her thigh just above the knee.

"You're damn right I do," she responded through a girlish giggle.

The sexual tension that characterized their relationship had risen to a very high level by the time they arrived at Costello's, a small Creole-Italian place on Magazine Street. The couple sat and ordered: lasagna for JJ and grilled chicken with portobello mushrooms over pasta with a cream sauce for Ren. JJ was purring by the time the waitress left to put their order in.

"Ooooh! You're gonna eat that creamy stuff in front of me, huh, you tease!" The look in her eyes betrayed that she was becoming aroused.

He laughed as he replied, "Hey, you're usually the one who goes for the 'heart attack on a plate' so don't blame me if you've got a craving for red gravy."

"Yeah, I sure do today." Her eyes followed a guy wearing jeans as he passed from the front door to his table. She raised an eyebrow slightly, and added, "I could learn to crave something like that as well."

Ren chuckled again. He was used to his friend's wandering eyes.

"You're such an ass babe, JJ."

She smiled back at him sweetly.

"Hey, the male tush is one of the greatest gifts the gods ever gave us mere mortals."

Ren noticed that JJ's nipples were poking out under her blouse, clearly visible in spite of the thin bra she was wearing. He pondered for a moment about how much fun it would be to cup her breast and massage one of those nipples. The visualization grew stronger as he sipped the iced tea the waitress had set in front of him, until he reached the point where he imagined giving her nipple a playful yet firm squeeze.

JJ looked straight at him. She was slightly startled, yet excited by the sensations she had just experienced.

"Did you do that?"

Ren saw the visualization he created vanish in a puff of smoke, just as in a cartoon.

"Do what, sweetie?" He tried to look innocent, but he knew he had been discovered.

"Renard Paul Alciatore don't bullshit me. You knooooow how much I love my nipples touched and somehow you were doing it just now!"

Ren continued to try to look innocent.

"Now how could I do that? I've never touched your nipples."

"Yeah? Well you just *thought* it straight through my blouse!"

Ren blushed a deep shade of burgundy.

"Well, the thought had crossed my mind, truth be told."

"Hmm. It felt like your hand crossed my boob, love. That was a helluva strong thought!"

It soon dawned on Ren that he had lowered his shield, his psychic guard, a fair amount whenever he was hanging out with JJ. He supposed it was a natural thing to happen when with a good friend, but it also had its consequences when friends were sexually attracted. At that though, he self-consciously raised his shields a little at that thought. The waitress' timely appearance with their salads saved Ren from any further immediate embarrassment.

Ren and JJ never discussed the sexual tension between them. It was by unspoken agreement that they simply did not go there. JJ was married and he was also friends with her husband, Joe. JJ Garrison was a major flirt when she was out, but Ren usually attributed that to her being a female engineer working daily in a very male world. They had talked enough about their personal lives that he knew she didn't cheat on Joe or, if she did, she would not be able to keep that from him. No, he thought, she doesn't cheat on him. I'd know it in some way if it were true. A flirt, Janet Julianne may be. But she was still a married lady from a prominent New Orleans family. She had obligations and responsibilities and was the type of woman who would fulfill those.

JJ poked at an olive in her salad as she looked at Ren and

smiled.

"OK, I suspect there's more to this than meets the eye, but my instincts tell me that it's better for us that we don't go there right now, dear. But we will revisit the subject at some point in the future." She smiled her sweet-and-innocent smile at him. The one she used when she knew beyond any doubt that she was going to get her way.

Ren smiled back.

"Promise. I'm still sorting out some of my own feelings on a lot of things, babe."

The rest of lunch was uneventful, both of them having put up walls to avoid revealing any deeper feelings. After lunch, Ren dropped JJ off at her building and headed back home. Nadine would be there by now and they had to go over a few business details. That would keep him busy until his 4pm appointment with a bride, and hopefully would calm down his libido.

***

Cecilia McIntyre tossed her empty yogurt container into the trash-can next to her desk and turned her chair around to face her computer. She regularly checked the various news sources on the Internet in the early afternoon, just in case something happened that might alter the format for the day's radio show. That was one thing about her boss, the Rev. Jay Hadley, that she really admired: his ability to bob and weave on his feet and to extemporize.

She switched from the regular news sources to the anti-Hadley websites that had cropped up over the previous two years. Cee was satisfied that nothing major had arisen that would give them problems for that afternoon. The information she had passed on to Ren Alciatore had made its way onto his webpage but she was confident she would be able to screen out any callers who might try to get this data on the air. What had truly surprised her, though, was the amazing level of silence on the Hadley matter being maintained by the Christian press. After all, there were a couple of Christian magazines that were actually calling into question some of the actions of various

Christian ministries. But Jay Hadley Ministries was not one of them. And that puzzled her. The stuff she was feeding Alciatore was much stronger than most of the allegations published in Christian "investigative" pieces. Still, she could not accelerate her schedule for providing Ren with more information. Not without exposing herself as the source.

"But the risk of exposure was a problem," she thought.

There were a number of legitimate Christian ministries in the New Orleans area alone which would welcome someone of her ability and experience. The pay may be less than JHM in most cases, but they were, for the most part, operations which were genuinely out to do the Lord's work and to help others. Still, there wouldn't be anyone who would hire her if they knew what she was doing. No matter that Jay Hadley deserved exposure and contempt; it would be an issue of loyalty for them.

Cecilia frowned at that thought, and took one last glance through the websites, closed down her browser window, and turned back to her desk to review her preparations for the day's show. She smiled. Today's theme was general attacks on the "New Age" movement, which would always guarantee calls from goofy women who sounded spiritually lost. Sometimes she would encounter some of these women who really were looking for help and she would get Hadley to lead them to Jesus while on the air. Damn. She was good at that!

Ren finished up with Nadine in his office just in time to answer the doorbell and welcome a client for a bridal portrait shooting. Even though her wedding was still a month away, she was already a nervous wreck and her doting mother was no help to her whatsoever. After the fourth attempt at getting her to pose properly for a formal portrait, her mother vented at him.

The mother wrung her hands, irritated. "I can't believe this is taking so long and is such a problem!"

"Mom, I'm trying, I just can't relax. And you're not helping things, you know!" The daughter was on the brink of tears.

"Jeez, the last thing I need now is the girl crying. That'll throw us off by an hour while she re-does her make-up," he thought. Ren had not had a bride this badly off for a couple of years. He took a deep breath and smiled at the girl.

"Annie, close your eyes for a minute. Yes, that's it. Take a deep breath, too. That's the girl. You and I are the only ones around now. Imagine that the wedding is over and you and Richard are off on your honeymoon. Just the two of you. Where are you going, sweetie?"

"To Jamaica."

"No problem, hon. we'll fix you up right good real quick." Ren's appalling imitation of a Jamaican accent made her smile. "C'mon now, meessie, let's get deeze shots done an' we'll get you to y'mon reel queek."

The bride was giggling now. Ren had lowered his shields and was filling the room with calm thoughts. He wasn't entering Annie's mind so much as he was projecting soothing feelings. Annie could reject them if she wanted to but he knew she would grasp anything to calm things down.

"OK sweetie. Now I want you to stand up straight for me, but don't open your eyes yet. Just relax. You're on that plane to the island. Great. Keep smiling. It'll be bikini time before you know it." Annie giggled at him again, and Ren smiled inwardly. This girl wasn't getting into a bikini any time soon, not at her weight. But the thought was what she needed right now.

"OK. Now hold the bouquet out in front of you. Nice and relaxed. Now I want you to open your eyes. Yes, that's m'girl. Great. Turn your chin towards the camera, love. And ready. And there!" He clicked the shutter release at that last word, the flash went off, and Ren had captured the first good shot of the girl that afternoon.

Which, of course, was her mother's cue to chime in: "I told you three times already, I don't want her shot from the left side. I have two other daughters and they are both posing left. This portrait must be from the right side. Are you deaf? Haven't you heard a thing I've sai– "

Ren whirled around on her in the midst of her tirade. He touched the mother's wrist gently and locked his eyes with hers. The mind-link complete, he began to send specific instructions to her mind while he spoke aloud. "Ma'am, we've finally got Annie smiling and in a good mood, so let's not worry about one or two shots as we work through what you need, OK?"

Mentally, his instructions were clear and concise.

"Look, woman. You are the problem here. Your sour attitude has your daughter on pins and needles. What should be a happy and exciting time for her, the time leading up to her wedding, you are turning into a living hell. You need to let her go now, ma'am, and give her the space she needs to make this commitment and be happy. Go grab a coke or some iced tea from the 'fridge if you like, but you're out of here for a while. NOW!"

He released her wrist and smiled as Annie's mother replied, "I think I need to go sit down for a while."

Ren smiled at her again. "No problem, ma'am. You're more than welcome to relax in the kitchen. I've got some soft drinks in the refrigerator as well as some iced tea. Help yourself. We'll be only a few more minutes here."

The mother smiled and left the room without saying another word. Annie was stunned. She had never seen her mother lose a war of words with anyone before.

"I just saw it with my own eyes," she said. "But still I don't believe it! How did you shut her up?" She was all but bursting out with laughter now, which made Ren worry again about her make-up.

"Oh, I've been dealing with the mothers of brides for years now. Don't you worry about her. She's just as nervous as you are and the fussing is her way of showing it. Now, let's get you turned around facing the other way so you'll fit on the wall right," Ren said, smiling.

Annie giggled again and got into the spirit of the moment. The remainder of the shoot was a total success. Without even seeing any of the photographs just yet, Ren just knew that the shots from that last half an hour would be winners. The kind of pictures he would eventually include in his portfolio.

Ren helped Annie out from the studio and into the guest bedroom so she could change out of her wedding dress and then went down the hallway to check on the mother. He arrived to find Msgr. Michael O'Donnell sitting with the woman and having a nice chat. The mother got up and went to the guest-room to join her daughter. As she left the room, Mike grinned a devious-looking grin.

"So, who's the 'Stepford Mom' I've been chatting with for the past fifteen minutes?"

Ren looked a little sheepish. "Was that obvious?"

"Hell, yes it was obvious. She must've been the ultimate bitch for you to turn her into such a complete robot."

"All I wanted to do was to calm her down so the girl didn't burst into tears." Ren looked concerned.

"Oh, you accomplished that! You did just fine. Remind me to work with you on the degrees of intensity of mind-links though. You've got to be a little more settled yourself just before you make your, ahh, 'suggestions' lest you wire into your subject too deeply. Don't fret, though. That one was probably a good one to go overboard with. I've seen the type and believe me, it's much more difficult to do what you did on the wedding day when it is all built up."

Ren was surprised. "I expected you to be angry with me for doing that, and here you're telling me you've done the same sort of thing?"

Mike smiled and clapped his hand on Ren's shoulder. "The Wiccans have a saying, Ren. It goes, 'And no harm done, do what you will'. It's their Rede, their main creed. Sort of a Pagan variant of the Golden Rule. Think on that and put your actions into the perspective of that Rede. Not only did you do no harm there, but you did a bit of good. Because you've freed-up that young lady so she can enjoy the time leading up to her nuptials without her mother crawling up her butt."

Ren breathed a sigh of relief. "I'd like to say that my motivations were that high-minded, Mike, but what I was really trying to do was to shut the bitch up before the girl cried and ruined her make-up."

Bursting out with laughter, Mike stood up from the table. "Well, as the kids would say, my friend, 'I can hang with that'. Go see your guests out and we'll get some work done this evening."

The bride had finished her changing and Ren helped Annie and her mother out to their car, with the dress and the make-up kit. The mother smiled as Annie gave Ren a big hug and jumped into the car, before the two drove away. Ren returned to the porch and waited for Mike to join him.

"What's on the agenda for today, Obi-Wan?" said Ren.

Mike scanned the porch and noticed a small ceramic bird in a flowerpot in the corner. He focused his attention on the bird and Ren watched it rise and float to hover in front of him. Ren extended his hand, and the ceramic bird landed softly in his palm.

"The technical term is 'telekinesis,'" said Mike. "Also known as 'mind-movement'. The idea is to use the force of your will to move objects."

Ren nodded, slowly. He had worked with Mike long enough that a demonstration such as this did not shock him anymore. Ren opened his mind to Mike as his instructions on mind-movement began to flow.

After receiving the "download" from Mike, he knew that he had the information in his mind now to perform mind-movement and he turned with a quizzical look on his face to his teacher and waited for the next instruction.

Mile pulled a pair of six-sided dice from his pocket and held them in his hand. "OK, you can see what these are. Dice have six sides with a set of dots on each side. This exercise is simple. You visualize which set of dots you want to show up on each die when I roll them on the porch here."

Mike shook the dice in his hand then rolled them lightly against the wall. Ren closed his eyes and visualized a five on one die and a two on the other. The dice hit gently against the wall and, as Ren opened his eyes, Mike began to speak in the voice of a craps-table croupier.

"Seven a winner, pay the line, collect the don'ts."

There was a five on one die and a two on the other.

"Now, let's try some other combinations." Mike worked Ren through a series of permutations of the two dice for over an hour. When he saw Ren rubbing his temples he knew it was time for a break.

The implications of dice manipulation soon dawned on Ren. "I guess this is how the Church manages to do so well at Bingo, uh?" He smiled as he picked both dice up off the porch and he and Mike headed back to the kitchen.

"Yeah, mind-movement and games of chance are wonderful and profitable combination for the experienced practitioner. But they're not the only application for such Talent."

"What do you mean?"

Mike smiled and said softly, "Well, let's just say that there are organizations who know how to muster this Talent on a much larger scale and can manipulate things for their own good as a result."

"Like, the Church?" Ren asked.

"Yes, for one. But not "The Church" as in the Pope and all those guys in the red and purple suits you occasionally see in public." Mike reached into the refrigerator and grabbed a Coke.

"Are you saying the Pope doesn't know of the existence of people with Talents?"

Mike shrugged his shoulders. "Well I don't know the guy well enough to know what he does and doesn't know, my friend. But it wouldn't surprise me if he didn't have any clue at all. The Roman Catholic Church is a huge organization, Ren, and there are many instances where the left hand of the Church is doing something the right hand doesn't even know about. With all the orders of priests, nuns, and brothers around the world, there are a lot of things that happen out the in the name of 'The Church' that Rome just can't keep track of. And, mind you, that's just the Catholics. That doesn't count other Christian denominations, as well as non-Christians such as Jews and Muslims. And then you've got to figure in all the Eastern religions as well."

The significance of all this was not lost on Ren. "Are there so many people with Talents out there that all this is important?"

"Yes. Enough to create a lot of good in the world as well as a lot of bad. And, as in other aspects of life, people who ostensibly profess to do good often disagree, sometimes even to the extent that their disagreements become destructive. Those of us who have Talents are still human, Ren. Never forget that."

Ren nodded. "Sure, but there must be higher authorities who regulate the use of Talents, right? After all, someone had to agree to the Protocols and such. That assassin deferred to your 'jurisdiction' and your authority. So that authority must have a source and structure, right? Is that authority based within the Church?"

"Partly based in the Church, yes. But it's grown beyond that over time, Ren. The use of Talents is an ancient art, an art that is becoming more of a science as we learn more about the mind and the body. Talents were discovered and harnessed at a time when the world was different and religion was a much more important component of life. People with Talents made great strides in bringing together people of differing religions as the Protocols were developed. It's a shame that the rest of us folks on the planet didn't follow their lead."

"I think I understand the background, but I don't know if I fully understand how this has made the transition to the present," Ren said, puzzled.

"Don't worry about that just now. Suffice to say that there are indeed governing bodies involved here and that those bodies work to maintain the Protocols and our traditions. Let's leave it at that for now."

"But what if I ever need to contact someone who is in a position of authority on these things?"

Mike smiled. "You're doing that right now, my friend. But I know what you mean. If you ever need to get in contact with someone in authority and you can't get in touch with me, always remember the Triple-7. There will always be someone there who can help. Trust me on that."

Ren nodded. He had been holding the dice throughout the conversation and he placed them on the kitchen table. He stared at them for a moment and willed one of the dice to rise slowly. It dropped suddenly and Mike applauded Ren's effort.

"Not bad Grasshopper." Mike grinned. "Now let's see you do that for another half-an-hour."

Ren groaned and got back to working on the task at hand. He kept at it for almost an hour before Mike said goodbye for the evening. Ren headed for his study, where he immediately activated his chat and email programs. His phone flashed as he scanned the screen. "Isis" was trying to "Kik" him.

"Hi."

"Hi yourself! Did you have a good day today?"

"Better than my boss had. :-)"

"Oh, he's been reading the blog, has he?"

"You didn't hear the show today?"

"No, I had a shoot this afternoon. ***I'll listen to the podcast later."***

"Well, you missed a fun one. Your friends flooded the donor lines and that really set Jay off. He just couldn't keep his cool, and had he been able to, nobody would have realized what was going on."

"Hmm. I can tell you that whatever happened today wasn't my idea, m'Lady. Sometimes things in the anti-JHM community just happen spontaneously. I guess today was one of those days."

"Sure, if you say so... :-)"

"I'm serious. Don't give me too much credit here. I'm still just a guy trying to earn a buck."

"OK. I believe you for now... :-)"

"Well I am glad for that..."

"So how's your research going?"

"Research?"

"Yeah. I figure by now you must be making a bunch of cyber-visits to the Lone Star State. :-)"

"Oh yes, that. Yes, I've learned some interesting things. Definitely some patterns forming there that are making more and more sense. Don't suppose you can shed any light on that right now?"

"Funny you should mention that... :-)"

The "new mail" tone on his phone beeped. It was a link to Dropbox, which contained a ZIP archive for him to download.

Ren opened the first of the documents, which were a series of memos from JHM personnel to various contacts at Marcus-Kayson Publishing. The contents of the memos were not exactly earth-shattering, but they did indicate a pattern of activity that posed more questions than they answered. The number of contacts within JHM who worked on Hadley's books indicated that more ministry staff worked on his books than on the various good works that Hadley's operation had ostensibly been created to do.

"Interesting from a tax perspective," Ren thought.

It was at times like this that he really missed Trip Kahn. Trip would know what all this meant and what its implications were, from both a business and a legal standpoint. "Isis" was giving him this information for a reason. But sniffing out the meaning of all this was now going to be more difficult.

"And that difficulty was no coincidence. JJ's right. Trip is dead exactly because of this. I'm pretty much slowed to a crawl, even though I've got an inside source," Ren muttered.

Ren added the newly-received documents to his growing data folder on JHM before moving on to other computer-based projects.

Meanwhile, "Isis" smiled to herself after having broken the connection to Renard Alciatore. Cecilia had admonished Ren to "follow the money", just like Woodward and Bernstein had done during Watergate, and it was paying off now. She led him electronically to M-K and he was no fool. She thought and smiled, *"One of these days, Renard Alciatore, you and I should have a drink or two together."*

CHAPTER NINE
Battlefield

"C'mon, let's get moving before my clothes stick to me completely," yelled Ren Alciatore back to Mike O'Donnell. Ren was already out of his Jeep and moving towards the back of the narrow strip of land that comprised the Chalmette National Cemetery. Located in St. Bernard Parish, just to the south of the city of New Orleans, the cemetery was right next to the site of the Battle of New Orleans.

Mike climbed out of the Jeep and paused at the curb for a moment. "I haven't been out here since the storm," he said, more to himself than for anyone else to hear. He raised his voice and called back to Ren: "Remind me what we're here for again?"

Ren answered without even looking back at his mentor. "We are taking photos of the final resting place of one Sgt. Jeremiah Wilkerson, who was in the Colored Troops of the Grand Army of the Republic."

"OK, and with all due respect to the late, distinguished, Sgt. Wilkerson, why do we really care where the man is buried?"

"Frankly, I don't," Ren shouted back. "But I'm a volunteer for the 'cemetery photos' group on Facebook, and a lady doing some 'roots' research asked if I could shoot some photos of the grave of ol' Jeremiah here." Ren walked through section 125 of the cemetery, looking at names and plot numbers on the headstones. He stopped suddenly in front of one of them and shouted, "Here we go. This is him!" He stepped back from the headstone and began taking photos of it from various angles with a state-of-the-art Nikon digital camera.

Mike watched with fascination as Ren practiced his craft.

The thought occurred to him that this was the first time he had ever been able to see Ren at work. “You know, this is going to sound a bit cold, but what’s in it for you?”

It was Ren’s turn to chuckle. “Oh, no direct financial gain, mostly just good karma. Also, it’s an excuse to take cemetery pictures. I sometimes have a hard time focusing mentally when I go to a cemetery to shoot stuff for the website. It’s different when I go looking for a particular grave. All of a sudden I am no longer a disinterested onlooker. Instead, I am trying to show the place for someone for a specific purpose. For some reason, the photos come out different when I do that. Combine that with the fact that most people who are into this genealogy shit seem to be women, and it becomes a cool thing to do.”

“You net-hound!” Mike laughed as Ren shrugged his shoulders and continued to shoot pictures in and around the grave that was his subject today. Mike walked over to the gap in the cemetery’s outer wall that joined it with the adjacent battlefield. He looked out at the British Union Jack fluttering in the breeze, sighed for a moment, then turned around slowly to find Ren just finishing up. “C’mon, let’s go out of the cemetery and into the Chalmette Battlefield for our work-out.”

“You make it sound as though there’s a difference,” Ren said.

“Oh, there is. Big time.” Mike nodded and continued, “All this area is sacred ground. It’s revered for many reasons: the cemetery is hallowed by those who have loved-ones buried here. The battlefield is hallowed by those who respect and revere the sacrifices made by men from both sides of the conflict. As a result of the differing reasons, the residual energy in the earth is different on either side of that wall. Since a lot of what we’re going to do today has to do with combat defense, it’s more appropriate that we tap into the energy out there on the battlefield.”

Ren bowed gracefully to his Teacher and held out his hand. “Well then, lead on good Father, lead on,” he said with a beaming smile.

Mike did just that, then he gestured for Ren to follow his lead. Once Ren was on the battlefield side of the low gate, Mike closed it behind them. He reached into his pocket and pulled out a steel chain and a small padlock. He wrapped the chain around the gate and snapped the padlock into the chain. After giving the lock a good tug he straightened up and turned to Ren smiling. "Locks and lock-picking is the lesson for today."

Without saying another word, Mike gestured to Ren to stand closer to the gate. Closing his eyes, his arms at his sides, Mike then raised his hands slightly and brought them in front of his chest, briefly making a praying gesture. He then held out his right hand, index and middle fingers extended and motioned them both in a small circle without moving his wrist. Mike exhaled and the padlock popped open with the slight sound of a click.

Ren was totally captivated by Mike's action and was immediately able to grasp the implications of what Mike had just done. "That particular feat has a lot of potential," said Ren.

"Well there's more to this than just popping locks, mind you," Mike retorted. "You have to know something about the type of lock and how it opens normally, so as to be able to figure out how to open it without a key. So, I can show you the basic technique here, but you're going to have to do a lot of homework to apply this to locks other than this little Master lock I brought with me. Open to me now, though, and let me give you the basics."

Ren closed his eyes and opened a mind channel for Mike to access. In under a second the knowledge he need to open the lock had been passed to him, and he began to practice repeatedly unlocking the padlock.

Mike stopped him after only a few attempts. "I'm still amazed at how fast you catch-on with this stuff."

"Well, it isn't all that difficult, you know. I might even have a new career ahead of me at this rate!"

"Hmm, if you're not careful you're going to be eating 'food loaf' up on the farm in Angola," Mike said in admonishment of his prodigy. "There are a lot of factors involved in lock-picking, such as the basic architecture of the lock, the mechanism surrounding it, such as the chain in this case, and then any other kind of security installed at the location you are attempting to enter."

"I hadn't even considered any of those," a visibly-sobered

Ren remarked.

Mike grinned. “I didn’t think you had.”

“But what if I don’t know how a particular lock works? Is there a workaround? Or am I screwed?”

“Well, you can always force the lock open, but that has two implications. First, it’s going to be a bigger drain on your power, and second, it will probably screw up the lock permanently, which means you’ll leave behind evidence of your visit. There may be times when that will make a difference to you, especially when you are somewhere you don’t want others to know you’ve been. Still, if you have to get in someplace, it’s fast and efficient.”

Reaching out his mind and stretching his hand out slowly, the older man locked the padlock at the gate. “OK, now I want you to open the lock and then pull the lock into your hands.”

Ren was curious. “Isn’t that an unnecessary energy drain? Seems to me I should just disconnect the chain manually.”

“Sure you could.” Mike nodded in agreement. “But my way doesn’t leave fingerprints.” He gestured for Ren to continue. “Let’s see you get the lock off and the gate opened.”

Ren closed his eyes and followed his mentor’s instructions which he received mentally. Visualizing the tumblers in the lock he moved each one as though the key was in and turning them. Once they were all aligned in the unlock position, Ren made a subtle gesture with his fingers and the body of the lock slid down. At that point gravity took over and the lock dangled on a section of the chain.

Ren extended a third finger now and gently lifted the lock off the chain without touching it. He could hear Mike’s voice speaking softly behind him.

“Remember, you will most likely be doing this at a time or in a place where you won’t want to draw any attention to yourself, so you don’t want things clanging into each other.”

Nodding, Ren continued, lifting the lock and making it float a few inches from the gate. He broke his mental connection with the lock at that point and allowed it to fall harmlessly to the ground. Turning his attention to the chain, he mentally picked up one end of it and caused it to draw out through the gate. Once it was in position Ren let the chain fall gently, producing only a slight tinkle as it reached the ground.

Ren opened his eyes, turned to Mike and bowed low. “Is this what you desired, Master?” he asked, in a mock-Chinese voice.

Mike grinned and replied in character. “Yes, young weed-hopper. You have done well.” He began laughing and reached out with both hands to draw the lock and the chain towards him, and pocketed them when they arrived in his palms. Back in his regular voice, Mike asked, “How are you holding up? Want to try a few more things?”

Ren nodded. “F’sure, what next?”

Mike led him further out into the battlefield and they continued to work on picking up objects for another hour. Ren was a natural when it came to telekinetic activity, so he peppered Mike with questions while he practiced.

“Try not to get wrapped up in the really arcane aspects of a duel so much that you forget some of the physical challenges that might confront you. It’s possible that your opponent will be so focused on casting their spell to summon some dark nasty on you that he won’t see the rock you’ve picked up mentally and thrown at his head!”

Ren was a little amazed at that. “You mean you can actually do that in the middle of a duel?”

“You bet. Once you have closed the ritual circle, just about anything is legal. You can whip out your dick and piss on an opponent if you want to. Of course, she might summon a hell-hound to snap your dick off if you’re not careful, so I wouldn’t suggest it as the first thing in your arcane arsenal.”

“But, throwing a rock sounds so juvenile.”

“Hey, it’s how David won the main-event match against Goliath, isn’t it?” Mike took the lock and chain out of his pocket again, hanging them on the gate.

“True, true.” Ren had hooked the lock onto the chain and was using his mind to swing the chain gently, ten feet in front of him. A quick shrug of his shoulders and the lock went flying, about thirty feet away.

“From a defensive standpoint though, your best bet is to

pick out a spot to cast the circle where there are no movable objects inside," added Ren's mentor.

As he returned from retrieving the chain, Ren asked, "Do the Protocols specify a certain type of site for a dueling circle?"

"No, the choice of site is very flexible. The general location would usually be laid down by the Challenger as in 'meet me at such-and-such a place at dawn'," explained Mike. "Unless the Challenge is spontaneous you can pretty much bet that the location will be a power nexus or other locale the Challenger is familiar with. This is important, because if your Challenger knows how to draw power from a location and you don't, then you could be at a significant disadvantage."

Ren nodded as he juggled the chain in his hands. "What's the best way to counter that sort of advantage from a Challenger?"

Well, the significance of some locations will immediately be obvious: a church, cemetery, or other power site such as this battlefield. For others, you'll have to do some historical research. Your background in history, Ren, combined with your ability to pull good stuff off the Internet fast, will help you immensely should you ever be faced with a Challenge which requires quick answers."

"How much time do you have between a challenge and a duel?"

"That will vary from one Challenge to another. But the minimum is the time between a sunrise and sunset, or vice-versa. So if you receive a Challenge at dawn, then it could specify a duel after sunset that day. The usual way of doing things, though, is to give both parties a couple of days to prepare."

"OK, I think I have this straight," said Ren. "I just hope all this is planning for a rainy day rather than something that will definitely happen."

"Me too," Mike agreed. "Let's go get a bite to eat." He led the way back through the gate into the cemetery. As they walked along the single lane that ran the length of the cemetery they both noticed a large SUV that was parked nose-to-nose with Ren's Cherokee. As they approached the cars, the driver of the SUV, a Suburban, got out of the car and began walking towards them. He cast an imposing figure, over six feet tall and looking like he weighed close to three hundred pounds.

"About fuckin' time you got back. This fuckin' Jeep of yours is blocking my way down the road!" The driver's face was red with rage.

Ren wasn't looking for trouble, especially in a cemetery. He nodded and replied, "Hey, no problem. Let me back up so you can get by."

"You assholes think you can just come down here and do whatever the fuck you want. You're all so full of fuckin' bullshit. I still oughta kick your ass!"

Monsignor Michael Aloysius O'Donnell had not said a word during this exchange. He was dressed in jeans and a polo shirt so his vocation was not evident to the big man. While his first instinct was similar to Ren's, that this was not a situation over which to make a big deal, this particular individual's foul mouth was beginning to grate on his nerves.

"Hey, sport, did your momma teach you those words? I know you didn't learn them from the teachers at Our Lady of Prompt Succor, when you were in fifth grade." Mike stared the larger man directly in the eyes. "This is a holy place, one you should treat with a bit more respect than your foul mouth seems to know how to do."

The face of the larger man was now contorted with rage. "I'll show you some respect, you little piece of shit!" He began to stomp towards Mike.

O'Donnell's upbringing in the Gentilly neighborhood of New Orleans was such that he rarely backed down from a fight, especially one which he knew he was going to win. He waited until the man was just over arm's length away, then he held out his hand like a traffic cop indicating "stop". The big man froze in mid-stride, his face now carrying a startled look. Mike turned his outstretched hand palm-up and locked his eyes again on those of his adversary. Mike began to cup his hand as if he was holding a grapefruit and, as he began to close his fingers slowly like a grip, the big man began to clutch at his chest.

"What's the matter, sport? Thought you were gonna kick my ass. Looks like all that greasy food you've eaten all your life has finally caught up with you. You a Veteran, sport? Maybe they'll plant you in here with these folks then. You can spend eternity wishing the people coming to visit you don't have mouths as foul as yours."

Mike's hand had closed in so that it now appeared to be holding an invisible baseball rather than an invisible grapefruit.

The big man had sunk to his knees, a look of fear now replacing the anger that was originally etched on his face.

"Please," he coughed, barely able to pick up his head.

Mike sighed, then opened his hand so that the palm was once again flat and facing the sky. The big man was on his hands as well as his knees now, and gasping for air. Mike motioned to Ren with his head that they should be leaving.

"Let's get out of here before he decides to pull out a shotgun and do something really stupid."

Once inside the Jeep, Ren turned to his teacher and said, "What the hell did you do that for?"

"Sorry, Ren. I guess the old neighborhood just came out of me. I hate people who are foul-mouthed in a cemetery. And I'm a lousy fighter. I learned to fight from a friend at college. He was Puerto Rican and his technique was to grab the first thing he could easily swing and start dealing on his opponent. Well, my technique has become a little more refined since then."

"I'll say it's become refined! Is that something you can teach me?"

"Eventually, yes. It's really just a variation on the theme we've been working on of moving objects. How about we go down the street to Rocky and Carlo's?" Mike smiled, "I've got a craving for macaroni and cheese."

***

Anita lay staring at the ceiling.

"This city is going to be the death of me. Eleven in the morning and I'm lying in bed," she thought.

No matter that the energy she had been drawing from Jay Hadley was good for her physical and psychic strength. But it simply offended the practical side of her nature to be lying in a hotel room half the day.

"My lover. No that's not right. My sex partner, yeah, that's better, will be out of the bathroom and will want

attention," she continued, in her mind.

Hadley emerged, smiled at her and mouthed a kiss towards her.

"Don't you think you should get up and get moving?" he asked.

"Yes, I suppose I should." She smiled. "But it's not easy."

He leaned over and kissed her gently. "I'm glad you're here, Anita. These past few months have not been good. Having you here helps a lot, on more than one level."

Anita sighed, inwardly.

"At least he's a guy. Not that female partners aren't fun, but a good pounding builds up a lot more power. Then again a woman wouldn't be thinking with a penis more often than not," she thought.

"I'm here for you Jay. You're important to me, honey. We're going places and all you have to do is just relax and be you."

The bed-sheet covering her slipped a little as she leaned towards him to return his second kiss. The sight of her breasts stirred him again, but she gently held up her arms to resist.

"You've got to get to the office, honey. It's important that every show between now and the book-signing tour should be live. We don't want to give the opposition any ammunition just now." She smiled sweetly at him as she climbed out of the bed and slipped on a very short terrycloth robe.

"Yes, you're right Anita. I want to get some things done before we leave next week."

He stood up and began to get dressed. "I'm excited about these book signings."

"They're all in very friendly territory, Jay. We're going to attract some good crowds, you're going to do some good preaching, and M-K is going to be very, very pleased with Jay Hadley the man, and Jay Hadley Ministries."

"Yes, and then I'll be allowed to go back to Dallas and run your life from there, you fool," she thought.

He smiled again at her, blew her a kiss, and left the hotel room. He had just a short walk from the hotel to his office suite in the adjacent building.

Anita sighed, still euphoric because of the level of power

she had raised through the act of sexual intercourse with Hadley.

"This could become addictive, especially since Jay is such good lover," she said, now that she was alone. Sex magic was supposed to be better when both partners are willing and aware of what is going on. She had to be careful that she pulled energy from the act and not from Hadley himself.

"The guy is the meal ticket, so couldn't have him aging prematurely," she observed, looking out the window.

Pacing around the room, she could not shake off the feelings she was experiencing. Damn, this was good! Sitting back down on the edge of the bed, she pulled the belt of her robe loose to let it fall open. She reached into her robe and cupped her breast and gave a light squeeze to the nipple.

"Well, you raise more power with two, but you can still raise a bit with one," she whispered.

***

As a rule, Ren didn't like talking on the phone and driving at the same time, but this was an exception. It never failed that is his appointments in the suburbs at opposite ends of the city fell on the same day. After his interesting morning with Mike in Chalmette, he was on his way across town to a coffee-shop in Kenner to meet another close friend.

He pulled into the North Kenner strip-mall parking lot and saw the black and white SUV that was his friend's work car. As he entered the shop, a diminutive Japanese man walked towards him and bowed ceremoniously.

"Konnichiwa, Ren-san," the man said in greeting.

Ren chuckled and returned the bow. "Konnichiwa, Bubba-san. Where y'at bra?"

"Nuttin' to it," Bubba replied as he grinned. He motioned Ren towards the counter. "Get something to drink and we'll chat."

Ren did just that and returned to the corner table Bubba was occupying. He took a sip of his latte and said, "So you done any thinking about this situation I've got here?"

Bubba nodded. "Done a little more thinking, my friend.

Did some checking around on your friends. There was no autopsy done on your friend Nick, which does not surprise me. After all, a heart attack on a guy like him isn't out of the ordinary." Bubba paused for a sip at his coffee. "The accident, of course, is a different story. The postmortem on your friend Trip indicates that death was caused by major trauma. Again, nothing out of the ordinary, and certainly nothing that would raise the eyebrows of any law-enforcement officer."

"Why do I have the feeling that the shoe's about to drop, then?"

"Ahh, Ren-san. Thanks so much for your faith in my ability to tell a mystery tale!" Bubba chuckled as he grinned widely. "Yessir, there's more to the story. The first shoe has to do with the driver of the rig. He was 24, worked-out daily, and was in the prime of his life. In fact, the St. Tammany detective with which I spoke was funny. He interviewed the guy's wife after the accident, and the descriptions of their sexual exploits she gave him formed an impression that if this guy was going to die of a heart attack, it was more likely it would have been while he was swinging from a chandelier. The autopsy confirms his good health, Ren. There were no genetic defects of any kind. It's not like when Pete Maravich dropped dead and they found that hole in his heart. Nothing like that on this guy. He just dropped dead."

"Well that sounded really strange to the detective up there," continued Bubba, intensely. "So he had the coroner's office run a battery of toxicology tests and such, on skin, blood, and hair samples. All came back negative, Ren. This guy hadn't even smoked the occasional joint or such. It's really bizarre. There's no medical explanation for this guy's heart attack, and there's no evidence of foul play either. Drugs that trigger a heart attack always leave tell-tale signs when you know what to look for. They went a-looking, but came up with nothing. So, we've got a guy whose death had to result from foul play, but absolutely no evidence of foul play. As Yul Brynner would say, 'Is a puzzlement'." Bubba grinned mirthlessly.

Ren had been listening equally as intently as Bubba had been relating the information.

"What's the other shoe?"

Bubba laughed. “Remind me never to go to a murder-mystery movie with you, Ren. You’re no fun at all! OK, most of my contacts up in St. Tammany are purely professional. You know how it is, the north-shore is like, ‘died and gone to the suburbs’. So, since I don’t have a true inside track up there, I sorta bounced around from one person to another at first. One of the secretaries I spoke with made a comment about how I wasn’t the first person to be inquiring about this accident. The hairs on the back of my neck stood up at that. So I asked who else shared my curiosity. She said it had been a secretary from State Police Troop A. That’s Baton Rouge, Ren.”

“Anyway, the deputies up on that side of the lake don’t get along well with the troopers. Has to do with the seizure of drugs, drug vehicles, and cash on I-12 through all the Florida Parishes. When I mentioned to some of the guys that troopers had been asking about an in-parish case, something that wasn’t even involving the interstate, several of them got more than a little indignant. They were more than happy to get me details about who it was from Troop A was in their business. What I found, my dear friend, was that the trooper making the enquiries was one John Hendrick. Ring any bells?”

Ren shook his head and Bubba continued.

“Well, he’s the younger of the two who tag-teamed you at your house. Hendrick is the partner of Donny Jeanfreau and both are assigned to the governor’s detail. Ren, ol’ buddy, my professional instincts tell me you have pissed someone off in a big way, and that someone has the wherewithal to get the governor’s staff involved. You been taking nekkid pictures of somebody or their wife lately? We need to figure out just whose shit-list you are on.”

The connections were coming together now in Ren’s mind. He spent a few minutes outlining to Bubba his contacts with “Isis” on the Internet, and her mentioning of the connection between Jay Hadley and Marcus-Kayson in Dallas.

“I’ve got transcripts of all this stuff back at the house, Bubba. I’ll email it to you when I get back. Hey, I really appreciate all your help with this, guy.”

“Not a problem, sir. As long as you pay up as we discussed.” Bubba laughed as he held out his hand.

Laughing with him, Ren reached into his day planner for four tickets to that evening's professional soccer match and handed them to Bubba. "Hell, I kinda feel guilty, that my 'payment' is something I got for nothing, but I know the kids love going to Jesters games."

"Oh, for sure, so does Didi. But just going to a Jesters game is one thing Ren. Karen can't wait to see 'Uncle Ren' in his blue 'professional' referee's jersey!"

"Hell, I'm only the fourth official tonight. You guys will have to come to a game in two weeks when I'm an assistant referee so she can actually see me do something," he laughed.

Smiling, Bubba looked at his watch.

"Jeez, I'd better get back to the office and make sure the world hasn't come to an end."

"Yeah, I'd better get over to the field as well. They always want us there for a proper pre-match conference for pro games."

As they both stood up, Ren's expression turned serious again.

"Bubba, you be careful, you hear? I don't want anything happening to you because you made a few phone calls on my behalf, OK?"

Bubba smiled.

"Hey, stopping bad guys is part of my job. Besides, forewarned is forearmed. We'll deal with things as they come up, Ren. Let's see what we can find."

Ren grasped his friend's shoulder gently, then released it and headed out towards his car.

A check of his watch showed that he might still have enough time to go out for some photos on the lakefront before heading over to the stadium for the soccer match. Even though tonight's match was just a "fourth official" assignment for Ren, it was a professional match. He should have been more psyched up for it. All the events of the previous few weeks had shifted his focus so much that he was unable to savor the enjoyment of his first summer refereeing soccer at a professional level.

Even though he was in Kenner, he was still on the Lakefront, which always helped adjust his attitude, and get some good photos.

A few hours later, the final whistle blew, indicating the

end of the soccer match. The New Orleans Jesters and the Nashville Metros were leaving the pitch at Pan American Stadium. Even though Pan American wasn't as large as the other stadium in City Park, Tad Gormley, a dragon could probably still land here.

"What made me think of that?" Ren wondered, just under his breath.

Ren collected his notepad and jogged to the center of the field to catch up with the two assistant referees who joined him in converging on the referee. It had been a difficult match, with some very physical play that had required several yellow cards and one red to maintain order among the players.

The officials' post-game discussion of their work for the evening was already so intense that Ren had not even noticed a young lady following his movements from the middle of the field to the locker-room entrance.

"Not that he would know by sight who I was by sight," whispered Cecilia McIntyre. "Still, if I'm going to let him know me at some point, I've got to lay the groundwork slowly." Her reverie was broken by the sound of her friend's voice calling for her to get moving. Her girlfriend had some serious drinking and man-chasing to do. And Cecilia was the perfect designated driver.

CHAPTER TEN
Shreveport

"I can't begin to tell you the extent to which I dislike Shreveport," Anita Delatorre complained, as she drove into the parking lot of the Holy Gospel Temple, just off I-20.

"Oh, c'mon Anita, the town does have a certain charm," responded Cecilia McIntyre from the back seat of Anita's Cadillac SRX.

"I'll remember that the next time I feel like being charmed," giggled Anita. "People in Shreveport even go to Dallas to do their shopping."

Jay Hadley was sitting next to Anita in the front passenger seat and chimed in, "This is true, but all of your Dallas folk go to Shreveport to do their gambling."

"Shush, Jay," Cecilia continued. "Those good Dallas Christians don't gamble!"

"Yeah right," retorted Anita as she laughed. "There are three or four churches in Dallas that could have their board meetings out at one of those casinos on a Saturday night. And I daresay my company could have a very productive senior staff-meeting at the same time, too."

They all laughed at that last remark as they got out of the car. The five-hour drive from suburban New Orleans to Shreveport had been a relaxing one, which made Jay happy. There had been a bit of tension between his publisher's representative and his producer, and he was relieved that whatever was causing it was taking a bit of a break today. The van which contained the other JHM staffers who were making the trip with them pulled-up alongside Anita's car. They all went into the church together to set up for the 3pm remote broadcast of "*Talk Live*". The book tour was yet another good opportunity to avoid taking live callers. The plan was to do a series of "teaching ministry" shows this week and broadcast them from cities north of New Orleans. The lectures would be on "Bible Prophecy", still a very hot topic on the Christian radio airwaves. The tie-ins abounded, since "*Bible Prophecy*" also happened to be the title of Jay Hadley's latest book. It was so easy to do a little preaching and then to hold a book-signing at a local Christian bookstore. That the bookstores just happened to be owned by a subsidiary of Marcus-Kayson was just icing on the cake.

With the staff rolling into action and getting this organized, Hadley settled himself into the office which the church maintained specifically for visiting pastors and other guests. People who criticized the Catholic Church for the extravagant lifestyles enjoyed by the Pope and many cardinals and bishops just did not realize the extent to which many in the evangelical community did the same. What seemed more amazing to Hadley was that while it had taken centuries for the resources of the Catholic Church to evolve, it had taken mere decades for the Evangelicals to develop their fiefdoms. The Catholic-bashing practiced by Southern Baptists and other conservative Protestant denominations over the previous 50 years had gone a long way to demonize the Catholics to the point where the Protestant preachers would get away with all kinds of fiscal excess. Hadley was now reaping the benefits of those excesses as he relaxed in an office that was better than those of most corporate CEOs. And this was the guest office!

It was not the money that usually got the Evangelical pastors into trouble, but their bedroom antics. And Jay Hadley was on the brink of developing such a problem himself. Over the previous few weeks, several of the anti-JHM websites, led by the "Jay Hadley Fan Club" site in New Orleans, had published a number of allegations about Jay Hadley's extra-curricular activities. It had been increasingly difficult for Cecilia to protect Hadley from hostile callers on the days when they went with an open-call format for the daily radio show. Despite the show being only two hours long, the tension of preparing for it, and the extreme anxiety of what cranks might call in, had made the previous two weeks of work very difficult. Remote broadcasts always meant a lot of extra work, not least with setting-up and breaking-down the portable studio equipment, but it was such a relief to use the no-caller format they would be over the next week and a half that none of the staff was complaining.

Hadley reviewed the program format for the day. Predicting the future was a hot topic today, just as it had been at the turn of the first millennium. The challenge now was to keep the gravy-train rolling as long as possible into the second millennium. Homeschooling families were the ticket. All Jay had to do was plant the seeds, and the Christian homeschoolers did the rest for him, buying his books, following the "curriculum guides" produced by his staff, and downloadable from the website. The entire homeschooling project was approaching critical mass, where Jay Hadley Ministries would be able to spin off an "education division". No more need for accountability to the radio broadcasters!

A light knock on the door roused Jay from his ponderings and heralded an update from Cecilia on the progress of setting-up the studio. JHM did remote broadcasts regularly, so the staff rarely had any difficulty with the operation. Neither Hadley nor Cecilia expected any problems today; the show itself and the lecture/prayer meeting that would follow that evening in the church were nothing special. The only downside Hadley could see in this trip was that, unfortunately, he had had to book separate hotel rooms for Anita and himself.

Later that evening Cecilia was relaxing in her hotel room, chatting with several friends on Facebook and congratulating herself for being able to convince Jay to buy her a notebook computer. Sure, there were the occasion when this particular computer system was actually used for ministry business, but the beauty of having the system was that she could stay in touch with friends whenever Jay went out on a road-trip. At ten o'clock, however, she said her goodbyes to her Facebook friends and logged off.

She reached for her phone and "Kik'd" Ren. Cecilia decided it was time to pass on some new tidbits.

"Hey there!"

"Hey yourself! What's up in your life?"

"Oh, not much. Been busy, but you can probably understand that."

"Yup, the traveling road-show must be a strain."

"Well, we get used to it, that's for sure. We pretty much have it covered. Still, there's always a bit of tension when you're on remote. What's new in the photography business?"

"Just the usual... brides and moms of brides... loads of fun... :-)"

"Does the soccer help you to take your mind off all that?"

"Jeez. You know about my refereeing? This is so unfair! You know so much about me and you're still the mystery woman to me. <pout>"

"Oh. We'll fix that in due course, don't worry. Now that I've seen those legs of yours in shorts I can assure you we'll fix that <evil grin>"

"Will we now? Hmm well, hopefully I'll find your legs as interesting as you do mine..."

"Oh, if it's my legs you want, I can show you those... hang on... :-)"

Cecilia initiated a file transfer to Ren's phone. The file was a picture of her in a one-piece swimsuit, but cropped so that she was visible only from the waist down. A few moments passed during which she knew Ren was checking-out the photo.

"Hey, not bad at all, but you're still trying to maintain the mystery, huh? :-)"

"Well, for now. I'm glad you like. I'll bet you figured I was some kind of ugly chick, uh?"

"Honestly, I didn't know what to expect. After all, there are some really good-looking women on those Christian TV shows, but then you've got the ones like that woman with the pink hair and three tons of make-up!"

"Yes, there are sure some of those <laughing>, but you should have realized that having good-looking women around is a priority for Jay Hadley. He's a major skirt-chaser, you know."

"This is very true. So whose skirt is the man chasing in Shreveport right now???"

"Actually, he's being very discreet on this trip. You guys have contributed a lot to that. In some ways it's made life in the office easier, but in other ways more difficult."

"But surely a guy with his sex-drive can't go long without being deprived?"

"No, that's for sure. But it's easy to get some when you bring it with you."

"Oh, really? And just what has he brought with him?"

"Well, let's just say that many authors in the Christian book business think that Marcus-Kayson fucks writers. In Hadley's case, it's the literal truth. :-)"

Cecilia closed Kik on her phone, breaking-off the connection. Sitting on the king-sized bed in her hotel room, she re-started the program and logged-on again, this time using a different alias, "Hot2Trot". The more she thought about Renard

Alciatore in his soccer referee's shorts and knee-socks, the more she needed to find someone to play with.

Back in New Orleans, Ren gazed at his phone, reviewing his recent conversation with "Isis". He jumped back to the M-K website and did a casual run-through of the profiles of some of the employees of the publishing house. He bookmarked some of the personal pages of the female employees who he considered might be attractive to Hadley. He made an entry in Evernote to look further into this. Hadley having a honey who worked for his publisher might explain a lot. It was a great way to keep him off the streets, as it were. The book-signings and production and sales issues would be more than enough justification for M-K to send someone to New Orleans to keep tabs on their rising star, Ren thought. And with a hotel right next to his office building... Ren did a quick Google search, found a phone number, and then made a call.

A female voice answered.

"Radisson Lakefront, this is Dawn, how may I help you?"

Ren took a deep breath.

"Hello Dawn, this is Harold Davidson from the Gray/Samuels Publishing Group in Melbourne, Australia. Yes, my boss wants me to express-mail a packet of information to the lady from Marcus-Kayson who is staying at your hotel, but the idiot just left without giving me her name. I'm hoping you can help me here. If I have to call Marcus-Kayson it will really embarrass my boss. I don't need that in my life at the moment."

"Oh dear. Well you know we're not really supposed to give out that information over the phone," Dawn said.

"Ah, but I'm begging, you don't want to leave a guy begging, do you Dawn? You're not that type of woman, are you?" Ren pleaded, rather proud with his flirting skills.

Dawn laughed.

"After all, I know she's there, and I'm not asking for her room number or anything. I swear, I just need to send her this envelope of stuff for Jay Hadley's next book project. He's right there in the tower complex with you guys. I'm sure you've heard of him."

"Yes, of course. OK, I don't think I can get in trouble for this," she said.

Ren could hear Dawn inhale deeply.

"Her name is Anita Delatorre," Dawn said, exhaling.

"Fantastic! Now I can get this stuff addressed and off to her! Thanks so much," Ren said, cheerfully.

"You're welcome. But I probably should warn you, she's not here at the moment. Ms. Delatorre came to the desk early this morning to say she was going to be upstate with Rev. Hadley and his staff for all of this week. If you send the package here, though, I'll be sure it gets up to her," Dawn said. Ren could sense she was reluctant to end the conversation.

"You're really a love, dearie. Thanks again for the help. Bye now!"

"Bye!"

Ren said a silent prayer to the patron saint of hotel night auditors as he hung up the phone. He immediately went back to his computer to look up information on Anita Delatorre.

***

"Another day, another hole-in-the-wall Louisiana town," thought Anita. If Shreveport was bad, Alexandria was worse. Half the population and double the stupidity. The only consolation was that it was Thursday and they would spend tomorrow and the weekend in Baton Rouge. This mini-tour was going well on all fronts, however. Hadley was in top form on the air with the pressure of not having to face callers ambushing him about his sex life for a few days. These Bible Belt towns may be a disaster for Anita's social life, but they were big bucks for her employer. Hadley's latest book was to be the bridge from fire-and-brimstone, "end times" preaching to "educational resources". Sales of those resources had more than one executive at Marcus-Kayson salivating.

Anita grabbed her purse and her keys from the table and headed down to the lobby, where she met up with Hadley and Cecilia. They had about 45 minutes in which to get over to the Celebration Assembly of God Church in Alexandria, the venue for Jay's "End Times Education" lecture that evening. Anita tried her best to hide her sour disposition, knowing the method in the madness.

With just ten minutes until the beginning of the evening's talk, one of the local volunteers knocked on the office door where Anita and Cecilia were making a final review of the checklist. A young lady entered, and with a sheepish expression handed Cecilia a flyer which, she said, several young men were passing out in front of the church. Cecilia scanned the contents of the page. It was titled, "What Jay Hadley Doesn't Want You To Know". The contents were some of the more lurid allegations that had been popping up on the numerous JHM website s over the previous couple of months. This move to distributing anti-Hadley literature at JHM events was an escalation, however.

Anita knew immediately which steps to take next. Turning to the volunteer, she said, "Try to identify who is passing these things out and have someone keep an eye on them. If you can, get their license plate numbers and descriptions of their cars. We want to know whether these are local folk or if we have agitators following us. "Anita realized the lady was quite nervous, so she released just a bit of soothing energy to put her at ease. "This isn't anything to worry about, hun, OK? You just relax and let's just find out who our problem is. Reverend Jay's work is will go forward tonight as planned, sweetie, and you're part of that effort. So grab some help and see what you can find out."

Anita's sweet smile was almost nauseating to Cecilia, but it had the desired effect on the volunteer, who left the office sporting a big grin and a determination to get to the bottom of the controversy. Cecilia was used to this end of the business; the trick is to find out whether you are dealing with a single nut-job or an organized group.

"My money's on this being isolated," Cecilia said to Anita. "Who the heck would come up to Alexandria for anything?"

Anita laughed.

"Not me, honey, that's for sure. And I'm inclined to agree with you. Still, there's some nasty stuff on that pamphlet. That's the problem with those damn blogs; they give even a single nutter too much ammo. Let's not tell Jay about this one OK, sweetie? He's on a roll this trip."

"Oh, for sure, Anita. He never used to let any of the negative stuff get to him like it does now. Of course, the stakes have never been as high as they are now, either."

"Truer words never spoken." Anita smiled.

"Maybe I'm winning Cee over after all," she thought.

The prayer meeting that evening was part college lecture, part tent revival. Jay Hadley was truly in rare form, not even missing a beat when a young man stood up and began to challenge Jay's ability to perform exorcisms. There were no exorcisms planned for this trip – it would be too difficult to control the situation in these smaller venues – so Hadley stuck to the prophecy themes that put money in his pocket. It was during one of Jay's better periods of his presentation that evening that Anita pulled out her phone and entered a Dallas number, , and and then held her phone out towards the stage so that the party on the other end could hear Hadley's preaching. Cecilia noticed this and smiled inwardly at how pleased with herself the book executive appeared to be. But there was no time for reflection as Hadley was working the crowd into such a frenzy that it was almost time to pass the baskets around. Churches that invited Hadley to speak did not usually charge admission, but preferred to rely upon donations to cover their expenses. With the millennium topics still big in the Christian community, Hadley was able not only to cover his expenses but also to turn a profit for many of his speaking venues.

Hadley, of course, made his money on the sale of his books, which was why Anita was so pleased. The van that had transported the road crew staff members had also towed a trailer containing several hundred copies of Jay's most recent book. Even in a town like Alexandria, the faithful were grabbing at the research flyers which Hadley's staff had thrown together.

The crowd was on its feet now, hands raised and shouting "AMEN!" as Hadley raised his hands to bless them in return. As the crowd waved and jumped up and down, Hadley's staff began to move in with collection baskets to pass down the aisles.

Jay jumped off the stage and circulated briefly among the audience then hopped back onto the stage and exited. He was greeted in the stage wings by Anita and an approving smile from Cecilia. Anita then went back onto the stage and, as the collection was continuing, she felt the power and energy Hadley had raised among his following. It was intense, yet at the same time, she thought it distasteful. As skilled in the arcane, and as hungry as Anita was, this power was unwelcome to her. These people might not merely throw her out of town if they knew what she was, but they might probably kill her.

"No, some energy is just not so good," she thought.

She sighed, returned backstage, and marshaled Hadley and Cecilia so they could see if they could get some supper. Her preoccupation with the crowd still distracted her, so much that she did not even notice the dark Chevy Impala that was shadowing their movements through Alexandria.

But the occupants of that surveillance car would learn nothing interesting about Jay Hadley that night. Anita had work to do once they got back to the hotel, and that meant Jay would not get his playtime. And that is not necessarily a bad thing, she thought. Being discreet is almost impossible in these small towns. She wished Hadley would realize this but, even now, he continued to behave like a hound. Anita would give him what he wanted tomorrow in Baton Rouge, both to settle him down and to help her to keep her power levels to a maximum.

They made the two-hour drive down I-49 and then I-10 to Baton Rouge without any problems. As they set up the road-show at the Cornerstone Christian Church just off Sherwood Forest, Anita settled into a small office in the churches complex so that she could check on responses to the enquiries she had made the night before about the flyer-distributors in Alexandria. A check of the license plate of the car the pair was using the previous night indicated that the effort was more than likely just local. Still, the owner of the car had a personal website which had links to a number of neo-pagan and Wiccan sites, as well as a prominent link to Renard Alciatore's "Jay Hadley Fan Club" blog.

Anita pondered her next move.

"Something must be done about Renard Alciatore, Protection or not," she thought.

***

Jay Hadley and his ministry were far from the thoughts of "that Alciatore fellow" that evening. He was pulling his

Mustang up in front of the Lucky Star Riverboat Casino – Ren always had to laugh at that name. The state legislature in their infinite wisdom had passed a law some years previously which permitted "riverboat casinos". What they had not specified, however, was that "riverboats" did not necessarily have to be on a river. So, the most successful casino in metropolitan New Orleans was actually situated on a lake, Lake Pontchartrain. The Lucky Star was a big boat adjacent to a large dockside pavilion that contained a restaurant, several bars, and a kids' game room. Ren tucked away the parking ticket the valet had given him and strolled casually into the pavilion to seek out his companion for that evening.

JJ found him first, however. She came up behind him, wrapped her arms around his waist, and pulled him close. She kissed his cheek. "Bonsoir, mon cher!"

"Hey baby, sorry I'm late. But you know about Metairie traffic."

"Yes, I'm afraid I do." She laughed before continuing. "No problem though, I made sure I wore jeans tonight just in case I was alone here for a while. The last time you and Joe didn't show up on time I was wearing a short skirt and the management thought I was a hooker."

"They should know better, love. Hookers around here aren't as good-looking as you." He chuckled. "Let's go in, shall we?"

Ren offered his arm to JJ and they walked into the larger of the two lounges, where the happy-hour cocktail party was in full swing. This was a fund-raiser for a local charity group that boasted JJ's mother as one of the members of its board. "I really do appreciate you coming along, Ren. With mom involved in this thing there was no way I could beg off and, with Joe out of town, that meant coming alone."

"Oh, no problem, baby. I have no problem being seen in public with a woman with a rack like yours."

The comment earned him a swift punch on the shoulder.

"Well, I'm sorry your friend couldn't come along. What happened to him?" JJ asked.

"Oh. Mike? I got a message on voicemail that said he had to run out of town for something. He sounded in a hurry."

JJ smiled sweetly as she teased him back.

"Teachers try to cram all their personal stuff into the summer. It's the only time they have, really, to do any traveling and such. They're not like you self-employed stiffs who can come and go as you please."

"It's a shame he couldn't come. One these days I want to introduce you to each other."

"You bet, Cher. Any priest whose company you can tolerate for more than ten minutes at a time is an OK guy in my book." JJ laughed and leaned towards Ren. "Besides, I need to meet anybody who is able to steal you away for lunch more often than I can!"

JJ and Ren mingled at the reception for about 90 minutes before JJ suggested they go into the casino itself.

"C'mon, she said. I wanna play!"

"I never thought of you as a high-roller," Ren said.

"Oh Lord, I'm far from that. I just like to put some coins in the slots. The engineer in me is fascinated by the craps table, too, but the mom in me can't bring myself to put money at risk," JJ said, wistfully.

"Well, you can watch me roll the dice, then," responded Ren. "You can be the hot babe on my arm who blows on the dice."

Still giggling together, the pair headed up the stairs to the non-smoking deck of the boat, and found a five-dollar-minimum craps table. Ren pulled out the two one-hundred dollar bills and exchanged them for chips as the crew member handling the dice pushed the chips towards a 30-something woman at the opposite end of the table.

"New shooter coming out!" he called.

Ren stacked two five-dollar red chips together and placed them on the PASS line as the woman rolled the dice. They came up a three and a one.

"Four. Four's the point," said the crew leader and gathered the dice with his stick.

Ren proceeded to place two green chips down behind his red ones on the PASS line, then handed to reds and two whites ($12 total) to the woman crew member working his side of the table, instructing her to place six dollars each on the numbers six and eight. Ren then placed a red chip on the COME box and waited for the roll. They turned up a four and a one, for a total of five.

The crew girl moved his COME bet to the number five on the table, and Ren handed her two green chips to put on the red one as an odds bet.

"See, this is what I don't like about craps," JJ said. "We haven't been here fifteen minutes and you've already put $122 at risk.

"Aw, cutie. That's what makes the game intense," replied Ren as he laughed.

"It's what causes people to lose their rent-checks, love." JJ smirked.

Ren placed another red chip on the COME box as the crewman passed the dice to the shooter. She rolled the dice down the felt and Ren focused on them. They both came up threes.

"Six. Hard six!" the crewman called.

Ren collected his winnings and his original chips for his number-six bet and pulled out another hundred-dollar bill to get more chips. Then he gave the girl two more green chips to put on the number-six come bet, as he placed another red in the COME box. The shooter rolled again. It was another six, and Ren again collected winnings.

Half an hour later, the excitement around the table had grown as the same woman was rolling for her sixth consecutive point. Ren had a stack of twenty or so green chips in front of him, as well as an equally large stack of red chips. Ren decided it was time for his streak to end, so he focused his concentration on the next roll. It came up seven, and the shooter was out.

Some of the crowd which had gathered at the table moved on. Except one, a young red-headed woman who moved from the center of the table to stand right next to Ren. "You're having some good luck tonight, uh?" she asked.

"Sure am. You don't look like you're doing too bad either," he said as he glanced down at the chips in her hand. He slowly took-in her figure, dressed in tight blue jeans and a thin light blue top.

"No. But I think I would be fun if I got luckier," she said, moving closer to him, her eyes twinkling.

Janet Julianne Garrison may have been a married woman, but there is a sort of instinct that kicks in when another woman moves in on her "date", even if that "date" is someone the woman really has no claim over. Smiling a smile that dripped with sarcasm and condescension, she said softly, "Well honey, maybe all that money you've won will attract you a guy or two at the blackjack table."

The redhead was not one to shy away from a challenge and she smiled back. "Well, sugar. I tend to like dice players. Sometimes I like their girlfriends, too." She gave JJ the once-over, her eyes traveling from head to toe and back again.

JJ flushed beet red and it was all Ren could do to keep from bursting out laughing. Ren knew JJ was no prude, but this girl's attitude had taken JJ completely aback.

While continuing to bet and observe the table, Ren began to chat up the redhead. He could feel the tension from his other side as JJ began to shift and become restless. She was obviously annoyed with him. The redhead excused herself for a moment, asking Ren to keep her place at the table.

Once, the redhead was gone, JJ wrapped her arm in Ren's and said, "Mon cher, if you dump me for that tramp I'll be inconsolable."

Ren laughed.

"Hey mon amour, I've got a better chance of getting lucky with her than with a married chick."

"Humph! Is that what this is about? Maybe I'll let me take you back to your place," she pouted.

Still chuckling, Ren held her close for a moment. "Aww, that's sweet, babe, but complicated. Tell you what, though. I'll make it up to you if you want. Let's have some fun when she returns."

"What do you mean?" JJ looked at him curiously. A twinkle in her eye betraying her interest.

"Remember the feeling you had the other day when we were at lunch?" Ren asked as he let his mind-touch caress her breast and pinch her left nipple gently again.

JJ gasped lightly as the realization dawned on her.

"You *did* do that, didn't you?"

Ren smiled.

"You little shit. I knew you did that deliberately!"

He kissed her on the cheek and whispered in her ear.

"I did it, but not deliberately. It was sort of an accident with you. But I've figured it out a bit more since then, watch."

He collected the latest stack of chips from the girl working the table as the redhead returned. Ren distanced himself a little from JJ to resume his casual conversation with the girl. JJ was startled to see the girl's nipples grow and push through the flimsy fabric of her top. So it was true! Ren was somehow getting the girl aroused without even touching her. She had to keep from giggling as the girl's body moved involuntarily under Ren's "touch".

For his part, Ren was finding it difficult to keep track of the roll of the dice and play this new game at the same time. He nudged JJ to keep an eye on the bets he still had on the table as he focused his mind on the girl. He visualized her sliding her feet out of the small white sandals she was wearing, then nibbling her ankle while running his hand up and down her other leg. She was squirming a bit now, squeezing her legs together in an attempt to remain in control of herself. Seeing her squeeze, Ren immediately sent the thought of him reaching up and gently grasping both her breasts, pressing her nipples as if they were buttons. The redhead forgot about the craps table and her bets and let out a small moan and began to get lost in the sensation.

Ren carried the visualization down to the waistband of her jeans, mentally unsnapping them and pulling her zipper down. The redhead's hips were swaying now as she physically felt Ren's "fingers" stroke her crotch and enter her. She let out another audible gasp and began to pump against those unseen fingers until her moans became loud, her orgasm apparent to everyone at the table. Her whole body shuddered and she grasped the rail to steady herself, her eyes closed and her teeth clenched.

When she eventually opened her eyes she noticed everyone on that side of the table staring at her. She could feel that the wet spot in her jeans was visible, and it was her turn to be embarrassed. Hurriedly, she gathered her chips and excused herself, leaving a five-dollar PASS bet still on the table.

Ren pointed out the bet to the crew leader and said, "My friend left that bet for the crew, she's not going to be back for a while." Ren chuckled behind his grin.

JJ was almost speechless as she stood on the other side. She eventually regained her composure and turned to Ren. "Good God Ren, what did you do to her? That was no fake orgasm on her part!"

Ren smiled. "Well I wanted to get rid of her for now without hurting my chances for the future, so I sent her away happy."

"Happy my ass. That was ecstasy!"

"Yeah, I suppose it was."

"That's amazing. I've always known people could have good mental connection. Hell, we have a good mental connection. But what you just did..."

"Yup. I guess it's a gift."

She punched his shoulder again, laughing as she did so.

"You shit. You're going to explain all this to me someday. Someday soon!"

He kissed her again, on the cheek and returned his attention back to the table. His winnings had reached over $1,100 and the pit boss, a cute blonde woman, took an increased interest in Ren's activities. Just at that point, something Mike told him came into his mind.

"Always remember to end an evening of gambling on a loss," his mind recalled his mentor saying. "Get your winnings to a certain point, and then lose ten or 20 percent of it in a short time. That will usually distract management enough that they will remember you only as someone who was momentarily lucky."

Ren heeded Mike's advice by increasing the value of his bets so that he now had over $200 at risk. He stared the dice down so that they came up five and two.

"Seven and out!" the crew-leader called as Ren's chips were snatched up by the girl on the crew. Ren tossed her two green chips as a tip, gathered his chips, and headed with JJ to the cashier.

Walking away from the counter, Ren counted five one-hundred dollar bills and handed them to JJ.

"Here," he said. "Give these to Mom and the kids at the hospital."

JJ looked him square in the eye. "Oh, Ren, that's so sweet, but I can't. You just won all that!"

Ren smiled back at her.

"Don't worry, mon amour, there's always more where that came from."

JJ froze in her tracks.

"WHAT?"

Ren placed a finger to her lips and she lowered her voice.

"You mean to tell me you're able to do something to the dice, just like you did to that girl?"

"Well... not exactly, babe. I didn't make the dice come," he laughed.

"You shit! You know what I mean. Renard Alciatore, I'm going to kick your ass if you don't start explaining!"

"Not here, love. Not now. But I will, I promise."

They walked to the front of the casino, Ren gave both parking tickets to the valet, and then pulled JJ close to him. He kissed her on the lips, holding her, until the valet pulled up in JJ's car.

"We're a dangerous team, love. I had fun tonight," he smiled.

"Mmm yes, we are indeed dangerous. And you, you little shit, are bad news. Very bad news."

Ren bowed gracefully.

"Why, thank you m'Lady, for such a high compliment."

Ren walked her to the driver's door. He kissed her again and wished her goodnight.

CHAPTER ELEVEN

Transport

"I'm not as familiar with St. Raphael as I was with Cabrini," Ren remarked to Mike as he got out of his car, parked alongside the church on Elysian Fields Avenue in Gentilly.

"Familiar surroundings always make the process of learning something new go more smoothly, Mike replied. "If it wasn't for the storm we'd be over at Cabrini for this little lesson."

Ren followed Mike to a side door of St. Raphael the Archangel Church, which had been renamed "Transfiguration of Our Lord" in the post-Katrina re-organization of parishes by the Archdiocese.

"The pastor gave me a set of keys while the post-storm repairs were in progress. I tried to give them back, but he told me to keep them, just in case. That was years ago now," Mike explained.

Ren's eyes scanned the high ceiling as he entered the church behind Mike and walked down the side aisle, towards the main entrance.

"Follow me to the baptismal font," Mike said.

"Don't you worry about being this open in a church like this?" Ren asked.

"Not at all," Mike said as he smiled. He pointed to his Roman Collar. "Firstly, this carries a lot of weight with the average passer-by. It makes me look as though I am supposed to be here. Secondly, I *am* supposed to be here, I've got the keys. And third, you know already that there are a few things we can do to deflect any attention should the need arise." Mike paused and turned with a grin. “Thus endeth the lesson.”

Ren returned the grin and followed Mike’s gesture to move to the back of the baptismal font. The morning sun was streaming into the church through a skylight, presenting a stark contrast to the dim lighting inside the rest of the church. Mike stopped in the entrance behind the font and raised his hands slowly in the classic “let us pray” stance of a Catholic priest. He whispered:

“Creator of lights,
Giver of the day.
Grant us short distraction
So we may be on our way.”

Mike then raised his hands fully over his head to make his invocation. As he lowered them a thin film appeared to follow them downwards and filled the entrance as though Mike were pulling down a shade. Once that film touched the floor, anyone passing the baptismal and looking in would see just an empty room and would also feel compelled simply to walk past and go about their business.

Mike turned to Ren. “OK, now we won’t be disturbed, so we can get things done. So far, you’ve done a lot with telekinesis and you’ve done well. I’m glad also that you took my gambling advice to heart.” He watched Ren blush then continued. “We’re going to take things a step further now, moving something bigger than a pair of dice or a lock mechanism. We’re going to work on moving *us*. From one place to another.”

Mike walked clockwise around the baptismal font to the eastern corner of the room. “Notice corners of the floor. Four of the tiles in each corner have a pattern that’s different from the rest of the floor. They are Gateways. It’s possible to teleport ourselves from one location to another, but it takes a lot of energy. More energy than we each possess. So, to use this Talent we employ the services of a Gateway. You with me? Cool. OK, the idea is simple. You step onto a Gateway, visualize your destination, then throw a mental switch. You channel your energy into the Gateway and it opens a path to the destination Gateway and sends you there. Once you’ve had some practice doing this, you'll be able to take another person through Gateways with you. That's how we're going to start this exercise. I'm going to take you with me so you can feel how it's done. Then you can try to come back."

Mike stood on the four tiles of the eastern corner and motioned Ren alongside him. "Take a good look at this corner," he said. "Then stand here and look out at the whole baptismal. Good. Now, just relax. Take a few deep breaths, lower your shields completely and yield control to me. Great. Now, just stay in that state... relax... ready... and... NOW!"

Ren felt his knees buckle slightly as he floated downward for what felt like a minute, then upward as though he was rising through deep water to the surface. The sensation suddenly ceased and he instantly knew he was no longer in the baptismal at St. Raphael's. It was dark when he opened his eyes. Much darker then where he had just been.

Ren shivered, and knew immediately where they were. "We're up at Holy Name!" he whispered, loudly, the amazement in his voice still there.

"Very good, weed-hopper," said Mike, smiling. "Yes, we started at a familiar location and ended up at another familiar location. Now, look around." Mike stretched out his hands to encompass the entire side of the chapel. "Feel your surroundings. Great. Now look down. Recognize the pattern of the tiles you're standing on? Both these Gateways were created by the same team."

"Team? What do you mean by team? And why are these Gateways in churches? Do they exist in any other places?"

"The church has long been a refuge for individuals with Talents. It's a sort of 'hide in plain sight' theory. Some of the things we can do would have gotten a person burned, so being a priest or a nun was an excellent cover for that kind of activity. So it's only logical that these folks would make a network of Gateways in their churches."

"Yeah, that does seem to make sense," Ren said, as he started to walk around the chapel, taking in all the details of the room.

"Also remember," added Mike, "a church has long been considered a sanctuary. As such, churches were the ideal place to seek help for someone with Talents who was on the run. Think of it as a variant of the Underground Railroad."

"OK. Gotcha. So, what now?"

"We'll make another jump. Are you ready?" Mike stepped back onto the Gateway, and Ren did so with him. "Relax again... give me control... and... we're... Gone!"

The same sensations as before overtook Ren as he seemed to fall through the floor at Holy Name, sliding through time and space. He knew Mike was in control and locked-in on his consciousness. Moments later, they surfaced once again. This time, in another familiar set of surroundings.

"Jeez, Mike. This is Our Lady of Perpetual Help in Kenner!" exclaimed Ren.

"I can tell you're a wedding photographer, the way you know churches," Mike chuckled in response. "This Gateway was created at a time when being assigned as a priest here was a punishment. Like being shipped off to the West Bank or down to Cut Off would be today. A priest with Talents can often fall foul of a more conservative pastor or bishop. The impact of such conflicts is that you may often find Gateways in churches off the beaten path."

Ren rubbed his eyes, nodded, and let out a sigh. "Amazing. But I can feel the drain on my system."

Mike nodded. "F'sure. And remember, teleportation is not something to do lightly, for a number of reasons. But, no big deal for today, since we're going to only one more place, and that's back to where we started." He gave Ren a few moments to get the "feel" for this particular Gateway, and then directed him to stand alone on the tiles.

"OK. Time for you to go solo. I want you to visualize the baptismal back at St. Raphael. See the tiles. See the room. Now, when you're ready, throw the switch mentally and feel the floor fall from beneath you and just float back to St. Raphael. I'll be right behind you, don't worry." Mike smiled confidently at his pupil.

Ren nodded, nervously. He stood on the Gateway tiles and did as Mike instructed. Seeing in his mind's eye the Gateway at St. Raphael, he pulled the lever mentally and visualized a trap-door opening below him. As he did so, he could feel himself floating, traveling back to their starting-point. Along the way, the sensation of falling changed to one of rising as he headed towards the floor of the destination Gateway. Ren gasped for breath before opening his eyes to see and feel the warm sunshine coming through the skylight of the baptismal in the Gentilly church.

He stepped off the Gateway and paced around to get his bearings. No sooner had his eyes returned to focus when a golden flash of light in the eastern corner heralded Mike's arrival through the Gateway.

Mike had a huge grin on his face. "Nice to see you!" He laughed. "I'm glad to see you didn't end up on the north shore, or worse! How do you feel?"

Ren swayed slightly. "Woozy. Queasy, Headachy." He leaned against the wall as he realized just how peculiar he felt.

"That's normal after a couple of jumps," said Mike. "Something else to keep in mind about teleporting: you're not going to feel a hundred percent right away when you get to the other end. The feeling you have right now will get better as you gain more experience using Gateways, but you'll never be able to just jump through and come out the other end ready to kick ass."

Ren rubbed his temples, slowly going through the exercises Mike had taught him previously to deal with headaches caused by psychic over-exertion. "You know, I've had headaches before after we've worked, but never as bad as this."

Mike nodded. "Well, you have just moved a large mass, namely yourself, through time and space. Are you up to driving home? What you need now is a nice nap and then maybe a bite to eat."

"Yeah, I can handle that. I took your advice, too, and didn't schedule anything else for today or tomorrow."

"Cool. I'll give you a buzz or come by tomorrow to see how you are doing. We'll practice this again later this week." Mike walked back to the entrance of the baptismal and reversed the concealment spell he had placed earlier. Ren watched the film rise and his view back into the church was clear again. Mike smiled, winked at Ren, and stepped back onto the Gateway tiles. He closed his eyes and vanished amid a golden flash.

***

Ren did indeed go home and sleep. He rested for most of that afternoon. When he woke up to grab a snack he checked his emails and found some more from "Isis" which contained some new interesting tidbits of information about the Rev. Jay Hadley. Smiling, he worked on adding them to the website until it was time for him to head to Metairie and meet up with the other referees who would be working with him on the professional soccer match the following evening. The referee for this match, a National Referee from Alabama, preferred getting together with his crew the evening before the match, to talk things over. A Premier Development Team such as the Jesters would not usually rate a National Referee but, as he was already to be in New Orleans on business, he was awarded the assignment.

Ren also preferred this method of getting ready for a professional match and was very comfortable when he arrived at the stadium the following afternoon to dress out and stretch. The officials would walk the stadium area as a crew, about an hour before kick-off, making note of any peculiarities about the pitch and the stadium, reviewing what they all knew about the two teams they would have charge of that evening.

Refereeing a National Premier Soccer League match was still a thrill for Ren. Even though he was an Assistant Referee, he was fully-aware of the compliment that was being paid to him by the people who assign the officials to matches and of the responsibility he had in order to live up to their expectations. As they took to the field, Ren walked to the right of the Referee, who was the senior official of the three. Ren would be running the line on the bench side of the field, in front of the two teams, who would, most likely, be most vocal in their dissension throughout the match. This was also the side with the majority of the crowd.

The two teams were introduced, the National Anthem sung, and the coin tossed at the halfway line. Ren checked the goal net on his side of the pitch and took his position on the line. From his standpoint as Assistant Referee, the match turned out to be a physical one, but his only challenge was to keep up with the second-to-last defender so he could properly adjudge offside violations. The forwards for the Baton Rouge team kept running as they constantly hammered the New Orleans defense. However, the game was scoreless at half-time and Ren was exhilarated and tired as he headed to the locker-room.

With the teams having switched ends after half-time, the second half began. New Orleans could not get the attacks going as much as Baton Rouge, so Ren didn't have the back-and-forth sprinting along the line that he had endured during the first half. Still, that did not stop the Jesters' forwards from pushing up as close to an offside position as possible, sometimes even crossing into what would have been an offside position and then retreating back when it looked as though play was about to move towards them. This continued throughout most of the second half. With only five minutes of the match remaining, the Jesters right forward, a twenty-year-old Honduran named Carlos Casales, was unable to get back quickly enough as his teammate passed a precise through-ball to him. He was a step and a half beyond the defender so Ren planted his feet, shifted his hand-held red flag from his left hand to his right and then raised it. The referee blew his whistle, halting play. Ren lowered his flag to a horizontal position, pointing across the field of play to indicate that the infringement had taken place around half way across the field. The referee raised his arm, awarding a free-kick to Baton Rouge.

Carlos had already begun his sprint towards the Baton Rouge goalkeeper as he received the pass when the whistle blew. Enraged, he turned around and yelled at Ren, "No fucking way was I offside!" With the match still scoreless, Ren had just shut down the best attack New Orleans had been able to mount, and this guy wanted a piece of him.

"Oh, I'm in the shit here," thought Ren. "If I let him get here, he's going to take a swing at me or try to push me. If he does that, his season is over."

A plan formed immediately in Ren's mind. Ren took a step back from the line and closed his eyes for a moment. He threw up a wall of energy between himself and Carlos, giving the young man a stare that would have made milk curdle. Carlos came to within six feet of him and stopped as if he had hit a wall.

Totally in shock at having been stopped, Carlos lost his train of thought for a second.

That was long enough for him to realize what he had been about to do. Carlos regained his composure and proceeded to stand there and yell at Ren. The referee ran up the field and stood between Carlos and Ren, pointing to the player to take his position for play to restart. The referee was not quite sure what it was that Ren had just said or done to disarm the young man, so he simply winked at Ren and ran back to restart the game with the free-kick.

A New Orleans midfield player trapped the resulting free-kick and immediately sent another though-ball to Carlos. This time, the forward was on-side and, after two excellent moves to escape the defender marking him, found himself one-on-one with the goalkeeper. The keeper committed himself too soon and Carlos struck a beautiful near-post shot that slid perfectly into the back of the net.

The crowd went wild and Ren couldn't help but feel a little guilty as he sprinted up the line towards the half-way line to indicate his agreement that it was a valid goal. Had he let Carlos approach him during that altercation, the player could well have been ejected from the match and that goal might never have been scored. Had he been justified in using his Talent to avoid the conflict? Ren thought. Had he unduly influenced the outcome of the match? The ethical implications of what he had done continued to distract Ren for the final two minutes of the match and as the officials went through a short post-game de-briefing. His feelings of guilt were not reduced when he heard the praise from the referee and the assessors who had been observing his performance.

"I thought for sure I was going to have to pull that kid off you," the referee remarked as they were dressing. "I've seen that guy in five matches at this level and he's a hot-head. I wish every Assistant Referee I have working with me could stop those guys like that before they get sent-off."

"I think he maybe just saw that end-of-career light flashing in front of him," Ren replied. "I didn't have to say anything. I guess he's smarter than we give him credit for."

"Hmm. He's a player, I'm not so sure," the referee said as

he smiled. "Anyway, well done, Ren. And I hope we get to work together again soon."

"Thanks, Miguel. I appreciate it."

They shook hands one last time, then left the stadium.

***

Ren jumped in his Mustang and headed over to Oscar's, a little pub on Metairie Road, to meet up with his friend JJ and her husband Joe. They had been to the game with their children, as Ren's guests. Their 17-year-old son dropped them off at Oscar's, and the plan was for Ren to give them a ride home. Ren pulled into the parking area in front of the pub and sat for a moment in the Mach One, closed his eyes, and replayed the incident with Carlos Casales in his mind. No, it was the right decision, thought Ren. Assaults on referees do nothing for the game nor the player, and they damned sure do nothing positive for the referee. Still, the speed with which he had reacted to the situation caused Ren some concern. His value system had seemed to be on auto-pilot when he had thrown-up that psychic wall.

But how is that different from a cop who draws his weapon to shoot at a criminal? No way was he going to resolve this tonight, he thought, so I should just as soon go and get a beer.

Ren found JJ and Joe sitting at a table in the left-hand side of the pub, munching on an order of onion rings and sipping on a couple of Abita Ambers. Ren waved at Gwen the bartender, who blew a kiss at Ren before drawing a NOLA Blonde ale from a tap for him. He pulled up a chair at JJ and Joe's table, grabbed an onion ring, and saluted his friends with it before popping it into his mouth.

"Good match, Ren," Joe said, gently slapping Ren's shoulder as he sat down.

"Thanks, Joe. I thought I was gonna get into it with Carlos tonight. I'm glad he held back before trying to run me down," Ren said, chuckling.

"Yeah, what was with that? Carlos is nothing but nice when he is coaching. I've seen you call penalties against his U-17 team without him letting out a peep," JJ added.

"Well, that's youth soccer, cher," Ren said with a wry grin. "It's different when he's actually playing. All bets are off then."

"Still, it was strange. Stranger still that he didn't slug ya!" Joe laughed.

Gwen came over to the table with Ren's beer and the three of them ordered burgers. Ren had not seen JJ since their outing at the casino the previous week, and Joe's travel schedule was such that he and Ren had not been out together for a couple of months. It was a pleasant opportunity for them all to be able to sit down and just relax for a while. They were able to catch up on lots of things going on in their lives, while polishing-off the onion rings as they waited for their burgers to arrive.

"Oh, Ren. Mom told me to give you a big hug and a kiss for your donation," JJ said as Gwen brought their food to the table. "She was very impressed by your generosity."

Ren felt JJ's knee bump him under the table and he blushed. "Thanks, babe. It was no big deal."

"That's because you don't have Joey's insurance bill to pay," Joe said as he chuckled. "The kid is going to break us, I swear!"

JJ slapped her husband lightly on the arm, and then curled her arm around his. "Oh, I don't want to hear it. You love it. You should have seen him back on prom night, Ren. You never have seen a prouder daddy as his boy went off with the car to pick up his date." JJ was positively beaming as she kissed Joe on the cheek.

Ren took another gulp of his beer and smiled at the two of them. The last thing he needed this evening was more emotional confusion. Firstly, he pondered, was his anxiety about his actions during the soccer match and then, secondly the sight of his best friend with another man just sent his head reeling. Oh, it didn't matter that "the other man" happened to be his best friend's husband; Ren's train of thought was behaving more from emotion than rationale. He knew JJ was a woman who could love more than one person in different ways, but even that thought was not coming through clearly for him. All he could think about was that he had the hots for a married woman, and the consequences of that were potentially disastrous for all involved. He sighed inwardly and was just finishing-off the rest of his beer when he realized Joe had been talking to him.

"...and I told him there was no way you would ever consider selling him the car, but I made a promise I would at least ask. Ren... are you there? Helloo? Earth to Ren!"

"Huh? Oh, I'm sorry, Joe. My mind was wandering a bit. I'm still decompressing," he said as he smiled sheepishly at both his friends.

"No problem, guy. I told my buddy I'd ask you. I didn't say you had to answer!" Joe laughed as he signaled to Gwen to bring them another round of drinks.

That round was their last. All three had things to do the next day. "The only bad thing about going out on a Thursday is having to work the next day, even if it is a Friday," JJ said from the back seat of the Mustang. She was leaning forward between Ren and Joe, her hands lightly massaging her husband's neck as Ren drove them both home. "Oh, look, baby. The kids got home in one piece." JJ was laughing, but the two men could sense the maternal relief in her voice, now that she knew her children were home safely.

Ren smiled and pulled the car into the driveway. Joe shook his hand and thanked him for the ride and the tickets. JJ pushed the front seat forward and climbed out of the back of the car and gave Ren a flirtatious wink as she threw herself into her husband's arms, and then walked arm in arm up the walkway to the house.

Ren lingered until the couple was inside and the front lights and been turned off, then he drove through the quiet Lakeview neighborhood back to the bayou and home. He dropped his referee's bag in the front hallway, kicked off his shoes, and headed for his study. Ren skimmed quickly through the email that had come in that afternoon and evening. As he chuckled at some of the off-color comments coming into the website, he heard his phone beep, a Kik from "Isis".

"You did a good job tonight. Congrats on keeping the players on the pitch."

"Thanks, I didn't know you were a soccer fan."

"I used to play when I was in school and my dad played when he was younger."

"Cool. Yeah, that goal Carlos scored was outstanding. It was fun to see him take that shot."

"And you had the best view in the house. :-)"

"Well, yeah, but that view is not without its drawbacks. So, when are you going to let me take you to dinner? There aren't all that many female footie fans around. We can sit around and talk some, one time."

"Oh, great! I get to have dinner with a guy who has legs like yours and we're going to talk about soccer? You must think I'm nuts!"

"Well, we could talk about other things. :-)"

"Careful now. What if I'm not that kind of girl?"

"Hmm. What kind of girl are you?"

"Well, not the kind who sleeps with preachers, that's for sure! :-)"

"Oh? And what kind of girl sleeps with a preacher, then?"

"Beats me. I prefer athletes."

"Oh. So I guess I'm out of luck then. Being just a referee."

"Well, they say that the ref runs more than any of the players on the field. Is that true? :-)"

"Yeah, as a matter of fact it is. So when are you going to put me out of my misery and go out with me?"

":-)"

Ren wanted to reply, but sensed that the conversation was over. He sighed and, as he finished checking his email, an anonymous message appeared in his "inbox". He opened it to reveal another series of internal Jay Hadley Ministries documents. More fuel to the fire. While they were all nice bits of information on the Rev. Jay's spending habits, none of them were, by themselves, the big gun that would shoot down Hadley's operation.

Ren smiled and went to his blog to start a new entry. Well, they aren't big guns, he thought, but getting shot at with a BB gun is still an uncomfortable thing. And making Jay Hadley uncomfortable was rather enjoyable.

Ren had grown to trust the "Isis" information to such an extent that he felt he didn't even need to take any steps to verify its authenticity. He finished formatting the new files into a blog entry and uploaded them onto the web-server.

This stuff should fire-up the talk lines with wonderfully inconvenient questions for ol' Jay, he snickered.

Just as the new pages had completed their transfer to the server, his Twitter client flashed a Direct Message from "Wynterbreeze".

"Je t'adore."

He sent back a <3, a heart, leaving his real heart to pound and his head swimming again. He sighed, got up from his chair, walked over to the bookcase, and pulled down a bottle of Bushmills Malt and a glass. Maybe a couple of fingers of the Water of Life would help him get to sleep, he thought.

CHAPTER TWELVE
Memphis

"Eight o'clock and the humidity is getting to me already," the older man said, wiping his brow as he turned to his younger friend. They had just completed a leisurely two-mile jog around Bayou St. John and were enjoying a cup of coffee on the front porch of his friend's home overlooking the New Orleans waterway.

"You've lived here all your life and you still complain about the weather?" Renard Alciatore poured his older friend another cup of coffee from an old-fashioned drip pot. "You can't tell me you expected anything other than this on an August morning, surely!" Ren's five-foot-ten frame was every bit as sweaty as his friend's and his thick black hair was already dripping with sweat, even though their run had barely taxed him.

Mike O'Donnell nodded his thanks to Ren and snorted. "Hey. I may bitch about the weather, but it's not like I'm moving away anytime soon. For openers, the coffee sucks anywhere else. Then there's the food. And there's nothing like running around the bayou or the Lakefront to get the day started." Ren only half-heard the litany of Mike's praise for the city as he became increasingly engrossed in a news story on his tablet. Mike could not fail to notice the lack of attention Ren was giving him and asked, "What's so interesting in the news today?"

Ren handed-over the tablet, which displayed a NOLA.com news article to Mike.

"Does it ever bother you to know you have Talents much beyond the average person and yet shit like this still happens?"

The article Ren was pointing to was a story about a kidnapping the previous day of an eight year-old girl from suburban Metairie. The girl had been playing on an empty lot near her home and had not returned within the half-hour her mother had insisted was the allotted play time for that day.

Mike O'Donnell digested the article and drew a deep sigh.

"Your reaction is typical of many people when they discover they have very powerful psychic abilities. For generations we've been identifying men, women, boys, and girls with the Talents. Once an individual discovers their telepathic and psycho-kinetic abilities and begins to develop them, the desire to help others in need soon manifests itself. You can't change the world all by yourself, Ren. There are things you can do to help people and things you can't. You have to learn how to choose the things where you can make a difference."

"But that's a little girl!"

Mike took a deep breath.

"Yes, she is. What do you think you can do to help her, though?"

"I don't know. But you read stories all the time about psychics who work with the cops. Maybe if we could talk to the cops or her parents. Maybe I could see something that would help." Ren looked at his friend and implored him to do something to lend a hand in the situation.

"It's not as simple as that. For starters, you don't have any credibility with either the parents or the cops in this area. They are likely to just dismiss you as a nut-ball. Secondly, you have no clear idea yet of what you can and can't do as an individual. And thirdly, be careful what you wish for. Let's say you found this little girl. The press is bound to pick-up the story, and then every parent in the nation with a missing child will be coming to you for help. You'll find you'll no longer have a life of your own as you run from one kidnapping or disappearance to the next. In many cases the victim will already be dead, so all you will have done would have been to assist the cops in finding a body. The emotional toll on you could be devastating. Take it from me, I know from personal experience."

Ren nodded, in acceptance of his mentor's wisdom. Still, the kidnapping disturbed him visibly.

"OK, I see your point, but there's just got to be a way to help without drawing attention to oneself. I have a buddy in the Kenner Police Department I could use to channel any information to. I really want to help this girl and I'm sure you can come up with a plan of some kind," said Ren, grinning.

Mike smiled back at the younger man.

"All right. Let's look at what we can really do and what we can't do. We know we can't simply wave our hands and bring her here. Now, can we get to her instead? Hmm...where does she live?"

Ren glanced back to the newspaper, then answered, "Metairie. It says 'Bissonet Plaza Subdivision'."

Mike cocked his head to one side. He was receiving data.

"St. Philip Parish." Mike reached for his phone, and punched a number.

"Jeannie Theriot! Father Mike here. Yes, I'm well. Yes, still teaching. So, little David really went off to Stanford, uh? Fantastic. Yup, I figured that when I didn't see him around UNO any more. Listen, Jeannie, I need a favor. The kids want me to offer Mass tomorrow for this little LeBlanc girl. You say her first name is Dana? OK, got it. I figure the family are St. Philip parishioners, right? Good. Could you give me their address? I want to see if I can get a picture of her for them to bring up with the gifts. Hang on; let me grab my pen...Yes, got it. Do you think she's home? Oh, for sure. No problem sweetie. I'll do that. Thanks Jeannie. You take good care of the rest of your gang. Talk soon. Bye!"

Mike chuckled in immediate response to Ren's bemused expression.

"Well, the Newman Center regulars are indeed going to be upset when I see them later. And you might not be as young as some of them but you're still a kid in some ways. Let's get moving. I need to get my uniform on."

Mike emerged from the upstairs bathroom 15 minutes later no longer simply Ren's running buddy but as Monsignor Michael Aloysius O'Donnell, Associate Director of the Newman Center at the University of New Orleans' Lakefront campus. The fact that the current Director of the Newman Center was a priest who had been ordained a mere five years previous didn't disturb

Msgr. O'Donnell, who was also Associate Professor of History at the university and had other responsibilities of which his church superiors were not aware. One of those responsibilities happened to be a certain Renard Alciatore. Now dressed in a bespoke black suit complete with the collar of his office, Mike sat back down on the front porch and waited for Ren to finish dressing. Ren had started out as a responsibility, but the speed at which he was developing his Talents was so great that he and Mike were able to spend a fair amount of time getting to know each other also. A strong friendship grew in the process.

"Well, he is friends with the 'me' he knows," Mike thought.

"Would he continue that way once he gets to know me better?"

As he reached for one of the bottles of water Ren had thoughtfully brought out with the coffee, he wondered about that prospect. Being a Teacher of those with Talents was a position of overwhelming responsibility. Sometimes, he had a duty to make some difficult choices and to take actions which the liberal-minded Renard Alciatore might not think necessary, much less moral.

Being a Roman Catholic priest did not help Mike in this instance. The Church's reputation for actions which were far from consistent with the New Testament's idea of what Jesus wanted people to do was one of its biggest hurdles in retaining young people with morals and principles. That, combined with hundreds of years of stupidity, along with more recent positions on women in the priesthood and a hard-line stance against homosexuality, and it was becoming increasingly difficult to convince intelligent college kids to remain Catholic. At least the pedophile-priest thing was beginning to settle down.

Mike sighed to himself.

The same bishops and monsignors with whom he had crossed swords were responsible for that debacle as well. The church had become a multi-national corporation run like a feudal kingdom. The clash of modern life and a modern situation with a medieval management structure was sometimes too much for him to take. Stupidity such as what those old men had perpetrated had cost the New Orleans area alone over $20 million. It was tough to explain to college students why so much money had to be spent to smooth-over incidents of priests buggering boys.

Ren Alciatore was also one of those who had difficulty understanding that.

"If I ever have to explain my duties as a Teacher of the Talented, I'm going to be screwed," Mike thought.

Ren would see it as a church conspiracy. The catch is, he mused, that was something entirely different. Now, if some people in the church hierarchy knew more about that side of the Right Reverend Monsignor O'Donnell, they would be more than a little upset. Hell, they would probably bring back the Spanish Inquisition! Mike couldn't help but to chuckle at that last thought.

Wistfully, Mike looked out over the bayou while mentally composing his thoughts and trying to decide just how best he could approach this poor mother who had already lost her child. No, not yet. The child was definitely still alive. Mike had no firm knowledge of this as fact, of course, but Ren's strong desire to help seemed to be an excellent indication that there was more than a little hope. If the girl were dead, Ren's emotions would probably be mostly of anger. Intense, but less urgent. The kid was good, but Mike didn't know yet just how good.

Ren, now dressed in a polo-shirt and khakis, went down to join Mike on the front porch. He was initially taken aback by Mike's formal business attire.

"Lucky you had your full suit in the car," said Ren.

Mike smiled.

"Oh, it's not luck. I always keep the uniform with me; you just never know in my business. Of course, there are other uniforms I can wear that show people I mean business." Ren was taken aback at that last comment, aware that the arched eyebrow Mike gave him meant that he was referring to the aura of light that was discernible to people of Talent. Ren started to head towards his 1971 Mustang Mach One, but Mike stopped him.

"Let's take the Jeep. We don't want to be rumbling up to someone's house in that old thing; no matter how much fun it would be to drive it on such a lovely day." Smiling, Ren turned towards the driveway and his less-conspicuous Jeep Grand Cherokee. The Jeep was Ren's work vehicle, and was the perfect size for his tools-of-the-trade as a photographer. He pulled the car out and the two of them headed towards the cemeteries and onto I-10 towards suburban Metairie.

Most of the traffic at that time of the morning was running in the opposite direction, towards downtown, so they were into Metairie in a matter of moments. A few stops and turns and they found themselves in front of the LeBlanc home.

As he climbed out of the car, Mike paused, gesturing for Ren to wait a moment.

"Follow my lead. She's going to be edgy. No doubt she has been prodded and poked by all the TV stations by now, so strangers will be the last thing she will want to have around."

Ren nodded in acknowledgement as they walked up to the door. He rang the doorbell of the suburban single-story house. The door opened to reveal a hard-looking woman in her early thirties.

Usually, she was a pretty-looking woman. But not this morning. It was clear that the strain of her daughter's disappearance for the past two days had taken its toll on her. The harsh words she was about to deliver to these intruding strangers died on her lips immediately when she saw that Mike was a priest.

"Good morning, Mrs. LeBlanc," Mike said as he smiled gracefully, doing his best to disarm the woman both physically and mentally. "I am Monsignor O'Donnell, a teacher at UNO and I also work with the kids at the Newman Center. This is Renard Alciatore, a colleague of mine. May we have a moment of your time? I realize you have a lot on your mind right now but I promise we'll only be a few minutes." Mike may have been a priest, but he was nevertheless a shameless old-school flirt. The smile he gave to Judy LeBlanc was almost enough to get him into her pants, let alone through the front door. She nodded and opened the door fully, inviting the pair in.

As she shut the door, she spoke, finally.

"Yes, Father. I've heard Mrs. Theriot at the church speak of you. What can I do for you?"

"Well, Mrs. LeBlanc. May I call you Judy? Thank you,

Judy. Well, we were on our way to Kenner and I just wanted to stop by to let you know that a lot of the students at the University are praying for you and little Dana. The kids want me to offer Mass for Dana tomorrow and we were hoping you could loan us a picture of her, to use at Mass. Oh yes, I know her picture has been used in the paper and all, but I was hoping you might have one that was a little less formal, if you know what I mean." Mike's smile had the desired effect and Judy settled back into the couch and exhaled.

"Sure, Father. Let me go and get you one of her soccer pictures. Dana has been playing soccer since she was five. In fact, I think I recognize your friend here as having refereed her teams on occasion."

Ren nodded and smiled on, in confirmation. Judy LeBlanc stood up and went to the back of the house and Mike turned to Ren and winked. Mike stood up and called back to Judy.

"Judy, while you're back there, could you also bring us something of hers, like a doll or a stuffed animal or something? You know, I was raised Irish-Catholic, so I'm still a bit superstitious. The Archbishop would knock me in the head if he heard me say this, but I still believe in some of the old magic. So having something of hers with me at the altar can't hurt." Mike saw her stick her head out from the door eventually as she gave a little smile. Mike turned back to Ren and winked again just like a schoolboy who was in the middle of the most successful prank of his life. Ren was trying to restrain his amusement.

"Damn, he's good at this shit," Ren thought.

Judy returned within just a couple of minutes with, in one hand, a picture of a pretty little strawberry-blonde girl and in the other a small stuffed animal, a baby deer. Mike pulled out a fresh white silk handkerchief and allowed Judy to set it down, not touching the toy, to insulate it from any further outside interference.

"I want to keep it clean and safe for her return," said Mike as he smiled at Judy. "Thanks so much, dear. This will be just perfect. Let's see if the prayers of some of those goofy kids can help get this little angel back into your arms real soon. We'll get out of your way now, Judy. Take care, and keep your chin up, now!"

***

Mike and Ren departed from the LeBlanc house with smiles and good wishes and climbed back into Ren's Jeep. Mike instructed his young friend to get back onto I-10 and head for downtown. "Get off at Orleans, right by the Auditorium. I think I know how to approach this problem," the priest said as he looked straight ahead into the summer sunlight.

"Well, I wish you'd clue me in a bit. I think I see the rationale behind getting a picture of Dana, but I don't get the stuffed animal. What's up with that?" Ren was easily navigating through the late-morning traffic back into the city. With the commuters by now safely ensconced in their downtown offices, the only interstate highways in and out of New Orleans was flowing easily again.

Mike did not acknowledge Ren's question immediately, but he then realized his protégé was waiting for an answer.

"OK, the concept is called 'scrying'. The idea is to focus on an individual and try to pick up psychic resonance from that person. If that person has Talents, you can then attempt to contact them mind-to-mind. At the very least, this technique should tell us whether or not the youngster is still alive. But what I have in mind is to go a step further and try to identify where she is. Don't worry about how we will accomplish that; simply accept for now that there may yet be a way to pull this off." He waited for Ren to nod, and then continued.

"So, the plan now is to get ourselves somewhere where we can amplify any psychic resonance we detect and get a feel for where it is originating. But, before we do that, I want you to be calm, collected, focused, and then we can continue with the game. Take us into town and park in one of those garages near the Saenger Theater."

Ren nodded again and they rode in silence for the rest of the trip. Ren began to breathe a little deeper, taking his mentor's cue to begin some basic relaxing techniques in preparation for the psychic work ahead of him. Mike closed his eyes and leaned back in his seat for a few minutes.

They exited the interstate on the outskirts of the French Quarter and Ren wheeled around into a multi-story parking garage just off Canal Street. Mike was already out of the car as Ren disconnected his phone from the car adapter before getting out and securing the vehicle.

The pair walked out of the garage and headed down North Rampart Street. Originally named for the wall that surrounded the northern limits of the French Quarter, Rampart Street was still the boundary that separated the original city from Faubourg Tremé. Once the location of the infamous Storyville red-light district, Tremé was for decades a poor neighborhood dominated by a public housing project. Now, the neighborhood was undergoing revitalization and gentrification. Just at the edge Tremé were St. Louis Cemetery No. 1, the oldest cemetery in the city, and Our Lady of Guadalupe Church, home of the International Shrine of St. Jude and one of the oldest churches in New Orleans. Mike gestured up the street towards the church and Ren followed his signal. The church was originally used as the Mortuary Chapel during the yellow fever epidemics of the mid-1800s, and then it became a parish church for the upper French Quarter neighborhood. The church was not a large structure, but it was steeped in New Orleans history and Catholic mysticism. This was the closest church to the cemetery that reputedly housed the remains of the Voodoo Queen, Marie Laveau.

The two stopped momentarily on the neutral ground in front of the church as Mike bade Ren to take out the photograph of Dana which her mother had given them that morning.

"Continue your deep breathing, but now I want you to focus on her face. Try to remember the last time you saw her. Think back to those soccer games. See her running, having a good time with her friends. Do you have the image? Great. Now, give me that little digital camera you always have with you. I'm going to take a few pictures of the church as you stand there. Go ahead and fall into a light trance, while you look at the girl's picture."

The priest stalked around Ren, ostensibly taking photos of the front façade of the church, while constantly monitoring his companion's condition. Perspiration was dripping off them both after fifteen minutes, and the older man decided it was time they entered the church. Grabbing Ren by the elbow, Mike escorted him across the street and to the small Lourdes shrine off to one side of the church.

A little confused, Ren turned to his mentor wondering why they weren't going right inside. Mike began to whisper.

"Some people see this shrine as a bit cheesy but I kind of like it. It's a good place to get out of the sun for a few moments. Continue your breathing and go a step lower. We're going to do some intense Work shortly, so stay focused and cool off."

Ren nodded again. He was smiling inside and thinking about how much trust he had come to place in the abilities and the judgment of his mentor. Mike stared at the small statue of Our Lady of Lourdes and felt Ren slip a further level lower into trance. If Ren were to continue at this pace he would soon reach the point where he would be unable to move around unassisted. Having sensed this, Mike nudged Ren's elbow to guide him into the church. He steered Ren to a pew towards the front, on the left, and then sat him down.

"Stay here a minute. I'm going into the shrine on the left, the St. Jude Shrine, to pay my respects," Mike whispered.

Once assured that Ren would be all right for a few minutes, Mike glided into the shrine. The heat from the votive candles was intense as he bowed to the statue of St. Jude, closed his eyes, and marshaled the power at his command. As he quietly implored the Archangels of the Quarters to keep out any of the old ladies who frequent the church during the day, Mike's aura began to manifest visibly as his concentration strengthened. A few minutes later he nodded to himself, took a deep breath, and then walked behind the shrine's main statue, and simply vanished.

Less than a minute later a brief flash of golden light heralded the priest-adept's return to the shrine. Shaking off the disorientation that usually accompanied teleportation, Mike stepped out of the shrine and went over to bring Ren to the shrine, where he began to whisper instructions.

"Stay in trance. I want you to drop your shields completely and open your mind to me. There is a Teleport Gate in the back of the shrine and we're going to use it to get to the sacristy of the church in Memphis. Yes, remember our work with teleportation. Keep your mind open to me and relax, I'll give you the data about the Gate as we jump and you'll then be able to use it on your own in the future. Just give me complete control now. That's it, drop your shields. Relax. Open to me. Now, we're going to walk right around the side here. Stay with me, open up. And... we're gone."

Different people react to teleportation in different ways. Most people with Talents report that the sensation of jumping through a Teleport Gate is akin to falling through a trap-door into a pool of water, but without the splash; just the sensation of being surrounded by water while floating through a pipe. Ren's feeling was intensified by the fact that he was not in control of his jump as he absorbed the specific "pipe" or pathway Mike was using to get them to the end-point of the jump. Even though the actual duration of the jump is negligible, those who have experienced the transit have said that it seems as though several minutes of floating pass before they materialize on the Gate on the other side.

Ren and Mike both gasped for breath in the sacristy of Calvary Episcopal Church in Memphis, Tennessee. Fully aware of the path used to arrive at this gate, Ren smiled at his mentor and gave him a "what next" look.

Mike smiled back and said to Ren, "Why Memphis? Well, that's easy. In addition to Dana's little stuffed animal we need a good map to help us to find her. Memphis has the perfect map for this kind of work. And, it's just a couple of blocks from here. Come on, we're going to Mud Island."

Ren was momentarily startled.

"Mud Island. Hmm, it's a nice mock-up of what it looks to be staring down at Confederate gunboats, but I don't see what it does for us in this situation."

Mike's expression changed visibly from that of a friend to one of a teacher.

"Do you remember me speaking of the concept of 'as above, so below'? We'll be relying on that concept for our scrying. You know the large map in the back area of the Mud Island facility, the area where the kids splash around in a swimming pool that represents the Gulf of Mexico? That area is a scale model of the Mississippi River. I'm betting that whoever took Dana has not yet taken her far from New Orleans. This isn't a parental kidnapping. So you're going to start upriver on the map and walk south. Hopefully, your meditation on Dana, combined with the resonance from that toy, will enable you to make a connection with her. Now, let's get out of here before we have to explain what two Yats are doing in this Memphis church sacristy."

Mike's reference to him being a "Yat" was from the popular old New Orleans greeting, "where you at?" which invariably came out as "where y'at?" So the people of the Ninth Ward and the Irish Channel became to be known as "Yats".

Ren snorted in response to Mike's comment.

"I grew up in Gentilly, not the Ninth Ward or the Channel, thank you very much," he said.

"You forget your roots, young Sir! The Brothers of the Sacred Heart got their start teaching Ninth Ward Italians," said Mike, chuckling.

The pair slipped out of the church quietly and walked the six or so blocks to the riverfront.

***

When they reached the main entrance to Mud Island, Ren was about to climb aboard the tram that takes visitors to the island itself. Mike grabbed his arm and indicated that they were to walk the distance of the covered pier which linked the riverfront reception area to the island.

The pair passed by the history tour and the exhibits and went immediately to the back of the facility to the Riverwalk, a five-block long outdoor replica of the Mississippi River. Starting with a mural representing the origin of the river to the north in Minnesota, the Riverwalk is a geographically-correct model that eventually runs to a wading pool that represents the Gulf of Mexico. Mike steered Ren, still breathing deep and clutching the picture of Dana, down to the edge of the wading pool, and settled Ren in the place on the map that represents the mouth of the river.

"OK, I want you to relax and continue your focus on

Dana. We'll begin in a moment, but first I want to put some protection over you and this site. Even though it's daylight and things appear to be quiet, I don't want you to be shooting any psychic flares that would draw attention to us. Always remember that there are people who really dislike when we try to do things to help people. So, always protect yourself from any outside influences."

Mike glanced over each shoulder to make sure the pair was unobserved, walked to the eastern side of the river model, and turned around. His arms slowly glided from his sides to an outstretched position of prayer as he lifted his eyes to the sky and began to murmur an invocation. The words were ancient and expressed a total commitment to the light. But they were the kind of words which would have sent chills up the spines of Msgr. O'Donnell's superiors in the Roman Catholic Church. Well, almost all of them, Mike mused as he sketched a banishing pentagram symbol in the air in front of him. To most who might have witnessed it, the gesture was but a quick sweep of the hand. But, to those possessing Talents, it created a five-pointed star of blue-white flame, burning fiercely yet controlled. Mike then moved to the south where he repeated the gesture to create a similar pentagram of flame.

After tracing pentagrams in the west and north also, Mike went back to the eastern position to complete his circuit, and then moved to the center of the circle he had just marked out. Again he stood, facing the east and, making another appeal to the Light he served, he turned around 360 degrees with his right arm outstretched and the first two fingers of his right hand extended. Still nothing was visible to the workers who were preparing the area for that day's visitors, but Ren's senses detected a searing bolt of blue light, the same hue as the burning pentagrams, shooting from Mike's fingers. The blue light extended out as far as the pentagrams, and a blue circle was forming, linking the pentagrams together. By the time Mike had returned to his starting position the light breeze which had been blowing around Mud Island could not be felt inside the circle and the sounds of the park were all but completely muted. They were ready to begin their work.

Mike returned to Ren's side and placed a hand on his

shoulder. "I believe we can begin now. Let's start with the picture. We're going to walk up to the Memphis section of the Riverwalk. That's a long day's drive from the city, so I don't think we will need to go any further north. Focus on Dana's picture. Hold it out in front of you and look at her while you walk around Memphis. Start at the north of the city and walk in concentric circles through the area of the city. After you have covered that area, move below the circle and repeat the process. Ready? Let's go."

Ren did as his teacher had instructed, slowly circling the replica of Memphis on the ground. His trance became deeper as he walked clockwise through the city and making sure his feet covered every inch of the map. Part of him felt as though he was actually floating, as if walking on clouds above the city map. He forced his thoughts to remain focused on his task and continued to walk. Nothing in Memphis. He moved down the map; nothing south of the city. Further down, through Natchez; still no sensations. Down the river into Louisiana and still no feeling of Dana LeBlanc. Into Baton Rouge, Ren repeated the process of concentric circles he had used with Memphis. He heard Mike telling him to take it even slower now in hopes of the girl being in the area between Baton Rouge and the Gulf. South of Baton Rouge now, into the mix of sugar cane plantations and chemical plants that is known as the River Parishes. Down to Donaldsonville, very slowly now. As he set his foot on the spot that that was the replica of the town of Donaldsonville, Ren felt a tingle. He stood still for a moment and that tingle became a chill; a shiver up and down his spine. Mike noticed a change in Ren's expression and the involuntary movement of his leg as Mike marked the location with a small dot made by a stick of white chalk.

Ren continued down the river into the metro New Orleans area. As he circled the city he had a strong feeling of warmth mixed with a measure of worry and concern over a section of Metairie. Mike marked that spot also, and Ren continued all the way to the swimming pool that represented the Gulf of Mexico. He felt no further sensations as he reached the symbolic end of the land.

Mike whispered into Ren's ear to begin again, but this

time to go north back up the river to Memphis. Ren stopped again at the mark made in Metairie on the map, and experienced the same sensations he had previously. He moved up river, and felt the same chill and shiver when he reached Donaldsonville. He heeded Mike's instruction not to look down and continued northwards as Mike marked the spots from the second trip across the Riverwalk.

"One more time now and stay focused," said Mike. "You're doing just fine. Try not to figure out what's going on at the moment, just ride with it and let things hit you as you go. She's counting on you." Ren smiled and started the third trip across the map. As he reached Donaldsonville again, the chill he had felt on the first two walks felt more intense, feeling more like a sense of fear. The sensation he felt when he got to the spot in Metairie was significantly different from the first, being now warm and reassuring. Mike made two more marks as Ren stopped. As he reached the end of his walk again and stood by the Gulf Coast, Mike touched Ren's shoulder lightly. "Just stay here for a moment in trance. I want to take a look at what you have accomplished here and think. This is going well, Renard. Stay at this level and don't come up. But don't go any deeper either, just now."

Ren nodded, closed his eyes, and relaxed his knees a little. He was becoming wearier by the minute but made sure he followed Mike's instructions. Meanwhile, Mike walked briskly back to the Memphis section of the map and walked along the model of the river, taking a direct course rather the circles Ren had traced. Mike stopped at the section of Donaldsonville which had caught Ren's attention and examined the marks he had made on each of Ren's walks. The little chalk dots were almost on top of one another. Had they been bullet holes on a paper target, the resultant hole would have been no larger than the hole left by just a single shot. The same went for the three marks left in Metairie. Given that Ren had been focusing on hardly anything except Dana since they had left her home earlier that morning, Mike's confidence was pretty high that there was some connection between the girl and Donaldsonville. That the three Metairie chalk marks were almost exactly at the location of the LeBlanc home solidified Mike's opinion. Mike walked back to his friend. There was one more exercise to be performed and their task here would be complete. Mike guided the younger man to the Metairie spot, reached into his jacket pocket, and pulled out the white silk handkerchief which had contained Dana's stuffed toy deer.

"I'm going to give this to you now. Hold out your hand and let any resonance you feel flow over you. Get ready now." Without touching the little stuffed toy deer, Mike unwrapped the covering and pressed it into Ren's hand.

Ren's expression turned immediately from passive into a big, warm smile.

"Home. It's safe here. Nothing can hurt her here. Her dad's here and he will keep Dana safe. Mom is nearby too. Her room is a fortress to her. Nothing gets in without her permission and her little stuffed animals protect her from anything that might hurt her. They're her friends; her confidants." Ren continued to describe her room in great detail even though he had remained seated on the couch in the LeBlanc's living room and had never seen any part of the back of the house.

Mike covered his palm with the handkerchief and held his hand out to Ren.

"OK, Ren. Put the deer back into my hand and come up just a little now. We're going to walk over to the other marks."

Ren did as he had been instructed and allowed Mike to guide him back to the Donaldsonville spot. "Now, take some deep breaths. Steady yourself and then lower your shields completely. Remember, we're warded here, so nothing can hurt you. Hold out your hand again. Relax. And... now." Mike turned his hand over and the deer fell into the palm of Ren's hand.

Ren all but doubled-over as the toy hit his hand. He forced himself with all of his will to stand erect as he started to shake. "She's here, Mike. Here. Scared. No-one has harmed her but she's so afraid. It's dark in the room even though it's daylight outside. The blinds are pulled shut. But she knows it's a nice day outside. Oh, God, Mike, she's so scared. They haven't let her see their faces but she knows there are at least two of them. They've grabbed her tightly by the arms but haven't done anything else. She's shivering, Mike. She's not cold, but she's shivering, Mike. It's fear. She thinks she's going to die."

Focusing on what else he could tell Mike, Ren continued.

"It's a trailer. No, not a trailer. It's a mobile home. The kind you see on the highway, with 'Oversize Load' signs. She's in a back bedroom. It's too dark to see any details, but she's on the bed. They've tied her leg to the bed. She can stand up but she's shaking too much. Mike, we've got to help her. They're going to do something to her, she knows it. She feels their emotions. Mike, this isn't just a kidnap/rape scenario, they're going to kill her. Not just yet, but they are going to. She knows it with every fiber of her body."

Ren clutched the stuffed animal tightly, grabbed his gut and almost doubled-over again. The four pentagrams surrounding them flared and roared, as though someone had fully-opened the gas jets fueling them. Mike raised his arms to pour more energy into the protective circle and the flames subsided.

Mike steadied his friend.

"Easy, Ren. Do not let this affect you physically. She needs you to focus, so you mustn't let any of her pain or fears consume you. You're worthless to her if you let that happen. Let the sensation flow past you, Ren. Nice and easy. Deep breaths. Now, yes, nice and easy. Settle into a rhythm. Good. Let's get back to work then."

Mike pulled out a small sound recorder.

"Describe everything to me. What has she seen? What has she heard?"

Ten minutes later, Mike turned off the recorder and sighed. The energy drain of supporting both Ren and the protective wards around them was taking its toll. As he rubbed his eyes he began to play the recorder. Ren sat down on a nearby bench as Mike paced around the Riverwalk within the confines of the wards. As he listened to the recording, nodding at certain details, he stopped occasionally to make notes. Twenty minutes after starting he returned to join Ren on the bench.

"Ren, let's get you up and out of your trance now. Your part in this is almost over, so it's time for you to return to complete consciousness and we can decide where to go from here. Pretend you're a diver coming up slowly. No pressure, no problems. Just come up nice and easy. Float to the surface.

Don't rush; you have enough air to make it slowly. No hurry. Just keep coming up. My voice is getting louder, Ren, so that you're no longer hearing me as a whisper in the corner, but at normal volume. Relax now and come up to join me." The older man took his hand off Ren's arm and moved over a little on the bench to give Ren more space.

Ren shook his head and turned to the priest with his now-familiar concerned expression. "What now?" He reached into his pocket for a handkerchief to wipe the sweat from his brow.

"Here, see what you make of these," Mike said as he handed over his notes. Ren read them through, twice, and then reached into his pocket for his phone. He hit the speed-dial combination for Kenner Police Department, and the phone connected him to the headquarters building in the suburban city. Ren rolled his eyes as he listened to the recorded greeting finish, so he could punch in Bubba's work extension.

"Hello? Bubba? Yeah, it's me. No, I'm not at home at the moment. Bubba, listen. You know the LeBlanc kidnapping? Yeah, I know it's not a KPD case, but I picked up something this morning that is relevant. Bubba, you don't want to know what it is, trust me. Yeah, something like that. Believe me on this, I wouldn't have called if I didn't think the information was accurate. OK, get your pen out..."

Five minutes later, Ren ended the call after giving his friend an extremely detailed description of where in Donaldsonville, Louisiana, two kidnappers were holding Dana LeBlanc.

"Bubba will take care of things from here. He'll tell the Sheriff's Office up there and the FBI that the source is a confidential informant. There's a life at stake here, so there isn't a judge in the parish who will give them a hard time about warrants. Jeez, am I hot! Let's get something cold to drink!" Ren stood up and turned in the direction of the snack bar.

"Whoa, Grasshopper, not so fast," the priest chuckled. You're sitting in the midst of some pretty strong wards. I must admit, I really was on my game this morning." Mike chuckled again. "These wards have to be dismantled before we head out of here. It's more than just common courtesy to clean up our mess or common sense that we should close down a magical working. Our psychic signatures are all over this circle now, particularly mine, and I don't want any potential enemy getting hold of that information. Come here and stand in the center, facing east. You can lend a hand as well."

Once the wards had been properly dismantled and thanks having been given to the Light from which they had been generated, Mud Island suddenly began to bustle with activity. It was as if a giant "KEEP OUT" sign had been taken down and people were now entering the Riverwalk to explore the history and majesty of the Mississippi. Kids were making tracks to the pool to get wet and play. Life began to flow there at its normal pace. Msgr. O'Donnell smiled inwardly at the scene and walked swiftly to catch up with his thirsty friend.

Two hours later, over plates of barbecue pork in Memphis International Airport, the two men reflected upon the day's activities. Mike decided they should fly home rather than attempt to Teleport. They had been lucky not to have been discovered when they had appeared in the sacristy at Calvary that morning and there seemed no sense in pushing that luck now.

Ren was three-quarters into finishing a large combination plate of pulled pork, ribs, and chicken, when he turned to his friend.

"You know, this whole process took a lot out of me physically and emotionally, but I never expected it to be this simple to find someone using a process like this. My main fear was that we'd take days to locate her and that we would just be too late."

The thought was not lost on Mike. He, too, had been musing over the same notion during the cab ride from Mud Island to the airport. "Well, you know, some people simply want to be found more than others. Do you remember the first night I met you?" Mike was referring to the night of the previous November when psychic "flares" sent up by Ren's will had drawn his attention from more than two miles away as he had been driving home.

Ren nodded without looking up from his meal. "Yeah, I suppose you're right. Well, good thing for us she wanted it badly enough."

Michael O'Donnell simply nodded. He would clue-in his younger friend about his suspicions later. No need to put something else on Ren's plate just now, he thought. Mike had been working with young people with Talents for a long time. At this point, all he could do would be to observe little Dana. They would do their best to keep her from harm. What concerned him most was that a girl with such gifts had been singled out for such emotional trauma and potential physical harm. That notion merited more close watch than did the girl herself. Oh well, he thought. Nothing's going to get done about it in this airport. Mike kicked up his heels on the spare chair at the table and took a good long pull on his beer.

CHAPTER THIRTEEN
Angels

Renard Alciatore stood under the shower, daydreaming. He'd been home for a while, after a morning of refereeing U12 soccer, but he still couldn't get the vision of one soccer mom out of his mind. Shaking his head, he realized that no amount of water was going to drown the memory, so he stepped out of the shower and proceeded to dry off and get dressed.

He didn't know any of the parents on the two teams in the last match, so Ren was a bit surprised when he heard a voice behind him offer him a drink. Closing his eyes to savor the memory, her looks were still vivid in his mind—tall, about 5'9", reddish-brown hair, thirties...nice figure. Not-too-short cutoffs and a t-shirt proclaiming her son's team name rounded out the fairly typical image of a suburban soccer mom. He gratefully accepted a bottle of water from her, and then he saw those eyes: hazel-green and deeper than he'd seen in a long time. Ren was spellbound; it was as if he could see a hundred lifetimes in that gaze.

She broke the eye contact first. Ren thanked her for the water, and she was off again, to give her son a big hug of congratulations. Not wanting to be obvious, Ren continued to the other side of the field, grabbed his bag, and headed home.

He tossed his head, more to shake off that memory than to dry his hair, but it was to no avail. It had been years since he had this feeling about a woman, and that woman was his best friend JJ. But Janet Julianne was married, and that situation wasn't likely to change. Pulling on some clothes, he pondered how to learn more about the mystery soccer mom. He fired off a quick e-mail to a referee colleague who lived in Mandeville with the description of her. The reply came back within minutes; his friend didn't know this mom. Sighing, he dismissed the thought from his mind.

An hour later, he still couldn't get the image of those eyes out of his head. Not only could he not shake the memory of her eyes, but the thought of those long legs in short cut-offs was stirring other desires in Ren. His erection was becoming distracting, so he got up from the desk and walked to the kitchen to get something to drink. Grabbing the phone as he walked, issuing it instructions:

"OK, Google," Ren said.

The phone beeped.

"Call Michael O'Donnell mobile."

"Calling Michael O'Donnell, mobile," the phone's female voice replied. A couple of seconds later, it rang.

"Hey, Ren, what's up?" Mike was his usual cheerful self.

"Not much. Was wondering if you had anything cooking for this evening."

"Not really, but Ren, do you really want to spend Saturday night out with a priest? Jeez, guy, you gotta be able to do better than that!" Mike laughed.

"Ha! Thought maybe I could talk something over with you. I've never had you over to the family place, have I?" Ren's voice betrayed his nervousness to Mike.

"No, you haven't, and it sounds so strange to hear the oldest restaurant in town referred to as 'the family place.'" Mike chuckled

"Well, I may not be in the direct-ownership part of the family tree, but I'm still an Alciatore, so I got some stroke," Ren laughed. "I'll be round to pick you up, oh, say seven?"

"Good deal, see you then!"

They parked Mike's Porsche 914 up along the riverfront next to the French Market and walked up past Jackson Square, down Rue Chartres to Rue St. Louis. They entered the Hermes Bar, just to the left of the front dining room.

"Where y'at, Davey?" Ren greeted the older man working the bar.

"Nutin' to it, Mr. Ren," Davey replied. "Slow-ass night.

What brings you in on a hot evening like this, son?"

"Been out with the kids all day, Davey, and I'm just too damn tired to chase women," Ren laughed.

Davey smiled at Ren. "Well, I guess you're not, running around town with a priest!" He wiped his hands on a pristine white towel, and then stretched his arm out to Mike.

"Hello, Father, welcome to Antoine's!"

Ren looked at Davey, a bit amazed.

"And just how did you know he was a priest?"

"Son, that's the problem with your generation. You don't learn nothing at those fancy-ass colleges you all get sent to. Some things you're just supposed to know, young Renard, and when to show respect to a man of the cloth is one of those." Davey shook Mike's hand and began to make a 'Death in the Afternoon'. He first poured a jigger of Atelier Vie's 'Toulouse Green' Absinthe into a Champagne flute, then filled it to the top with Moet et Chandon Champagne.

"Got this local Absinthe in the other day, give this a try," Davey said, as he pushed the glass towards Ren.

"Just like Hemingway would like it!" Ren said, sipping the cocktail.

"You were right, Mike, he likes Champagne cocktails," Davey said, with a smile.

Mike looked at Ren's continued expression of amazement and laughed. "Davey here is jerking your chain big-time, Ren. He knows me because his daughter brings him out to the Newman Center for Mass occasionally. I knew you were a bartender, Davey, but I never knew where. What a small world!"

"For sure, it is. Now, Father, what can I make for you? I have this local gin, same distillery as the Absinthe. How about a French 75?"

"That sounds perfect for a summer evening," Mike said.

Davey poured gin, simple syrup, and lemon juice and ice in a cocktail shaker. He shook the shaker like the pro he was, then strained its contents into an iced champagne glass, topping the glass off with the Champagne.

As Davey made the second drink, a young man in his twenties came up to greet Ren. Giving a wink to Davey, the newcomer said, "You know, Daddy says we gotta take care of family, but jeez, sometimes I wonder," he laughed, reaching to embrace Ren in a big hug. "What's up, cuz? Haven't seen you since the boys' soccer season ended in the spring. Where you been hiding all summer?"

"Weddings, Jim, weddings!" Ren said, as he introduced his cousin Jim to Mike.

"Ren, it's a weird night. I've got a party in the Rex Room, and another in the 1816 room. The Dungeon is full, but you've never been one to 'be seen,' so I figured you wouldn't want that anyway. I can put you upstairs if you like, or you can have the Escargot room, unless you just want to sit in one of the dining rooms."

"Jeez, Jim, I hate to see you have to deal with upstairs just for us, but I wouldn't mind a little privacy. How about Escargot?"

"Done, cuz," Jim grinned, and motioned for them to follow along. Ren and Mike worked their way through the maze of hallways and rooms that is Antoine's, back to the first-floor room called the "Escargot Room." The room gets its name from the big snail that is etched into the wood paneling on the back wall.

The three men were followed into the room by a tuxedo-clad man in his 40s, whose nametag proclaimed him to be "Albert." He held a small basket in his hand which he set down on the table as he turned towards his boss and the guests.

"Well, well, well. Look what the cat dragged in!" The waiter shook Ren's hand firmly as the younger man clasped his shoulder.

"Al, you're looking good, that's f'sure," Ren said.

"Thanks! You and your guest munch on those, and I'll be back in a bit with some appetizers," Al said, pointing at the basket.

Ren grabbed one of the puffy, pillow-like treats from the basket and popped it into his mouth. Mike did the same and said, "Soufflé potatoes. Boy, I forgot just how good these things are."

"Not just your average French fry. I've had people over for dinner at times, and they always want me to make them at home, if they know about the family business," he smiled.

It wasn't long before Al was back with a bottle of white wine and glasses, followed by an apprentice waiter who had a plate of appetizers in each hand. "Brought a couple of things for you to get started on. I know what you like to pick on, Ren, but I don't know your friend here, so let him grab first. You can always go get more if you want." Turning to Mike, Al continued, "I'm Al De France, by the way. If I wait on this one to introduce us, I'll be over in St. Patrick Cemetery with my momma!"

"Mike O'Donnell," Mike laughed, "and I've learned that my friend here tends to lose his manners when he's hungry!"

"Be nice," Ren cautioned, "Or I'll eat all the Oysters Bienville!"

Pouring them each a glass of Pouilly-Fuissé, Al explained each of the appetizers, then asked about entrees.

"Well, I'm in a steak mood, but I've got to referee some more games tomorrow, so I don't need that sitting in my stomach all night," Ren smiled. "Give me the Chicken Rochambeau. Mike, what are you in the mood for?"

"Steak sounds good to me. Rare, please, good sir," Mike requested.

"Wine sauce or Béarnaise on your steak, Mike?" Al asked.

"Oh, Marchand de Vin sauce, of course!" Mike replied.

"Good deal. And I'll bring you each a cup of gumbo. I'll have one of the guys bring you some bread and leave you to chat for a bit, then. I know you, young man. You're usually out in the Dungeon staring at women's asses unless you're talking business, so I'll make sure you get some privacy." Al winked and partially closed the door behind him.

"Nothing like the red-carpet treatment," Mike said once they were alone.

"Well, you know, I spend so many weekends in the spring and summer away from the restaurant that they want to fuss over me when I do come in."

"What's this 'Dungeon' that your cousin and the waiter both referred to?"

"Oh, it's the section of the back dining room that's separated from the main area by the back hallway. The four tables back there are sort of prime real estate. The table in the corner is very private, almost like having one of the private rooms. The middle two tables allow you scope out the entire back dining room. It's the perfect place in the restaurant to watch the comings and goings of all the babes in the place," Ren smiled.

"Neat. You'll have to bring me over here on a busy night, then," Mike said. "Nothing better than checking out babes in short skirts."

"I don't know if I'm ever going to get used to comments like that made by a priest, Mike," Ren chuckled.

"Hey, one of the biggest public-relations problems the Church has these days is this perception that priests are pedophiles and perverts. Well, shit, I'm here to prove to the world that you can be a priest and still appreciate the intricacies of the female tush," he smiled.

They devoured the rest of the appetizers, and Al's crew deftly cleared the plates and returned with steaming cups of dark, thick seafood gumbo. Al then came in with a bottle of a mid-priced California Pinot Noir. Once they were alone again, Mike said, "OK, what's up that you wanted company this evening?"

Ren relayed his experience from the afternoon, using a mind-link. He didn't hold back the intensity of the moment. Mike ate his soup for a moment quietly before saying anything.

"You know, human emotions can be tricky, especially when they're influenced by your dick. Sometimes it's just good karma to let sensations like you felt today go and leave it at that. Fantasy is healthy, Ren, and there are a lot of times where it's better to let fantasy stay that way. Reality often falls way short of our dreams," Mike advised, as he took a sip of wine.

"Yeah, I relate to what you're saying, but still...there was just something about that look in her eye. I've had tons of chance encounters and such over time. Some yeah, you let them go. This one, though, needs to go a bit further before I can say it's no big deal," Ren said, frustrated.

Mike broke off an end from one of the small loaves of bread on the table.

"This is a bit more complicated than the scrying we did to find that girl. We're going to have to do work on a higher plane. That's going to require some preparation, as well as some consideration of the issues involved."

"Issues?" Ren asked, curiously.

"Yes. You want to find a grown adult who doesn't consider herself lost. And you're doing it for a very personal reason—to get into her pants."

Ren flushed, embarrassed at that last statement. "Mike, you felt what passed between us. I understand, but this one is more than just idle curiosity. This could be something good for the both of us."

"OK, let's say you get together, and you're having a good relationship. Do you ever think you'd confide in her the steps you took to find her? You're potentially on shaky ground ethically here, and you don't know if her values system is going to deal well with this kind of thing."

Mike cut his train of thought short when he saw the door to the room push open a bit wider. Al and his apprentice served up the entrees and salads. Mike continued when they were once again alone.

"Look, I'm not saying you can't do this, Ren. I'm just saying that you have a bit more to think through here than some of the other uses of your Talents we've been developing. We've been doing so much nuts-and-bolts work that the ethical and moral issues behind this stuff aren't arising as quickly."

"I see what you mean," Ren said, as he dipped a piece of bread into the brown Rochambeau sauce that flowed down over the slices of chicken on his plate. "So far I've focused on developing my Talents to save my own ass rather than for other purposes. That whole thing with Dana really made me see that our Talents have serious potential for doing good work. I just thought I could piggy-back on that good work for a little personal gain."

"Let's play with some of the concepts and work up to the ethics. That might be a good approach. No way we can really do the kind of full-blown Work you're looking for after a dinner like this. So, let's relax, enjoy this good food, and have a little fun as we go. Maybe you'll learn something along the way."

They chatted amiably through their mains, with Al occasionally popping in to re-fill their glasses with the Pinot Noir he brought in earlier. As the dishes were being cleared,

Mike looked over at Ren with a mischievous twinkle in his eye.

"Ready to play?" He asked.

"You bet!" Ren nodded.

"OK, what we're going to do is some Astral Projection. Or at least, that's what the new-age types call it. Some call it taking the High Road or the Second Road, others call it having an 'out of body experience.' The idea is to stretch your soul out beyond your body, without actually leaving it and doing the physical body harm. We'll start small and see how you adjust."

Mike put down his wineglass and laid both hands flat on the table.

"Close your eyes and try to focus your thoughts." While Ren's eyes were closed, Mike waved his right hand towards the ceiling, making a gesture of power. A thin shield of energy formed above them near the ceiling, then spilled down the sides of the room. The shield protected them from outside influence on both the physical as well as the higher planes. Mike began to issue instructions to his pupil.

"Keep your eyes closed. Now, see your soul as a white light that's enveloping your body. Take that white light and move it six inches above your head, so that if your soul is in tandem with your body, it will be six inches above your head."

Ren did as he was instructed, feeling his astral self rise a bit as he concentrated. He looked at the world as if he were driving a bus or a large SUV, just above everything in the room. Mike continued.

"Now, stay relaxed and let's expand your view of the universe a bit. Let your astral self rise and float to the ceiling of the room. Visualize the silver cord of your life rising with you, and flowing out from your astral body as if it's the tether used by an astronaut doing a space walk. See the cord lengthen, but relax, it can't be broken so easily. Continue floating up. What do you see?"

"I see the room, looking down. The snail etching in the rear, the big table, and the greeting area. I see you, Mike, sitting, twirling your glass in-between your hands," Ren whispered.

"Verrry good, but how do I know you're not just saying that because you were peeking." Mike smiled.

"Mike, my eyelids are so heavy right now that I don't

know if I'd be able to pull one over on you!" Ren smiled, as he replied.

"OK, I'll buy that this time. Keep relaxing and float yourself over to the door. Just keep paying out your silver cord behind you...that's it...how does it feel?"

"Interesting. I can see back into the room as if we just walked in."

"You've done it again, Ren—you've managed to surprise me with how quick you catch on. OK, now move around the restaurant a bit...just for a few minutes...nice..."

Mike waited a few minutes, continuing to sip his wine.

"Now bring yourself back to this room, Ren. Take a nice direct route from where you are in the building now to the door of the room. Great...move into the room and float up to the ceiling again. Feel the energy from your body and slip right over it...feel your soul overlaying your physical body...relax and rejoin your body. Open your eyes and talk to me!"

"That was incredible!" Ren exclaimed. "I could see and hear everything people were doing and saying. I saw what they were eating and drinking. And they had no idea I was standing there, looking over their shoulders!"

"Now you should start to see what I mean by issues. It would have been so easy for you to go up and start rubbing a gal's leg, or maybe squeeze a boob or two."

Shivering, Ren reached for his wine and took a big swallow.

"Yeah, I see." He began to rub his arms and shoulders to warm himself up.

"Why is it so cold in here?"

Mike laughed and poured the rest of the red wine into Ren's glass.

"You left your body! Your soul is partly responsible for keeping you warm. When your astral self went for a walk, your body sat here, almost lifeless. It started to get chilly. Remember that when you're doing this kind of work. Don't go out on the astral for more than your body can absorb, I'd say no more than two or three hours at a time."

Ren wanted to ask for more details on this, but was interrupted by Al, who was bringing in a tray with what appeared to be a small loaf of bread.

"Anybody for dessert?" he asked. That small loaf of bread was actually a Baked Alaska, an Antoine's specialty. Ren shivered again at the thought of eating ice cream, but this was a treat that he had never passed up in his life, and didn't intend to start now.

***

The next evening found Ren and Mike sitting quietly in the chapel of the Newman Center of the University of New Orleans. Mike was not quite sure that Ren had thought this through all the way, but he was still insistent on finding this woman.

"He probably could do it on his own, but I'd just as soon stick around and make sure he doesn't get in trouble," Mike thought.

"Where's your boss, Father Adrian, anyway? Did he abandon the Newman Center to you totally?" Ren asked.

"Oh, he's off in Chile or Peru or something, with a couple of his seminary buddies. They're doing some missionary work down there. He's being groomed to take over a parish here in the area, so there's no way those vultures at the Archdiocesan office would ever let him get away to do some constructive work in another country." Mike grimaced. "Well, you ready to give this a try?"

"Yup!"

Mike activated the protective warding that he had built into the chapel.

"I've built permanent wards into this room, which makes it easier to Work here. The room's dedication to the Light and the regular Masses we say here have really built up the strength of the shield, so activating the wards takes almost no energy expenditure."

Ren nodded and began deep-breathing so he could go into trance. Mike observed him for about five minutes and then touched him on the side of the arm.

"Stay in trance for a while...let your mind float first. Now, just like last night, slide your astral self up a few inches. Once you're up a bit, move above your physical body." Mike closed his eyes and let his own Sight observe Ren's progress.

"Fantastic, you remembered. Move now to the ceiling. That's right...nice and easy. You're in no big hurry. We need to get you out past the wards now, so let's do that in the North Quadrant." Mike pointed with two fingers at a spot in the wards about thirty degrees above the floor. He sketched a symbol, then drew a simple image of an iris valve. The image opened, allowing Ren's astral body to float past the shield. Mike closed the gateway in the shield and reached out to monitor Ren's pulse.

"You're doing fine, Ren," he said. "Now, float out into the neighborhood, then start heading across the lake. What do you see?"

Ren sat in trance, the candles around the small chapel sending shadows dancing across his face. He spoke, but it sounded as distant as he actually was.

"It feels like I'm looking out an airplane window. I see the lake and the lights of the north shore in the distance. There's the end of the Causeway now...I'm over Mandeville."

Mike continued to monitor Ren's vital signs.

"Shift your focus a bit now. Come down in altitude."

"Yes, I can see more detail now, but I don't have a feel for which direction to go in."

"Stay in sort of a hovering state...good...now, remember your encounter with this lady. Remember turning around...see her eyes...look up at the sky, Ren, and see her face against the black sky. Good, look back down slowly and tell me what you feel."

"It's so peaceful like this, Mike. The ground doesn't seem as cluttered. I feel something...not terribly focused, but I feel it. Over off by Pelican Park..." Ren shifted his astral presence and swung a bit eastward.

"Yeah, this is the right direction. It feels right, but I can't lock it in. I'm over three or four streets, but I can't lock into this feeling."

"Stay relaxed, Ren. I want you to look away from the ground, back up at the sky. Change what you're looking for. You know how you can take night-vision goggles and switch around what they see, from regular light to infrared? I want you to do something similar."

Ren closed his astral "eyes" for a moment. He opened them, looking at the stars. The sky was unchanged. Below, most of what were well-lit neighborhoods a few minutes ago were all but dark. There was the occasional small glow from one section or another, but nothing that stood out and demanded notice.

Just then, a blue-green "flare" shot up just a couple of miles north of where he was viewing. He focused his attention on that flare as it subsided into a glowing light, deep green in color. The color of the glow was exactly the color of the woman's eyes!

His excitement must have spilled over into the reality of where his body sat with Mike, because his teacher softly admonished him.

"Whatever you see, Ren, slow down a minute. If you're not in danger, take a moment and collect yourself. Don't go do the psychic equivalent of breaking down the door."

Ren took a deep breath.

"I've found her, Mike. I see a flash and a glow that I'm pretty sure is her. Moving over to fix on that glow now...OK, I'm here...it's a nice, two-story house not far from the seminary."

"Close in and come down over it so you're hovering just above the roof. Careful in case she's aware of her abilities and has some protection set up."

Ren came down easily on the location, settling on the lawn in front of the house. He moved towards the door, and passed through the front door into the main hall of the home.

"This is what Mike meant about ethics. Now I'm a home invader," he thought.

Still, he just had to know about this woman. Continuing on into the house, he passed through the hallway, back to the family room. It was a typical den in a typical suburban home, with toys and books on the floor Ren found a man sitting back, his feet up on the coffee table, dozing softly as a movie played on the DVR.

The object of his search was there as well, stretched out on the sofa, long legs curled under her, head resting peacefully on his side. She sensed his presence in the room, and looked up at him with a smile. Wordlessly, she began to speak to him.

"Well, you've gone through all this trouble to find me," she said in his mind as a smile danced across her face. *"I knew that we would meet again, but I didn't expect it to be so soon. Are you in need now, my friend? Is there something I can do to help?"*

Stunned speechless, all Ren could do was send a wordless negative.

"Ahhhhh...ok, now I get it! It must've been the shorts. Yeah, I look pretty good in those shorts if I do say so myself." Ren felt her laugh, but the sensation was one of tinkling raindrops, pleasant but powerful.

"Well, I'll say again, I'm flattered. But I'm sorry to disappoint you. Here, at this moment, in this place, my attention is focused on this man."

Ren's astral self nodded to her, amazed at her perception and disappointed with her statements.

"Oh, don't be sad, sweetie! We will come to know each other in time. There are varying levels of friendships and relationships. You and I will develop one, I'm sure." The green aura around her began to grow, conveying him a message.

"You have some serious trials ahead of you, Renard Alciatore. Your Teacher is a worthy man, but he is nonetheless a man, and can only help you so much. Always remember that there are others willing and able to help and pick up where your Teacher leaves off. But that's all for now. You are mortal, young Ren, and you must take care that you do not over-extend yourself with these newly-discovered Talents of yours. Go now, sweetie. Thank you for the high compliment you have given me, and be at peace."

The green light grew and enveloped him till Ren could no longer see the woman or the house he was "standing" in. The surrounding light seemed to form a cylinder that shot skyward, opening a way home for him. He closed his eyes and allowed himself to flow up through that cylinder until he was hovering over the lake once more. Sighing, he shot back to his physical form. He merged the two with a whoosh. Ren opened his physical eyes and looked over at a very-worried Mike O'Donnell.

"Welcome back. I was beginning to get concerned. Just a

few minutes after you stopped talking, your pulse went nuts, then slowed down to a point where I thought I might have to pull you out of this myself."

Ren rubbed his arms again, feeling that same sensation of cold he felt at the restaurant. Mike tossed him the warm-up jacket that was sitting on top of Ren's gym bag—they came prepared for that contingency. As he warmed up, Ren felt able to relay some of what happened.

"Mike, it was incredible—she was—well, let me show you." Ren opened his mind to Mike and passed the experience inside the house to him.

Mike didn't say anything, instead reaching over to grab two bottles of water, handed one to Ren, and took a long swallow on the other.

"There was a lot of power in that room with you, Ren. It was well-shielded; so much so, it's difficult to see if that power serves the Light or the Dark."

"How could anything that beautiful serve anything but the Light, Mike?"

"That's something you need to keep in mind, Ren. Some things can be at once beautiful and evil. Catch is, whoever or whatever you were talking to this evening is powerful enough to mask its feelings thoroughly, not to mention having the ability to send you back here when she was done with you."

"I don't think she's human, Mike."

The priest smiled.

"Neither do I. But we're not going to solve that puzzle tonight..."

CHAPTER FOURTEEN
Plano

"Well, yeah, she's cute, but what are we going to talk about later?" Ren asked as he took a pull on his beer. The Hooters restaurant in Plano, TX, was jumping on Labor Day evening, mostly around Ren and his referee friends.

"This is SO true," laughed Dan Nugent, a Navy officer originally from New Orleans, who was now stationed in Pensacola, Florida. "That one looks like she could be my daughter!"

"Careful, Admiral. For all you know, maybe she is!" Terry McNeill, a high-school English teacher from Houston admonished him. "Watch this..." He motioned for their waitress, a very well-endowed blonde who stood all of five feet tall.

"Yes, sir?" she smiled.

"Sweetheart, have you ever been to Las Vegas?" Nugent inquired.

"No, sir. My boyfriend wants to take me, but he's in Miami right now. He says when he gets back we're going to travel all over the place."

"What does your boyfriend do?" Ren asked.

"Oh, he's a model and a dancer. He's going to be in Miami for a year. But I really love him, so I'm going to wait for him." She smiled again.

"That's wonderful, hon. Tell you what, why don't you bring us another pitcher while you're waiting?" Nugent suggested.

She smiled and walked away with the group's empty pitcher. There was a collective gasp as the three men at the table exhaled, deeply. The lone female of the group was not impressed.

"You guys are sick puppies sometimes. Messing with that gal is like pulling wings off a dragonfly." Barbara Eagan was a 42-year-old engineer who was not much taller than the waitress. "Sick puppies, for sure."

"Aw, B. Sometimes you're just no fun. If you weren't such a friend, I'd threaten to ditch you right here in Plano!" Ren exclaimed as he laughed.

Barbara looked at him sternly.

"Renard Alciatore, you don't need the amount of deep shit and bad juju you would get from me if you even half-considered leaving me in this god-forsaken shit-hole!"

"Such a thing to say about our neighboring state!" Ren said, with mock shock in his voice.

Barbara threw a curly French fry at him and lifted her glass as she pretended to ignore him. The other guys laughed.

"Hey, Ren," said Dan. "You're not gonna get any sympathy from that one. I worked two games with her yesterday and she's brutal! She tossed a coach in an Under-14 boys match without a second thought," McNeil commented.

"Don't I know it!" responded Ren. "She's a bitch, but she's my bitch." Ren laughed and put his arm around Barbara. She punched his shoulder and kissed him on the cheek. "So, mister 'I'm-driving-to-Plano-by-myself'. What's up that you decided to do that rather than fly with the rest of us? It's not like the air-fare is expensive."

"Oh, I had some research I wanted to do for a possible magazine article, so I wanted to have the car and a little flexibility. Besides, I hadn't taken the Mach out on the open road for some time, and you just can't leave a car like that to putt-putt around in city traffic all the time."

"Very true. I used to have a 1980 'Vette I felt just the same way about. You have to run it up over a hundred occasionally or you don't feel you've got your money's worth for the vehicle," Dan said, excitedly.

"Testosterone cars," Barbara sneered. "You're married," she said, pointing at Dan. "And you," she turned and pointed at Ren, "You're decent-looking enough that you don't need a car to get laid. No excuse for these cars."

"Don't believe a word she says, Dan," said Ren. "You're talking to a woman who drives a BMW Z4."

Barbara smiled but was not going to give in. "Yeah, you don't pick up women in mine!"

"No, but I sure as hell could," laughed Ren. "Shame you didn't bring that little thing up here. Me and Dan coulda borrowed it and had all sorts of fun."

"Not a chance, sport! I know how you drive. You're not touching my baby. Back to your research." She paused as she took another sip from her glass. "What kind of article?"

"You know about the web project I've been working on? The radio preacher? Well, I was contacted by a magazine doing some investigative work on the same guy. They want to use some of the information I've gathered in a piece they're doing on radio preachers. In exchange for that information, they gave me the photo assignment for the article. I'm off tomorrow to get some architectural shots of the headquarters of this Christian Publishing House that publishes Jay Hadley's books. If you've ever gone out to Arlington, you know, where the Rangers and Cowboys play, you can see this office building with a big cross up on it."

"Yeah," said Terry, interrupting the conversation. "I know where you're talking about. That cross is lit up beautifully at night. It's a deep blue that makes you think it's not attached to the building at all. Gorgeous."

"Really? Cool. Maybe I should run over there tonight, then. Traffic shouldn't be too bad from here, should it?"

"Well, it might be a little heavier than the average Monday night because it's Labor Day," said Dan. "But if you want some company, I'll ride over there with you."

"You bet. I'd love that. D'you think we can leave these two alone together?" Ren asked as he cocked his head in Barbara's direction.

"Hm. Well, Terry's a hound, but I think he wants to keep all his body-parts attached, so he'll be a gentleman," Dan chuckled. "C'mon. Let's roll!"

Ren and Dan pulled out their wallets and left enough money to cover their portion of the bill and the tip, with Barbara and Terry. Ren blew Barbara a kiss, gave an off-hand salute to Terry, and he and Dan headed towards the door. They reached the Mustang and climbed in. As they made their way around downtown Dallas over to Arlington, the conversation remained focused on the main thing the two men had in common: soccer, association football, "the beautiful game".

"You're a Leicester City supporter? How did you come to support a lower-tier team?" asked Dan as they approached I-30.

"Well, Dan. That's the thing," Ren explained. "For all the notoriety of an Arsenal or a Manchester United, there's something neat about a team like City. And the Internet is a great leveler in terms of getting information about a team. I've made some great friends from the online forums and email lists for Leicester City fans."

"You know, I have an email at the office and I rarely use it for anything outside of Navy business," said Dan in response. "I guess I'm stuck in the past with regard to the Internet. My staff often tells me about the great wide world out there online, so I guess I really need to get into it. 'Can't have these 20 year-old sailors show me up too much," he laughed.

"You got that right, Dan."

Dan reached over in front of Ren to point to their left.

"It's over there. See the cross?"

Ren nodded. "Yeah, that is pretty."

"Next exit, and then I'll curve you through to where you need to go," Dan instructed.

"Gotcha. I appreciate you taking the ride, Dan."

"No problem. This is a great car. Haven't been in a kick-ass Mustang in ages."

Ren followed the exit signs and worked his way off the highway to the service road. After a few turns, the pair were approaching the 12-story building that was the international headquarters of Marcus-Kayson Publishers, the largest Christian Publishing House in the world.

"Take a left here and you'll be at the far entrance to the parking lot. You should be able to get some good shots of the entire building from there," Dan explained.

"Cool," Ren replied as he turned the wheel and gently eased the powerful Mustang over to where Dan had indicated.

As he looked up at the building he began to feel a twinge of uneasiness. He shook it off immediately, turned off the car's engine and began to climb out.

"Let me get my camera out of the trunk," he said to Dan.

"Need any help?" Dan asked as he joined Ren at the back of the car.

"No thanks, I've got this down pat." Ren said as he smiled to his friend.

"This digital camera is perfect in low light and the parking lot and the building are lit up like a prisoner-of-war camp. I won't even need a flash."

"Ha, yeah. I was thinking that these people must have one heck of an electric bill!" Dan chuckled before continuing.

"I'm going to walk around a little while so my bones don't get too stiff; I shouldn't have refereed five games today!"

"That's for sure! I feel just about the same way!" Ren concentrated on setting up his Nikon digital camera on the tripod. As he began to focus the camera on the building he again felt that same uneasy feeling that had come over him a few moments earlier. But he couldn't simply shake it off this time. He turned around to look for his friend and saw Dan at a distance, walking briskly, having turned around to make his way back to the car. Ren shook his head again at the uneasy feeling which was engulfing him as he continued to position the camera.

Ren shouted to the distant figure approaching him.

"Hey, Dan! Do you feel anything strange about this place?"

"Heck yes I do! This whole place gives me the creeps, but I get like that just from walking past a fundie bookstore in the mall!"

Ren laughed.

"I hear ya. I was wondering if it was just me," Ren replied.

He finished positioning the camera, aiming it upwards and with a wide-angle lens. He crouched down a little behind the set-up, removed the lens cap, and looked through the eyepiece to focus. Ren made slight adjustments to the camera's position until he finally had the entire building in the viewfinder.

"Hey Dan. You were right. This view is really..."

"Ren! Man, are you alright?" he heard Dan say as his friend eased him into a sitting position.

"I think so. But I'm not too sure. I think I blacked out for a moment."

Dan looked into his friend's eyes.

"Ren, are you in pain?"

Ren winced and nodded.

"Yeah. My head is killing me all of a sudden. I don't get it. One minute I was looking up at the building, to focus, and the next thing I know I'm looking up at you!"

Well, it's been a hot weekend. Top that off with the beers we had tonight and there's a perfect recipe for a bit of light-headedness."

Dan looked Ren over, and then closely into his eyes.

"I think you'd better pass on taking pictures tonight, though. Let's get you back to the hotel so you can crash."

"That's a good idea. Thanks. D'you mind driving us back?"

Dan laughed and gave Ren a boost up to his feet and helped him to pack up his camera and equipment. "My friend, I wouldn't wish you injury for anything, but this does save me from begging you to let me drive the Mustang!"

That was exactly what Ren needed at that moment, to help him lift his spirits.

"You go for it, El Capitan," he replied, as he broke out into the best he could muster for a grin.

Dan casually saluted him, in acknowledgement to the allusion to his naval rank.

"You're a gentleman and a scholar, sir. Now, let's get moving. We'll get you back for a good night's sleep and you can put all this behind you."

Ren nodded. He was in agreement about the sleep but, his concerns weren't going to go away.

"There's something going on here that needs additional expertise," he thought. He would have an important phone call to make before he climbed into bed that night.

***

As Monday dawned it was hot and humid in suburban New Orleans. But that did not stop the activity in the offices of Jay Hadley Ministries. Even though New Orleanians soon learned to deal with walking in what usually felt like a sauna, for Anita Delatorre it was something she still could not get used to.

"I swear, Jay," she said as she brushed her hair aside with her slender fingers. "I just don't know how you people handle all this humidity!"

"Oh, you get used to it my dear," replied Jay Hadley in perfect macho man mode. "But, I do agree that I'd rather be on the beach if I am going to be this hot. So, what do you think our best attack to this problem should be?"

"By 'problem', I am assuming you are referring to the ongoing information that's making its way from the office and onto the Internet?" asked Anita as she again ran her fingers through her hair.

"Of course, Anita. There aren't many problems for this Ministry that don't seem to lead to the darned Internet as their source. We really need to address this. I know you have tried some political connections to shut down this Alciatore fellow, which I applaud of course. But this is not going the way we want it to."

"Oh, Jay, I appreciate your diplomacy, but we both know that trying to shut him down using the company's connections was a major rat-fuck." Anita smiled at his reaction to her using profanity.

"For all your attempts at being cosmopolitan, Reverend Hadley," she thought, *"You're still just a tent preacher."*

"Alright. So things got... messed up. Still, maybe we can still do something at this end about the problem."

He picked up the phone and touched a button.

"Cee, can you come in for a moment?" He hung up the phone, and added, "I'm going to get Cecilia in on this."

Anita nodded, although she was not altogether happy.

"Sometimes I wonder about that girl. But she is the logical person for this step."

Cecilia entered the office without knocking.

"You rang, Master?" she asked, in a mock-Lugosi voice.

"Take a seat, Cee. Anita and I have been discussing the continued flow of information out of this office to 'The Jay Hadley Fan Club' website."

Cee replied immediately.

"Yeah, it's been getting pretty serious. Most of what they've been posting is internal memos. Not the kind of stuff you can just pick up off the street."

"Exactly. I want you to start an internal investigation into this. You know the computer system here well-enough to get this started, Cee. This is something I don't have the skills for, and neither does Anita. Let's see if we can get to the bottom of these leaks before they cut any deeper into our fund-raising."

Anita glared at Hadley, annoyed with him suggesting she had shortcomings of any kind. Cecilia completely maintained her composure, and exhaled gently.

"You got it, boss," she said. "It shouldn't be that difficult to nail down the computer system. Hard-copy, though, will be a different story. But the website isn't showing scans of any actual documents, so their source is probably computer files, anyway."

Anita spoke for the first time since Cecilia joined the meeting, "Well, you've lost me already, Cee. But I'm sure you know how to handle it. Jay tells me you've become quite the computer wizard."

"Well, it does help to have a good laptop, you know," Cecilia said.

Yes, I'm sure it does," Anita responded, sweetly. "I'd offer to help, but I'm just not a 21st-century woman with all this."

Cecilia smiled as she rose from her chair. "OK, folks, I'll see what we can learn. I'll get with our network consultant and get back with you about the security measures."

"Thanks so much, Cee," Hadley said, as Cecilia turned and walked out of the room.

"Well, honey?"

Anita turned-up one side of her mouth at hearing Jay's term of endearment.

"She is good at the computer side of things, but I suspect that whoever is pulling those documents is no fool. In fact, it could even be Cecilia, for all we know."

Hadley laughed.

"Preposterous. Cee would be the last person to sell-out the ministry like that!"

Anita smiled back at him. She had expected that reaction from Jay, and really did not have a response to it. For all her Talents, her attempts to read Cecilia properly had indicated that the woman had been sincere and had been telling the truth.

"Well, then, why don't you take me over to Starbucks and buy me an iced mocha?"

"Deal," said Hadley.

***

Renard Alciatore was ready for far more than just a cup of coffee by the time he had reached Shreveport on his return trip from Plano. He had left early and had stopped at a small diner for breakfast, just as Mike O'Donnell had suggested he should. The coffee was indeed as good as the coffee at home, while the waffle he dug into was excellent.

"I told you it was good. I'm glad you have finally decided to be reasonable and take my advice on occasion," Mike O'Donnell remarked as he pulled out the chair opposite Ren and sat down with him at the table.

Ren shook his head.

"You know, I really should be past being speechless about all this shit. But it still blows me away."

"Well, I'd show you the Gate over at Holy Trinity, but I'm sure you had something important on your mind when you called. You sounded pretty bad, Ren. So let's have the story."

"That's the problem, Mike. I don't know just what to tell you because my memory is pretty blurred. It's one of those things where I feel as though I saw or did something I need to know more about, but I just can't pull the memory back. It's all very confusing and frustrating at the same time."

Mike casually looked over his shoulder to check what everyone else in the restaurant was doing.

"I don't want to rush you, but I don't want to draw any attention to us, either. This is Shreveport, you know. OK, reach out with your mind and give me your thoughts."

Ren did just that. He closed his eyes and allowed himself

to transmit his memories of the night before to Mike. Mike stayed focused on Ren's closed eyelids as he took in the mental images until Ren reached the point where he almost blacked-out.

"Hold it, Ren," said Mike, as he touched the younger man gently on the wrist.

"Do a freeze-frame of the image, right there, and stop sending. I want us to go somewhere else before we go any further."

Ren opened his eyes and exhaled gently as he acknowledged his Teacher's wish.

"No problem. You have the same bad feeling about this, don't you?"

"I sure do, m'boy. I want us to be under more protection than what a diner can offer. Why don't you take us over to Holy Trinity? Maybe I'll get to show you their Gate, after all." Mike smiled, through the grim expression that was on his face.

The pair arrived at the church in less than ten minutes.

"A colleague is pastor here, and when I say 'colleague', I'm not simply referring to him being a fellow clergyman," he said as he winked.

They took a seat in one of the rear pews.

"He's out of town at the moment but the staff knows me well enough that if anyone notices us they will leave us be. Now, let's start this little exercise from the beginning, shall we? Why don't you go back to when the Hooters girl first came up to your table?"

Ren smirked.

"Liked her, did you?"

"While I share your taste for tall brunettes, I wouldn't kick out a short blonde," Mike said through a broad smile.

"Relax now. Think of this as rewinding a video, and then hit the 'play' button at that point."

Ren inhaled deeply and hit that imaginary "play" button as he exhaled. He again began transmitting images by using the "playback" method as Mike had suggested, and the images "played" forward. But there was an obvious gap: Ren was able only to send his conscious memories.

"All right, hit the 'pause' button now, Ren. Relax for a

moment, but stay focused on the place we have reached so far in this recollection. I want you to pass control to me for a short while. You saw and remembered much of what happened, but I want to probe what you saw and were unable to remember. Stay relaxed. We'll see what can be learned. You still with me? Good. Take a deep breath and drop your shields completely. Excellent, Ren. I'm going to take a little look at your memory now. Stay just like that."

The priest reached into Ren's mind as though it was a book and picked up the page where Ren had bent over to take a look through the camera. He went forward in small increments of time and braced himself for whatever it was that had caused Ren to black out when first recalling the memory. He saw the image of the M-K building through the lens and moved further forward. Mike felt a tingle as the façade of the building seemed to become transparent to reveal the activity within. Moving further forward in Ren's memory, he saw a gray-green glow on the upper floor, before the image through the lens changed from an overall view of the building to zooming in on just that one floor, eventually to shift to the corner as it homed in on the source of the glow. The view zoomed deeper in so that the glow Ren was tracking grew to fill the entire view through the lens as it became brighter, burning his eyes. Even Mike winced as he shared the experience of the memory.

The burning subsided after a moment, but the light did not go away. The creator of the light seemed to attempt to enter Ren's mind but backed-off. Most likely because of the imprint Mike had left there indicating that Ren was under his Protection. A sense of doubt seemed to grip the unidentified presence within the building and a bolt of deep-green light shot out of the corner office, to strike Ren harshly in the eyes through the camera.

It was all Mike could do not to collapse onto his haunches in the same position that Ren had fallen into when that bolt of light had actually hit him. He summoned additional inner strength and held the link with Ren steady as he continued to review the memory while the bolt of light maintained contact with Ren's eyes despite Ren having dropped away from the camera. The presence had been unable to blot Ren's memory because of the Sigil of Protection around him. So the presence settled for generating a fog that blurred Ren's memory and prevented it from looking into the domain of the presence.

Mike sighed, and released the mind-link with Ren. "Well, you were right to get me up here, Ren. You did remember a few things after you looked up into that building."

"Cool. So I take it these memories were not of a brunette in a short blue dress then?" Ren smiled.

"That's a very specific fantasy," Mike said. "What brought that on?"

Ren shook his head and smiled again. "Oh, I saw a brunette the other day and it's been difficult to shake-off her image."

"Jeez, you're a hound!" Mike retorted. "C'mon then, I need to get back. Let me show you the Gateway before we leave."

"Wait. What about what you dug out of me?" said Ren, lightly touching Mike's arm.

"I've got some things to do, and then I'll get back to you, OK?"

"No. Not really, Mike. I'm entitled to know what it was that zapped me back there. What aren't you telling me?" Ren looked his Teacher square in the eyes.

"Ren, I've been straight with you ever since we've met, and I'm not going to lie to you now."

Mike turned squarely to Ren to match his stare, eye-to-eye.

"This is way bigger than I want to bring you in on, my friend. You're still in the rookie league on a lot of things and you just had a brush with a major-leaguer."

Ren looked at his mentor with a confused expression.

"What?"

"Let it go for now, Ren. I need to act on what I've just learned but I'm really not at liberty to go into what I have to do. I'll fill you in when the time is right for both of us. Please trust me on this, Ren."

"I do, Mike. I don't understand this for shit, but I trust you. Believe me on that."

"Yes sir, I do." The older man smiled.

"OK now, come with me and learn another place to Gate

to."

They walked back to the sacristy of the church, where Mike took Ren through the steps of learning a new Teleport Gateway location. Satisfied that his pupil had it straight, he stepped into the Gateway himself and vanished. Ren shook his head in amazement and respectfully retreated from the church to make his own return trip home in a more conventional manner.

Just as Renard Alciatore reached the outskirts of Alexandria, Louisiana, on I-49, Cecilia McIntyre planned how to initiate an investigation into a target she knew was herself. She had gone to great lengths to ensure that the information she had passed to Ren and his colleagues could not be traced back to her. Her problem now was how to proceed. She sighed and turned on her laptop. Rather than use the office system, she jumped through two proxy servers to access an anonymous email account. Ten minutes later she had her message completed.

From: Isis
To: PhotoGuy
Subject: JHM Information

There have been some changes at JHM that will make getting new information to you difficult for the foreseeable future. JHM has started an internal investigation into the source of the information you've been posting and I don't want my source there to get into trouble. There's still plenty of potential for passing along internal information, but we're going to have to be patient on this. There's going to be a good bit of turnover at JHM in the next couple of weeks (one person is leaving because her husband was transferred to Houston, another is going out on maternity leave, and a third is just quitting to stay home for a while). With all these departures, it will be easy to cast doubt on the actual source of the information.

I know you understand where I'm coming from on this, and I appreciate that. Look for some new goodies by the end of the month.

Thanks,

Isis.

Cecilia read the message twice over before hitting the SEND button and letting it go its way. She closed-down the outside Internet connection and began to type a preliminary "to-do" list of items to get the ball rolling towards the finding out just who was the leak from the ministry.

CHAPTER FIFTEEN
Wards and Probes

St. Louis Cathedral in the French Quarter is not the biggest church in New Orleans by far. Arguably, it is not the fanciest, either. And, given all the repairs to it in the 1840s, it is not the oldest. None of that mattered to local Catholics; as far as they were concerned, it was still the religious center of the city. Non-Catholics usually had a soft-spot in their hearts for the Cathedral, too, considering that the scene of Jackson Square and the surrounding buildings, including the Cathedral, was the subject of so many paintings, postcards, and snapshots.

Daily Mass, at the Cathedral, particularly the one on Saturdays, was also a splendid occasion. The building was too small for many of the big ceremonies held there, but that was never a problem in the average weekly round of services. The eight-fifteen Mass on this day was a special occasion for a couple of reasons. Firstly, Ren did not usually attend Mass and, secondly, the celebrant for this particular worship was Monsignor Michael O'Donnell.

Mass, for Ren, had become an off-and-on thing since he had left college. He had sometimes felt the energy and vibrancy around him but, at other times, he had been almost completely smothered by the apparent indifference and apathy of the congregation. The crowd at the Cathedral on this occasion was somewhere in-between. He could hear several older ladies around him reciting their rosaries, but merely going through the motions of their ritual. Others were fully into it, and Ren's Talents were able to detect a slight glow, an aura, around those people as their worship contributed good feelings to the world.

The glow around the celebrant on this morning was rather more pronounced. Mike always had an aura around him, but his aura became much stronger when he took his place at the altar. It was clear the Mass was important to this priest; he was not there simply to help people meet some arbitrary obligation. No, this ritual was, to Mike O'Donnell, a celebration of Light, and his enthusiasm for that Light was contagious.

His homily was short and to the point. It was, after all, a weekday service and there was little point in droning on to these parishioners. They would simply tune him out or leave before Mass was over. Still, his talk made several good points about modern life that were well-taken by some of the congregation, and were not offensive to the little old ladies with their rosary beads. The shortened homily enabled Mike to regard the rest of the ritual with the solemnity it deserved.

Ren's thoughts had wandered a little following the homily, but they were brought into sharp focus as Mike began the prayers which led up to the consecration of the bread and wine into the Body and Blood of Jesus Christ. He watched as Mike bowed over the large round Host and recited the words of the ritual. There was no great flash from heaven as the pronouncement was made, but it was clear that Mike believed something had happened to the thin wafer of unleavened bread lying on the altar in front of him. His personal aura expanded, spreading out beyond the width of the altar, as he picked up his chalice and used his priestly magic to transform the cup's contents from wine into blood. Ren had become cynical about this: if that was blood, and Jesus was a man, then didn't that make Catholics vampires? That cynicism vanished today, though, as the energy that Mike poured into the ritual had become so captivating for Renard Alciatore.

Once the climax of the Mass passed, Ren listened intently as the Great Amen was sung and preparations were made for Communion. Ren walked up to Mike to receive Communion, and smiled to himself as he remembered Mike's specific admonishment not to eat anything before attending Mass.

"Yeah, just like back in the Dark Ages, when you had to fast between midnight and Communion the next morning. Trust me, there's a method in my madness," Mike told him, on the phone the night before.

When it was his turn to stand in front of the priest to receive the Body of Christ, Ren smiled as Mike extended his hand to place the Host into Ren's outstretched palms. The exchanged looked just like any other one that had come before it on that day, but Ren could discern a distinct golden glow emanating from the Host as it left Mike's fingers and rested on Ren's palms. Upon consuming the Host, that golden glow briefly manifested itself around Ren's body too, before settling down again into the regular aura usually projected by a person with Talents.

Communion complete, Mike began the process of cleaning up his chalice and proceeding with the closing section of the ritual. There was no speeding-up the rite at this point; all magical ceremonies had to be brought to a conclusion properly, with any power that had been raised absorbed by the participants, grounded to the earth, or both. Mike took advantage of the Blessing to disperse much of the power the Mass had raised, passing it back to those in attendance. When it was clear that there was no more external power that could be absorbed by the people in the church, Mike used the flowing gestures of the Dismissal to focus any remaining power into the Teleport Gateway which was off to the side of the sanctuary in the Cathedral. One of the reasons Gateways in churches are so potent is that a skilled practitioner who was also a clergyman could easily raise power and then re-direct it into the Gateway.

The organ in the loft of the cathedral began to belt out the recessional hymn as Mike bade the altar boys to lead the way before him down the main aisle of the church and to the front doors which opened on Rue Chartres. Ren watched as Mike worked the crowd, shaking hands and chatting with parishioners. Once everyone who looked in to catch the priest's eye had moved on, Mike gestured subtly to Ren that he should follow him back into the church.

"Take a walk while I get out of the vestments and we'll get on with our day," he said.

"Works for me. I'm starved," said Ren, with enthusiasm.

"Not so fast, grasshopper," replied the priest as he laughed. "I said, 'get on with our day'. That doesn't necessarily mean we go and eat."

Ren smiled. "You know I don't mind. I really enjoy learning about all this stuff."

"Excellent then," responded Mike as they reached the sacristy. They went in and Mike began to remove the layers of vestments he had donned for Mass, hanging them up and putting them away until he was down to his basic priestly attire of black shirt and slacks. "Have you ever been out into the garden behind the cathedral?"

"No, come to think of it, I haven't. I've shot pictures of it through the fence but have never gone in."

"Well, let's walk back there. It's a good spot for what I have in mind for this morning. Not that there's anything wrong with here in the church, but people will start coming in from off the street again now that Mass is over and I'd rather not have the distraction."

Ren followed Mike out of the side door of the church that led into Pere Antoine Alley. They turned left into the alley and walked about six steps to the wrought-iron gate that provided access to the small garden. He used his Talents to "pop" the padlock on the gate and removed the lock, swung the gate open, and motioned Ren to step inside. He closed and locked the gate behind them to guarantee they would have some privacy for a while.

"This might tick-off a few purists who want to poke in and get photos of the garden without having us in those pictures, but they'll just have to suck it up for a while. I want to work a bit more with you on mind-links and I prefer to do that sort of work in a protected environment. He waved his right hand clockwise around them and Mike sent power to the wards that surrounded the garden. "Nice. This place has a very nice feeling to it when it's warded. OK, I want you to do some shield work this morning. You need to get ample warning that someone is coming after you psychically, but not everyone plays by the rules. So, there are a few things you can do to detect a psychic attack before you're hit. Lower your shields a little, just below your regular level. Where you put them when you're trying to 'feel' something in a public place."

Ren nodded his head and followed instructions.

Immediately, Mike's regular aura began to glow just a bit brighter and the perimeter of the garden appeared hazy to him.

"Yes, that's good," said Mike. "Feel where your shields are now. This is a good level for when you walk into a restaurant or a crowded room. You can see and feel your surroundings, but you can easily raise your shields if you don't like what you feel." The priest closed his eyes and sent a gentle mind probe towards the side of Ren's head.

Ren blinked his eyes as his head whirled around in the direction of the little energy shot and he snapped his shields up tightly. "Did you do that?" he asked.

Mike smiled. "Good reactions, young Padawan! That was a simple probe, the kind of thing someone with Talents might do to a stranger when they meet. Lower your shields a little again and feel for it. Get yourself used to it so that you don't snap-to quite so fast. The speed you did it made you look like an amateur."

"But I am an amateur, Obi-Wan," retorted Ren, chuckling as he complied with Mike's directions.

The pair went back and forth with short mind-link probes for almost an hour. When Ren began to rub his temples Mike slapped on his thighs and stood up to pace around.

"Let's take a break," he said. "You should have a good idea of what both sides of this connection feel like. This isn't a threatening move, just something more like two strangers eyeballing each other, measuring each other up." The heightened perception of the Teacher detected that Ren was relaxing his shields again, lowering them to the level just below that of the daily routine. Just as Ren was settling at that level, Mike sent a short energy zing to the side of his head.

Ren's shields snapped up immediately, as quickly as they had the first time Mike had probed him. "Whoa!" Ren exclaimed. "What was that for?"

"Noticed that, did you?" said Mike, grimly. "That was something a little less benign. You did well there, grasshopper." Mike sent another simple probe, which bounced right off Ren's shields. "You distinguished well between a basic probe and something stronger. Let's work on both of those for a bit, so the difference between benign and threatening becomes instinctive to you."

"OK. But, if I know it's coming, is that an accurate measure of my reactions in a typical encounter with a stranger?"

"Well, no it's not. But we can work on that in time. You'll find that most people who are trained in the use of their Talents will engage the simple probe just to find out whether they are dealing with a normal human being or someone with Talents. You'll see how this works as you meet others. What concerns me is that you might run into others who are less than friendly before you meet my friends." Mike smiled and gestured to Ren to again lower his shields.

After another hour of work, Ren was yawning and Mike had a sense of accomplishment. "This has been some good classroom work. You've got a good feel for this now, so we can move on from this topic." Mike waved his hands again to drop the protective wards from around the garden. The sky was brighter as the morning sun rose higher.

"I hate sticking to the subjects of attack and defense, especially with a pupil of your creative abilities. Still, we need to keep on this until I'm comfortable that you are able to handle any challenges you might encounter, fair or foul. Had you begun this training when you were younger, we would have taken a much different approach, by working on your senses and perception from a variety of angles," Mike said. "But don't worry, we'll get to the fun stuff in due course."

"Good," responded Ren. "Because I can sense that there's more to all this than just throwing lightning bolts at someone's head. Even sitting in church this morning was a different experience. I want to be able to translate some of that feeling into my work."

"Definitely," the priest said. "But, for now, let's make sure you stay alive long enough to do all those neat things. Stand up and stretch, then we'll move on."

Ren did just that, while walking around the small group of tombstones and monuments in the center of the garden. He pulled out the small digital camera he usually carried in his pocket and shot a few frames, then joined Mike on the bench at the rear of the cathedral. "You know, I feel good about being able to raise my shields when necessary," he said. "But what about a more physical attack? I mean, what if someone tries to toss one of those energy zingers you sent at me, but they aim for my balls or some other part of my body I'd prefer to hang on to?"

"You're good at anticipating where I'm going with these lessons, you know that?" Mike grinned. "Well, so far, you've been able to cope well with raising the more substantive defenses by instinct. But those were in situations where your life was in immediate danger. I want you to be able to raise that 'aura-armor' on demand. Take a deep breath. Now hold it a second and we'll do a basic visualization. OK. Exhale, and then another deep breath. Good. One more, but this time visualize drawing-in the sunlight into the top of your head as you inhale." Mike stepped back and watched a thin shaft of golden sunlight steaming down from the sky and brush the top of Ren's head. "You're looking good, grasshopper. Stay relaxed. Don't drop your shields, but just absorb the solar energy. Feel it filling your head then open up your chest area to it."

As Ren did just as he had been instructed, Mike observed a golden glow which began to emanate from Ren's chest. "Still looking good, m'boy. Keep absorbing the light and let it continue to flow lower down into your body. Nice. Yes. You got it. Do you feel the glow of the energy as it courses through you? Yes, like that. What do you think?"

"Feels good," said Ren. "It's like an adrenaline rush, but not quite as intense. More like how I feel when I'm going out to referee a little-kids soccer game."

"Not a bad analogy," Mike observed. "Now, go ahead and ground this energy. Don't drain yourself, just ground any excess. Keep some of it so that you maintain that comfortable feeling rather than on 'overload' level." He watched as Ren exhaled. The golden glow flowed from Ren's hands and feet and poured into the ground in a puddle of light, before being absorbed into the earth. "You're definitely on a roll today, Ren. Try the process again. Hold the energy then release the excess."

Ren repeated the sun-capture three more times. As the final pool of light vanished into the ground, Mike smiled. "Well, now you see why the sun is so important to you. I want you to pull some of that solar energy inside you every day, just like you have been doing. It doesn't have to be a 'tank-up' like we've just done. But if you're sitting by the water, for example, you can draw on that energy as well, just like we did when we were out on the river. Either way, try to maintain a level of personal energy that's higher than usual. When you do, you'll be able to draw on that extra energy to do a number of things."

"Sounds like a segue to me," Ren replied as he chuckled.

"You got me. Yes, it was. The idea now is to project some of that energy and to shape it around you. Focus the energy inside you and draw it towards your head. Do it slowly so you don't mess up your equilibrium. Can you feel it manifesting in your chest? Wrap your heart in it. Yes. Good. OK. Now let that energy flow outward from your heart and encircle your chest. Continue to pump it out, slowly, and let it surround your arms and head. Now, go lower with it and let it flow easily around your legs."

Ren felt the energy leave his chest and saw the golden-white glow that began to take shape around him. "I can see it, Mike. I feel as though you could throw a rock at me and it would bounce off this Light all around me!"

"It would indeed," the priest noted. "But you also know that it can be penetrated if you're not careful. You need to be mindful of that when you are in a duel. Your aura-armor will repel a random energy attack, and even most physical attacks. But the slow, deliberate attack that comes right at you will penetrate you, for sure."

"And what is the correct defense for such an attack?" asked Ren.

"Keep your sorry ass far enough away from your opponent that you don't get into that position to begin with!" Mike roared.

Ren sighed and looked at Mike with a pained expression, "Gawd, there's nothing worse than a Channel rat who thinks he's funny."

"Oh, I am funny, thank you very much," retorted Mike, grinning. "You need to hear me preach a proper homily sometime. Now, pull your aura back inside you. Visualize something out of a sci-fi movie, where a layer of skin folds back and is absorbed by your body. You don't want to dissipate this energy; this is what you'll be using to project the armor layer again." Mike noted that the glow around Ren had been absorbed before he let out a sudden command: "Good. Now let's put it up again. NOW!"

Ren was startled by the sudden harshness in Mike's voice, and he immediately shut his eyes and projected energy outwards from his chest. His aura-armor re-appeared in the same sequence it had the first time, but the overall covering popped into place in a fraction of a second.

"Hm. It looks like you didn't forget that night in front of your house," Mike said.

"Who the shit would?" Ren asked, rhetorically. "But still, I don't know where that just came from! It was like an autopilot reaction or something."

"It's nothing more than your strong instinct for self-preservation, Ren. It takes a bit more than that to develop such an instinct in a child. But you did just fine. I'd wager you've had a few dates recently with women looking to rope you into marriage," said the priest as he snickered through his words.

"Hey Mike, what's the penalty for telling a priest to 'kiss my ass' in a church garden?" Ren said wryly.

"None that I've been hit with. And you have done it before," Mike laughed. "Let's sit and center for a while, just to get a grip on everything we've done here this morning, and then we can go to lunch."

"Lunch? That's a fascinating notion," Ren grinned. "I'm starving. Muffuletta at Napoleon House?"

"That will do just nicely," responded Mike as he waved his hand to unlock the padlock on the garden gate.

***

They both walked back along the alley to the front of the cathedral and strolled casually up Rue Chartres for two blocks to the corner of Rue St. Louis and the former home of Nicholas Girod, the sixth mayor of New Orleans.

"D'ya think Napoleon would have consented to live here, had Girod been able to pull off his desire?" said Ren, thinking out loud as they walked past K-Paul's restaurant.

"Oh, shit yes," Mike replied. "St. Helena was already so

far away from France, and a number of his officers had come to the States after the war anyway. And, you've got to admit," he added, sweeping his hand in front of him, "this isn't all that bad a house by early nineteenth-century standards."

"Yeah, I know. But this is such a far cry from Paris," Ren added.

"And they didn't even do the muffuletta here in those days!" Mike laughed. "Let's get a sandwich and chat some more."

As the pair walked through the dark hallway connecting the bar and the courtyard Ren noted the single two-person table in the corner, with a chess-board embedded into the top. "One day, I'm going to put that legend to the test," he said.

"Hm, you mean the one about Napoleon showing-up to play chess?" asked Mike. "That's one I'd like to see myself. I'm not too good a chess player though. Are you?"

"Second chair on the Brother Martin team. A good friend was first chair but I ended up getting his girlfriend, so I can't complain," Ren smiled, as the waiter showed them to a table in the courtyard.

Mike smiled as he sat down. He caught Ren's eye as he turned to the waiter. Ren nodded, and Mike ordered for them. "Half a muff for each of us, and two Abita Ambers." At that, the waiter whisked away and left the pair to contemplate the lush courtyard surrounding them.

"The hanging plants and that running water are going a long way towards easing my headache from the workout you put me through this morning," Ren said.

"Oh, I think there's more than a little credibility to the concept. You already know the power of flowing water in terms of relaxing and energy. After all, isn't your favorite relaxing spot out at the lakefront?"

"Yeah, Marconi and Lakeshore, to be specific," Ren replied.

"Ever go out for one of Brother Augustine's 'star parties'? We used to get so very drunk doing that," Mike laughed.

"Yeah, us too. Sometimes a little more than drunk."

Mike understood Ren's meaning immediately. "You know, I never gave that much thought, but it does come to mind now. Pot and Talents aren't a good mix. I don't know if you indulge that habit much at this stage of your life..." Mike paused for a few seconds at Ren's shake of the head, then continued, "But if you do, make sure you set-up a bit of protection around yourself before busting up. Getting high can really do a number on your shields."

"I'll remember that. JJ and I used to get high on occasion, back when we were in grad school, but we haven't done that in years."

The waiter returned with their beers at that point, so Mike hesitated before replying.

"Well, you'll find the Pagan community a bit divided on that subject, and many who follow the traditions of Western mystics are adamant about not using drugs of any kind. They're in a different spot on this subject, though. They're trying to nurture abilities that are barely there when compared to what you have. The Talents are much different. Your abilities are there, but pot in particular will just blow away your shields. If you get high with someone else who has Talents you'd better make sure you're with someone you trust totally, otherwise they will be able to read every thought you ever had."

"Wow, you're that defenseless?" Ren asked.

"Definitely. That's why I said to put some protection around you. Don't get me wrong, sitting down with a pipe full of primo weed is one of the finer pleasures in life," the priest said, smiling. "But make sure you maintain a very controlled environment around you."

"I'll remember that, too. I'd be the type to partake of a hit or two at a party or something."

Their sandwiches appeared just as Mike nodded back to acknowledge Ren while taking a hearty sip of his beer. "Well, I can safely say that indulging in a muffuletta is only bad for your waistline and your cholesterol count, and definitely will have no significant impact on your Talents."

Ren grinned. "Yup, the muff is proof that there is indeed a superior being." With that, he dug into the creation in front of him, which was made up of olive salad, provolone cheese, salami, and mortadella, all surrounded by good Italian bread. The pair both ate in silence for a while, their exertions of the morning having made them both ravenous.

Ren finally came up for air and broke the calm between them. “I’ve always preferred a warm muff like this one over the cold ones you get at the grocery stores on Decatur.”

“Hmm, that’s a religious debate I would not usually participate in,” Mike said. “I prefer discussions about easy topics, such as Thomas Aquinas or the like.”

Ren smiled and signaled the waiter for two more beers. “I’m going to cut it off at two today,” he said. “I’m refereeing two men’s league matches tomorrow morning, so I don’t want to be hung-over later.”

“No problem. I’m going to a fundraiser for UNO tonight. One of those ‘brie and chardonnay’ things that Republicans like to sneer at,” Mike said as he laughed. You’ll have to come to one of those things with me some time. There’s lots of great potential for you to score some business.”

“I’ll do that. Thanks, Mike. The family thinks my photography business is just a hobby. They don’t realize that I actually make a decent living from it.”

They tapered off into silence again as both men contemplated the quiet of the courtyard. There were a few other diners around the perimeter, but they were so caught up in their meals that the only voices to be heard were two very spirited folks at the bar. The waiter had discreetly placed the check on Mike and Ren’s table as they were relaxing. Ren reached for his wallet but Mike stopped him.

“I was out on the boat across the river last night. Charity party. But we did go on board and I rolled the dice for a while. This one’s on me.”

Mike paid the check and they both parted just outside the bar. “Practice raising those defenses daily, Ren. I can’t begin to tell you how important that is.”

“Will do, Mike. Can I give you a lift anywhere?”

“No thanks. I’m going for a stroll, then sit up on the Moonwalk for a while. I’ll catch the Elysian Fields bus back home.”

“Gotcha. Thanks, as always, Mike. Catch you soon!” Ren waved as they went in separate directions, he turning towards Decatur and his car, Mike turning up the street and back into the heart of the Quarter.

Ren was in no hurry to get home as he took his Mach One up Esplanade. He thought of stopping in St. Louis Cemetery No. 3 to shoot some pictures, but he decided to wait for a weekday when it wouldn't be so filled with tourists. He turned back along the bayou and pulled up in front of his house. Rather than settle down, he grabbed a bottle of water from the fridge and went back out, to sit on the bank of the bayou. Ren received the email from "Isis" notifying him of the change in the information flow, but he had not been able to catch her live to discuss it. Entering the Kik app on his phone, he tapped on her name and began to type a greeting.

"Hi. You've been hard to connect with the past few days."

"I'm sorry about that. I know you got my e-mail, though, so you know what's going on."

"Yeah, it's no problem. I don't want to get anyone in trouble over there. JH is going to fail eventually, and folks there are going to need to be able to find new employment."

"Do you really think you can bring Jay Hadley down?"

"I can't see how a guy like him can stay in business when he's so full of shit."

"Ren, people buy into shit all the time. It's part of what makes the world go around."

"That's a scary thought."

"Well, it's true, and a lot of these homeschooling families don't believe the "real" media."

"That's even scarier."

"So, you going out to stare at soccer moms tomorrow?"

"Soccer wives and girlfriends, actually. Mens' league games tomorrow."

"Out in Metairie?"

"Yeah."

"Cool. I dated a guy once who played in that league. It used to be fun to lie out and get some sun while they were playing."

"That's one of the reasons I love to referee, dear. Some of those WAGs look pretty good in shorts and less :-)"

"You're a hound. D'you know that?"

"Oh, I've been told that before."

Well, it's true

"<Blush>"

"You? Blush? Yeah right."

"Huh, maybe you'll find out, one day."

"Maybe I will at that..."

He once again sensed the conversation was over, and did not reply. Ren sighed. His chats with this woman, while interesting, had given him no clue as to her identity. He smiled at the screen, and then turned to go inside. He needed to get back to the images he was in the process of enhancing.

***

"Damn good thing I made an early night of it," Ren

thought, as he followed the play down-field during the second half of his 8am men's match. The game had been a bit more difficult than usual. Several of the lads on the field had been more interested in beating on each other rather than playing the ball. After six cautions and two sendings-off, one from each team, Ren looked at his watch and began to count down the final ten minutes of the match. The team in red had taken a three-goal lead over the white team; a score-line which had dramatically taken the wind out of the white team's players.

It was at this point that Ren was finally able to look around a bit and check out the crowd watching the game from the far-side touchline. He noticed one woman who appeared to be in her late twenties, maybe early thirties, sitting on the grass. Her legs were stretched out in front of her with her short skirt hitched up even shorter. Yup, Ren thought, that's why I referee men's soccer. It was interesting, though, that a gal as cute as that was sitting on the far side. Men's soccer matches didn't usually attract crowds, and the hardcore fans, that is, wives and girlfriends, usually stayed on the players' side with their men. A couple more uneventful trips by Ren down-field and back up again confirmed that she really was interested in the game but that she didn't appear to be affiliated with either side. Well, he thought, maybe she's here for the 10am matches. He continued to look at her through the corner of his eye but was distracted as two players went down, sprawling. He signaled for the foul and awarded the free-kick to the white team. While waiting for the players to re-arrange themselves for the re-start of the game, he stole a glance at the woman. He found it curious; nobody watches the referee during a soccer match.

The white team took the kick, sending the ball to the corner of the field where she was lying. Ren again glanced her way while waiting for a red player to take the throw-in. This time the girl smiled at him, obviously approving of his interest in her. Ren looked down at his watch. Twenty-five seconds of the match remained. He followed the play as it went up-field, and then blew his whistle to indicate the end of the match as his watch showed 45 minutes played.

Both teams' players came together, shaking hands, slapping backs, and migrating to their respective teams' bench areas for water and to sit down. Ren met his assistant referees near the half-way line, shook hands with them, and led them off the field. He thanked them for their performance during the match, grabbed a bottle of water, threw his bag over his shoulder, and headed across the field to where the woman was still sitting. She smiled a most welcoming smile of greeting and motioned for him to sit down and join her.

His initial assessment of the attractive legs stretched out was confirmed upon closer inspection. At about five feet four inches tall, the woman was what Mike would call "curvy", meaning she wasn't thin, but not too heavy. She also had a better-than-average-sized chest to go with her pair of deep brown eyes and well-tanned complexion.

"Hi," he said. "I'm Renard Alciatore."

"Yes, I know. It's a pleasure finally to meet you."

"Do I know you somehow?" he asked.

"Sort of. How does it feel to meet an Egyptian goddess in person?"

He was startled, but then recovered quickly. *Isis*?"

Smiling again, she extended her hand. "Cecilia. My friends call me Cee."

Taking her hand gently, he replied, "Well, it is indeed a pleasure, Cecilia."

"Cee," she corrected.

"OK, Cee," he smiled. "How did you find me here? Oh, that's right, I told you last night, didn't I?"

"Yup. You did. I figured this would be a good way for us to meet face-to-face for the first time. I have a bunch of friends on the Cyclones, and they're playing on the other field at 10am," she said.

"Makes sense to me. Are you a soccer fan yourself?"

"Just a little. My mother's maiden name is Gonzalez," she giggled. "My brother played in the International League here in town, as did two of my uncles."

Ahh. Well, I'll try to watch my Spanish profanity, then, since that's about all the Spanish I know."

She laughed, stood up, and fished around with her foot for the sandal she had kicked off earlier. "Well, Ren Alciatore, I thought you might be interested in walking with me over to

Field Four, where my friends are playing."

"That would be lovely." He waited until they were moving a while before continuing the conversation. "So, do you work for JHM?"

"Yes."

"And what do you do there?"

"I'm Rev. Hadley's radio producer and chief-of-staff," she replied.

Ren was surprised at her rank within the organization. "If you are that high-up in the ministry, why are you trying to put yourself out of a job?"

"Oh, I can get a job just about anywhere, either in the non-profit sector or working for a commercial radio station. I originally came to JHM with all sorts of idealistic notions, but things have changed a great deal over time." She turned to him with a serious expression on her face. "I'm very impressed with your willingness to take JHM on, Ren. That's why I want to help. Also..."

"Yes?" he asked, encouraging her to continue.

"Well, at first, I thought I could be just like 'Deep Throat' and feed you information anonymously. But, the more I got talking to you, the more I wanted to meet you. I hope you don't mind."

He smiled. "Oh, no. I don't mind a bit. I'm just a bit surprised. Aren't you taking a risk, being seen with me?"

"Well, if Jay saw me with you, I'm sure he'd fire me. But that's no problem; I'm ready to move on. If that happens sooner than later, I'll cope," she said, again smiling.

"I'd hate to see you lose your job, Cee, but I'm sure glad you looked me up, I've been terribly curious about the person behind the words. It's a neat added bonus to discover that she's as pretty as you are."

She smiled and blushed. "Thanks."

"Hey, I have another game to work now. Would you like to get together later and have some lunch?" he asked.

"I don't think that would be a good idea, because I'd rather we weren't discovered together," she said.

"Oh," Ren replied, unable to mask his disappointment.

She thought for a moment. "Do you know 'The Steak

Shoppe' in LaPlace?"

"Yeah."

"How about we have lunch there on Tuesday?"

His eyes gleamed again. "That would be very nice."

"Well then, I'll leave you now, Ren Alciatore. I'll message or email you if our plans change." She extended her hand again. "It's been nice to meet you in person."

"Same here. Enjoy the game," he said as he shook her hand.

Ren turned to head off to the next field over and meet up with his colleagues for the 10am match. During the pre-match conference, both of the other referees noted that Ren seemed to be on another planet.

CHAPTER SIXTEEN
Communications

Between thoughts of Astral Projection and women at soccer matches, Ren's Monday was a blurry mess. The only thing that saved it from being a total waste was that he had resolved to begin, at Mike's urging, a regular regimen of meditation and general psychic exercise. He was sitting at a coffee shop in the Garden District, remembering some of Mike's instructions from Saturday.

"It's going to sound silly to you at first," Mike said, "But I want you to start focusing on the position of the sun at various times of the day. When you awake in the morning, face towards the east, and acknowledge the rising sun. At noon, stand, facing south, and acknowledge the midday sun. In the evening, turn towards the west and bid the sun farewell for the day. And finally, before you go to bed, greet the North Star and the rising moon and draw their energy to you. And if you can't remember all of that, do your best to focus on the moon. That's the one that's most important to you right now."

"Jeez, that almost sounds like you want me to convert to Islam, bowing and praying all day," Ren remembered smirking, as they lingered over their beers at Napoleon House two days earlier.

"Shit, I don't want you to get into some routine boring prayer ritual, Ren. I just want you to think about two of our main sources of both physical and psychic energy and make them work for you. Besides, praying to the sun and the moon isn't Muslim, it's Pagan," he laughed.

Ren was still a bit skeptical. "All right, I'll start

tomorrow...Monday for sure."

It was approaching high noon as Ren sipped his café mocha approvingly. This place had changed management recently, and he was pleased that the change had not impacted the quality of the beverages. In spite of his fixation on tomorrow's lunch with Cecilia, Ren still remembered his mentor's directions this morning, and now was considering an appropriate place to perform his noontime solar oblation.

"The cemetery will do, providing it's not filled with bloody tourists and vampire wannabes," he thought.

Finishing his beverage, he stood, exited the coffee shop, and walked the half-block down Washington Avenue to the entrance of Lafayette Cemetery No. 1.

This high-walled cemetery occupied the square block bounded by Washington Avenue to the downtown side, Coliseum Street on the river side, Prytania Street on the lake side, and Sixth Street on the uptown side. (New Orleanians don't have 'north' and 'south' in their vocabulary, so things are expressed according to their relative position to the two bodies of water to the top and bottom of the city.) Ren made a quiet appeal to the archangels to shoo away the tourists, sighed, and stepped into the cemetery.

It was a warm afternoon for September, which probably had more to do with the fact that the cemetery was all but empty, rather than his prayer, Ren mused. Still, whatever the reason, he wasn't complaining as he wandered to the southwest corner, into a little open spot. Why no tombs or graves had been constructed on this series of plots, he didn't know. It was fortunate for the various television and movie production companies who came to the city, though, because they could set up some of their larger equipment in this area. The Lafayette cemeteries were city-owned, so the movie folks were able to secure permission to shoot inside here.

Ren stood in that little clearing, facing towards the river. Strictly speaking, he might have been facing more east than south, but he figured that the sun wouldn't mind too much if he used New Orleans geography. Extending his arms and stretching out his fingertips, he closed his eyes and raised his face to the warmth of the sun's rays. Ren quietly reflected on the heat and energy he was allowing to enter his body through his skin. Pulling a bit of it in consciously, he gave thanks for it, and acknowledged the power of the Light that created it.

As he stood there, Ren felt a tingle in the back of his brain that moved down to the base of his neck. It wasn't a negative feeling, but it was clear that the source of the energy tingling his neck was another human. Smiling, it was the same feeling he experienced when he was with his buddy, Janet Julianne. He figured that standing here communing with the sun functioned like a transceiver, sending out energy with his particular psychic signature, and receiving warmth and pleasant thoughts from his friend. Just as he was enjoying the sensation, a second tingle scratched the back of his head. This one was different; again, not negative, but the emotions being sent to him were...ummm... much more passionate than his connection with JJ.

Allowing this link as well, Ren's breathing began to get a bit heaver. It was clear that the sender of this signal was indicating an interest more than "just-friends". That was more than obvious to Ren, whose manhood began to stiffen as the external energy worked its way down his body to his crotch.

This sensation startled Ren, who raised his shields a bit as he lowered his arms. Opening his eyes, he adjusted to the change in light, allowed his shields to balance, and began to seek the cemetery's exit. Well, he chuckled inwardly, it's nice to know you're appreciated. Now if I can just find out who is doing the appreciating...

***

One place where Renard Alciatore was most decidedly not appreciated at the moment was the corner office in the Metairie suite of Jay Hadley Ministries. Anita Delatorre was reviewing a report she had obtained from her company's contacts in the Louisiana State Police about the enquiries being made by one Lieutenant Toshihiro Watanabe of the City of Kenner Police Department. Said Lt. Watanabe had acquired a good bit of data through official channels on two deaths in St. Tammany Parish. The author of this report had been instructed to relay to Anita any activity at all with regard to either of these deaths, since they happened to be two of the three principals involved with the most popular anti-JHM website on the Internet. That a suburban cop from the South Shore was taking such an interest in these two North Shore deaths was a major concern to her, one that merited some further research and possible action. She sighed and made a mental note to get someplace private for a phone call later.

"You look like you've seen a ghost!" Jay Hadley said as he swept into his office, lightly kissing Anita on the cheek after closing the door behind him.

"Oh, it's nothing," she said, folding the report up and returning the pages to their envelope. "I just didn't sleep very well last night, and I think it's catching up with me in a big way now."

Hadley stood behind her and lightly massaged her shoulders. "Well, if I didn't have to get moving with the show, I'd offer to take you home and give you a nice massage," he purred, softly kissing her ear.

Anita sighed. "Mmmmm...that would be nice, Reverend Hadley, suh," she said, putting on her thickest Yellow Rose of Texas accent. "But, as usual, we both have obligations which require our attention."

His hands left their resting place on her neck and moved slowly but deliberately to cup both of her breasts. Gently caressing her nipples through her blouse and thin bra, he moved to one side, brushing his erection against her shoulder.

"You're a bad man, Reverend Hadley, suh," she said, staying with the heavy accent. "It's gonna be hard foah me to continue to be uh lay-dee if you don' stop your actions, suh." She smiled sweetly.

He pinched her nipples and she gasped, but suddenly stood up. "I'm sorry, Jay," she said, lapsing into the accent-less speech of the corporate world, "but we really don't have the time. You need to get your prep work done and I have to call the office and get a couple of other things done. I do like the attention, though...maybe we can have dinner?"

Hadley acknowledged her wordlessly, kissed her cheek, and hurried down the hall to the studio. Composing herself, Anita gathered her paperwork from the conference table in

Hadley's office, straightened her blouse, and headed down to the lobby of the adjoining hotel. Making herself comfortable on a small sofa, she reached over to the low table in front of her and dialed a cell phone number that originated from the DFW area.

"Ryan," the Irish-accented voice said curtly.

"It's Anita. I have something that needs your attention... can you talk now?"

"I'm just finishing lunch...I'm in Houston at the moment."

"How fortunate for me," Anita cooed. "Can you join me in New Orleans tonight?"

"Tsk-tsk," he said. "Such haste. Haste just breeds mistakes, dear. You sure you want to move so quickly on whatever your latest need is?"

"Yes, I'm sure," she said firmly. "Get one of the afternoon flights and meet me at that pizza place you like here in Metairie, OK?"

"You mean Tower of Pizza? Sure, I can do that, but I'm not convinced it's a good idea."

"The stipend I have in mind will convince you," Anita said, seductively. It was mostly an act with Hadley, but when money was involved, her seduction was always real.

He sighed. "I know that tone of voice, therefore I will not argue further. All right, I'm on my way to the airport, love. I'll see you this evening."

"Thanks." She hung up the phone and headed upstairs to her room. After setting down her purse and getting out of her business suit, she donned a robe from the closet and stretched out on the bed. Closing her eyes, she began to project a golden aura around her body. To one without Talents, she appeared to be just having a quick nap. To the Talented, her aura was a visible defense against any kind of attack, both physical or psychic. The golden light strengthened, becoming opaque around her.

Anita's chest rose up and down slowly as she continued to gather strength and project her aura. Once she was satisfied that the aura would keep her safe, she turned her attention to the Astral Plane. She reached out with her mind, and visualized herself sitting on a bench on Boston Common. Once she held that astral scene firm, she used her mind to "call" one of her superiors.

Just a couple of minutes later, Anita felt a surge in the energy nearby, as the astral image of a man that looked as if he just walked off Fleet Street in London approached her, then sat down on the bench.

"Thank you for joining me, sir," Anita said, hesitantly, mind-to-mind. She was physically still in suburban New Orleans, while the man was in suburban Dallas, their thoughts merging, crossing the distance at the speed of light.

"My pleasure dear. Now, please update me," he replied.

Anita opened her mind to this man, as she had done countless times before.

"So, you would like to re-engage the assassin, then?" He asked.

"Yes, sir. This is his area of expertise."

"But what you have in mind isn't his typical sort of operation, and you're already creating a trail of bodies," the man stated, as he adjusted the sleeve of his shirt, under his suit coat.

Anita cringed. He could sense it.

"I know, but this next target is...well, sensitive. If not handled properly, this could lead to huge complications," she explained, anxiously.

"Relax, Anita. I know what you mean. There is a lot riding on Hadley. We are ready at all levels for our push into homeschooling. Hadley, for all his faults, is the right choice to bring these people to us, and encourage them to buy our materials. A few incidents in metro New Orleans aren't going to be noticed in the long run. I don't share the beliefs of these people with their huge families and desire to remain ignorant of the world around them, but I prefer that we manipulate them rather than leaving them to the influences of others. You have my permission to go forward with the assassin. I will make sure the funds are available to you to complete this," he concluded, with a nod in her direction.

Anita's presence on the bench exhaled deeply. Her body on the bed in Metairie did the same.

"Thank you again, sir. I will meet with Ryan this evening and he will get on this immediately," she said, her confidence picking up.

The man nodded, rose from the bench, and walked away, fading from the astral plane.

CHAPTER SEVENTEEN
Isis Revealed

LaPlace, Louisiana was situated just north of New Orleans, on the up-river side of the Bonnet Carré Spillway from the city. The spillway is a strip of land that runs from the Mississippi River to Lake Pontchartrain. When there is a threat of the river overflowing its banks and endangering the city, the US Army Corps of Engineers will open the mile of floodgates along the river, causing the water to divert from its normal course to flow in-between the two levees on either side of the spillway, and out into the lake.

Ren was driving up US Highway 61 (Airline Highway to locals) from the city, and was crossing the bridge over the now-dry spillway. The need for major intervention with the river only happened once a decade or so. Most of the inter-city traffic between New Orleans and Baton Rouge now used I-10, making US 61 a nice, quiet way to get from the city to LaPlace and other points just north. Ren was in no hurry this morning, having stopped at his favorite film-processing lab in Metairie before making the drive. He should have been very relaxed, since he started the meditation routine suggested by Mike the previous day. He was doing his level best not to be anxious, but the thought of the young woman in the short skirt from the other day was causing him to press down more and more in the accelerator. The Mach One hit one of the expansion joints in the bridge across the spillway pretty hard, jarring him back to reality for a moment.

Smiling at himself, Ren slowed down a bit and tried to relax his mind. It was just lunch, after all, he thought. Lunch with a pretty woman. Lunch with a pretty woman who knows me. Lunch with a pretty woman who likes me. Lunch with a pretty woman who...oh, shit, who works for the people I'm trying to...

"Oh, shit!" He said audibly. He called to his smartphone, telling it to call JJ's office number. Just as the call was about to start, he ended it, and told the phone to dial another number.

"Dr. O'Donnell."

"Hey, Mike."

"Ren, what's up, my friend?" Mike said cheerfully. "I don't have but a minute...going over to the University Center for lunch with a grad student. Nice butt on this one, you want to join us?"

"Figures you make an offer like that when I've already got a lunch date," Ren chuckled.

"Oh, cool. And just when are you going to introduce me to your friend Janet, anyway?"

"My lunch date isn't JJ today, and the answer to your question is soon. She still can't believe there's a priest in this town that neither she nor her daddy knows!"

"Oh, I know her daddy, Ren. He just probably doesn't remember me. OK, let's set something up with the three of us soon. So, who's lunch with today?"

"With the woman who is Jay Hadley's chief-of-staff," Ren said. "Actually, I'm a bit embarrassed that I'm just telling you about this."

There was a very pregnant pause before Mike replied.

"Embarrassed, huh? I take it that it's finally just dawning on you that you might be walking into some kind of setup?"

"Well, at least credit me with coming to my senses before I got there."

Mike O'Donnell could see the sheepish grin on his student's face even though he was on the other side of town. "Fine, fine. You wised up. I'm glad. Next time, be a little suspicious a little earlier."

"Yes, Obi-wan, I'll do that. I'm heading up to LaPlace, by the way. This is just lunch, and I have a four o'clock appointment with a bride back at the house. If I don't make it back to the house, I'm going to tell Nadine to text you. Of course, if it looks like I have a chance of getting laid, I just might cancel the four o'clock and text you myself," he smirked.

"Well, if you do get laid, I expect a full report, so I can live vicariously through your adventures," Mike said, laughing. "That sounds like a good deal. And don't forget the Triple-7 if you need me and I don't call back in a reasonable amount of time. The odds of me getting laid are considerably less than yours, but I still am out-of-pocket on occasion."

"Thanks for the reminder, Mike. Talk to you later." Ren switched off the phone after Mike's final good-bye and began to keep his eyes open for his destination. The Steak Shoppe used to have three locations, one uptown and one in Metairie, in addition to the LaPlace restaurant. A beep-beep from the watch he kept in the glove compartment signaled noon as he pulled into the parking lot. He could see her waiting by the door, in a blue oxford blouse and a khaki skirt that was significantly longer than the shorts she had on out at the park on Sunday.

It took a lot of will power for Ren to slowly exit the car and walk over to the front door without running up to her. Doing a quick deep breathing exercise, he closed the distance deliberately, then reached both hands out to her. She extended her arms to grasp his hands, and they stood for a moment like that, looking each other in the eye.

Whatever doubts Ren possessed about this being a setup vanished rapidly as he saw the look in her eyes. Seizing the opportunity, he leaned in and kissed her, gently brushing her lips with his.

She squeezed his hands a bit tighter as he kissed her, her emotions a combination of startled and excited. "Hi," she said, a bit breathless.

"Hi," he replied. "You having an OK morning at work?"

"Yeah. The show is taped today, so things were much less hectic than usual around the office. No live callers, and Jay taped all the 'impromptu' pledge solicitations last week, so I took the afternoon off."

"Great, so I don't have to worry about you running out on me mid-meal, then," Ren smiled.

"No worry at all," she said.

They went in and were seated immediately. Both ordered iced tea as they settled in. Their waitress, a thirty-something blonde, smiled and walked off briskly to fetch their drinks.

"I haven't been to one of these places since the one up by Baptist Hospital, excuse me, 'Ochsner Baptist Medical Center', closed, years ago," Ren said.

"Oh, my sister lives out here, so we come out this way all the time. I'm going to baby-sit her kids tonight, so I thought it might be a good place for us to get to know each other," Cee replied.

"Not to mention that it's away from most of the lunch places your colleagues frequent," he winked.

"Well, yes, that was a bit of a concern for me. I've already started looking at other possibilities for jobs, but I want to leave quietly and peacefully, not under the cloud that being seen with you would bring."

"Then why be seen with me? Why the risk?"

"Well, I could say because you look good in knee socks, and that would be correct," she said, "but sometimes I feel like I have to do something. It sounds too trite to just say 'YOLO' like a teen, but that's exactly how I feel lately. First I felt that way about passing JHM information to you. this might sound a bit crazy, but sometimes I feel a connection with people I chat with on the 'net."

"Not crazy at all. I know exactly what you mean. Happens to me occasionally, like when this 'Isis' chick started messaging me."

She was grinning as the waitress came to take their order. She ordered a burger and he a Chicken Caesar Salad.

"Now that's a switch," she remarked. "You normally expect the woman to be grazing and the man to be the carnivore."

"Well, believe me, I'm not against the consumption of tasty animals in any way, but I try not to eat a lot during the week. Slows me down too much when I run in the evenings."

"Where do you like to run?"

"Oh, either along the bayou or up on the Lakefront. Do you run?"

"Well, sometimes," she giggled, "But most of the time I prefer a brisk walk. I banged my knee up a bit in high school, playing basketball, so I try not to put too much stress on it."

"Ahhh, so you like to be on your back then?" Ren said softly, with a wink.

"Sometimes...but sometimes it's fun to be a cowgirl." She

winked back at him.

He smiled back, enjoying the directness of her response. This was going to be fun, he thought. “So, you said you’ll be watching your sister’s kids. How many does she have?”

“Two, one boy and one girl. The boy is ten and the little girl seven. My sister’s the next oldest up from me in our family. I’ve got one brother older than her and one brother younger than me. Jackie, my sister, works downtown, so sometimes I’ll pick the kids up for her and keep them so she can work late or go to happy hour as the occasion dictates.”

“Happy hour? What does your brother-in-law have to say about that?”

“Oh, he’s in the Navy. They always have him going off to one place or another for work, so Jackie’s often at home alone with the kids. I love them both, so it works out all around.”

“And Cecilia, does she ‘happy hour’ often?”

“Not as much as she would like,” she giggled. “It’s that Christian employer thing. I’m better off going to the health club to work out and have a smoothie or something there.”

The conversation continued on health clubs and running until the waitress arrived with their meals and another refill of their iced teas. Ren dug immediately into his salad as Cee began the ritual of dressing the massive burger sitting in front of her.

“Looks good,” Ren commented, gazing down at her burger, but also allowing his gaze to pass over her breasts.

“Tastes good, too,” she said, licking her lips suggestively, then biting deep into the burger.

“Jeez, you bite!” He laughed.

“Yeah, I sure do...sometimes I draw blood if the meat is rare,” she winked.

“Hmmm...I’ll keep that in mind, mademoiselle,” he smiled.

The magnetism they were generating spilled out from the table and was immediately sensed by their waitress as she came to check on them. She smiled at both of them in such a way that Ren wasn’t quite sure which one she was expressing an interest in.

“Maybe it’s both of us,” Cee said.

“Huh?” Ren asked, caught totally off guard.

“The blonde. I think she likes the notion of doing either one of us."

DAMN! Ren thought.

She giggled again. "What, Mr. Alciatore, you didn't expect such thoughts from someone working for Jay Hadley Ministries? It is possible to be Christian and not be a 'nutball,' as you would say."

"Well," he stammered, "I really haven't given it much thought. Your boss tends to carry on to such an extent, and your callers..."

"Our callers are the true 'nutballs', Ren. Most of the women who work at JHM are just trying to earn a living. Oh, they believe in the positive things that the ministry does, but they are moms and wives who need to feed their families and want to have a little enjoyment in their lives."

"And you want to mess that up for them?"

Cecilia's expression turned serious for a moment. "There is enough going on behind-the-scenes by this man that just has to be stopped, Ren. Your instincts are spot-on, as you footballers say," she smiled briefly.

"You have evidence of things more dramatic than the stuff you've shown me up to now?"

"Yes."

"OK, I can see that this is the wrong time to press you further on that. But rest assured I won't forget."

"Oh, I won't let you, kind sir, take my word on that," she said, as she finished the last bite of her burger.

The waitress noticed both were just about finished with lunch, and made a discreet appearance. "Would y'all be interested in some dessert?"

Ren looked across the table. "Dessert?"

She gave him her best wicked glance. "Oh, I could go for a little dessert...but they don't have anything I want on their menu..."

Startled once again, Ren muttered something to the waitress to decline her offer and handed his credit card to her. Cecilia's gaze had turned from wicked to something approaching angelic so quickly that Ren wondered if he was hallucinating. "You know," he said, regaining some of his composure, "I always try to get up to the river and shoot some pictures when I get up this way. Would you like to come up there with me?"

"Bringing me some place wide open and public, huh, where I can't take advantage of you?" She said, the wicked look returning now that the waitress was gone.

Ren chuckled. "Oh, feel free to take advantage of me wherever you like, mademoiselle." He signed the receipt left by the waitress on the table and stood, extending his hand to assist his date with a most chivalrous gesture.

"Thanks," Cee smiled. "Tell you what," she added as they walked out of the restaurant, "I know a great spot along the levee, not too far from my sister's house. Why don't you follow me over there?"

"Works for me," Ren said.

"Good. Don't get lost on me," she smiled as she kissed him gently on the cheek. She turned to head for her car, and he did the same.

They arrived at a nice spot on River Road just opposite an upscale subdivision. She waved for him to pull his car up behind hers, and they both got out, Ren grabbing his camera bag. Cecilia was already jogging up the hill that is the levee. Ren followed, but at the pace of a more leisurely walk. She was already sitting down on the top of the levee as he set his camera bag down and retrieved his Nikon F3, one of his film cameras. A tugboat pushing a chemical barge was gliding up the river, and Ren snapped a couple of shots as it passed. A gust of wind caught Cee's hair and Ren managed to get a good shot of her tossing her hair back out of her eyes.

"Hey, who said you could do that?" She giggled.

"I did," he said, finally feeling like he was getting the upper hand.

"Well, if you're going to take my picture..." She unbuttoned the top two buttons of her oxford blouse, then sat back on her hands.

More than Ren's imagination was stirred up by the sight of a bit more of her chest, even though that glimpse wasn't all that revealing. He snapped a couple more pictures of her, as she smiled beatifically for the camera.

"I often get some nice shots up here," Ren said, "But I'm always amazed when I get really high-quality shots."

"What an optimist!" She said, giggling.

"What a sense of humor you have!" He smiled in return, returning the camera to its bag and sitting next to her.

"And this surprises you?"

"Well, it's not something I expected to see from 'Isis'."

"Well, 'Isis' tends to be a bit more open than Cecilia. That's to be expected, after all—she's a 'net persona. However, Cecilia does have her moments..." She turned to kiss him, gently at first, as she pulled his head to hers and pressed her lips firmly onto his, her tongue parting his lips and exploring his mouth.

Ren returned the kiss, his fingers moving to touch her cheek as his tongue found hers and they began an ages-old dance. He slid his hand up the side of her head as his fingers found her hair and ran through it. Not breaking the kiss, she turned towards him, pressing her breasts into his chest, her hands running up and down his back slowly. They broke the kiss by mutual agreement, and Cee leaned in to kiss Ren's neck. His hands encircled her now, fingertips caressing her back on the way down, fingernails digging in lightly on her back on the way up.

A moan escaped her lips as she kissed him again, both of them holding each other close as their tongues met a second time. They allowed the kiss to linger, neither wanting to really stop. His hands wandered up and down her back, then to her sides, where he could feel the thin fabric of the bra that was separating her breasts from her blouse. She pulled her body away from him slightly, making room for him to extend his caresses. Correctly reading this signal, Ren's fingers lightly danced over her breast, pausing to flick her nipple, which was erect under her bra. She moaned softly again, still kissing him as she did, then she pulled her lips from his, kissing his cheek, then his neck, then running her tongue up to his ear.

Their passion built up in the afternoon sun. He became bolder, hand reaching under her skirt to caress her thighs. She parted her legs slightly to allow this as well, and reciprocated by reaching down to caress his butt and dig her fingernails into his back. His fingers lightly ran up and down her thigh, barely brushing her panties on the upstroke, reaching all the way to her knee on the down stroke.

Cee's breathing was becoming ragged now, but suddenly she grasped the hand that was exploring her thigh in hers and pulled it up to her lips for a kiss. Her reply to his enquiring look was to cock her head to one side, in the direction of two riders on horseback that were now about twenty yards ahead of them.

Ren realized that the spell had been broken for the moment; he simply smiled and reached for his camera, setting up to photograph the riders as they passed.

"Ever the photographer, aren't we?" She laughed at him.

"Well, it gets in the blood. Besides, I have to protect your honor by not engaging in any untoward behavior, at least until they're out of sight," he smiled as he adjusted the lens.

"What a sweet man, to be so concerned about my honor," she giggled.

He gave her a mock half-bow and began to take pictures of the horses. "Beautiful creatures," he said. "Maybe one day I'll learn how to ride one."

"You've never ridden a horse?" she asked. Upon seeing his negative nod, she continued, "We shall just have to correct that situation one day. My uncle has a farm up near Folsom. I've gone up there with my family for years."

"Cool. If you don't think I'll be much of a burden, I'd love to give it a try," he smiled.

"You'll only be a burden, Ren Alciatore, if you decide you don't want to kiss me anymore," she smiled.

"Ahhh, then we won't have any disagreements on that subject, my dear," he laughed. Turning around, he snapped a couple more pictures of her, now that she had adjusted her skirt and blouse and was sitting upright. The riders had passed, so he sat back down behind her, spreading his legs so they slid around either side of her. He wrapped his arms around her waist and kissed her neck gently.

"Mmmm...that's nice," she purred.

"I'm glad you think so," he replied.

"What's up for the rest of your afternoon?" she asked.

"I have a bride coming over for a portrait shoot at four."

"I don't know how you do that. My sister was such a bitch of a bride."

"I have lots of patience. You'll see how that works as you get to know me," he said, lightly kissing her earlobe.

"You behave, sir. I just don't have time to take advantage of you today," she laughed.

"Yeah, I must admit, I didn't figure on you taking advantage of me today, that's for sure."

"Well, neither did I, but, you know, sometimes things just connect. And I don't believe in wasting time anymore."

"Well, that's quite obvious!" He exclaimed.

She disentangled herself and whirled around on her knees to face him. "No! This is what I was trying to say at the restaurant," she said. "Ever since I turned 30 I've felt like I need to be more aggressive with guys. But lately, I feel like things have speeded up for me." She paused for a moment, then pressed forward. "Have you ever watched how some candles burn? Some burn steadily all the way down, but some start giving off an average amount of light, then they hit a point where their light suddenly increases radically, just before they burn out. I've been feeling that my candle's been burning brightly now for some time. Lord, I must be making absolutely no sense!"

He rose on his knees to meet her eyes, and said, "You know, it's just possible that you're not a candle that's going to burn out, but just one who has found its proper brightness." He reached out and took her face into both hands, then pulled her to him for another kiss. While not as passion-filled as the ones earlier, it was deeper emotionally as she accepted his thoughts. She wrapped her arms around his neck and hugged him tightly.

"I hope you're right, Ren Alciatore. I hope you're right."

They both sat back down and watched the river traffic go by. First a tanker, riding high, on its way downriver, heading back out to the Middle East where it would be filled up again. Then came a number of barges, going both up and down river. They talked, arm-in-arm for some time, until Cee looked down at her watch and then stood up.

"Three o'clock. I need to get moving so I can go pick up the kids, and you have a bride coming."

"Ah, so you have a practical side as well," he smiled.

"But of course. I'm a radio producer. I may be many things, but I'm always punctual," she grinned.

He stood up, and pulled her into a quick embrace. She brushed her skirt off, and they walked down to the cars holding hands. They walked over to her car where he pressed her up against the door and kissed her deeply.

"Thanks for a lovely afternoon, cutie," he whispered in her ear as he gave her a final peck on the cheek.

"Let's do it again...real soon, Ren," she said, not without a bit of urgency in her voice.

Nodding, he kissed her hand and turned towards his car. She blew him one more kiss, jumped in, and proceeded to drive off. Ren got in the Mach One and sat there for just a minute. He composed his thoughts, started the car, and headed up to the access road that linked LaPlace with I-10. He had decided to take the faster route back into the city so he had time to get organized before his appointment.

CHAPTER EIGHTEEN
Shots Fired

Bubba laughed as he finished his po-boy at Smitty's Seafood Restaurant in Kenner.

"No, no, I love both kinds of crab, Louisiana and Maryland," he said to the woman at the table next to him.

"I don't like that seasoning, you know, that seasoning they put in their stuffed crab up there," the woman told him.

"Old Bay."

"Yeah, dat's the stuff! I like our crab boil here. Gimme Zatarain's any day," she said.

"I can't argue with that!" Bubba said, smiling. He was used to random people chatting him up when he was working. While it meant that he didn't get much time for his own thoughts during the day, it was important. He could develop trust with people who talked to him. He worked hard on this with his platoon, and it pleased him when he stopped in a place like Smitty's and received a warm welcome from the diners.

He left an extra dollar on the table for whomever would clean up, and headed out to his patrol vehicle. Bubba appreciated the size of the Ford Explorers that were assigned to patrol supervisors, but he wished the department would buy them for his officers as well. The use of the larger vehicles was always the subject of discussion and debate at the various FBI and Federal Law Enforcement education courses he'd attended in recent years. He pulled out of the parking lot of Smitty's, heading down West Esplanade Blvd., to Loyola Avenue. Another feature about his vehicle he appreciated was the good-quality "hands-free" mobile phone system built in. Without taking his eyes off the road or his hands off the wheel, Bubba instructed the phone to call Captain Mike DiFranco who supervised all patrol duties in the department. The distraction of the phone conversation contributed to Bubba not noticing the blue Hyundai that followed him. West Esplanade Blvd. was a busy street, so a car going the same way for as much as a mile was no big thing. Even when he turned off West Esplanade onto Loyola Drive, it was no big deal for the Hyundai to turn as well, then pull over so the car was next to him in the left lane.

Bubba took note of the car and did not sense anything beyond someone in Kenner going from place to place. Will Ryan's shielding was at a level where anyone glancing into the rented Hyundai would see just a fuzzy image of a white guy. As his chat with Captain DiFranco continued, the phone flashed, indicating an incoming call from his friend, Renard Alciatore. Bubba let the call roll to voicemail; he wasn't going to cut off a business conversation for a personal call.

He pushed the steering wheel button to end the call, but suddenly his left rear tire blew out, forcing him to slow down. He rolled on the rim for two blocks, and then pulled into the parking area of Kenner City Park. The area by the lagoon was empty, so he eased the Explorer to the side. Bubba radioed in that he had a flat, requesting a service crew come out and fix the tire. That call made, he climbed out of the vehicle, not noticing at all that the Hyundai pulled into the park entrance a block further north. He leaned inside the car again to retrieve his smartphone when he heard the screeching of tires as a Chevy Suburban accelerated half a block down on Loyola Drive, turning into the park.

Bubba enjoyed street patrol, but he was also an expert on anti-terrorism tactics both here in the US and in Japan. The fast movement of the Suburban approaching him was bad news; he dropped to the ground and rolled under the patrol car, emerging on the opposite side, pistol in hand. As he was coming up from underneath the car, Bubba heard the fast pops from an AK-47 assault rifle and felt the thumps as the rounds fired hit the side of his vehicle. Keeping his composure, he popped up from behind the car, aimed his standard-issue Smith & Wesson pistol, and fired three rounds at the passenger with the rifle. He then shifted aim and fired three more rounds through the windshield at the driver. The Suburban swerved and skidded into the park lagoon.

Bubba remained behind his vehicle, pistol aimed at the Suburban, not relaxing a muscle. He moved from the rear of the SUV to the side, using the vehicle as a shield, the passenger in the Suburban emerged, firing two shots from a pump-action shotgun. He was wading out of the edge of the lagoon, still trying to use his vehicle to get some cover. Bubba popped over the hood after the shotgun discharges and put three rounds right in his attacker's chest. The shotgun fell to the ground and the attacker followed right behind it, legs splashing in the water.

Bubba immediately kicked the shotgun away from the attacker, who lay either dead or dying. Pistol cocked and ready, he waded to the driver's side of the Suburban, where he found the driver, slumped over, either unconscious or dead. Satisfied the immediate threat was over, he pushed the microphone unit clipped to his shoulder.

"110."

"110," the operator replied.

"Signal 108, shots fired. Situation is under control, two suspects down. Send two EMS units for suspects. Officer unhurt. Repeat, two suspects down, officer unhurt."

"Roger, 110," the female voice said. She knew his position from the satellite tracking system installed in the trunk of the vehicle. "EMS, backup, and Kenner 1 on the way."

Bubba sighed. Kenner 1 was the chief, his boss. "Roger. Standing by."

Bubba opened the door of his unit and sat back down. Exhaling again, he instinctively reached for his cell phone. His first call was to home, leaving a message on the home machine.

"Hi, honey, it's me. I've had a bit of excitement today, but if you see anything on the news, don't worry, I'm fine. Really and truly. Will call you later. Love ya, bye."

He ended the call and took another deep breath. Bubba then called a reporter at Channel 6 to whom he owed a favor and told him where to come to get a scoop. Those two tasks done, he instinctively hit the button to retrieve voicemail. Listening to Ren's message from just a few minutes earlier, he began to get the post-trauma shakes. Thumbing in Ren's number, he heard the call roll to voicemail.

"Konnichiwa, Ren-san," he said respectfully. "Thanks for the kind message. Seems as you were on the money on that one, but unfortunately I didn't hear your message until it was all over. Check the Channel 6 news this evening for details, or try to call me, if I'm still sober. Once I'm done with de-briefing on this, I'm going over to the pub and having several pints of Guinness. Thanks again for your intuition, Ren-san. Talk to you soon."

He heard the sirens of the units coming up the street as he closed his eyes and tried to settle his shaking, not at all noticing the infuriated young man pulling out of the park in the Hyundai.

***

"...And that's all we know now. Scott. Lt. Watanabe was looked over by paramedics at the scene and Chief Moscone drove him home personally. Both of the lieutenant's attackers were killed in the shoot-out and Kenner detectives are sorting through the scene now. This is WDSU Rapid Response Reporter David Brown. Back to you, Scott."

Ren flipped the TV off with the remote and reached for the phone to call Bubba's house. "Didi? Hi, yeah! Yeah, I'm doing fine, thanks. No, don't wake him. I just caught the news. Oh, he told you? Yeah, I figure it wasn't more than ten minutes before they attacked him. Weird isn't the word for it, Didi. Yes, I know. Well tell him to call me when he gets up if his head isn't pounding too hard... thanks love. Talk to you soon, bye!"

Ren tossed the cordless phone aside and reached for his very full glass of Bushmills which was sitting on his desk. He took a big swallow and shivered as the whiskey flowed through his veins. He turned his back to his workstation as he heard the chime on his phone from Kik.

It was Isis. He responded.

"Hi. I'm on my way to becoming very drunk."

"I don't blame you. May I join you?"

"You bet! C'mon right over."

"Give me 15 mins"

"You're serious?"

"Very."

"OK. Come on over. :-)"

"Bye."

Ren didn't know whether he'd been put on or not, but he didn't have much time to think about that, though, as Twitter chimed with a Direct Message.

Ren, I just finished watching a replay of the news. Jesus!

Wynterbreeze this time.

"No shit, love. And you don't even know the whole story yet!"

"What's the whole story?"

"I'm too drunk to tell it now... can we get together tomorrow?"

"Let's...xoxo"

He stood up and headed upstairs to splash some water on his face and comb his hair. The part of his mind that should have been very excited that Cecilia McIntyre was coming over to his house had been blunted by the booze. But another part of him did remember that he should be at least presentable. He had just about reached a satisfactory level of "presentable" when the doorbell rang.

He hurried down the stairs and opened the door,

revealing Cecilia in a t-shirt, shorts, and sandals.

"I hope you don't mind me barging in," she said as she grinned.

Ren bowed low, as an old family retainer would do. "Not at all, ma'amoiselle, come right in." Ren made a sweeping gesture of welcome.

Cee giggled. "You're drunk."

"Oui, ma'amoiselle, that I am," Ren spluttered, smiling. "But I am still a gentleman and I will do my utmost to respect and defend your dignity and honor."

"Why, I am flattered, kind sir," she responded, again grinning widely. "But don't try too hard with that." She wrapped her arms around him and kissed him on the cheek. She pulled him to her as her kisses migrated from his cheek to his lips. As she reached his lips she stood on her tiptoes and kissed him deeply, her hands reaching behind him to grab his butt and squeeze him there gently.

He responded as most men would. She sensed the bulge and shifted her position so that her thigh stroked against it gently. His arms wrapped around her and he held her closely for a minute. His hands then went in opposite directions; his fingers running through her hair, while the other to her butt to caress her there and to pull her hips into his a little tighter.

Cecilia let out a faint moan, then kissed him again, touching his cheek then running her fingernails up and down his arm and shoulder. She broke the kiss after a while and stood back from him a little, smiling.

"I feel a lot better knowing you're OK," she said, still smiling as she regarded him.

"Yes, and you do feel pretty good," he said in response, leering at her a little.

She smacked him playfully on the shoulder. "You're silly. Show me the house."

"Cool. Bedroom first or last?"

She giggled: "You decide. But remember I said 'show me' not 'do me'."

"As ma'amoiselle wishes," he said, bowing as he had done when he first answered the door.

She giggled again and he proceeded to show her around

the downstairs rooms.

"So this is where the assault on my employer takes place," she said as she spun herself around in Ren's computer-room chair.

"Yup. But the 'assault' actually took place in the minds of myself, Trip, and Nick, and usually in a bar or coffee-place. This is just where the server resides."

"How come a photographer got hooked onto computers to this extent?"

"Well, I am kind of a mutant in that regard. I was always good at math and computers in high school, even though my heart was in taking photos. I think that's why my daddy agreed to allow me to study photography; because he always talked about how technology would change the business and such. That, and because I figured I could get a 'real' job if I ended up losing my shirt in photography."

"Cool. How did you manage to get this wonderful house, Ren? Something in the family for years?"

"Would you believe, I was driving by one day and saw it up for sale."

"You're kidding."

"Nope. I've always loved this neighborhood, so I took down the agent's number from the sign and the rest is history. Daddy helped with the down-payment so my note wouldn't be outrageous."

"What a nice dad!" she exclaimed as she laughed.

"Yes, he is that, to be sure." He extended his hand to her and her up from his chair. She came into his arms and nuzzled at his neck before kissing him again.

"So... let's see upstairs." She was beaming the naughtiest grin.

He led her up the stairs and showed her the three bedrooms there.

"I use this room as a dressing/changing-room for my clients. They like it better if I am downstairs so that they can come up and have more privacy when changing. It has its own bathroom; the other two share a bathroom. My bedroom is the one on the end."

"Makes sense." She turned the knob on the door to the

middle bedroom, but it was locked. She turned to him with a questioning expression on her face.

"That's my meditation room. It's my private space, so I keep it locked. Mothers-of-brides can sometimes get curious and wander around up here," he explained, chuckling.

"Show me?"

Ren smiled, then reached into his pocket for the key. He slid it into the old-fashioned lock and turned it, then opened the door so Cecilia could enter the room.

It was the smallest of the three bedrooms, sparsely-furnished and with a large armchair on one corner, several bookcases along one wall, and another wooden chair in the other corner. In the center of the room was a small table shaped like one cube stacked upon another. A single white candle stood in the center.

"I was expecting a bunch of statues and one of those mini-altars in here, since you're Catholic."

"Oh, that's never been my style," Ren replied. I prefer to sit and think and relax. I usually do that out on the lakefront but this room is handy for me when I'm not in the mood to go out there or when the weather isn't co-operating."

"I can feel your energy all over this room," she said, as her breathing became a little heavier. "It's nice." The intensity of the moment was building up inside her, and she subconsciously began to caress her left nipple as she slowly turned around in the room.

"Would you like something to drink?" asked Ren.

"Yeah, that would be great." With the intensity of the moment broken, they left the room. Ren locked the door and led the way down to the kitchen.

"I got a couple of different kinds of beer in the 'fridge," he said. "And there's a bottle or two of wine in there. I've also got some reds if that's more to your liking."

"Mmm... some white would be nice. I'm not much of a wine snob so I'll let you choose." Cecilia looked at him with an intense smile.

Ren removed a bottle of white wine from the fridge.

"This is a Riesling from Eberbach Abbey, in the German Rheingau region. If you ever see the designation 'Kabinett' on a

German wine, indicating the driest of the different types of 'quality' wines, that name originated in Eberbach."

"You don't go into all that detail when you're in a bar, do you?" She asked, giggling.

Ren blushed.

"Shit, that was a bit douchey of me. My apologies. I've been drinking," he said, bowing.

"OK, you're forgiven. Are you having some of this wine?"

"I think I'll stick with my whiskey," he replied, toasting her with his glass.

"Good idea. You're not supposed to mix grain and grape. What kind of whiskey is it?"

"Bushmills, the single-malt. I have a bottle of 21-year-old, but that is for sharing with someone else, rather than for drinking alone."

"OK, anyone in particular?" She asked.

"Hmmm...Oh, I see what you mean! No, I mean, a bottle of good whiskey is an invitation to, at a minimum, good conversation," he said, smiling.

"Oh yes, I agree with that sentiment." She sipped her wine, and began to run her tongue over the rim of her glass seductively.

He matched her stare and smiled in return, then eyed her from head to toe. As his gaze arrived at her feet she kicked off one sandal and ran her foot up his bare foot and massaged his calf.

"Nice toes," he said as he admired her neon-blue nail polish.

"Thanks," she blushed. "The more conservative women in the office tend to get shocked by my choice of colors."

"Well, blue is the color most associated with the Blessed Virgin Mary, so just tell them you've developed a new sense of dedication," he said, with a smirk.

"Oh yeah, right. That'll go over big in an evangelical ministry office!"

She laughed then finished off her wine and held her glass out to Ren for a refill.

He grabbed the wine bottle and leaned towards her to pour. Once he had filled her glass, he leaned across her to set the bottle down and then moved to kiss her on the cheek. She turned at the same time and their lips met gently, just a peck, then another, then another, until they parted to kiss deeply.

She broke the kiss momentarily, stood up in the kitchen, and pulled her t-shirt off over her head. She unhooked her front-fastening bra and let her clothing fall to the floor. She sat in his lap, wrapped her arms around him, and kissed him again as she rubbed her bare breasts into his chest. She pulled away from him a little again, this time to remove his t-shirt. She then pressed close to him, allowing her now very erect nipples to brush his. Ren was now squirming in his seat as she moved her body against him now in slow circular rhythm to continue to arouse his passions.

After another sip of wine she set the glass back down and kissed his cheek, ear, then nibbled on his neck; letting her fingernails scratch firmly into his back. He arched at her touch and she reached her hands to her breasts to rub her nipples against his nipples as he moaned.

That was enough for Renard Alciatore. He slid her hands to her sides, stood her up, got himself upright, then scooped her into his arms and carried her back upstairs to his bedroom as she flung her arms around his neck. They giggled as her other sandal fell to the floor as they made their way to the bed. Ren laid her down gently and ran his tongue quickly from her left ankle and up her calf to her inner thigh. She continued her circular motion, as she had in the kitchen, as she sighed contentedly. Ren reached for the snap on her denim shorts, unzipped them, then hooked his thumbs into the waistbands of both her shorts and her panties beneath them and pulled them both down and off.

He slid back up to lie beside her on the bed and they kissed again, passionately. Her hand wandered to his crotch to stroke his erection through his shorts. He responded and ran his tongue over her breasts, down her stomach, until it found her wetness. She continued to moan as he tasted her and his tongue picked up speed. It wasn't long before her moans turned to cries of ecstasy as the rush of orgasm washed over her. As her body continued to throb and gyrate from his ministrations, he sat up for a moment to remove his shorts. He took his erection in his hand and rubbed it over her as he moaned again, building up a second time. Just as she began to cry out, he entered her. The orgasmic wave flooded her again, more intense than the first, drowning her in orgasm.

It was only a few lunges before Ren felt the pressure building up within himself and he exploded within Cecilia, calling her name and pounding his hips against hers. As his orgasm subsided he collapsed on top of her then rolled over to one side as she kissed him and pulled him close to her, wrapping her leg around his.

The combination of alcohol and sex immediately betrayed itself as he involuntarily began to yawn. He laughed, a trifle embarrassed.

"Oh, jeez, I'm sorry about that, Cee. It's certainly not the company!"

"I know, sweetie. Just lie back and relax." You're exhausted, and I didn't do much to help that."

"Yeah. But it was damn fun. Thanks, Cee."

She kissed him deeply again. "You're welcome."

Yawning again, he said, "I can't keep my eyes open."

"I know. Stay here, Ren. Go to sleep. I'll let myself out."

He smiled weakly, closed his eyes, and was asleep almost immediately. She stood to gaze at him for a few moments in the darkness before gathering her clothing. She dressed, left the house, and drove off.

Celia McIntyre was much too pre-occupied in enjoying the afterglow of sex to notice the dark blue Isuzu Rodeo down Moss Street whose engine started just as she drove her yellow VW Beetle away from Ren's house. Anita Delatorre, who was behind the wheel of the rented Isuzu, tried to remain calm and process the scene. Anita had driven to the bayou area, primarily to evaluate any wards or defenses that might have been placed around Ren's home/office. While her stalking did not reveal any magic around the house, she just observed Hadley's chief of staff leaving the home of one of the ministry's enemies. Well, she thought, tomorrow will be an interesting day at the office.

CHAPTER NINETEEN

Marconi and the Lakefront

“Jeez, you look wasted,” Mike O’Donnell exclaimed as Ren sat down at the University Center cafeteria. “I feel wasted. As soon as I heard from Bubba last night I started on the whiskey. Then I had some company over; I didn’t stop.” Ren laughed, “My company was my friend Isis, by the way.”

“No shit! Well part of me wants to press you for all the gory details but it would just depress me today.”

“You’re a trip, as priests go.”

“I’ll take that as the compliment it was intended to be, of course,” said Mike through a sarcastic grin. “I’m glad you had a little fun, though.”

“Yeah, it would have been better if I had not been so drunk.”

“Well, you’ll just have to do better next time. Ready for a bit of instruction?”

“Yeah.”

“Let’s go for a walk up on the levee,” Mike said, grabbing his coffee as he stood up.

They left the building and headed up to the levee which separated the campus from Lakeshore Drive. Mike broke the silence after a couple of minutes: “Well, it’s time for us to discuss a new topic. The night we first met, you were being engaged in a formal magic duel, Ren.”

“Yeah, I’m aware of that.”

“Those duels are controlled by very strict rules, which we call the Combat Protocols. The Protocols were developed a very long time ago and for two main reasons. The first was to prevent indiscriminate challenges among people with Talents. There had been entirely too many little 'street-fights' among us, and they were costing the lives of the best of us."

"If that were the case, I'll bet the second reason for the rules was to keep those duels from drawing public attention, right?" Ren asked.

"You got it, grasshopper. Duels with swords and other weapons were difficult enough to keep quiet. Can you imagine the spin-doctoring that had to be done to keep a magic duel under wraps? Well, that's the background to the Combat Protocols. They lay out in detail the behavior expected of all parties involved; from the time a challenge is issued to the point when the duel is concluded."

"Sounds complicated."

Mike stopped walking and gazed out over the lake.

"Not really," he said. "Open up to me and I'll give you the full Protocols."

Ren nodded, closed his eyes, and opened his mind to his Teacher. He absorbed the information being transmitted from Mike. After two minutes of connection with him, Ren opened his eyes.

"That doesn't seem so bad."

Mike chuckled: "Told ya!"

"One question: what is the incentive for someone with Talents to obey the Protocols? Surely there are rogues out there who don't respect the rules?"

"Yes, there are occasional problems, but not as many as you might expect. You have by now deduced that I have an affiliation with a group that is involved with these issues."

Ren nodded.

"Well, that group is an Assembly of some very experienced people who provide advice and mediate disputes. In fact, the Delegates appointed to this body come from all walks of life, as well as from a number of religious and ethnic backgrounds. The Assembly enforces the Protocols and deals with anyone who violates them."

"How are the problems dealt with?"

"We hunt them down, to the far corners of the earth if necessary, and eliminate them."

Ren started to laugh, mainly out of disbelief. But seeing his Teacher's serious expression, he stopped suddenly.

"You're serious aren't you?"

"Very much so, Ren. This is not something to be fucked with. One of the Oaths that the Delegates take upon becoming part of the Assembly is to uphold all the Laws and Protocols. There are rewards for both the individual Delegate and for those he represents. The system has worked extremely well for quite some time."

"I see. But I take it that this Assembly isn't like Congress, is it?"

"Hardly." Mike laughed as they resumed their stroll. "No, it isn't exactly a democratic institution, but it works. When you're ready I'll present you to the Assembly and you'll fully understand how things work. In the meantime, if you feel the need to 'call your Congressman', just give me a shout."

"Gotcha. Well I don't plan on challenging anyone to any duels, but thanks for the knowledge."

"Well, I'm pleased to see you are exercising some common sense on that score. And that leads to the other thing I want to discuss. When I barged into that little encounter on your front lawn, I placed you under my protection. The reason I did so was to keep you from being chewed up and spit out by anybody who chose to do so. It's a standard thing while you are in training. With kids, it's really easy, since we simply impose restrictions upon them that block their ability to mess with each other. With adults it's a little different. The Protocol of Protection is as specific as the Combat Protocols.

Anyway, without going into all the legal mumbo-jumbo with you at the moment, once I had placed you under Protection I was obligated to instruct you and to prepare you to use your Talents to their fullest. One of the other obligations of the Teacher is to determine when his student is ready to go out into the world on his own. It's a solemn obligation, Ren, and one I am prepared to exercise with you now."

"You mean, you can't teach me any longer?"

"Oh goodness not at all! But, I must formally release you from my Protection." Mike stopped again on the levee and turned to face Ren. "Renard Alciatore, I hereby declare you to be aware of and trained in the use of your Talents. As such, I remove my Sigil of Protection from your aura and admonish you to take full charge of your life. May the Author of Lights shine her grace upon you and grant you guidance all of your days."

Mike concluded the Declaration and signed Ren with a three-fold benediction of a pentagram, a triangle, and a solar cross.

"There. That's done. You are now at risk of Challenge, Ren. But I firmly believe you can handle yourself."

"Well, I am a bit confused by all this, Mike. But I do understand you can't hold my hand forever."

"That's a good way to sum it up, my friend. Always remember, though, that we are here to help you down the path. You must choose that path, of course. But we'll gladly give you guidance along the way."

"Thanks Mike. I just hope I don't run into any bad guys right away."

"Me neither." Mike chuckled. "Look, I've got to get back. Catch up with you later?"

"Yeah. I think I'll stay up here for a while and go over those Protocols in my mind again."

"Cool. I'll call you this evening."

"See ya, Mike."

The priest trotted down the bank of the levee and walked briskly back to his office. Ren sat on the levee and gazed out over the lake for some time, assimilating in his mind all the information that had been passed to him from Mike that morning.

***

Jay Hadley was also assimilating information, and he didn't like what he was hearing.

Anita began to say something, then held back. "Well honey," she said, "what matters now is how we handle it. She did sign the standard Ministry Confidentiality Agreement, right?"

Hadley nodded.

"Good. Well, we have grounds to terminate her, then. Let me handle this, dear, you've got too much on your plate now as it is. I want you to stay on target for making your next deadline. The "course enhancement bundles" for homeschoolers are going to be quite lucrative. I've already made some calls and I've got a new producer coming in from Dallas next week. By the weekend both Cecilia and Alciatore will no longer be problems to the Ministry."

"Dear God, Anita. What do you mean by that?"

"Why, sugar, you don't honestly think we can allow this to continue, do you? But don't worry about the details, Jay. You do what you do best; I'll clean up the mess."

Jay stood up at his desk, horrified. "You're going to kill them? Oh my God, you killed those others, didn't you? This is unbelievable! You can't..."

Anita stood up and slammed her hand onto the desk. "Not only can I do this, Reverend Hadley, but I will! I've been instructed by my home office to deal with problems on this issue, and I most definitely will deal with them! It's your stupidity that generated this whole mess, remember? This is so far out of your hands it's not funny. You're under contract, and management wants that contract fulfilled. We're talking about a large amount of money here, Jay, and my career as well. You will sit your ass down and behave, mister. This will be taken care of by me, and on my terms!"

Jay recoiled from Anita's words and slumped back into his chair. "Yes, Anita. I understand." He sighed, aware that his acquiescence sealed the death warrants of two more people.

***

Ren lingered atop the levee for a while, and then headed back to his car by the University Center building. It was getting closer to lunchtime, but his body was still not very interested in food. He grabbed one of his Nikon digital cameras; he had decided he would walk around for a while and take a few photographs. A college campus is a great place for people-watching, he thought. He made his way from the UC to the Earl K. Long Library building, then over to the Science building, along his way shooting photos of both the buildings and of the people coming and going around them. Ren thought at first that his age would immediately isolate him as a non-student, but he had forgotten that urban schools such as UNO attracted students of all ages. He shot several pictures of a very pretty blonde woman in her thirties who looked like a mom returning to school herself, now that her kids were in school. He smiled at her and gestured with his camera, mutely asking permission. She smiled back and nodded, and Ren continued to snap several shots of both her and passersby.

Ren's body and his overall disposition had greatly improved after an hour or so of wandering around, so he jumped back into his car and drove to his first afternoon appointment; an indoor shoot at a large Uptown home. The clan matriarch was approaching ninety and the children had decided that a family portrait would be the perfect birthday present. Ren was in-and-out in about an hour and a half, leaving more than enough time for his second job of the afternoon, which was to photograph a newly-renovated house in the Irish Channel. Ren had already shot "before" pictures of the house several months ago. He would send those pictures, along with "after" shots he would be doing today, to the Preservation Resource Center. The PRC had several programs to encourage home-buyers to consider moving back to the city rather than out to the suburbs. This renovation was so good, the PRC might even consider adding this house to their shotgun-home tour.

Ren stood in front of the small house and admired the quality of the workmanship. These houses were called "shotguns" because of the linear construction. One room opened into the next, with no hallway. If all the doors were opened, front to back, you could fire a shotgun from the front and it would go straight out the back. He shot pictures from various angles but none of them really gave him the feeling that he had captured the soul of the property. Maybe I'm just hung-over, he thought. He set the camera back onto its tripod, closed his eyes, and began to meditate. His mind now a little clearer, he lowered his shields slightly and turned his attention again to the house.

With his shields now relaxed, the house took on a fresh glow. Ren picked up his camera again and began to shoot more pictures. It was as if the house itself was telling him which angles would best capture its essence. As he imagined how he would Photoshop some of his pictures into black-and-white, he lowered his shields even more and resumed shooting. Suddenly, Ren became aware of another presence nearby. He felt no immediate danger, so left his shields in their lowered state and looked around. Nobody on the street but himself, he thought, and no sounds to indicate anyone in the backyard. Still, the sensation of someone being nearby would not leave him. He sighed and continued with his shoot, while making a note of the feeling so that he could question Mike about it later. Ren concluded his assignment and gathered up his equipment to reload it into the Jeep.

"It could have been a lot of things," said Mike O'Donnell, as they chatted on the phone. "Once you dropped your shields, you opened yourself up to all sorts of psychic input."

"OK, I'll buy that," Ren said as he maneuvered his Jeep from Uptown to the Lakefront. "But can you take a guess as to what specifically this could have been?"

"Given that is was an old house, and you have always held a passion for things historical, my bet would be that those impressions you received are something from the past. Perhaps someone who used to live there had strong Talents and you're feeling the residual powers from that."

"I wonder why I've never felt anything like that before."

"Bear in mind you are still developing your Talents, Ren. Besides, perhaps you did, and you simply didn't realize it."

"Huh?"

"You know, critics have often said that you know how to capture inner sensations within your photographs, whether they are of people or of inanimate objects."

"Never thought of it that way," Ren murmured.

"Well, once I've got some of the business I've got to do completed, Ren, I'll introduce you to a friend who is better than I am at past-life and historical resonances."

"Sounds cool. Anyway, thanks Mike."

"No problem. Anyway, where are you heading this afternoon?"

"Oh, no place special. I'm meeting JJ up at the lakefront.

"Ahh... the fascinating Janet Julianne"

"I haven't forgotten my promise that the three of us go

out," Ren replied with a chuckle. "Talk to you later."

"Bye."

JJ was perched on the trunk of her car as Ren pulled his Jeep next to hers. M&L – Marconi and Lakefront – was empty except for the two of them, which was unusual for such a pretty afternoon.

"Bonjour, mon ami," he said softly as he kissed her on the cheek.

"Bonjour," JJ replied, pulling him to her and giving him an affectionate hug. "How are you doing?"

"Better now," he said. He took her hand and led her towards the water's edge, before briefly relating the events of his previous afternoon and evening.

"Hmm... sounds like the gal knows how to take care of a man," she quipped. "Do you really think that what happened to Bubba is related to all this shit with you and your website?

"Looks that way to me," Ren replied. They were walking alongside the sea wall now, slowly.

"Well, I'm not going to gloat and 'I-told-you-so' just yet. This shit is too serious for that."

"It sure is," Ren agreed. "But there's more I want to talk with you about all this. JJ, do you believe in psychic ability?"

"Well, Ren, my engineering training almost always forces me to look for a logical and scientific explanation for most phenomena, but I don't rule out the possibility that we have only begun to tap the power of the human mind."

"What if I were to tell you that I have some very powerful and psychic Talents?"

They continued their walk in brief silence before she answered. "I'd say that it would make sense, given your ability to 'read' me and my emotions. I'm sure I'm not the only one you've been able to do that with. You can get inside my mind and make my skin crawl sometimes!" JJ laughed, tossing her head back.

Ren stopped walking and gestured for her to sit on the bench they had been approaching. They both sat down and he took her hand in his.

"Close your eyes for a moment, babe. I want to show you something. Good. Now take some deep breaths..."

JJ inhaled and exhaled deeply at Ren's request. As she

made one inhale of breath, Ren reached out to her mind and touched her.

"Don't jump back," he sent, via his mind to hers. "This isn't going to hurt. I need to do this to convince you of the truth of the story. Keep breathing, sweetie..."

Ren proceeded to send her the full story of his Talents. The images flowed slowly at first, but he increased the speed gradually as he sensed she became better able to absorb them. As he got to his previous evening he finally spoke, softly, "Relax babe... did you get it all?"

"Renard Alciatore, that was incredible! How did you do that? No, wait, don't try to explain it. I can't believe you can do that!"

"It's still kind of spooky to me, too," he admitted. "But it works. And I'm worried babe. These abilities have spilled over and are posing a danger to the people I care about."

JJ stood up and began walking again, and Ren followed. "I'm not so sure that's a cause-and-effect at work here. Shit was happening even before you knew you had these abilities, and that shit was related to that stupid website of yours. If anything, your Talents have actually helped rather than hurt your friends. Look at Bubba: I'll bet he managed to pick up on your concern when you called, even though he didn't talk to you."

"I suppose. Still..."

"Still, schmill. I'll admit it's an incredible situation, but it's very plausible. After all, there are so many things about the mind we just don't yet understand."

"So you don't think it's all crazy?"

"Well I might have thought that if you had simply told me the story. But that was one helluva practical demonstration just now!"

"OK then. But what now?"

"Use your Talents, love. Just like you use your skills as a photographer. Have fun with them, and kick ass with them if you ever have to."

Ren smiled and hugged her closely. "Thanks babe. I needed that encouragement." He gently squeezed at her butt as he kissed her cheek.

"Beast!" she said, laughing. "Now get yourself home, and

I'll do the same!"

"Yeah, kiss the kiddos for me babe."

"Bye Ren."

CHAPTER TWENTY

Never Change

“I really used to enjoy New Orleans,” thought Will Ryan. “Lately though, this city has become more trouble than it's worth.” Ryan's mind flashed back to his previous conversation with Anita Delatorre as he eased his rental car out of the Starbucks parking lot.

"Well, sugar, I have some very upset bosses - and they're upset with us both. You've never let them down before, which is about the only reason we are both not back there having to explain ourselves.”

"My business is not an exact science, Anita. There are dynamics involved in each job. And you, as an employer, have not given me full details as to what is going on behind the scenes here!"

"Yes Will, I know this, and I have made the situation very clear to my superiors. They are aware that the situation has escalated to a much different level as a result of the discovery of Renard Alciatore's Talents." Anita paused momentarily to take a sip of her latte. "My superiors have always been results-oriented, so the next task has to be completed quickly and efficiently. There is no margin for error here, Will. You have a week to get the job done, so don't force things. I will also make sure that you have more than sufficient opportunities to get this done."

"Very well, love. I'll get on it right away. Now, are you quite sure you have given me all the details on this one?"

Anita sighed. "Yes. The brief I've prepared is very comprehensive; not only in personal details, but it also includes a great amount of background information. I know there's a lot in there that you should have been given sooner in this process Will, but I was instructed not to. You'll also find that your fee for this job has been increased. It's my boss' way of expressing his appreciation for your patience."

"How gracious..."

"Try not to let the sarcasm drip too much, Will. That increase is a message as well - good performance will be rewarded; poor performance won't be tolerated."

"On that note, love, I will take my leave. I have reading to catch up on." Will Ryan arose from the table and walked out.

The brief was indeed detailed, right down to specific destinations the target would very likely visit over the next three days. The document all but guaranteed the target would be en route to these places, almost down to the minute of the day.

But he was not going to be dwelling on the big picture this morning - there was work to be done right away. As he hit Causeway Boulevard, he accelerated his car to match the speed of the others there, and then shuddered again at the thought of the threats Anita had implied. On the face of it, this was, or should be, a straightforward hit, with little or no complications. But this target was involved with Renard Alciatore, and Ryan's track record when dealing with Alciatore had not been good.

That was about to change, however. Ryan picked up the subject's car at the south side of the Lake Pontchartrain Causeway and followed it across the lake, to Mandeville. The destination of the errand in the brief was accurate; Ryan proceeded to drive ahead, returning to the 24-mile bridge. He paid the three-dollar toll and casually drove southbound. About halfway to the south shore, he chose a target at random and followed it. Will closed his eyes briefly and visualized a break in the radiator hose of the car in front of him. Immediately, steam began to rise from the hood of the car and the driver pulled over to the side of the bridge and stopped. The driver got out and walked towards the emergency call-box not far in front of the car and Ryan passed him slowly and carefully. He then eased his car into the next crossover between the northbound and southbound bridges, not far from the breakdown, and parked.

Once he alighted from his car, Ryan immediately began

to move his arms in a sweeping gesture and focused his mind on the area around the broken-down vehicle. With his arms still outstretched, he began a spell:

"Daylight glow,
Breezes blow,
Invisibility confound,
All those around."

Ryan muttered the verse three times, focusing his thoughts and energy on the breakdown a hundred yards to the south of him. A haze fell over both the car and its driver, becoming thicker each time he chanted the words, until the car and driver appeared not even to exist.

Once the steam had dissipated sufficiently for the driver of the disabled car to open the hood, he could see clearly that the radiator hose had come undone and the car had overheated. He continued to inspect the engine for any other damage until a service van arrived.

A yellow VW Beetle was moving swiftly along the southbound span at 85mph. Ryan focused, and the Beetle accelerated faster, to 90mph. Ryan closed his eyes and then clenched both fists in front of him. The Beetle's front tire decompressed with a loud "bang", and the driver did well to control her vehicle and steer it to the side of the bridge. That work was for naught, though, as the Beetle stopped dead, crashing into something unseen.

Will Ryan nodded grimly, as the driver of the Beetle was ejected, flying up and over the parapet and into Lake Pontchartrain. Casting out with his Talents, Ryan should have felt his target's silver cord part, but the shock of impact combined with crashing onto the surface of the water below the bridge was too intense. Ryan drove off, certain his work ended Cecilia McIntyre's life.

***

Janet Julianne Garrison was driving home when she heard the news on the radio:

“Traffic is still stopped on the Lake Pontchartrain Causeway, two hours later, as divers are in the water around the bridge in an attempt to recover the body of the owner of of a yellow Volkswagen beetle. Our sources on the bridge say the vehicle belongs to Cecilia McIntyre, an employee of Jay Hadley Ministries, whose offices are located in Lakeway Center.”

The shock of the news almost caused JJ to have an accident of her own.

"Oh fuck!" she exclaimed as she reached for her phone, hitting the photo that would summon her sister. "Hey, Vicky! You hear about that wreck on the Causeway? Yeah, well, the woman that was killed is... um... was Ren's new girlfriend. Yup, that one! Look, Joe's in Dallas till Friday. Get the kids for me, sis, I'm going to look for Ren. I don't want him to be alone right now. Love ya, sweetie." She ended the call and looked at her watch.

“Fuck-fuck-fuck!"

JJ turned into Canal Boulevard and headed towards Lakeshore Drive. She slowed down as she approached the intersection with Marconi, but didn't see either of Ren's cars.

"Fuck!"

She turned down Marconi and headed along the western edge of City Park, then turned onto City Park Avenue, following the northern boundary of the park. As soon as she turned right onto Moss Street she could see him, sitting on the bayou. She parked her car in front of Ren's house and walked slowly to where he was sitting as he stared out over the water, then sat next to him.

"I heard what happened, on the radio."

There was no reply.

"Ren, you don’t know how sorry I am."

Still no response.

"Do you want me to leave?"

"No," he said, finally. "I'm sorry JJ, I didn't mean to shut you out."

"Yes you did.” She smiled, weakly. "But it's all right. I understand. I've broken up with lovers before, sweetie. But I've never lost one. I can tell she was a more than a little special to you."

"Thing is," said Ren after a long pause, "I didn't really know her all that well. I mean, most of our conversations were on the computer. But I still felt something strong. And when I finally met her..."

"Yeah, I've had similar sensations," JJ said. She sighed as if lost for what to say. "This is a terrible thing, Ren. Did she have much family?"

"Her parents and a couple of brothers and sisters."

JJ took his hand in hers. "Ren, I know you were attracted to her. I could feel it from what you shared with me about your Talents..."

"Mike says I need to learn to pick and choose what I share with people about those," he said, a short sigh revealing a little embarrassment.

JJ responded with a snort.

"Excuse me, but, I am bloody well not 'people'. I am me!

"Ain't that the truth!" Ren said, with a half-smile.

"Well, we've talked about your amorous liaisons before, sweetie. But this time I got more detail than I've ever beaten out of you in the past."

She gave him a droll look as she said that, and this started him smiling, then giggling slightly.

"Oh, JJ, thanks for being you." He raised her hand to his lips and kissed it gently.

"Anytime, love. Anytime. Hopefully not under such tragic circumstances as this, though."

She disengaged her hand from his and pulled him to her to hug him closely. Ren responded by leaning his head on her shoulder. They remained in silence, for several minutes, as she just lightly ran her hand up and down his back. He sighed and raised his head to kiss her cheek, but as he did so she turned her face towards him and his kiss landed on the edge of her lips. He tried to back out of it for a second, but JJ turned a little more and returned his kiss, lightly. Their eyes met. She made it quite clear by her actions that to go a step further was not only allowed, but encouraged. She closed her eyes and ran her hand up behind his head to pull his mouth to hers and kissed him, caressing his lips with her tongue while she ran her hand through his hair.

Ren was at first surprised by the passion that had stirred within him from JJ, but he forgot his sadness and lost himself in the moment, returning her kisses and caresses with equal passion. They both stretched out on the cool grass and she rolled from her side to lie on top of him. The pressure of her body awoke his manhood; she encouraged it by grinding her hips on to his, gently as she stroked him softly with her thigh.

Suddenly, he sat up, whispering, “Cee...”

JJ held him tight, as the lights of a car passing along Moss Street reminded them of where they were. JJ climbed off him, brushed her skirt as she stood up, and reached out to help him to his feet.

"We should go inside," she said with a smile in her eyes.

He nodded, wordlessly, as she wrapped her arm around him and led him into the house. She kicked off her shoes and stretched out on the couch in his office, while Ren went to the kitchen to fetch a bottle of wine.

"Lost in thought?" Ren asked, handing her a glass of Pinot Noir.

"Just worried about you,” she answered, enjoying the aroma of the wine.

"I'm glad you are here for me." He pulled her up a bit and sat down, letting her head fall into his lap.

"Joe's out of town, you know," she said, still staring at the ceiling.

"Who's got the kids?"

"Vicky."

"Then you can stay a while, can't you?" He looked at her and kissed her again.

"Sure," she replied, smiling.

Ren awoke the next morning to the sound of activity in his kitchen. He decided to stay in bed. The kitchen grew quiet, as JJ returned to the bedroom, clad only in one of Ren's t-shirts; a souvenir of a soccer tournament.

"Good morning, sleepyhead," she said as she kneeled on the foot of the bed.

"Hey, gimme a break, it's only seven o'clock!"

"Sad, sad. I've been up since six." She smiled climbed under the covers with him.

"I made coffee and a little something to eat."

"Looks like I've got a little something to eat right here," he said.

"Beast!"

"Moi?"

"Oui, cherie. Toi." She kissed him.

"JJ, I..." She put a finger to his lips.

“Shhh...we don’t have to talk about this. I’m OK with crashing next to you for the night. We're friends, Renard Alciatore."

"OK, I'll leave it at that. What's in store for you today?"

"I'll run home, change, and go into work, I guess. What about you?"

"I'm shooting some pictures over at Oak Alley today."

"Not the nicest house, but you can't beat the trees."

"F'sure. as long as the weather holds out."

"Yeah, I agree. I've got to be a soccer mom this evening and I don't want to do it wet."

"Hmm... but you do wet well," he said as he tried to pull her towards him.

“BEAST!” She said, jumping up to organize her clothes.

***

It was noon by the time Ren got to the Plantation. Oak Alley was arguably the most recognizable of the plantation homes on the river between Baton Rouge and New Orleans. The live oak trees in front of the main house were in their third century of life and they were often the subject of photographs. Ren pulled his Jeep into the visitor parking lot, grabbed his camera bag and monopod, and walked towards the old main gate on River Road.

He stood there for a moment to take in the scene before beginning to shoot some long-distance shots of the house. The parties from the bus tours that had come over from the city were still in the house or were enjoying lunch in the restaurant.

“Peace and quiet. Let's see what this old house has to say,” thought Ren.

Ren lowered his shields a little way and immediately felt

light on his feet as he reached out for any sensations that might be there. Once satisfied that the plantation grounds were benign, he lowered his shields further and gazed into the viewfinder of his camera.

The current mauvish-pink paint on the main house blurred and faded, eventually to become a bright white. The two rows of oak trees leading up to the house looked virtually unchanged, but the horse-drawn carriage that was moving behind the main house towards one of the brick outbuildings indicated that Ren was actually viewing a scene from at least a century-and-a-half earlier. Ren remained relaxed, feeling that what was happening would be no threat to him. He panned the camera to follow the moving carriage, which eventually came to a halt at an outbuilding about two hundred yards behind and to the left of the main house. A middle-aged man driving the carriage jumped down with the vigor of a teenager as he moved to assist his passenger out of the back.

Ren zoomed-in the camera lens, in at attempt to get a closer look of the alighting passenger. Even though her dress was a bright yellow, Ren was conscious of a pastel-blue aura surrounding her. The young lady possessed Talents! He gasped and tried to remain calm so as not to lose sight of the scene. A couple of deep breaths more and he noticed that the blue aura of the young woman was turning to a purplish hue whenever she got close to the groom. Ren shifted his focus back to the groom and the reason for the color-change became clear - his blood-red aura was mingling with this woman's hue whenever they got close to each other. A slave with the Talents? Amazing! Mike would be fascinated.

The groom went into the outbuilding and the young woman ran off towards the main house. As she did so, she met up with a young man who had been running towards her from the house. Her arms wrapped around the man and at the same time the scene faded from the viewfinder of Ren's camera. The color of the main house returned to the pink of modern times, as a woman of thirty-something and wearing a full hoop skirt came skipping towards him.

"Renard Alciatore, you come up here and you don't even stop to tell me hello!" The woman said, wearing a mock pouting expression. Her accent was authentic Cajun.

"You you never work on a Thursday, Catherine Marie Desetreaux, you silly Cajun," Ren replied as he laughed and held out his arms to encircle the lady with a hug, hooped-skirt and all.

“Well, Cherie, you are the psychic one, so you're supposed to know I'm here," she retorted, giggling.

"What do you mean, psychic?" Ren looked at her curiously.

"Cherie, my momma taught me a long time ago to show respect towards people who are a little off, and you're more than a little off," she replied, laughing. "All it takes is a quick look at your photographs to realize that you have the ability to see a bit more than what's visible to the rest of us underprivileged folk."

"Hmm... I've never really given it much thought, Cathy. Tell me, how much do you know about who owned the place before the Zoe family?"

"You mean the McKinney's? They owned the place from the early 1800s until just before the First World War.”

"Just before the war, sometime in the 1850s or so... was there a young woman living here? A girl, really, maybe in her late teens or early twenties?"

"You watch that girl stuff, Ren Alciatore. I was a woman by the time I was that age, thank you very much!" Exclaimed Cathy through her giggles.

"OK. Point taken, sweetie. What about my question?"

"Well, yes. there was Elizabeth McKinney, cousin to Angus McKinney, the only one they called ‘young master’ back then. His father, Ewan, passed away in 1852 when he was oh... 22. Elizabeth was 19 at the time. She had come down from Scotland two years previously."

"Thrown out of the Old Country?"

"Sort of. Her dad was just about fed up with her headstrong attitude."

"Sounds like a typical Oak Alley woman!" Ren chuckled.

"Careful, Cherie, or I'll smack you!"

"You be careful, Cherie. I just might like that!" Ren matched her stare for stare.

Cathy burst into laughter. "You are the most terrible flirt

I know, Ren."

"Aw shucks," he said grinning. "So, what became of the young Miss McKinney?"

"Oh, she ended up marrying a man from the city. Last name was Delatorre. I can't remember his first name. A wealthy man, invested in a number of different ventures. Killed in the Civil War, during the Battle of Gettysburg. Specifically, on Little Round Top, I think. I believe the family ended up in Shreveport and several branches moved over to Texas, following the oil business that way. Dallas, if my memory serves me correctly."

"Interesting. You're so damned smart, Cathy." Ren grinned as he kissed her cheek.

"And you'd do well to remember that, Ren Alciatore," Cathy said as she burst into giggles again. “Do you want me to take you inside?”

"Depends on what you have in mind once we get there," he said with a leer in his expression.

"Stop that! You know what I meant. Is today just outside pictures?"

"Yeah, I think so. And the fresh air is good for me. Besides, I want to get some different angle shots today. The straight-on shot through the oaks has become so clichéd."

"OK, I'll leave you to it," she said. She kissed him on the cheek before adding: "If you need anything, just come over to the office and get me or one of the ladies."

"Thanks, cutie. I'll come say goodbye before I leave."

"You'd better." Cathy grinned and blew him a final kiss as she pivoted and skipped back toward the main house in a whirl of skirts and petticoats.

Ren made two circles of the house as he followed his plan to shoot the house from a variety of angles. Once he was safely alone again he dropped his shields as he scanned the house through his camera for additional sensations. Interesting, he thought, that his less expensive camera brought out the psychic resonances he had detected both here and in Dallas. He could all but hear Mike O'Donnell admonishing him that coincidences are few and far between, so Ren made a mental note to check out the history of his less expensive camera.

One of these days, in my spare time...

He finished up with his photography and packed up the small camera bag, swung it over his shoulder, and stopped off at the plantation's office to say goodbye, as he had promised. As he headed back to the city, traffic on I-10 through Metairie was dreadful, as usual, but he eventually arrived home at around four o'clock. He spent several minutes organizing the equipment he had taken up to the plantation, and then settled in at his computer for a while.

Ren scanned the messages from the various mailing lists to which he subscribed. He paused, halfway through his list, to read a message which contained some very interesting information:

From: BubbaKPD@gmail.com
To: PhotoGuyNOLA@gmail.com
Subject: New Info...
Hey guy. I know you're still hurting, losing your friend, but I thought you would be interested in some information I've come across. Let's try to get together soon, like tomorrow if possible. I don't have all the pieces of the puzzle, but maybe between the two of us we can sort them out.
Bubba

To which Ren replied:

From: PhotoGuyNOLA@gmail.com
To: BubbaKPD@gmail.com
Subject: Re: New Info
Lunch tomorrow works for me. Let's say Lopinto's in Bucktown at 12:30? Oh, and I'm going to invite a friend to join us, the priest from UNO I told you about. If he's available, that is. Make him welcome if he beats me to the restaurant.
Ren

He clicked the "send" button on the screen and continued to read his emails. Half an hour or so later, a direct message came through from "Wynterbreeze".

"Hey."

"Hey, Wassup?"

"Not much. Getting ready to head home."

"Wish you were coming back here actually. :-)"

"You OK, Ren? You want me to come back?"

"Sure I do. But not for reasons of platonic friendship."

":-) We'll see how that goes, luv. But for now, I have kids to fetch."

"Fear not, I'll cope... :-)"

"I'm sure you will. Ciao!"

Once he had completed dealing with his email, Ren sat down to the task of writing a memorial to a good friend, on his JHM website. The memorial would be short and simple, but his regular readers would no doubt wonder why such a major player in the attacks on Hadley would be paying tribute to such a key member of the JHM staff.

"Let them wonder," he thought.

CHAPTER TWENTY-ONE

Parrotheads

There are all sorts of theories about how Bucktown got its name. But the old fishing neighborhood along Lake Pontchartrain had become more well-known for being part of the legislative district which had elected former KKK wizard David Duke to the only public office he had actually won. Not that everyone in Bucktown was a racist; but the local Republican Party had not been that smart in fending off the challenge from a charismatic figure like Duke. Restaurants such as Lopinto's were more than happy that Duke had taken his traveling roadshow across to the north side of the lake in recent years, allowing the whole thing in Bucktown to die down. Now, there wasn't much left to old Bucktown, but there was still Lopinto's, with its menu of fresh lake seafood, pizza, and other Italian culinary creations.

Ren parked his Mach One at the levee that protected the neighborhood from the lake, jogged across the street, and entered through the front door of the restaurant. His lunch companions were not difficult to spot: a Japanese man in a cop uniform and a priest in a short-sleeved black shirt with a Roman collar. The two appeared to be engaged in a very animated conversation as he walked up to their table.

"Well my favorite album from the old stuff is 'Living and Dying in ¾ Time', but I am still a fan of his newer discs as well," the policeman was saying as he shook his head vigorously.

"Hmm. My pick for an older album would be 'Havana Daydreaming'. I just love the title cut..."

"Stashed his cash in Ecuador, bought a good suit of

clothes..."

"...Flew on up to Mexico, standing by the shore." The priest finished the line.

Ren stood next to their table in disbelief, and turned to Msgr. Michael O'Donnell.

"No. It can't be true. Say it ain't so, Joe. Please tell me you're not a..."

"Parrothead?" The priest smiled and laughed. "Guilty as charged, Ren! Bubba was humming 'He Went to Paris' as he was walking in and we discovered that we are both, indeed, Parrotheads."

"Heaven help me. Not one, but two friends who are Jimmy Buffett fans. I don't know how I'm going to cope!"

"You will cope just fine, Ren-san," Bubba Watanabe laughed. "I took the liberty of ordering for you. I hope you're in the mood for the combo sausage meatball po-boy?"

"Double cheese?" responded Ren expectantly.

"Naturally!" Bubba replied.

"What a man you are! OK, I guess I can let the Buffett talk slide, given your impeccable taste in ordering lunch." Ren reached across the table and took two packets of sugar, which he proceeded to dump into his iced tea. "So, what's the new information? Just so you know, Mike knows everything that's going on here."

Bubba nodded to both of them. "Right then. Something has been bugging me for a while now, about this whole situation, and it goes back to when those two state troopers showed up at your doorstep, Ren. I couldn't help but wonder why it was that cops from the governor's personal staff were taking an interest in you, especially given how apolitical you've been the past five years or so."

"It's a funny thing about cops who you know. We have a lot of friends who are also cops. I know the good Father here knows how it goes: you call a friend, he calls another friend, and pretty soon everyone you know is keeping in the back of their head what you are looking for. Well, a conversation I had with a state police lieutenant who's a professional acquaintance of mine, triggered a thought in his mind and so he dropped me an email. According to my acquaintance from Shreveport, several prominent members of some big-ass Southern Baptist church up there pumped a bunch of money into our current governor's campaign fund; as well as into a number of political action committees that supported the governor. I'm talking some very righteous dollars here, my friends." Bubba paused as a waitress appeared with three plates of sandwiches: roast beef for Bubba, Italian sausage for Mike, and Ren's sausage-meatball combo. Bubba's monologue was placed on hold for a few moments while all three dug into their lunch. After devouring half of his sandwich, Bubba continued.

"Of course, once the election had been won, these gentlemen from upstate were after a return from their investment. That's when the governor created his little investigations unit. The guys on that unit were never particularly liked by most of the other troopers. Combine that with the nature of things they've been working on recently and the loyalty level towards them isn't what you might expect among fellow officers. What got the attention of my acquaintance was a duty status report that he came across. For the past six months, all of the activities of the governor's team have focused on places north of Alexandria, and mostly in the Shreveport area. But with one exception..."

"Me." Ren finished the thought.

"You got it. I had a couple of other colleagues do some checking into the men who pull the governor's chain regarding these cops, and found that two of them have a major stake in a Christian book publisher in Dallas. An outfit called Marcus-Kayson. Heard of it?"

"Yeah. I've even stopped by to check the place out, last trip to Dallas. Go on."

Bubba nodded and bit into the second half of his sandwich. "One of these guys is even on the Marcus-Kayson board of directors. I've got a brief file on each of them here. Maybe it will jar some memories for you, Ren."

Ren took the folder from Bubba and glanced at the contents for a moment before passing it to Mike. Mike nodded and began to read.

Bubba continued: "Further inquiries revealed the name of their primary contact at M-K, as the place is referred to in

Christian publishing circles, to be Anita Delatorre. A blonde looker from Dallas." Bubba handed a second folder to Ren.

Ren's eyebrows immediately picked up as he heard the name Delatorre, and he became wide-eyed as he looked at Anita's photograph. She was the woman he had seen through his lens at Oak Alley!

"D'you know this babe, Ren?" Bubba asked.

"Umm, no. But she looks a helluva lot like an historical figure I've been researching. It's remarkable!"

"Family resemblance?" asked Mike.

"Most definitely," Ren replied, shooting a quick mental image of the plantation scene to Mike. Mike's expression remained unchanged as he received this new visual information. He nodded.

"Anyway," continued Bubba, "the attractive Ms. Delatorre has an assignment that brings her to New Orleans. Metairie, specifically. Quite often. She's the executive-in-charge of production for various media projects, books, tapes, public appearances and so on, of one Jay Hadley, of Jay Hadley Ministries."

Ren pondered. "Fascinating, as one Mister Spock used to say," he said, in a dry tone.

"Now, to tie all this together," Bubba continued. "I have found no references to any State Police involvement with you prior to my initiating inquiries into the death of Nick and Trip. My guess is that the folks in Dallas did make a call to the governor's office, to get you to back off from further digging. The attacks that resulted in the deaths of your colleagues do not appear to have involved the State Police."

Ren frowned. "I take it that the trail is still cold in terms of any hint of foul play in these two deaths."

"Afraid so, my friend," replied Bubba with a sigh. "There's nothing there. I wish I had better news on that front. I firmly believe you in that there is a strong possibility that Trip was murdered. I don't share the same belief in Nick's death, but the circumstances that wrap around all of this do make me wonder. Still, it's no more than a feeling, and there's no concrete evidence whatsoever to support that feeling. There is also no evidence at all as to who might be behind your friend Cecilia's death, or the attack on me."

His report concluded, Bubba finished off his sandwich.

"This is all very interesting but I still have the feeling we know a whole lot of nothing," said Ren.

"Same here," Bubba confirmed.

"Not much new here," Mike agreed. "But I do know one of these two guys," he said as he tapped on the folder in front of him. "This guy, Daniel McCain. He's a major player in Christian enterprises, not the least of which is Marcus-Kayson. If memory serves me correctly, he even maintains an office at M-K in Dallas. His interests extend well beyond Christian publishing, too, and into Christian recording, Christian radio, and a number of secular ventures as well. As I said," concluded Mike, "he's a major player in the Bible-belt world."

"Would he kill to get what he wants?" Bubba asked.

"Personally, I doubt it. But he is sufficiently wealthy, and well-connected to know how to order a hit."

“But this wasn't just any hit, Mike," Ren added.

"Very true. And while that aspect of this requires a lot more research, I intend to find out some specifics soon. This has not gone unnoticed and will not pass without some action being taken," Mike said firmly.

Bubba returned to his presentation: "Well, to sum all this up, I think we've identified those involved in this little excursion into the seamier side of Christian publishing. The question now is, what do we do with this information?"

"Well I can't imagine that any of this is even close to being able to be used as evidence," Ren stated flatly.

"No indeed. This is all second-hand data and cop intuition. But even though it isn't evidence, it is enough to enable us to take steps to protect you, Ren. From any further stunts these folks might pull."

"Works for me," Ren said.

"Ren, don't get too comfortable with this knowledge," Mike cautioned. "We won't be out of the woods for at least another month."

What's a month got to do with these folks?"

"The 31st day of October is significant to people of many different religions, particularly those whose interests lean towards what the mainstream media refer to in guarded tones as 'the occult'. All Hallows Eve, better still, 'Samhain' to the Wiccans, is, to many, a day of power. Given that your enemies appear to dabble in things arcane, Ren, I'll feel a lot better once we're past Halloween."

"Surely, Mike, you don't believe there is an occult motivation for all this, do you?" Bubba asked, with a skeptical expression on his face.

"I do indeed, my fellow Parrothead," said the priest as he smiled grimly. "But, I'll know more after making a few enquiries."

"Jeez, how ironic that people involved in various evangelical Christian ministries and businesses should be involved in all this stuff!"

"Stranger things have been known to happen," added Mike as he began to stand up. "Well gents, I'd best be running along. I have a two o'clock class and it's shockingly bad form for the instructor not to show up." Mike offered his hand to Bubba: "It's been a pleasure, Bubba-san. We need to go get a beer soon and talk music."

Bubba stood also and grasped Mike's hand firmly. "For sure, Father. Talk to you soon." Mike nodded to both men at the table, turned, and walked out of the restaurant.

"A very interesting friend you've acquired there, Ren," Bubba said as he sat back down at the table. "Very interesting indeed."

"Yeah, he's something, that's f'sure."

***

Mike O'Donnell had fully intended to teach his class that afternoon but something from his otherwise pleasant lunch conversation was nagging him. He reached for his phone as he turned his Porsche 914 onto Lakeshore Drive to head back to the University.

"Yeah, Jeri?" he asked of his graduate assistant. "Could you take my 2pm class for me? Something's come up I have to deal with this afternoon. You're sure I'm not imposing? OK, cool. I owe you one, cutie. Thanks much. No, I won't be gone overnight, don't worry. Thanks again, Jeri, see you tomorrow." Mike ended the call and turned the car down Canal Blvd. As he cruised along the wide boulevard with its mixture of houses, churches, and schools, he decided to make one more call.

"Bishop Thompson's office," chimed the cheerful voice at the other end.

"Hi Marie, Mike O'Donnell from New Orleans calling. Is Himself in?"

"Father Mike! Long time no talk! Yeah, he's here today. Hold on, I'll get him for you." The phone clicked and paused as Mike turned into Harrison Avenue.

"Michael."

"Can we chat?"

"Yes. I've got a few minutes. What do you need?"

"Meet me at the Basilica in ten minutes."

"As serious as that?"

"Potentially."

"OK. Well, at least you've picked a quiet afternoon for it. OK, see you in ten."

"Can do."

"Adios, amigo."

"Right." Mike shut off his phone as he pulled his car into the parking lot in front of St. Dominic's Church. He locked the car and waked around the church building to the side door, slipping in quietly and heading towards the sacristy. Catholic churches are usually empty during the middle of the day, and Mike gave a quick thanks, mentally, that today was not an exception to this rule. He pushed open the sacristy door and made his way back to the priest's dressing area. He still had six minutes to kill before his rendezvous, so he sat down in a chair across the room, closed his eyes, and focused on what he had to report. He took several deep breaths to build up personal energy and drawing from the power nexus that the church had become after years of service to the Light.

When the appointed time arrived, Mike walked over to the four ornate tiles in the corner that did not match the rest of the floor. He made a quiet invocation, closed his eyes, then pulled the mental lever which sprung the trap door in the Teleport Gateway. He felt a rush downwards as he vanished into nothingness, then suddenly felt the rising sensation as he appeared at his destination. He blinked several times to restore his eyesight. He found himself standing in the sacristy of the St. Mary's Basilica in Phoenix, Arizona.

"Any cute flight attendants on this trip?" a voice from across the room inquired.

"Funny man," said Mike. "Thanks for seeing me, Dwayne."

"No problem, Mike," said Dwayne Thompson, Auxiliary Bishop for the Archdiocese of Phoenix. "Some people can be so full of shit when it comes to needing something of me right away. But you are not one of them, by far."

"I've encountered a bit of a situation and I may need your help."

The bishop nodded. "Let's go sit down in the church."

Unlike St. Dominic's in New Orleans, the Basilica was bustling with activity. Thompson led his guest to a side chapel near the main altar, where they both sat on a pew. Both men began to focus and, at Thompson's nod, Mike began to send his thoughts and impressions concerning Ren Alciatore and his enemies. After a few moments both men opened their eyes. A grave look veiled the expression on the face of Dwayne Thompson.

"Did you take the afternoon off?" he asked.

"Yes. I thought it might come to this."

"Your instincts in these matters are usually correct," said Thompson. "You up for another trip?"

"But of course."

Thompson stood and then led the way to the sacristy.

"I realize it's considered rude for the host to leave first but, in this case, I suppose I had better." Thompson stepped onto the tiles where Mike had first appeared in Arizona.

Mike immediately followed Thompson by stepping on the tiles again and setting the Teleport energies. He materialized in what appeared to be the library of a large home or manor house. The windowless room made it difficult to determine its location, but Mike appeared to feel immediately at home. Turning around to gain his bearings, Mike found his traveling companion already settling into an easy chair. Thompson nodded, as Mike slowly paced over to a straight-backed chair next to a low table full of books.

"Well, I made the Call as 'urgent'. Hopefully we're not disrupting their routine."

"They'll cope," Mike said. "Although I must admit it's a refreshing change that I'm not the one who has been caught in the shower or some other ritual that involves my being unclothed."

Thompson laughed and nodded in agreement. "Yup, the same has happened to me also. In fact..."

His story was cut off before it had begun by a flash of light that announced another arrival through the Gateway. Another priest appeared on the tiles, this one dressed in a charcoal-gray suit, with a black shirt and a Roman collar. Once he had oriented himself he turned to greet his colleagues.

"Dwayne. Mike," the newcomer said, with a nod towards each man, in turn. The newcomer sat down in a stuffed chair, a mate to the one Thompson had claimed. He picked up a copy of the *New York Times* and began reading.

Twenty minutes passed without a word being said between the three men, when the Gateway flashed again and a woman in her mid-thirties alighted from the tiles. Her long black hair, which grew almost to her waist, flowed behind her. She was a dressed in a light cotton skirt, a knitted top, and sandals. She, also, took a moment to get her bearings, then nodded to Thompson and the newcomer before, the formalities completed, she whirled to face Mike.

She immediately started laughing. "I should have known. If you're going to pull me out in the middle of the day, the least you could do is give me a lift!"

Mike shrugged and cocked his head in Thompson's direction. "I came via Phoenix, Meg."

"OK. You're forgiven then." She smiled and held her arms outstretched, demanding a hug. Mike stood up and embraced her curvy body tightly.

"I firmly believe you have the most infectious smile on the planet, my Lady," Mike said as they separated. He immediately bowed to her.

"Why, thank you my Lord!" Meg responded, returning his

chivalry with a graceful curtsy. "Dwayne, Ian, I hope you are well?" she added, acknowledging the other two men in the room.

"I'm doing well, thank you, dear," the priest in gray said. "I was in the middle of watching the Blues playing on Sky, but no matter. That's what we have DVRs for," Ian Whitman added, smiling.

A knock was heard at the door to the library. Bishop Thompson got up and gently opened the door, to accept a note that was being passed to him.

"Well, Derek can't get away so it's just the four of us," Thompson said. "I initiated the call for this meeting after Mike came out to see me earlier. That said; Mike, why don't you take this from here?"

Mike O'Donnell rose and bowed his head, first to Thompson and then to each of his colleagues at the meeting. "I know that each of you have kept up with my reports regarding Renard Alciatore, my current protégé. When I first met Ren, it was clear that his actions not related to his Talents were sufficient reason that someone involved in some way with Jay Hadley Ministries wanted him dead. That the assassin hired to do the deed made use of fairly well-developed Talents in the ply of his trade did not surprise me that much. What remained to be determined was whether this assassin was working for parties who were unaware of the true reason for success in his business, or whether he was hired specifically because of his Talents."

"Further investigation into the backgrounds of several people involved with this case have led me to believe that this assassin was not acting alone. If you will open to me, I will share this information with you."

His three colleagues silently acknowledged his request and all closed their eyes. Mike reached out with his thoughts and found three familiar minds ready to accept what he had to share. He submitted the images Ren had passed to him from his Labor Day excursion to the Marcus-Kayson offices in Dallas, as well as various conversations with Ren, culminating with details from his lunch conversation that day with Ren and Bubba.

"You're a Parrothead?" His Excellency of Phoenix inquired, chuckling. Mike blushed.

The woman giggled. "You haven't ridden with him more than a couple of blocks then, Dwayne, or you'd know that already! Still, that's not as much a revelation as that we've got someone with Talents in the US conservative Christian community. I'm not quite sure what to make of that just yet."

"I would have thought you'd be upset by such a notion, Meg," retorted Ian Whitman.

"Personally," she responded, "I'm appalled. In my capacity as member of the Executive Committee, however, I've learned to temper my initial reactions when it comes to the behavior of some of you Christians."

"None of us doubt your objectivity, m'Lady," Mike said. "The reason I'm bringing this to you in this forum is to decide what action, if any, to take from here. I take it that I'm correct in assuming that none of you are aware of anyone with Talents working out of Marcus-Kayson in Dallas?"

Each member of the meeting shook their head in negative response.

"That being said, we must therefore determine a course of action."

Meg cocked her head to one side before speaking. "Why do we need a course of action, Mike? If someone wants to swim in a sewer, I don't see how this committee has a need to deal with it."

"We have to deal with it because it is a threat to the authority of the Assembly!" Mike exclaimed.

"How so?" Meg responded.

"We have people using Talents who are outside the jurisdiction of the Assembly," replied Mike.

"That may be true, Mike, but this is not the first time we have encountered this situation and it won't be the last. Yes, it sucks that someone is distastefully using such a front for their operations. But it isn't clear whether these people are refusing to acknowledge the Assembly's jurisdiction. After all, the attacker did withdraw from combat when you asserted your authority."

"Well, in my opinion, I simply managed to rattle his cage."

"But you don't know that, Mike. While I'll be the first to admit that this entire episode makes the hair stand up on the back of my neck, I don't see any reason for us to take any action; including bringing this before the entire Assembly."

"Well I'm extremely concerned that Ren will be Challenged to combat by someone who won't respect the Protocols!" Mike responded, forcefully.

"Be that as it may," Meg replied, "we have an obligation to the policies of the Assembly to allow that scenario to play itself out."

"That attitude could cost Renard Alciatore his life!" retorted Mike vigorously.

Meg smiled, wryly: "Hey, that guy's cute. If he makes it past Hallowe'en I'll be asking you to introduce me to him, don't worry. Still, we need to keep things in perspective, and there's no need for intervention at this time."

"I must concur with m'Lady Meg," Ian said. "Dwayne?"

The Auxiliary Bishop of Phoenix sighed. "This is a very serious situation, and my gut says Mike is right. However, Meg is absolutely correct that we indeed have no justification for any kind of preemptive action."

"Well," added Mike, "as much as I respect Derek's input and thoughts on this committee, I don't see his opinion changing any minds here. So we'll leave it at that. If you folks will excuse me, then." Mike arose from his chair, bowed curtly, and walked to the Gateway. A moment later he was gone.

"He's pissed," Ian said.

"He's struggling to be objective," Thompson added.

"Well I feel we made the right decision," said Meg. "I just hope it turns out that way for the two of them."

CHAPTER TWENTY-TWO

Formal Challenge

Anita Delatorre blinked several times as she stepped down from the platform where the Gateway was located. She held the handrail firmly to navigate carefully the three steps from the platform to the floor.

"Sorry," she said to the man greeting her. "I'm a bit rusty. What with all the field-work I've been doing, it has been over six months since I've used a Gateway."

"Yes, there's always an extra bit of disorientation when you've not used the skill for some time," the man said. "But your work has been going well, Anita. We'll be away from those people and back in the office soon, so don't worry."

"I hope so. New Orleans is so dominated by Catholics that it truly is difficult to find a Gateway I could use without drawing anyone's attention. How did you come to be in a Baptist church in Old Metairie, anyway?"

"My grandfather had it constructed. He had come to the same conclusion about the Catholics as you did. Pops figured that the organ loft would be a safe enough place, and Baptist churches usually stand empty except on Sundays. All in all, it's a good place for a Gate which the priests don't know about. Come, let's go in and deal with the business at hand."

The man led the way from the Gateway chamber and into the lobby of what appeared to be the upper floor of an office building. Anita and her guide crossed the lobby and made their way to a conference room. Anita's guide gestured to a chair at one end of the table. She sat down, looking at those already seated. There were three women, and one man, along with her guide, who now sat in between two of the women.

"Thank you for coming in so promptly, Anita," said a woman in her mid-forties, seated on the exact opposite end of the conference table. She was dressed in a hunter green suit that Anita recognized from the Marshall Field's department store. She had passed on it herself, mainly because of its $1,500 price tag. "You have done well in your management of our interests in Jay Hadley Ministries and you are to be commended for that. However, there are some aspects of our involvement with Hadley that have not gone too well..." The woman paused for a few seconds. Anita did not speak, as she had not been invited to do so.

"And we would like to understand, from you, exactly what has happened, so that we may decide a proper course of action for the future."

Anita replied in a formal manner. "My Lady, as per instructions of this Lodge, I took upon myself the task of eliminating certain opposition to Jay Hadley Ministries, specifically the principals behind an anti-Hadley website. I engaged the services of William Ryan, an assassin we have used before. He succeeded in eliminating two of the principals but encountered serious obstacles with the third."

"Yes, we know this," said the man who had been her guide. "The obstacle is that your third target, Renard Alciatore, evidently possesses Talents and has been discovered by a priest."

"Not just a priest, my Lord," said the other woman at the table; who was most likely in her mid-twenties. "Alciatore was saved from the attack by a Michael O'Donnell, a Teacher who is affiliated with the Assembly of Mainz."

Anita sat up straight.

"The Assembly is involved! This is new information! This is bigger than just homeschool publishing, if an order dating back to the Templars is in play!" She thought, as she schooled her body to maintain an outward calm, projecting no concerns to the room. The meeting was suddenly taking a different turn than what she had expected.

"I was not aware of the priest's affiliations, my Lady, nor was Mr. Ryan. He judged it prudent to respect the priest's decree, which had placed Alciatore under his protection, so he broke off the action and departed."

Anita continued. "Following the revelations concerning Alciatore, I determined that it would be better to try to use some of our political contacts in order to shut down the Hadley efforts. Unfortunately, this was only a temporary solution since Alciatore comes from a New Orleans family who is fairly well-connected. In my opinion, the best way forward is to eliminate Alciatore."

"This Lodge and the entire Council would concur with you, Anita," declared the man at the head of the table. "Renard Alciatore should be eliminated. But, obviously we cannot simply put a bullet in his brain nor have him succumb to 'an accident'. Mr. Alciatore will have to be Challenged and defeated in Magickal Combat."

"But, my Lord, what of this priest and his Decree of Protection?" Anita asked.

Her guide turned his head to face the woman on his left. He nodded, indicating she should report.

The younger woman returned his nod.

"One of my agents in New Orleans has determined that the priest, O'Donnell, has lifted his Sigil of Protection on Alciatore. As such, Alciatore is now fair game for anyone who has Talents."

Anita was again taken aback, both by the knowledge about Ren and by the fact that the Lodge had other operatives in New Orleans. "Surely the priest knows that removing protection from Alciatore might surely mean his death, my Lady!"

"More likely that he believes his protégé is capable of answering a Challenge and of defending himself," said the other man at the table, who had remained silent up until that point. "From what we have learned about Monsignor O'Donnell, he is a formidable Teacher. His name has come up in connection with other projects in which we have taken an interest in as well. If he has been working with Alciatore, it is highly likely that he has imparted a great deal of knowledge to the younger man already."

"I'm not sure I follow your thinking here, my Lord," Anita said, cautiously.

Her guide to the meeting responded in a take-charge tone. "The bottom line here is simple, Anita. Alciatore has to be eliminated, and we don't want the job botched. Therefore, someone who has strong experience in Magickal Combat, someone who thoroughly understands Combat Protocols, will challenge him; that person, Anita, will be you."

He leaned forward in his seat, facing Anita. "Alciatore will be issued a formal Challenge to arcane combat, which will take place on Samhain. You will choose the site and circumstances for the combat. And you will compose the Challenge. Until a day or so before the combat you will remain here as our guest. We will get word to Jay Hadley that you have an urgent project to deal with right now, so don't worry about him."

His look turned from neutral to quite serious.

"Anita, this situation has become far more serious than anyone expected it to. Now that the Assembly has expanded its alliances, the involvement of an Assembly operative this close to one of our projects requires immediate and direct action. This cannot be entrusted to a youngster, such as your Ryan. Bringing in someone from the Council could be construed by others as an escalation of our conflict, which would be an act contrary to our current goals. So I want you to handle this with the skill and efficiency you have shown in all your previous operations."

Anita bowed her head as she sat. "I thank you for your confidence in my abilities, my Lord."

"Very well then. You have our leave for you to begin your preparations." The man rose from the table and bowed low towards Anita, before turning to one of the other men; Anita's original guide.

"Daniel, if you would be so kind as to see to all Anita's accommodations and needs." Daniel nodded, arose from the table, and gestured to Anita for her to follow him.

Once outside the conference room, Anita turned towards her guide. "You might have warned me, Daniel."

"My dear, you are a wonderful person and a good friend. But you know we are all bound by oaths which prohibit discussion of certain subjects without permission. Believe, me, I personally felt that you should have been given all the information we have on this matter, but it isn't up to me."

"No matter," she replied. "You know what I need, of course. Find me a place to settle into, and I'll get to work."

***

For Renard Alciatore, the school year moving into full swing meant more work for him, as well as lots of soccer matches to officiate. Even though so many people were taking an interest in him, he welcomed the intense activity. It diverted his attention away from the loss of Cecilia and the mixed emotions about JJ swirling around him.

It was on a beautiful Tuesday morning that Ren jogged alongside Bayou St. John, then past Beauregard Circle, in front of the main entrance to City Park, before altering his usual running route to go around the art museum in the park instead of following the bayou eastwards. Ren pondered that New Orleans doesn't display quite the dramatic change in color that the northeast does in the fall, but what little color there is at this time of year usually shows best in the park. Exiting the park at the intersection of Esplanade Avenue and Wisner Boulevard, he turned towards his home on Moss Street. He picked up his pace now that he was back alongside the water and, as his home came in sight, Ren noticed a man walking up the steps to his front door. Ren slowed down so as not to attract the man's attention, and watched as the man went up to the door. Rather than knocking on the door, the mysterious visitor removed an envelope from one pocket and what appeared to be a small knife from the other. He placed the envelope on Ren's front door, impaling it with the knife, then walked quickly down the steps and into a waiting car which pulled off as soon as the man was inside and the door shut.

"Son-of-a-bitch!" Ren exclaimed as he started running now, up towards his house. He was about to grab the knife when something in his brain stopped his hand just before it touched it. As Ren's fingers came near, he felt a strange vibration in them as if he was passing his hand over an electrified fence. He withdrew his hand immediately then unlocked the door and went inside.

A moment later Ren returned with a silk handkerchief, which he used to remove the knife carefully from the door. He caught the envelope in his other hand and took them both into the study. The knife turned out to be a dagger with an elaborate pattern, inlaid with gold in the handle. Even though it was wrapped in the silk handkerchief, Ren could still feel an intense amount of residual power. The design on the dagger appeared Celtic in origin, an intertwined knot, but with small thistles interwoven. Scottish rather than Irish. There were small cairngorms also inlaid in the handle. The gold pattern extended down the handle, continuing onto the blade. This was no inexpensive trinket!

He turned his attention to the envelope. It was plain vellum and, unlike the dagger, gave off no vibrations. However, Ren raised his shields to full protection, then picked up the envelope to open it. In what appeared to be a brownish ink, a strong hand had written a short verse:

"You have become a nuisance, my Lord Renard,
A nuisance I mean to end.
By magic in accord with the Red Protocol of Combat
To another world I will you send.
On the eve of All Hallows, at sunset we will meet
Before the dead come out to play.
The monument of the Virginians will mark our combat
And you will not see another day."

The back of the envelope was marked with an address in the Garden District. Ren read the note through twice, then reached for the phone. He grimaced as the call rolled to voicemail.

"Hi. This is Dr. O'Donnell. I will be out of the office until next Thursday. If you need immediate assistance, please contact Ms. Morgan at on-campus extension 6944. Thank you."

"Mike, this is Ren. I've received an interesting note that I'd like you to look over. Please give me a call. Thanks."

Ren sighed as he leaned back into his chair. It had not

been all that long ago that Mike had been reviewing the Combat Protocols with him, and the details of "The Red Protocol for Single Combat with a Magical Foe" were still clear in his head. He had 48 hours to answer the formal Challenge. Failure to answer meant that the Challenger would then be free to come after Ren in any manner they wished, since he would then no longer be considered a person of honor.

As Ren pondered, he realized that drafting a formal response to such a Challenge was a task that was beyond him. It looked like his mentor might well be out of touch for more than the time he had to reply. Part of Ren's brain went into panic mode, while another part reminded him that he had Mike's local support system. But it was a bit early in the day to go to a bar, particularly after a five-mile jog. And there was more than enough time for Ren to take a shower and collect himself. “Shit,” he thought. “If I'm gonna drive all the way Uptown, I might as well make the morning a productive one.”

Twenty minutes later, Ren tossed his small camera bag into his Jeep and headed for the Irish Channel. He was much calmer now, and he decided to drive straight down Canal Street into downtown, then turn onto Magazine Street to get to the Channel.

The Irish Channel was not really all that Irish, even when the families of the men who had built the New Basin Canal had all settled in the neighborhood north of the French Quarter between Magazine Street and the River. In addition to the Irish, a large contingent of German immigrants had also moved in, which had created a clash of cultures when it came time to establish a Catholic parish. The Irish did not want to celebrate Mass with the Germans, and vice-versa, so they built separate Churches across the street from each other. The Redemptorist priests assigned to the parish would say Sunday Mass at St. Alphonsus Church for the Irish families, and would then go across the street to St. Mary's Assumption Church to preach to the Germans. Now, when tourists drive down Constance Street, they automatically assume that one of the two large churches is Catholic and the other is of a different denomination.

Ren parked his vehicle in front of St. Alphonsus School, down the street from his intended destination, where children were in the yard for morning recess. He twisted a wide-angle lens onto the body of his camera and crossed the street to stand just down the block from St. Alphonsus, so that he could capture the entire facade of the church in his photo. He clicked off several shots, then let the camera dangle at his side and sighed as he took in the beauty of the building.

A voice behind him startled Ren. "It is still a gorgeous building, isn't it?" Ren turned sharply and encountered a man in his mid-fifties who had been just a couple of paces behind him.

"Oh my. I am sorry. I certainly didn't mean to startle you," said the stranger with a smile. "I went to school here, you see, and then to high school down the street. I was in town visiting and wanted to come back down to the old neighborhood."

"Oh, no problem," said Ren. "And yeah, it's a wonderful church. I love photographing both of them."

"You look like you would have enjoyed going to school down here," said the man.

"How do you know I didn't?" responded Ren mischievously.

"You're too young! Redemptorist High closed in the spring of 1980. Besides, you're wearing your Brother Martin class ring," said the older man, laughing.

"You got me there," Ren responded, grinning.

"Well, take some pics of these old ladies that will make 'em proud, my friend. Have a good day." The man turned and walked off down the street.

"You too!" Ren called back. He continued to photograph around St. Alphonsus. As he rounded the corner once again, he turned his attention from the Irish church to St. Mary's across the street. As he let his shields drape around him like a cloak, he could discern the psychic "glow" of the Gateway located in the church's sacristy. As interesting as he found the effect, this "glow" distracted his ability to focus clearly on the overall shot. With a shrug of his shoulders, Ren brought his shields back to a normal level and the image faded, allowing him to see the bell tower clearly in his viewfinder. He clicked the shutter on his camera and then moved further up the street to catch a shot of the front of the church in all its glory.

Ren spent another full hour taking photographs of the churches and the buildings around them. The Gateway in St. Mary's was the only psychic sensation he experienced in that time. That's odd, he thought. Given the rich history in the neighborhood he wondered what he was missing. He looked at his watch and decided that this was not the day to try to answer that question. It was just past 10am and time for him to set about the task at hand. Ren made his way back to the Jeep and headed further uptown along Constance Street, turning left, then right, onto Annunciation Street. A couple of blocks later, and he parked in front of a green-roofed building that was the Triple-7 Bar and Grill.

The Triple-7 was a typical New Orleans street-corner business establishment. The style of the building is what is known locally as a "camel back", where the bar and restaurant are towards the front, with a residential area in the back and on a second story, above the business. The entrance to the bar was right on the corner of the building. Ren took a deep breath, pulled the door open, and went inside.

There was more light in the bar area than Ren had expected. The bar ran down the left side of the room and a couple of small tables were placed to the right. Three video-poker machines stood against the back wall as if on watch over the establishment. Ren kept his shields up as he stepped up to the bar.

"Well, young man, we meet again." It was the same gentleman he had met outside St. Alphonsus earlier that morning. "Father Mike gave me a heads-up about you some time ago. I had a feeling you might be coming over here today when I saw you at the churches." The man extended his hand across the bar. "Jacob Harrigan," he said, smiling.

"Renard Alciatore, but you probably already know that," Ren replied as he grinned sheepishly. "Mike said I could come over here if ever he wasn't available and I had a problem..."

"Of course, Ren, of course," said Jake. "But first let me buy you a cup of coffee upstairs, OK? We'll have bit more privacy to chat, up there." He winked at Ren and nodded his head towards the corner of the bar to indicate a doorway which led to the rear of the building.

"F'sure."

Jake gestured for Ren to follow him and they walked up the two steps to the doorway connecting the bar with the restaurant behind it. After another six steps up to the restaurant, Jake opened another door and revealed another set of stairs, this time leading up to the second floor of the building. Once on the second floor, the older man led Ren into a room at the end of the hallway.

"This is my office," Jake explained. "The wife runs the business out of the larger bedroom at the other end of the hall. She has graciously permitted me to have this humble space for other purposes."

Ren looked around as he walked into the office. It was furnished in a stark, hi-tech style, which was in marked contrast to the old, Irish Channel style of the rest of the Triple-7. He noticed several expensive computer workstations, a small server rack, and a host of communications equipment, around the room.

Ren's observations were interrupted by Jake's voice: "Coffee? I hope you don't mind a basic drip-pot. I don't get any fancier than café-au-lait."

"Hey, I'm more a fan of Morning Call than anything else," retorted Ren.

"Good!" He poured coffee from a small pot on the sideboard, then added warm milk from a second pot which stood next to the coffee-maker. Jake slid a mug over to Ren and followed it up with a spoon and sugar dispenser. The two men prepared their coffee, and then he looked Ren straight in the eye.

"All right, young sir, you didn't come over here just to have coffee. What's on your mind?"

Ren removed the note from his pocket, along with the dagger that had impaled it to his front door. As he showed them to Jake, Ren recounted the events of the evening before in great detail as he listened intently. Jake was reading through the note for a second time as Ren came to the end of his tale. Both men then sat in silence for a few minutes.

"Yes," said Jake, breaking the silence. "You have indeed been Challenged, young Mr. Alciatore. This note invites you to

Magickal Combat; Combat to the death."

"By whom?" Ren asked.

"By the person who wrote this note. The Red Protocol does not require the Challenger to reveal themselves to the Challenged until the time of combat. So let's not worry about what we can't figure out, and instead focus on what we know from the note."

"OK."

"Good then. Well let's do this by the numbers. We can't answer 'who'. ‘What' is a magical duel; and 'when' is Hallowe'en, October 31st, at sunset. 'Where' has me foxed at the moment. The line about 'the dead' indicates a cemetery, but the reference to 'Virginians' has me."

"It's the Tomb of the Army of Northern Virginia, in Metairie Cemetery,” Ren said.

Jake looked thoughtful as he gazed blankly at the wall. "Is that the one with the tall monument? The one where Jefferson Davis was temporarily interred?"

"The very same."

"Ok, I know where that is, and it makes sense as a location for a duel. Battle monuments are usually places with lots of power, that have plenty of natural energy for combatants to tap. Given how many cemeteries we have in town, I would guess that this monument is of particular significance to the Challenger."

Jake began to prepare a second pot of coffee. "You've got fifteen days until the duel. That's more than enough time to do some background research about the monument and who is buried beneath it."

Ren reached across the table and picked up the Challenge note to read it through again, carefully. When he had finished, he consulted the notes he had been taking during the meeting then looked up at Jake with an expectant expression.

"Jake, please don't be offended by this, but I really wish Mike was here."

"Ha! No offense taken, dear Ren." Jake smiled as he responded. "I know a great deal about these things, Ren, but I agree, nobody in town is quite in Mike's league. But no fear, we'll do just fine here. Now let's work on getting you a response

I can take to that address on the Challenge envelope."

"You'll take it?"

"That's right. Part of the formalities, son. Think of me as your Second in a duel. It isn't dignified to have this thrust upon you and then have to schlep around at their beck-and-call. Humph!" Jake said, snorting with mock indignation.

Fifteen minutes later, the reply had been written. Ren read through the handwritten note while Jake poured himself another cup of coffee.

"You know," Jake said, "we had all this high-tech stuff set up and configured in here, and then it seems like it always comes down to using pen, ink, and paper for the truly important things. Mind you, Renard Alciatore, I didn't have all this put in here merely to satisfy the whims of Monsignor O'Donnell. Now that you know what we have here, please feel free to come and make use of it."

Ren nodded. “Thanks Jake, I can't begin to tell you how much I appreciate your help with this. If there's anything I can do by way of returning your generosity..."

"Yes. There is indeed something you could do: you can win this friggin' duel!" Jake laughed as he extended his hand. "I'm going to stay up here and check my email and see if I can get in touch with Mr. Mike. Do you think you can make your way back down OK?"

“Sure can Jake. Thanks again. I'll talk to you soon."

"You damn well better!" The older man chuckled in his reply, and as he turned to face one of the computer monitors on his desk.

***

Back in the sanctuary of his home, it took almost every bit of self-control in Ren's body to attempt to maintain a regular work schedule for the following week. His desire to delve into the history of the Army of Northern Virginia Monument and the men buried there would have completely overwhelmed him had he not received daily phone calls from one Jake Harrigan.

Ren pondered Harrigan's most recent call: "It's only natural for you to be anxious, Ren. But remember, you need all your wits and Talents focused and relaxed for Combat. If you're exhausted you will give your opponent an advantage. He's already got a jump on you, so your focus is important. See your clients this week, continue with your computer work, and take things as they come, day-to-day. Look, Ren, I've never been in your position, so I can't give you reams of sage advice here. But I can give you some good old-fashioned Irish Channel advice: keep your wits about you!"

Ren smiled inwardly as he stood up from his computer desk, walked into his hallway, then grabbed his camera bag before heading out to the Morial Convention Center, in the Central Business District. On his way, Ren told his phone to call the number of a particular office on Poydras Avenue.

"Janet Garrison," came the reply.

"You know, a thought just occurred to me as you answered your phone."

"Oh, I'm just happy to know I exist to deal with these wild-ass thoughts of yours," JJ replied.

"Oh don't know why I have never really thought of this before, but do you always use your maiden name?"

"Well, duh! It's me, you fool! I am NOT Mrs. Janet Beckman, *thankyewverymuch*. What are you up to? You sound like you're in the car."

"I'm on my way to the Convention Center."

"You're heading down here? C'mon over babe. I'll clear off my desk and we can do it right here!"

Ren chuckled. "Sorry, love. If I do that I won't be able to shoot 'grip and grin' photos of doctors at this medical trade show. Anyway, the reason I called you was to find out what you are doing later."

"Hmm, no soccer today, methinks. Kids can fend for themselves for a bit. So what do you have in mind?"

"Oh, just a little conversation. More would be tempting, to be sure, but I really could use someone to talk to for a while."

"You got it, babe. M&L?"

"Yup."

"K... See you about five then. That way, I don't have to listen to that damned preacher you like so bloody much!"

"Deal, babe," Ren replied, chuckling. "Later then."

"Bye love."

Ren ended the call and continued to navigate through downtown traffic towards the Convention Center. The trade show job was totally uneventful and, after having lunch with his client, a young woman who was supervising her company's booth at the show, he headed back home to continue his research.

The Internet yielded little information about Metairie Cemetery. In fact, his own website was the only source of any detailed information about the place. He sighed audibly and moved from his computer to the extensive array of bookshelves behind him. He chose two books from the shelves, both of which were about the cemetery. One was a coffee-table style picture book which contained some beautiful photographs but was of little factual substance; while the second book presented a number of interesting architectural facts about the Army of Northern Virginia Monument and its tumulus. But there was no information about those who had been buried there. Most references to the cemetery mentioned that Jefferson Davis, the only President of the Confederate States of America, was initially buried there. However, there were no details about other burials at the monument. Ren closed the book, placed it on the small round table in his study, and stretched his legs out. He tried his best to control his frustration by practicing one of the deep-breathing exercises Mike had taught him.

Ren was barely two minutes into his relaxation regimen when the computer on the other side of the room emitted a chime to indicate that new email had arrived. Realizing that his concentration on his breathing had been blown, he stood up and went over to retrieve the message.

From: Flintlock@yatmedia.com
To: PhotoGuyNOLA@gmail.com
Subject: Metairie Cemetery

Hello. I have attached the data from the Army of Northern Virginia which you requested. Good luck in your search!

Ren smiled as he read the message and loaded the database sent by his Civil War research contact. The list was over two thousand names.

Twenty minutes spent trying to scan the list proved to be futile. He sighed, then decided on a more methodical approach. He proceeded to assemble a list of employees' names at Jay Hadley Ministries, which he then augmented with the names of anyone who had been involved with JHM and his dealings with the ministry since the time of Nick's and Trip's deaths. He then added the names of several Marcus-Kayson employees, which he picked off their website as having dealings with JHM. Arranging all these names took Ren a further twenty minutes or so, and he then ran his list of names against the database he had received.

There were 19 matches. Eight were Smith and seven were Jones. While these names could not be ruled out totally, he turned his attention first to the remaining four. The first was Braedon, then Delatorre, Jameson, and Wagner. Three of the names did nothing for him. But Delatorre?

Ren closed his eyes for a moment as he sought the memory. Yes, Delatorre. His hand reached for his phone and thumbed in a local number.

"Jake? Yeah, it's me. Listen, I want to run something past you. I've come up with what may be a genealogical connection between an M-K Vice-President and a man buried in the Army of Northern Virginia tumulus. The name? Delatorre. Major Luke Arthur Delatorre Junior. He was killed at Gettysburg, and brought back to New Orleans and buried in the Protestant section of St. Louis No. 1 Cemetery. He was re-interred into the tumulus on its opening. What I'm looking for is a connection beyond last name, to one Anita Delatorre, who is the M-K person. Yeah, she's involved with Hadley. Looks like she's his M-K point person. Yup, that's right. Great. Yeah, email me back the details. Thanks, Jake."

Ren hung up the phone and went across the hall to the interior room he used as a darkroom, to process some black-and-white film. An hour later, he jumped into his car and was soon sitting on the sea wall at Marconi and Lakeshore Drives, taking a few photographs and returning calls from his clients.

He was doing his level best to follow Jake's advice to keep up his routine. That meant setting-up and keeping appointments, placating brides-to-be and their mothers, and schmoozing his corporate clients as much as possible. These were all things at which Ren was very good at, but they were still tiring to him. He was rubbing his eyes and hanging his head down when he heard an amused voice behind him.

"You started drinking without me? I'm devastated," JJ said.

"Hey baby," Ren groaned, without even looking up. "How was your day?"

"Looks like it was better than yours. You OK?"

"Yeah. Just been on the phone with clients for a while." Ren chuckled. "That always gives me a headache."

JJ sat down next to Ren and began to rub his neck and shoulders gently.

"Mmm, I thought that was my job to do to you," he remarked.

"It is indeed, love. But some days you deserve a little treatment in return. So what's on your mind?"

It took Ren about 15 minutes to explain to JJ the full situation regarding the Challenge. When he had finished, they sat in silence for a moment or two as she absorbed the information. Then she was ready to ask a few questions.

"So you're quite sure the person who is Challenging you is this Delatorre woman?"

"Yes I am. It makes a lot of sense. For openers, the likelihood that one of the staff members of JHM would have Talents is pretty slim. They're all a pretty reactionary lot, and that would really get on their nerves. Then there's the genealogical connection between our Miss Anita and the Major Delatorre who's buried in Metairie Cemetery. Finally, the resemblance between Anita and Elizabeth McKinney is uncanny. They're dead ringers."

"That would suggest she has Talents, yes," JJ agreed. "I would never have thought that a Christian publisher would be so ruthless as to be ordering hits on their opposition, much less these 'Magickal' duels you've got yourself into. Still, you have been a good deal of trouble to them, damaging their hot radio commodity as much as you have. There's no reason to believe that 'vindictive bitch' isn't one of Anita's strong qualities."

Ren laughed, this time throwing back his head. "Spoken like a third-generation bitch, love."

"Well, you take it to heart, then, dear Ren. I've invested way too much in you as a friend to lose you now."

Ren smiled at her and turned to hug her tightly. "I'll be fine, JJ, don't you worry a bit."

"I do worry! You're taking this way too lightly, my friend."

"Believe me when I tell you I don't. I feel like I've been pulled into a strong current and can't escape. In spite of everything, though, I'm not worried. I don't have a cocky attitude but I still feel everything will be OK."

"Huh. 'Don't worry, be happy'? That went out in the Reagan years, dear." JJ wrapped her arms around him again. "Just remember you are fighting a female, Ren. Male types like you have notions of honor and chivalry when having to fight a woman. If you treat her with that same sense of honor she will take advantage of that and nail you. This woman is your enemy, Ren. Treat her with contempt."

Ren pulled away for a moment. "I've never seen you like this, JJ."

"Momma-bear syndrome, dear," she said smiling. "Just do what you have to do and come back, OK?"

"I promise," he said as he drew her to him again and kissed her deeply.

CHAPTER TWENTY-THREE
Protocol

"It's about time you got back into town!" said Ren as he stood up to meet Mike O'Donnell at Koz's Restaurant in Lakeview.

"Yea, I'm sorry about that, Ren. I wanted to call but the circumstances of the trip wouldn't allow it." The older man motioned Ren back into the rear dining room and they each took a seat at a table against the wall. Mike was carrying two po-boys wrapped in white butcher's paper, and he tossed one of them onto the table, in front of Ren.

"What's this?"

"Lunch."

"Jeez, Mike, I can't eat a thing. I'm on pins and needles."

"I know." Mike pointed at the sandwich. "Eat."

"But..."

"Eat. It's barbecued beef, dressed."

Ren sighed. "You don't play fair."

"And that, sir, is the first lesson of the day. Magickal combat is about bending your opponents will to yours, and then destroying him. I worked you down just now and you gave in. that's the last time you will do that on any issue, large or small, until this affair is over. Still, you need to eat."

Ren unwrapped his sandwich and Mike did the same with his. The priest took a bite and sighed.

"For all the good food in other cities, I still enjoy the simple pleasures of home. Now you eat, I'll talk. Jake briefed me in email and on the phone. I wish I could have been there when the Challenge came in, but you'll find sometimes these trips of mine just can't be avoided."

"I understand, Mike. Besides, I'm a big boy now. I can't come running to you all the time."

“On the contrary laddie, you can indeed! That's why I worked up a local support system for you. You're to come running or call Jake whenever you feel the need. Please don't feel like it's an imposition." The priest's eyes twinkled as he delivered that last remark, and Ren caught it.

"Hmm. No imposition, uh? What's in it for you then?" Ren smiled as he made the verbal challenge.

"Ah, you're starting to get to know me, Ren," Mike chuckled through a mouthful of beef. "I'll have to work on becoming less transparent to you. Yes, my friend, there is a catch. Just as you might call upon Jake on occasion. he or I might call upon you for certain.. ahhh, 'situations' which may arise."

"Is this an example of a 'situation'?" Ren responded, his expression now quite serious.

"Well, yes. But we wouldn't be asking you to fight a duel, Ren. Let's say, for example, that another member of our little support network had been Challenged in the same manner as you've been. Perhaps Jake might want to give you a call to pick your brain about some history. You know, background research. Or maybe we might occasionally need a photo or two taken. Trust me when I tell you that I am certainly not requiring a blood-oath from you."

“At least not yet,” the priest thought to himself.

"OK, I can handle this then," responded Ren, becoming more relaxed as he finished of the last bite of his po-boy. "Jeez," he said as he sighed contentedly. "When I came in here there was no way I could even eat a bite!"

"Stress and tension can do that to you. You need to continue your relaxation exercises morning and evening. There are times you will need to banish tension and calm any fear. The disciplined mind can do this without any difficulty."

Mike switched tacks. "Let's talk about this duel now. First, open your mind to me and give me your memory of receiving the Challenge." Mike closed his eyes and stretched out his hands across the table towards Ren, who mirrored Mike's actions and gently touched Mike's fingertips with is own. He began to download images of the incident of receiving the Challenge note.

After just an instant, Ren withdrew his hands and opened his eyes. In turn, as was his custom, Mike remained in his trance a moment longer, absorbing and processing the new information he had received.

"Well," Mike eventually declared, "they certainly have done everything by the book. "That tell us your Challenger has most likely read the book, or been taught it well, as you have."

"Is that a good or a bad thing?"

"Good and bad. Good in that they will probably follow the rules and not resort to any sort of treachery. Bad, in that your Challenger is obviously trained in the use of their Talents. They may even already have Combat experience."

"In other words," Ren said, pondering, "she feels she can do things by the book because she thinks I'll be easy to deal with?"

"Yes. That's about the size of it. I noticed you referred to your Challenger as 'she'. I take it from that you still believe she is this Delatorre woman?"

"Yes I do," Ren said firmly.

"I'm inclined to agree with you but I wouldn't go as far as to bet my ass on it, just yet." Mike chuckled. "And I don't think I want to bet your ass on it yet, either! Let's continue your overall preparation for this Combat a little more generic manner. If your opponent is the lovely Ms. Delatorre, that will be great for your ego. If it isn't, then we need to make sure you won't be totally freaked out when someone else shows up for the duel," Mike concluded.

"Speaking of which, Obi-wan, how many people will be showing up anyway?"

"Oh, just your Challenger. The Protocol is quite specific about that. I'll be glad to give you lift to the combat ground, in this case the cemetery. But I won't even be coming in. Given that they have followed the book, I think you can expect a solo appearance from her too." Mike stood up from the table. "I'll be right back" he added, and he began to walk to the front of the restaurant.

Ren took the opportunity to gaze around Koz's. The sign from the old, flooded, location in Gentilly was up against the wall. Ah, memories, Ren smiled, but then immediately felt a pang of anxiety. If the outcome of this duel did not turn out as planned then this could be the last time he ever ate here.

"Don't look like that, Renard!" Mike exclaimed upon his return to the table. "You know I'm not a mind-reader but I can sure tell when some gets into that 'I'll never see this place again' mood. I don't want any part of it, d'you hear? It's too easy for that shit to become a self-fulfilling prophecy."

"OK, I'm sorry. I just got a bit melancholy for a moment."

“If you want to be melancholy about something, be sad that we can't finish this meal with a Hubig's Pie. One of Koz's sandwiches just wasn't complete unless it was followed by a Hubig's Pie." Mike laughed.

They continued to muse about Simon Hubig's fried pies, and other "ain't there no more" memories of growing up and living in Gentilly. After a few moments, Mike looked at his watch and frowned.

"Ren, I've got to run. I've been away from school so darned long that I'd better check on my grad students. We'll get together again for sure before Halloween, and I'm serious about being there for you as much as I can on the night itself."

“That's great, Mike. You know I can't even begin to tell you how much I appreciate your help. I've no idea how I'll ever repay you a fraction of what you've done for me."

"Oh, don't worry," The priest grinned at Ren with a mischievous look on his face. "I'll figure out how you'll repay me. Don't be startled, this isn't some Faustian bargain. Just remember the support network. That in itself will be the best way of repaying me." Mike patted Ren on the shoulder. "Discipline, Ren. Practice controlling your fear and releasing the tension in you, and you'll have a major advantage over your opponent. They don't know exactly who or what you are. They're going to be cocky and that's the weakness you can exploit. I'll call you during the week to check up on you." Mike waved twice has he departed; first to the owner, at the side, and then back to Ren.

As Mike left the restaurant, Ren went back to the drink

dispenser, refilled his drink, and then checked the messages on his phone. It seemed all so simple. Could it really be just so?

***

"So, I still don't know whether I'll be going back to Dallas tomorrow night, Jay. My assistants are loading me up with tons of meetings in November, so I may need to get a jump on prep work for them. I'm just not sure." Anita Delatorre knew full well where she would be spending the next night, but she had no intention of revealing those plans to Jay Hadley. She and Hadley were sitting on the small sofa in the private study/bedroom he kept behind the main office, on the shore of Lake Pontchartrain.

"It's just that Halloween is such a big day for the Ministry, Anita. You know that. The Halloween show is one of the most fun times of the year."

"For you, maybe, Jay. But it scares the shit out of your staff."

"What do you mean?" Jay replied as a puzzled look developed across his face.

"There are two types of people who work for you, Jay. True believers and all-business. The true believers actually think the day is a dangerous one, where the spirits are going to come out and take them over. Or they buy into all your stories about occult rituals being held on the 31st to seduce their children into witchcraft and pure evil. The day really does scare the shit out of them."

"And the all-business ones?"

"They know that Samhain is a great day for Pagans and others to fuck with you. You revel in it. But they are scared to death that someone will get on the air and make some revelation or other about your personal life or the Ministry's finances. Not only do those kind of comments break your rhythm, but they also discourage the fringe element of the true believers, which causes a dip in the number of pledges and that ding to the bottom line makes them nervous. None of them are as financially secure as you, Jay, so they need their jobs. You've been good to them but you do make them very nervous."

"I see. Do you think I should change anything about

tomorrow, then?"

"Oh no, indeed, you silly man! They might have their fears and concerns, but they still love the show. For the true believers it's like a hot roller-coaster ride; and for the all-business it's the rush of being at the top of their game while you perform."

Jay grinned. "Sometimes I just don't understand you, Anita. But that's OK as long as I get to hold you."

"Why Reverend Hadley, what a nice thing to tell a lady!" she responded in a mock sugar-sweet southern accent. She leaned over to him and kissed him gently on his cheek. He turned towards her and their lips met, tentatively at first, but then his passion for her overtook him and he kissed her deeply. His hands began rubbing up and down her back, then found the buttons of her suit jacket. She helped him to slip it off, but then backed away, so he didn't damage her silk blouse. She moved closer again, allowing him to slip off her bra. She lay back as he began to kiss her erect nipples as she gasped. Anita knew this encounter would be quick and physical.

She pushed him away gently a second time and stood up from the couch to remove all but her thigh-high stockings. She moved over and lay on the bed, seductively, as if to dare him to come and take her. The sight of her, naked, on the bed drove him towards a near-animal state; exactly how she wanted him.

It turned out, indeed, to be a physical and rough encounter. While Hadley could, at times, be a very gentle lover, the subtle signs which Anita had been depositing into his subconscious throughout the day had finally consumed him. So he mounted her like a beast. She accepted his forcefulness fully, capturing the sexual energy he released and storing it within her body. By the time he was about to explode she was like a battery on a 110 percent charge. He screamed as he thrust his orgasm into her then collapsed on the bed.

"God, Anita, I've never been so overcome with lust! I don't know how you manage to drive me wild like that without it killing me. I'm not a young man any more!"

"Oh, sweetie, you're doing just fine. Don't you worry."

"Besides," she thought, *"I don't want to destroy a renewable energy source if I don't have to."*

She kissed him on the forehead and then rolled out of bed.

"You rest, sugar. I need to run back to my room and check my email. You'll have a wonderful show tomorrow, and hopefully we can do this again tomorrow evening."

***

The day before Halloween was, fortunately for Ren, a busy one. Autumn brought with it a steady stream of work; conventions and various school events. In between his morning appointments he took the opportunity of having his daily phone chat with his mentor.

"It's more than a little important that you be your usual laid-back self when you take this Challenge on, Ren," Mike said. "There's no more time to teach you anything substantive with regards to using your Talents. You know what you need to know, and you feel what you need to feel. The key now is to maintain your state of mind so that you can focus on what you need to and mount active defenses based on those feelings."

"You do realize you're not making much sense, Obi-wan," said Ren as he chuckled.

"You might think so, Weedhopper, but I still want you to relax. When you get there, you'll still have one of those revelations that you're supposed to have at times like that and you'll appreciate all this psycho-babble then."

Ren laughed as he steered his Jeep through the narrow streets of the French Quarter. "If you say so, Mike. Hey, do you say morning Mass tomorrow?"

"Yes, I do mornings. But I'm going down to St. Raphael's, umm, 'Transfiguration', on Elysian Fields tomorrow to cover for the guys there. My friend, the pastor has a problem. His assistant has the day off, but he wants to go to a golf tournament for one of the oil companies. You know, the kind of tournament where everyone wears costumes and the golf carts are loaded up with ice-chests of beer?" Mike laughed.

Ren laughed with him. "Oh, I know those events quite well. I'm glad you're resisting the temptation to join him, then."

"Surely you jest, my friend. I would not miss my small

role in tomorrow's activities for all the gold in the world, much less all the beer in New Orleans. If you're serious about joining me for the Eucharistic Liturgy, as the Mass is now known officially these days, c'mon over to St. Raphael's for eight-thirty, OK?"

"Cool Mike. I'll see you then!" Ren switched off the phone.

"Jeez, it was a good thing this mother-of-the-bride is such a bitch. I'll need all my wits to deal with her so I won't be dwelling on the fact that tomorrow might be the last time I ever attend Mass," he thought.

Halloween dawned foggy, and it was still a bit gloomy when Ren pulled his car into the Prentiss Avenue side of Transfiguration of Our Lord Church, formerly St. Raphael the Archangel Church, in Gentilly. St. Raphael (he still couldn't wrap his brain around the parish's new name) was not one of his favorite churches in town, but it still held some special memories for him, from his high school days, down the street.

As was the case with most weekday morning Masses, there were no more than 20 people arranged in the first ten or so rows of pews. He took a seat just forward of the halfway point along the main aisle and scanned the church. His eyes focused on the flickering Presence Lamp just off the left of the church, behind the altar. The flame of the candle was filtered by thick red glass and its soothing bounce caused Ren to drop into a light trance. He could feel the fear and doubt rise within him as the trance made him more vulnerable. But after several deep breaths, that fear was dispelled and he became more relaxed. Mike's techniques were working; he was able to banish his concerns and focus.

Ren's reverie was broken by the chimes of the bells that announced the beginning of the small procession that started the morning. Two altar servers, a boy and a girl, preceded Msgr. O'Donnell out of the sacristy towards the front of the main altar, where they stopped and bowed, before Mike moved to the other side of the altar and the servers took their assigned stations.

Mike began to deliver the prescribed liturgy for the Eve of All Saints with a crisp efficiency. The regular congregation stood for the Profession of Faith even before Ren realized that Mike had completed the readings, the gospel, and had preached the brief homily. Ren shook his head gently and refocused his attention on the Mass rather than on the emotions which were swirling in his conscious mind. Mike invited the congregation to stand once again and, with the Preface complete, everyone began to kneel for the Consecration. As Mike began the ancient prayer, Ren again noticed the energy visibly swell up around the priest as he cast the spells to change the bread and wine into Flesh and Blood. In spite of all Ren had seen and experienced, he still found his Faith lacking. Seeing the energy shift from celebrant to the Host and chalice, however, convinced Ren that, indeed something was happening. And that "something" would be with him that evening when he faced his enemy.

The remainder of the Mass blurred past him, and Ren found himself walking around the side of the church to catch up with his friend. Mike beckoned to Ren to join him in his Porsche.

"Did you eat breakfast?" the priest asked.

"No."

"I figured as much. C'mon, let's run down to Blue Dot on Canal Street, I've got a craving."

"For...?"

"For bacon donuts!" Mike explained through his laughter.

The pair zipped to Mid City, where they grabbed donuts and two pints of milk. When Mike had stuffed the last of his donut into his mouth he turned to Ren.

"This is one of the great guilty pleasures of life, don't you know."

"No kidding!" Ren agreed.

Mike started the car and swung it around to drop Ren off back at his car. "How about I pick you up at around four-thirty at your place and then give you a lift over to the cemetery?"

"Thanks, Mike. I appreciate that. I hadn't given a single thought about how I was to get there."

"Understandable. I'll drop you off and you can meet me over by Greenwood Cemetery when you're done."

"You're sure I'll make it?"

"To be honest, no. But I'm sure you're ready for this, Ren. And I know you'll do your best. That, and I'm superstitious. I've got this awesome bottle of port that I've been dying to drink for some time. Graham's Vintage 1960, from Portugal. I'll have it waiting. Walk over there and we'll have some, OK?"

Ren took a deep breath and grinned. "Will do, Mike. I'm going to run home for a short while. See you there at four-thirty?"

"You know it! See you."

Mike sped off towards the Lakefront as Ren climbed into his car and headed for home. Upon arrival he reviewed an email message from his attorney, which dealt with the will he had put together the week before. All his affairs were now fully in order and he was ready to face whatever would happen that evening. He was about to close his computer down when a Twitter message popped up:

"All set for tonight?"

"As well as I can be, luv."

"Well, I expect a full report in the morning, love. I'm trying to get a grip on what this is all about."

"That's assuming I'm around in the morning to give you that report."

"Don't even talk like that, Ren. You WILL be here in the morning."

"Why is everyone so sure, except me?"

"Ren, I may not have all your abilities, but I do have awesome intuition. And that intuition tells me that it's simply not your time yet. You go out to that cemetery and kick this woman's ass into another plane of existence, or whatever the hell you're supposed to do!"

"Hmm... I'm supposed to kill her, love."

"Then fucking kill her before she kills you!"

"Yes, ma'am!"

"Sorry, love. That was a bit of a momma-bear reaction, wasn't it? :-)"

"It was. But no momma-bear ever looked as good in a short skirt as you do."

"Isn't that the truth. And damn, do I look good in mine today! Tell you what, I'll wear one tomorrow when we have lunch, OK?"

"You're on, JJ! :-)"

"Be safe, love. See ya tomorrow...."

"Xoxoxoxo"

One email message had come in while Ren had been chatting with JJ; a final note of good wishes from Jake Harrigan. Ren could just hear the older man's voice as he read the words. Ren smiled and shut down his workstation, then took the nap Mike had suggested.

***

In Metairie, Anita Delatorre was not napping. As a trained occultist, she knew her abilities and limits very well. Trying not to develop too much of a sense of over-confidence, she had no misgivings as to the outcome of the evening's duel.

Mentally, Anita walked through her plans for the combat at least a dozen times. She knew that Alciatore had been under the protection of a very skilled and powerful Teacher, but she also knew that Teacher's main weakness. Unlike those who had been her instructors, the priest would not have schooled her pupil in the Black Arts. That would be his undoing, because Anita had been fully-trained in the ways of the Dark.

But maybe it won't even come to that, Anita thought. He

may just fold up and panic. Once again dismissing any feelings of over-confidence, she sat in the armchair in her hotel suite, closed her eyes, and brought herself into a light trance. The energy she had recently drained from Jay Hadley swirled around within her body, caressing and teasing her. Anita's skill should have enabled her to push those sensations aside, but the energy level was simply too high for her to ignore. As a result, she was tense; almost hyperactive.

After checking her email for the fourth time in an hour, she finally settled down in her chair and began to meditate. Since she had given up hope of any peaceful meditation, she once again reviewed the Protocol that governed the duel that evening.

The Challenge having been issued and accepted, the two parties would enter the dueling area separately. They would also be alone; no other human beings would be allowed within five hundred yards of the place of Combat.

"The priest would most likely drop him off," she thought.

The person in her life whom she considered her mentor lived in San Francisco, and she was not going to call him about a Combat she figured would be over in ten minutes. Anita made a mental note to contact him the following day to catch up on things, and then she continued with her review.

Once the combatants had reached the place of Combat, an area would be warded by mutual agreement; each combatant would put forth a matching amount of energy to seal the wards. From that point, there would be no chance of any outside interference, and they could begin the combat. The Protocol did not restrict them in any way once the wards were complete. If they chose to throw stones at each other, then that was just as acceptable as summoning demons and any other fantastic creatures.

Once the Combat came to its logical conclusion, Protocol demanded that the victor dismantle the wards and psychically "clean" the site. She would, of course, have ample energy in reserve to deal with this. Still, the overall energy drain from Magickal Combat was such that she would have to exercise extreme caution that she would not fall asleep on her drive back to the hotel.

Once she was satisfied that she had the situation well in hand, Anita shifted over to the desk and called her office to book her flight back to Dallas the following afternoon. That would give her sufficient time to get a good night's sleep and then a nap on the plane. “Yes,” she told her assistant, “definitely first class, and have a limo meet me at DFW. Yes, everything here is fine; I’ve simply been away from the office too much for my own taste lately, so I need some time to catch up on things there.”

Once the travel arrangements were completed, Anita went back to the large armchair on the other side of the room. She closed her eyes and resumed her meditation, shifting the energy around her in an attempt to settle things down. Even it if wasn't working, it was a simple enough diversion to pass the time.

***

Two-thirty in the afternoon was not a regular time for Renard Alciatore to be at home. If he wasn't actually working on a job for a client at that time, he would be out and about in the city shooting photos of whatever took his fancy. Today obviously being different, he lacked any motivation to get out and go. Mike's admonitions about his mind dwelling on the duel got the better of him, however, so he grabbed one of his Nikon cameras and headed out towards the bayou.

He walked down to the corner of Moss and Esplanade, having decided to shoot a few pictures of the statue of the Civil War general, P.G.T. Beauregard. The statue stood in the middle of a small traffic circle that joined Esplanade, City Park Avenue, Wisner Boulevard, and the entrance to the New Orleans Museum of Art.

Dueling Oaks is right there, he thought. A much more appropriate venue for that evening. He sighed, dismissed the thought, and took several shots of the statue from different angles and distances. Despite the concentration required to compose the shots, it was still difficult to dismiss thoughts of the duel. Beauregard was the problem, The guy was buried right there in Metairie Cemetery, bringing his thoughts back to the duel. At least Beauregard was buried in the Army of Tennessee tumulus, which was not the site of the duel. Beauregard had been a popular figure in the post-war city, in spite of his involvement with the crooked lottery of the Reconstruction period.

Once he had taken several solid shots of the General's statue, Ren turned to walk into City Park towards the museum. The oak trees offered some shade so he headed towards a large one near the lagoon in the south-eastern corner of the park. City Park was originally part of a plantation, and the lagoons were the result of WPA work in the 19thirties. Ren sat down on the grass below the oak tree, stretched his legs out, and enjoyed the peace and quiet. An hour passed with him doing absolutely nothing and, finally relaxed, he prepared to do what had to be done.

Anita Delatorre grabbed her keys and walked out of her suite at precisely four o'clock. It was a short drive from her Metairie hotel to the Cemetery, but Friday afternoon traffic in New Orleans was always a mess. No harm in arriving a little early, she thought. Once on I-10 she made a quick phone call to the office to check her travel arrangements for the following day, then another call to JHM where she received a brief report on the day's show. "End-times" panic and the Halloween threats from occultists had combined to make this one of the most successful October 31st shows in the history of the Ministry, and Jay was quite pleased, according to the show's new producer. Anita smiled and hung up before guiding her rental car through traffic to the Metairie Road exit, where she double backed around and pulled into the Pontchartrain Boulevard entrance to Metairie Cemetery. She pulled the car into the parking lot of the funeral home on the cemetery's grounds and walked slowly from this newer section over to the "racetrack" section of the property. Yes, this is a good day. The ministry is on track, the book projects are back where they should be. Sales of homeschooling materials were skyrocketing.

And now the problem of Renard Alciatore would soon become part of the past.

Ren was stretched out on the couch in his den when he heard the honk of a horn outside, heralding the arrival of his mentor. It was four-thirty on the dot.

"Right on time!" he said as he climbed into Mike's Porsche.

"Did you expect anything less?" Mike smiled. "I'm glad you took my advice about what to wear. I was afraid for a while that you might decide this was some sort of formal event and dress accordingly."

"Well, you know, this does feel like something you should wear a suit to," Ren said. "But you had a point that the comfort and ease of movement is key."

"Yeah. The Protocol is significantly silent on the subject of dress code. The history of Magickal duels has shown that combatants have worn anything from swimsuits to white-tie formal wear. My experience in these matters is that you don't want to be thinking about how tight your shirt collar is or that your shoes are too tight. Besides, there's always the possibility that there will be enough of a physical dimension to any Combat, so it is better to go for clothing that won't be a hindrance."

The ride from Ren's house to the Cemetery was a short one; just a hop across City Park Avenue, past the foot of Canal Street, and under the Interstate.

"Ren, I'm going to make the U-turn right under the overpass and then let you out on the corner at Metairie Road," the priest said. "You can climb the steps on the corner there and enter the Cemetery through the old gate. That is the original entrance, so focus on the history of the grounds as you walk in. Remember, your opponent has most likely chosen this location because of some particular meaning. Soak in the history of the Cemetery as best you can and turn it to your advantage."

"Will do. Mike, let me just say thanks one more time."

"You're welcome. You can show your appreciation properly later when we break out that port. I'll have it ready to go for you. Just walk back over to the other side of the overpass by Greenwood, OK?"

"Got it."

Mike swung the car around and stopped momentarily on the corner.

"Here you go, Ren. Stay focused and positive."

"See you in a bit, Mike."

They shook hands and Ren climbed the concrete steps up to the old main gate. There was a chain wrapped around the gate, with a basic Master lock, blocking his way. Just as he raised his arm to unlock the lock, it popped open and fell silently to the ground, followed by the chain.

"I figured you didn't need to worry about the additional energy drain. Go with the blessings of the Light and Her Angels and Archangels, Renard!"

Ren could see the little car speeding away with the priest at the wheel, so he knew no reply was necessary. Mike's final blessing, however, had not been a casual one: Ren could feel the firm confidence of a Presence lightly touching his shoulder. He smiled as he walked through the gate and on to face his Challenger.

CHAPTER TWENTY-FOUR

To The Light

His Challenger might have a connection with Metairie Cemetery, but any such connection was more than offset by Ren's attraction to the place. He admired the Army of Tennessee tumulus to his right, and the old receiving chapel to his left. He walked slowly through this, the finest of New Orleans' "cities of the dead", and took-in the remarkable mixture of simplicity and grandeur. Many of the tombs in this part of the cemetery dated back to its opening in the 1870s; a time when families were still bringing home their dead young men from the battlefields of the Civil War, to bury them alongside their loved ones.

Ren continued his slow pace along Central Avenue, the street that cut across the older part of the cemetery and which connected it with the new main gate further along Pontchartrain Boulevard. He stopped at the first intersection, the outside ring of the former "racetrack". Before this piece of land became a cemetery it had been Metairie Race Track, a "gentlemen's club" where the men of antebellum New Orleans went to watch and bet on horse races. According to local legend, one of the founders of the cemetery association had been blackballed from the club that owned the racetrack. So he swore that one day, he would buy the place and turn it into a graveyard.

The cemetery layout followed the oval of the racetrack, with three concentric rings in what would have been the track's infield, and which encircled prominent monuments and tombs. Ren turned left into Avenue A, the outer ring, and moved in a clockwise direction around it. He never ceased to marvel at how serene this place was. He took a deep breath as he rounded the curve in the eastern portion of the oval, continuing with a steady slow pace.

He turned into the eastern curve of the oval and stepped up the pace as he approached Central Avenue again, and walked up the short section of road towards Avenue B, where he repeated the curve around the racetrack on the middle road. This was the location of the massive tombs where the various benevolent societies buried their members. Tombs were not cheap, even in the 1900s, so many families would pool their money to build large structures that could hold dozens of their departed loved ones, thereby ensuring that their people had a proper place to go to when their time came. Ren bowed his head while passing through this section. As the son of an old New Orleans family, he had no doubt that he had a number of friends and relatives buried in these vaults. As he worked his way past the society tombs, he marveled at the quality and the workmanship of the individual family tombs on the western curve of Avenue B. Intermingled with the tombs were a few in-ground graves which were built up around their edges with small brick or stone reinforcing walls. Most of these graves were owned by Jewish families, whose burial rituals call for in-ground burial rather than the above-ground burial which was common in New Orleans.

The sun was rapidly getting lower in the sky, an indication that the appointed hour was approaching. Ren completed the walk along Avenue B and turned back onto the connecting road, then on to Metairie Avenue, before taking his walk along what was know as "Millionaire's Row". This interior section of the racetrack was the prime real estate of the old cemetery. The size and beauty of the ornate tombs here bore testimony to that. He took the western curve past the pyramid-shaped Brunswig tomb, ignoring for now the Army of Northern Virginia tumulus to his right. As he went along the "back stretch" he slowed his pace a little as he passed several war memorials, bowing his head slightly once again, this time to honor the men and women who had given their lives for what they had believed in.

"Maybe this is where I'll end up when my time comes, That might be today for all I know. Will I be next to give my

life in such a cause? But what do I believe in? I know what Mike has taught me, but is that a set of beliefs or merely a set of instructions? Half of what the Brothers taught me about religion was just so much crap, according to many of the priests I've listened to. Still, Mike's a priest, he believes in God. 'The Light' is how he refers to God. And he says, 'Her Angels and Archangels', as if God were a female. Well shit, maybe She is. That would certainly explain a lot, wouldn't it?"

He shook his head gently and quickly banished that thought. I've still got lots of time left. These Talents of mine have so much potential for doing good, I can't let them go to waste simply because I didn't focus on the task at hand.

Ren turned slowly through the eastern curve of this final oval and began working his way to his destination, taking notice of carious statues of angels as he walked. Mike must believe in those as well, he deduced, since he had asked them to bless me. Or is that just Irish superstition. Nah, Mike O'Donnell may be many things, but he's not superstitious. But, angels? Do angels ever look after me? Who knows, maybe so. I'll give that more thought the next time I'm meditating.

Ren sighed and stopped walking to stand in front of the Army of Northern Virginia monument and its tumulus. Built on a hill about 20 feet high was a column that rose up thirty-eight feet. Atop that column was a statue of Thomas Jefferson "Stonewall" Jackson; Robert E. Lee's best general during the Civil War. He looked up as the column cast a long shadow eastward. Ren approached the hill and walked around it to its northern side. The base of the hill was open on this side and an archway led in to the burial chamber carved into the mound. The hill was a tumulus whose vaults housed the remains of around 2,500 soldiers and officers who had fallen in the Civil War. In addition to those, one empty vault marked the original burial place of Jefferson Davis, the only President of the Confederate States of America. Davis fell ill while passing through New Orleans in November, 1889. He died on December 6, 1889, and was interred in Metairie Cemetery, until his wife decided to make Richmond his final resting place. Two vaults down from where Ren stood was the final resting place of one Major Luke Arthur Delatorre, Junior.

Ren looked up from the entrance to the tumulus to see a golden-haired woman waiting for him on the mound, at the northern side of the column's base. He nodded his head again in respect for all the men who had died for their country, and then walked around to meet the woman on the eastern side of the monument. As he began to ascend the steps, his thoughts formed a brief prayer, formed in the style of his mentor.

"Creator of Lights, protect me as this day ends. Guide me on the path of the Light and grant me wisdom to overcome the obstacles in my path."

Ren reached the base of the column as he completed his prayer, and turned to face the Challenger who was waiting for him. He looked Anita Delatorre in the eye and stopped short. He had known to expect a woman who looked like the Elizabeth McKinney of his encounter at the plantation, but the reality of this woman's resemblance was something that just could not be done justice by a mere mental image compared with a photograph on a webpage. He broke eye contact to follow her frame down to her low heels, then back up to her face again.

"Well, I hope you like what you see my Lord, " Anita said, chuckling slightly. "What a pity you won't be around to sample the goodies."

Ren smiled at his opponent. "Actually, I was thinking about how striking your resemblance is between you and Elizabeth."

"Ah, you've been doing your homework, I see. Congratulations on your deduction. Not that it will matter much in terms of the final outcome."

"Cocky bitch," thought Ren.

"Still, she's probably done this before. Perhaps she has a reason to be cocky?"

"It's your show, Ms. Delatorre," he said, bowing slightly. Ren took three steps back and stood firmly in the south-east arc of the circle that surrounded the column. Anita stepped forward and took her position on the north-east arc.

"Down to South versus North again," Ren mused.

"Not that I'm complaining about the position, since the South is the domination of Michael, Fire of God, the patron of warriors. I'm not much of a warrior, mighty Archangel, but

I'm certainly one today. I'd mightily appreciate any help you can send my way."

Behind him, the ground that was the southern arc of the circle suddenly flashed bright red-green-red, as if the ground was the floor of a disco.

"Disco imagery; an Archangel with a sense of humor." Ren could swear he discerned a wry chuckle in the distance.

Anita either did not see the flashes of light or she chose to ignore them. She nodded to Ren then stretched her right hand out in front of her.

"In accordance with the Red Protocol, I will that this duel commences, my Lord Renard. I command that all persons other than you and I be gone from this place of Combat and entreat you to complete the Circle of Power."

Anita lowered her right hand, then raised both her hands in front of her to a position above her head. She extended her arms out from her sides, and drew them together in front of her.

Ren knew what to expect once those motions were complete, but he gasped nevertheless. A globe of gray-white light formed at the northern compass point of the circle upon which they were standing. As Anita's arms came together in front of her, a thin line of light extended out from either side of the glowing globe. It started with the gray-white color of the globe, becoming gray-blue halfway through the north-west arc, then blue-orange, terminating in a blue-orange globe at the western compass point. The light crawling out through the north-east changed hue to gray-yellow, then yellow-violet, where it merged with a sphere of yellow-blue light at the eastern compass point.

Ren was impressed, but he knew what the proper response was. Extending his arms in a mirror-image of Anita's gesture, he again asked the Archangel for guidance as he visualized a globe of green-red light behind him at the southern compass point. Red-green light followed the arcs northward, turning red-blue then blue-orange as it terminated in the west; and red-yellow, then yellow-violet in the east.

The two trails of light Ren had originated merged with the western and eastern halves and, at that instant, four arcs of white light shot up above the statue on top of the column. An umbrella of white light then dropped down over the column to completely cover it, the two combatants, and the circle on which they stood.

Anita nodded to acknowledge Ren's closure of the circle. She stretched out her arms to either side of herself as she began the next phase of the duel.

"In further accord with the Red Protocol, I challenge you, my Lord Renard, to join me in single combat. I stipulate that this combat will be complete when one of us lies dead within the circle. I entreat you to join me in sealing this circle so that death is the only means by which it can be dismantled."

As she completed the words of her challenge, Anita raised her arms above her head and a flash of golden light emanated from her fingertips and rose to the white canopy above her, to spread down over her half of the Circle of Combat.

Ren felt the desire to say something in response as he began to raise his arms in order to complete the inner canopy, but as he did so, he thought back to the advice given to him by his mentor:

“When some people enter into a magical duel, they get all poetic, closing the circles in verse and casting spells in rhyme. others are much more technical, meeting the obligations of the Protocol in a brisk, short format, as if they were a lawyer presenting a motion before a judge. Personally, I don't care for either approach. Verse requires you to concentrate on form over substance; the technical approach is better but you still tend to telegraph more information to your opponent than you really want to.

“Your best approach is to keep your mouth shut. Let your actions speak for you. You can fulfill all of the requirements of the Red Protocol and conduct your duel without ever saying a word. Do that and you'll give yourself a double advantage: you won't telegraph very much, and you will also really piss of the bad guy."

The combination of the memory and the look of annoyance on Anita's face as he wordlessly lowered his arms back to his side made him smile.

"It appears that protégés of the Assembly are no longer taught manners."

Ren shrugged his shoulders in response.

Regaining her composure, Anita continued: "The first strike is yours to claim, my Lord. Art thou ready to begin?"

***

Ren again eyed Anita from head to toe. She was dressed in all black. A clingy black sweater, full-cut black skirt, black hose tucked into black riding boots. There was a marked contrast between the black clothes and her fair skin. Had Ren encountered her in a bar, he would no doubt have been extremely attracted. Ren ran his eyes over her once more, lingering upon her breasts for just a little longer than he would ever do in polite company.

"Thank you, my Lady, but it would be rude of me to claim first strike after all the trouble you went through to make yourself pretty for this evening." He bowed and smiled.

“Well, I see that I was wrong in my initial assessment of your manners, my Lord. We will begin then." She assumed a modified martial-arts stance and began to weave a spell with her hands, just in front of her face.

Ren could not hear the words which she muttered under her breath, but her body language made her intentions clear. On the third pass of her hands in front of her, a blue-gray cloud of mist coalesced around her hands forming a barbed bolt of light that slowly crossed the space between the two combatants, and crawled towards Ren, hissing and spitting flame as it went. As it got to within ten feet of Ren's body, its speed increased tenfold. Ren was ready for this and threw out his hands to conjure a shield of blue energy in front of him. Anita's bolt of darkling energy crashed into the shield and shattered harmlessly.

Ren did not waste a second. As soon as the threat had gone he raised his hands and cast his own testing spell. Extending his fingertips towards Anita, ten red slivers of light shot out at her like small blood-tipped darts. Anita had been expecting one of the standard testing spells rather than one involving such a quick attack. She cast a midnight-black shield in front of her and was able to deflect nine of the ten darts. But the tenth was just a little faster than the others and it zipped past her shield. She ducked her right shoulder slightly and the dart grazed the fabric of her sweater, leaving a slight tear.

She threw a look of pure hatred at Ren as she settled the damaged sweater back as best she could. Waving her hands and muttering again under her breath she brought up another cloud of mist in front of her; this one taking on the form of a small winged lizard. The creature beat its wings three times, hovered in the air in front of her, then began to fly right at Ren, belching fire and smoke before it.

Ren immediately began a deep-breathing routine and focused on a counter-attack for the beast. He waved his arms briskly in a series of circles to gather the air in front of him into a horizontal vortex about two feet across. He pointed the vortex with his two forefingers and guided the swirling mass of air forward. As the vortex approached within a foot of the spectral lizard it accelerated and engulfed the creature before imploding without a sound.

The testing spells continued for another half an hour. Anita launching an attack, then Ren deflecting the spell and countering with one of his own. Their spells varied between energy bolts and the small creatures. First Anita's lizard, then a snarling wolf from Ren. Anita followed with another energy strike which was deftly turned off and countered by Ren with a dazzling display of blue-gold lightning.

The sun had by now set completely, but the glow of the protected circle illuminated the area of the memorial with a deep off-white glow. Anita looked up from blocking Ren's latest energy bolt, smoothed out her skirt, and looked across at her opponent.

"I'm very impressed my Lord. I had not realized that the priest was as good a teacher as he appears to be."

Ren favored her with a curt half-bow and finally broke his silence. "I'll be happy to pass your compliments on to Monsignor O'Donnell tomorrow, my Lady. Bear in mind, however, that it's possible his student knows a thing or two on his own."

Anita replied with a quick curtsy. "You are quite correct, my Lord. But you will certainly understand if I beg your pardon and disagree with your plans for tomorrow." Her smile was wicked, almost non-human, as she turned to strike once again.

This time it was no simple creature or energy bolt. Anita spent a full three minutes weaving the spell with her hands as she muttered a string of commands in a low, guttural tone. The creature that emerged and sent charging in Ren's direction was hideous, the same basic shape and size as a bull, fire-engine red, with three horns, six eyes, and nostrils that spewed forth flame. Its black hooves thundered towards Ren without so much as a starting trot.

Ren parried the raging creature, which passed by him to stop short of the southern perimeter of the circle before turning to charge him again from the opposite direction.

"Shit!" he muttered. "Bitch be moving up a notch!"

He turned to face the beast as it moved to attack him again. Ren placed both his hands down at his side, turned sideways sharply, then swept his arms upwards. A sheet of white light sprung from the ground to his arms and continued upwards for a further ten feet and outwards ten feet. As the creature ran through the sheet of light it changed from a hideous beast to a striking white steed. It was now the kind of horse you would expect a medieval king to come riding in on to save the day.

The white steed ran past Ren for a couple of feet then paused. The horse turned its head towards its new master then nodded in acceptance of its new task and turned to charge the pretty blonde at the other side of the circle.

Anita was again surprised by Ren's skill, but she still had ample warning of what was happening to counter the spell. She wove her hands in a complex motion, and a magical net appeared in front of the steed and caught it well in advance of any contact with her. The net collapsed around the horse and completely stopped its forward motion. When the net had completely surrounded the animal, a puff of dark smoke swallowed both horse and net, which burst into flame. The flames rose to the top of the protective canopy of light then subsided to a height of around ten feet. A red-orange phoenix rose from the flames and immediately flew at Ren.

The speed at which the flying beast moved towards Ren took him totally aback. He panicked for a second before thrusting both arms towards the phoenix to discharge energy bolts strong enough to destroy ten times the power and size of that phoenix.

Clearly shaken, Ren took a deep breath and moved for a more complex strike of his own. He closed his eyes and raised his hands slightly at his sides, and began to draw a gray mist together in front of him. He stood still for several seconds more as the mist grew into the shape of a small human. Using his hands, he continued to sculpt the mist until it was clear he was forming the body of a woman. As he stretched out his hands in front of him, golden light flowed from them in two streams. One touched the top of the misty form, the other touched the bottom, as the golden light surrounded the gray mist. When the two swirls of light met they dissipated immediately, revealing the form of a blonde woman in a pastel-blue hooped skirt. The resemblance to his opponent of the ghostly form in front of him made it clear that he was conjuring Elizabeth McKinney, the ancestor of Anita Delatorre, and the first person in her line to be trained in the use of Talents.

The image now complete, Ren gestured with his hands in a pushing motion towards Elizabeth's back. She began to walk forwards and to speak to Anita in a bright Scottish brogue.

"Ah, my bonnie Anita, why have you gone and forsaken your heritage with this fool notion of power and lust? Come back to us, my dearie, your journey on this earth is complete. Be with us and we will make you whole once again."

Anita stood fast. "Do you really think a cloud of smoke would change my plans for this evening, dearie? Surely you know that Delatorre blood long-ago eliminated any trace of your do-good McKinney beliefs. In token of that, I will be gone in the manner your own life was taken - by the hand of your own husband!"

She clapped her hands violently as she spoke her last word, and a bolt of gray-gold light flashed in front of her. The bolt struck the ground and expanded, turning quickly into the misty form of a Confederate officer.

Luke Arthur Delatorre was a handsome young man, 5'9" tall with a muscular frame, and wearing the uniform of a CSA cavalry major. As he turned towards Anita, the figure drew his curved saber and saluted her. She smiled, nodded, and gestured for him to move towards Ren.

His conjuring the image of Elizabeth had bought Ren sufficient time to regain his composure. In spite of the drain the spell was placing on his energy resources, Ren willed the image to bow to the form of her husband and to speak.

"My husband. It has been too long since we have been together. Why the sword, my love? Surely you have nothing to fear from your wife. Come to me, my love. You are tired from your journeys and from the war. Rest in my arms, my love. Lose yourself in me and I bring you healing and salvation."

Anita laughed. "Oh, Renard. You are so green. Do you really think young Luke here will listen to you? No, that's not going to happen today. You are just throwing your energy reserve down the drain making that silly woman speak."

Major Delatorre's form sheathed his sword and walked towards the female form which was blocking his way. Ren frowned, but focused again on the shadow under his control.

"Come to me, my husband. Open to me and let us both leave this place," the form of Elizabeth said. "Come to me!"

The male image did indeed go to her, his arms open to embrace. Just as the embrace was complete, the cavalry major reached down to his hip and opened a holster flap. His arm drew up once again, now with a Colt .45 revolver in his hand. Quickly, he cocked the hammer, pointed the gun at the woman's stomach, and fired. The female shape gasped and coughed as blood poured from her stomach and spread on her dress.

Ren was startled once again by this and he immediately stretched his arms out to pour energy into Elizabeth's shadow. The flow of blood stopped from the wound and she stood up straight. Anita snarled and wordlessly commanded the image of Luke Delatorre to fire twice more; once into the woman's heart and once into her head.

The attending mess was exactly what you would expect from gunshots at such close range. Ren reeled and rocked back on his heels when he saw the second shot all but blow Elizabeth's head off her shoulders.

"Now, my doomed follower of the Light, you will see what it means to cross paths with one of our kind who knows how properly to use our Talents!" Anita's voice was harsh, with her anticipation of the kill edging every word. She gestured for the image of Luke Delatorre to move forward again, slowly, step-stop, step-stop.

"Yes, you foolish man, this is your death approaching. Your energy levels are much too low to counter his strike, my poor little Renard. Every step brings you closer to the abyss that is awaiting you. There is no Light, no hope. Just death."

She raised her right arm and the shape drew its sword. Luke Delatorre cocked his sword-arm back in preparation for the strike and took another step forward.

Cavalrymen did not engage in the deadly-accurate swordplay of the Samurai or other famous warriors of history. Rather, they usually hacked at their opponents as they rode past them, bringing their blades to bear on whichever part or parts they could hit. The image's face developed a feral look as he was a mere six steps from striking Ren. Anita's face seemed to match that of her creation. Moving in for the kill was as much a thrill for her as it had been for her ancestor.

Ren tried to erect a barrier between the image and himself. Three times he tried to cast a shield wall and three times the wall cracked and fell in shards to the ground, where it dissipated. Breathless now, and knowing he had nothing left in his bag of tricks, he took several steps backwards. Panic had truly set in.

He was going to die.

That much was very clear to Renard Alciatore. With five more steps the ghostly sword would hack him down, and he would die.

Anita Delatorre knew it too. She maintained her focus to make sure that the spectral form of Major Luke Delatorre would move forward at less than a snail's pace. She absorbed the panic which emanated from Ren as easily as she had absorbed the sexual energy from Jay Hadley.

Four steps.

Ren's mind searched frantically for something else, something different he could muster. As much as he did not want simply to give in and surrender, he realized that he had run out of energy; and of ideas. He thrust his hands forward in a gesture of warding-off, so that what little energy he had remaining would form around him in a last-ditch effort to hold back Anita's spell.

She laughed at him again. "Such a feeble attempt to delay the inevitable, my dear. It's a shame, because you had so much potential. You would have made a formidable ally."

"There is nothing, nothing you could ever offer me that could persuade me to give in and become your ally."

Three steps.

"You continue to amuse me, little man. There is no turning back now, you know. You can bluster about your convictions all you want, but this is a fight to the death. Even if you wanted to turn over your life to me now, it just can't be my dear. The circle cannot be broken by any human from the outside, and cannot be broken from the inside until one of us lies here dead. Your adherence to your principles does you credit, dearie, even if it has been foolishly-placed. It will ultimately cost you your life."

Two steps.

Ren looked around as his final shield just about held together.

"Goodbye, Mike, I wish I could have done you proud, my friend. I am sorry," he thought.

One step.

The shape sensed the ward around Ren and it stopped abruptly, awaiting instructions from his mistress. She knew that victory was in her grasp as she raised her right arm theatrically, and then lowered it in a fast sweeping motion.

The misty sword came down on Ren's shield. As it struck, the shield shattered, making Ren stagger helplessly. Ren had no more energy to put into his defenses and he sank to his knees. His mind was still defiant and searched for a way to salvage his situation. Anita raised her arm again and the creature followed suit, pausing briefly before its strike; Anita lowered her arm in the same theatrical sweeping motion and Major Delatorre's sword came down towards Ren.

The misty sword came to within inches of Ren's head and was blocked with the sound of a CLANG which both Ren and Anita felt reverberate through their bodies. Stunned, Ren looked next to the figure of Major Delatorre and saw a beautiful woman dressed in tight red pants, a fitted red jacket, and red boots. Her right hand wielded a flaming red sword which was dripping with green fire. The woman's aura grew upwards until it reached the top of the protective circle's canopy as she turned to swing at the creature. Major Delatorre's shadow turned in an attempt to block the woman's flaming sword, but the shadow was no match for the power of Ren's benefactor. Her sword flared and changed shapes from a cavalry saber to a samurai katana as she held it in her hand. She grasped the handle with two hands now and planted her feet as she swung and deftly beheaded the evil shape, causing it to burst into a bolt of gray light which shot upwards toward the canopy and almost knocked Anita off her feet.

Time seemed to freeze for Ren as the woman sheathed her sword and approached him. The clothes she wore seemed to change color from deep red to a soft golden hue as she walked around him. She reached out an arm to him and helped him to stand up. As she kissed him gently on the forehead Ren could feel his strength return and his energy levels increase to where they were when he had entered the cemetery. He opened his eyes, looking directly into her eyes, then regarded her up and down.

"You? This is almost as good as the cut-offs at the soccer field," were the only words Ren could manage. Her clothes changed color again, this time to a deep forest green. The color was the perfect compliment to her dark hair and hazel eyes.

She chuckled gently as Ren gawped at her. "Such a cheeky thing to say right now! And yes, I must remember those shorts. Anything that can turn a man's head this much is something I will definitely be including in my arsenal." Her lips never moved as she spoke directly into his mind.

Once satisfied that Ren was indeed OK, the woman gave him a firm hug. "I told you we would meet again, Renard Alciatore. But I didn't expect you to need our help in quite this way," she said as she smiled sweetly at him.

"Hmmm... Deus ex machina? You come sweeping in to save the day for me. Thank you!"

"'Deus?' Hardly, sweetie. 'Angelicus' would be more like

it. We can get into that discussion another time. And no, good sir, I am not here to rid you of your little problem over there," she said, gesturing with a nod towards Anita. "This duel is far from over, and I get only the one chance to lend a hand. I've been watching, but that last spell of hers really did a number on you, so I had to intervene." She looked at him with an expression of concern. "You look as though you have been through the wringer, but your energy levels are back up again. When I'm gone, time will speed up to normal again so be prepared to throw your next spell at her immediately."

"Well, I certainly thank you for your help, my Lady. Hmm... umm...what do I call you?"

"Not now, my friend. You have other matters you need to be concentrating on. Go with the Light to victory, Ren Alciatore!"

Anita stood on the opposite side of the circle, stunned to see that her opponent was even alive, appearing to be conjuring up another spell. Her attack having been thwarted, she stood ready to counter another spell in return. Her own energy levels were still very much solid and intact; none of Ren's attacks had come even close to her since that one testing bolt had grazed her shoulder. I'm glad I rode ol' Jay like a broke-down horse, she chuckled. It's only appropriate that it should be his life-force that would be used to eliminate his opposition.

"That's just what I expected from you, my Lord!" she said, as the image of a young virile woman bearing a sword of Light appeared within the circle and began a sweep of her sword towards Anita. Ren's adversary responded by waving her arms almost in a counterpoint to his spell, and as she did so a figure of her own appeared.

"You continue to thrust these symbols upon me, my Lord. That is your choice, of course. But now you must suffer the consequences of your actions. Behold the Light-bearer, the bringer of joy and sadness to all of Creation!"

Anita's counter-image appeared on the final word of her spell; a majestic angel robed in what appeared to be all-white. As the figure turned towards Ren its robe shifted color from white to every hue of the rainbow, then back to white again. The transformation happened so quickly that the rainbow colors appeared only as an after-image in Ren's consciousness.

Ren stood firm and focused his thoughts on the figure he had conjured. "This image is merely a creation of your mind, my Lady," said Ren's young angel-figure, flatly. "It is not the Light-bearer and we are not moved by your shadows." The angel-image displayed a great deal of bravado as she raised her arms and cast out a net of light in an attempt to ensnare Anita's figure.

"Shame on you, my Lord, for your horrid lack of respect. The Light-bearer, Lucifer of a thousand names, stands before you! Bow now and accept your destiny, lest you perish in his flames for all eternity!" As Anita nodded gently, her figure of the great Archangel raised a finger as well and sent Ren's flying net into a thousand sparks.

"THAT is not Lucifer, my Lady, and you know it!" responded Ren's non-angel shadow.

"Your voice betrays your concern. Truly, you are aware of the power of the Light-bearer. Now bow down and cover your head and pray that Lucifer of a thousand names will accept your worship and grant you mercy!" Anita's voice never once betrayed her belief that angels were just so much bullshit.

“Master was right, play the devil card against these Light-believers and they crumble,” she thought.

Renard Alciatore was not exactly crumbling in the face of the image of the greatest Angel. But he was not exactly a figure of supreme confidence, either. He closed his eyes and cast a mist around his youthful angel-child, which re-shaped the image into that of a woman of considerable maturity. He sighed audibly at the extent of the energy transfer this took, and waved his hands as he formed a blue-orange image in front of him.

"Behold Gabriella, sister to the Light-bearer and consort to the Captain of the Hosts of Light!"

The woman who stepped out of Ren's cloud was more than a match for Anita's male figure. As tall as the Light-bearer, Gabriella was attired in a robe of glowing blue and orange light. She held a long trumpet to her lips and blew a single shrill note which shook the foundations of the tumulus upon which the human combatants stood. The trumpet blast completed, she threw the instrument high into the air and, as it reached its zenith, it broke into three lightning bolts as it returned to earth and blasted Anita's angel-image.

Anita gasped and moved with slick skill to counter the force of this latest attack. "That was no child's strike, my Lord. I commend you on your ability to control elementals. You should be proud. While your Angel of the West is no match for the Lord of the Angels, she is nevertheless a formidable contender. But I have no patience to play with you or your shadows, my Lord. The Light-bearer suffers no Challenger, and he will make you pay for your arrogance!"

As she raised her arms again, Anita tapped a significant measure of her combat energy and poured it into the figure standing before her. Her image of Lucifer rose another foot in height as it moved towards the center of the circle. The image stretched out its arms as to draw a cloud of mist around itself as it began to spin. The spinning motion quickly caused the mist to become a funnel cloud, which rose above the image of the mighty Archangel.

"Your pitiful concept of what an angelic form is mocks me, Renard," the image boomed, as the magical twister hovered over its head. "I appreciate flattery but I cannot abide mockery, and I will not tolerate it in a Magickal circle. I alone control the angelic hosts, and they obey my will. Even in shadow form!"

A lightning bolt shot out of the twister and struck Ren's angel in the chest. The force of the bolt forced his Gabriella to her knees. Fearing another strike, she began to stretch out in a position of supplication.

"She's got it wrong, you know." A female voice spoke softly in Ren's mind.

"Huh? Who's got it wrong?"

"This rather arrogant chick you're fighting. The Light-bearer was indeed the leader of the angels, but control of the hosts belonged both then and now to the Light. The Light-bearer was a second in command, if you will. We had listened and obeyed, but the Light was always in the background."

"You mean, like a voice in his ear, telling him what to do?" Ren thought.

"Ha! I detected your smirk, there, Ren. Yes, something like that," She said, giggling.

"But you're totally not God."

The sound of her laughter was like the tinkling of a wind chime.

"Let me assure you that the Light is much sexier than I am. Let's put that down on our list of things to chat about some other time. You have a duel to finish."

"Yes, I sure do, and my Archangel isn't doing so well. I thought you said you could intervene only once."

"I am not intervening. We are simply having a nice chat about history. Besides, I hate seeing my former boss, that image she's conjured up, get a bum rap from this tart. I'll talk to you later." Her departure was pleasant, but almost audible as she popped from his consciousness.

"Former boss?" Ren asked.

But she was gone. Anita's image of Lucifer was poised to attack his angel with another lightning bolt. Ren stood at attention and gestured for his angel to rise.

"Get up, sweetie. He has no authority over you. You answer to the Light, not the Light-bearer. Stand up now!"

The angel-image, bolstered now by Ren's words and a surge of energy, got up to her knees, and then onto her feet. She turned to Ren and nodded thanks, then turned to speak to the image of the Archangel.

"Oh, mighty Light-bearer, you forgot your place. I do indeed answer to the Light, and I obey the Light in all its manifestations." She stepped towards the center dividing line of the circle. "Will you join me, great one, and re-dedicate yourself to the Light?"

Lucifer's expression changed from that of sublime complacency to one of complete anger. "How dare you address me in such a manner! Back on your knees before the Light-bearer!" Another lightning-bolt reached out from the cloud above his head but Ren's angel deflected it, turning it into a shower of sparks.

Anita exhaled and took a step back. "I have no idea where you are getting the power to manifest such defenses from. Very well, my Lord. You have escalated this duel, and it is now upon me to take it further. She pointed both arms towards her image of the greatest Archangel. "The Light-bearer suffers no rival, good sir. Your images of the Light will now suffer the consequences of their failure to submit to the Light-bearer. He demands compensation for your insults!"

Dramatically, she swept her arms skyward then, bringing them down swiftly, Anita willed the funnel cloud above her angelic image to engulf Lucifer. The gray light of the twister became lighter then turned silver-gray, finally to become a shade of burnished gold. The winds of the twister spun faster and faster so that it became impossible to recognize the shape of the angel inside. The spinning increased the temperature inside the twister, and its light changed from bright gold to a fire-gold, then to a deep burning red. Flames shot forth from the top of the twister, spilling over the top and ripping to the ground. The volume of flames increased as the speed of the circular winds began to decrease. Ren could feel the hot blast as the twister stopped and burst into a fireball the height of the protective shield which surrounded the dueling ground.

A mighty roar ensued from the flames. This was followed by a great sucking sound as the twister imploded. What was left caused Ren to gasp as he saw it. Before him was no longer Lucifer the Light-bearer, but the Devil of his Catholic upbringing, poised now to attack and destroy him. The sight of the red-black image before him shook Ren to the core.

"It's time your shadow left this place, my pretty sister!" The voice of Anita's modified shadow was so much harsher than it had been in its angelic form. The shadow took two steps forward and nodded before shooting flames from the horns on its head, blasting forward to engulf the image of Gabriella.

"You have long supported the causes of women on this feeble planet, good sister. It's time you suffered the torture men have placed on some of your 'sisters' because they dared to believe you and other angelic manifestations. Now let your shadow leave this place in the same manner!"

Ren's immediate attempt to block the flames was only partially successful. The flames singed Gabriella's gown and engulfed her in smoke. Coughing and spluttering, her shadow managed to remain upright, but beating back the flames was a losing battle for her as they climbed up her gown. Anita sensed the momentary buckle in Ren's will and shot another blast of fire at Gabriella from her demon, until the Archangel's form was completely consumed by the evil fire.

Ren gathered his energy into himself again and let go of the image. He expected to see Gabriella's image simply vanish, but Anita's demon grabbed control of the archangelic shadow. Extinguishing the flames engulfing the figure, Lucifer formed a cloud of mist within the space between himself and Gabriella; a mist which he then directed to surround her form. Just as the winds had been used to transform Lucifer from Archangel to demon, so these mists were changing Gabriella from Archangel to woman.

Satisfied that the transformation had been completed, Lucifer spread his arms apart and the mists cleared to reveal the image of Cecilia McIntyre. The image, dressed in a short navy blue skirt and a white cotton blouse, bowed to her new master, then turned to face Ren.

"Don't you think I look cute today, Ren? I think I look darned cute." The image standing before him smiled coyly. "And I'm so horny, Ren. It's been so long since we did it. Did you enjoy doing me, Ren? I sure did like the feeling of you inside of me. It makes me feel so hot remembering that, Ren. Real hot." The image unbuttoned two buttons of her blouse and reached one hand in to massage her breast. "Uhhhh..." the image sighed.

Ren stood still, in a mixture of surprise and arousal. Arousal tipped the balance, however, as the image of Cecilia continued to unbutton her blouse and pull it up from out of her skirt.

"Yes, Ren, I'm really hot. I need it, Ren, and I need it soon. It's been too long, Ren. A woman can't go long without it, my love." Her hand moved from her breasts to under her skirt. "Ohhh, Ren, I have to have it..."

Ren was transfixed, but the sight of Cecilia so aroused gave him an erection he could not disguise. Anita could see his discomfort from the opposite side of the circle, and she smiled.

Anita raised her hands and opened a channel to the sexual energy she had been storing, and directed that energy at the demonic image in front of her. The demon extended his arms to either side, and two figures appeared, wearing hooded black robes. Both wore upside-down crosses, as those often affected by Satanists. Lucifer brought his arms together in front of him to create an image of a rough stone altar near the middle of the circle. Once satisfied with his handiwork, he gestured to his subordinates and they all began to move towards the image of Cecilia.

"No!" Ren shouted, and he raised his hands to conjure a defense.

The image of Lucifer laughed in response. "So, you know how this little play concludes, do you? Oh, don't worry, my arrogant little creature, she will enjoy our play, trust me. Indeed, she will enjoy it so much she will want to stay with me for all eternity!"

By now, the dark acolytes had escorted Cecilia to the altar and disrobed her. Even though he tried to convince himself that it was not truly Cee there, but only an image, Ren's revulsion at the scene before him grew even stronger. He directed several energy bolts in rapid succession at the demonic images approaching the altar but the robed figures merely deflected each one. Ren paused, breathless, and rested his hands on his knees momentarily.

Anita was smiling again as she sensed her opponent's drain of energy, and poured more energy into the scene playing out in the center of the circle. The robed acolytes had taken positions at the head and feet of the now naked female figure they had stretched out on the altar. The demon was approaching, his erection prominent as he prepared to mount the image of Cecilia. But just before the demon could copulate with her, the acolyte at her head produced a large knife and plunged it into her heart.

Cecilia gasped as the dagger opened her chest, convulsing as her blood shot into the air. The demon mounted her and emitted a feral growl as he thrust into her furiously. His growls ended in a horrifying blood-curdling scream as he climaxed into the now unmoving form lying on the altar.

"NOOOOOOO!!!" Ren again attempted to send bolts of energy at the demon in an effort to stop his attack, but the acolytes continued to defend their master. Recharged as he had been by his protector, Ren was furiously squandering his energy.

Even though his attacks on the demon were not reaching their target, they were nonetheless a nuisance for Anita Delatorre. She was now forced to deflect Ren's attacks lest one of his energy bolts should escape and actually make contact with her. She was unable to focus completely on the tableau in front of her and was pouring even more sexual energy into the demon so that his lust forced him on independently of Anita's thought processes.

The drain on her resources were well worth it, however, as her attacks had shaken Ren to the core of his beliefs.

"You bitch!! How dare you violate the love I had for Cee!" he shouted, instantly regretting the weakness that had overtaken him.

Anita smiled, but declined to respond directly. Instead, she motioned for her creation to climb down from the altar and to stand before Ren. "She was adequate, I'd say," the demon growled. "Of course, I was the best thing she has ever experienced. Perhaps I should put her back together again and have another go at her. What do you think, human?"

Ren took a deep breath then exhaled slowly. "Do what you have to do, foul creature, and I will do what I have to so that you will be struck down. I am weary of your antics and will tolerate them no further." Lucifer growled: "Brave words, from such a pitiful creature as yourself. Surely you know there is nothing you can do or say to challenge my power! No being can stand before me and survive!"

Anita Delatorre winced as she poured still more energy into her demon, providing him with the strength to re-animate the bloody female form on the altar. First to be removed was the carnage caused by the knife, then the naked form began to twitch and writhe. Sensing the energy renewal in the offering, the acolytes resumed their positions, pinning her to the altar. The knife re-appeared in the hands of the robed figure at her head and prepared to plunge it into her yet again. But before it could descend, the blade of the knife turned white hot and vanished in a wisp of smoke, leaving the acolyte holding just the hilt. Confused, he turned to his master, who in turn looked up from his prey in anger and disgust at the figure now standing before Ren.

"So, young man, you think you can pick up where my sister's shape left off? You don't have the power, you pathetic human creature."

Ren stood fast, bringing forth more energy from his reserves. With a sweep of his hand, his anger created a gust of wind that blew away the entire scene in front of him: altar, acolytes, even the image of Cee.

The demon image staggered back two steps as Anita fell to her knees. Ren stepped forward to match the demon's movement, advancing on him,

"The tide has turned, my Lady! It is time. Time to bring this game to an end. Now!" Ren thrust his hands upwards and two lightning bolts struck the top of the protective dome of light surrounding them. The lightning ricocheted off the dome and bore down upon the demon-shape Anita had conjured. Her Lucifer began to transform from the classic devil image and back to the form of Lucifer the Light-bearer.

Anita had just regained her footing when the sight of her demon returning to the form of an Archangel against her will sent her reeling yet again. Gasping for breath, she staggered back to the far end of the protective dome. She directed another burst of energy towards her creature, but it glanced off the reflective light of the image of the great angel.

Ren directed another bolt of light at the image in front of him.

"I take control of this creature, my Lady. The Light-bearer was a great Being and you have corrupted his memory. Let your foul images be gone!"

Ren joined his outstretched hands together and pointed them at the image, willing it to turn around to face Anita. Still defiant, Anita stepped forward to confront the image that was originally hers to control.

"Come back to me, mighty Light-bearer. Yes, I brought you to this place to destroy my opponent. Come to me and let us finish the task at hand." As she reached out with her right hand, a green mist sprung from her fingertips and began to swirl around, slowly approaching the shadow. "Come to me... join with me..."

The green mist became a barrier to the advancing image

of Lucifer. Ren pulled his hands back a little, causing the image to halt just in front of the mist without touching it. Ren stared directly at Anita, and he willed the image to speak.

"You have no respect for me or my power, my Lady. It is wrong of you to pervert my image into the demonic form so feared by the Christian world. It is not my memory that should be feared, but the real evil of you and your associates. You have given up the right to control this shadow. Submit now, my Lady, and this will be over as quickly as possible."

Anita coughed and gasped for breath, but still managed to laugh at Ren.

"You think you can end this quickly? Not hardly, little man. You will not defeat me. I have re-asserted my authority over the image of the Light-bearer, and I now command he return to me."

Waving her arms forward, Anita moved the green mist so that it started to wrap around Lucifer. When the mist had formed a complete cylinder around the archangelic shadow, she wrapped her arms around her body and the cylinder collapsed onto the shadow.

Ren held his hands steady, emitting a constant stream of energy to the shadow. "You may not have this creature back, my Lady. I will not allow you to continue." Ren pointed his index finger at the back of Lucifer and shot out a stream of white light which pierced the green mist and engulfed the image. The white light pushed the green mist away from the image, causing the green cylinder to break up and return to the shape of a smoky barrier between Lucifer and Anita.

"You may not retain control over that which I created!" shrieked Anita at him. "I renounce the Light and all it represents. I will not submit to it!"

She poured her remaining energy reserves into the green mist. As the mist wall thickened, the color drained from Anita's face. Her skin became almost translucent as she wavered on her feet, desperately trying to hold off what would surely be Ren's final assault.

Ren reached out through the angel-image and tested the green barrier. The angel's hand moved to within less than an inch of the mist, then fell to his side as if he had put it too close to a fire. Ren willed the image to speak.

"You have created a formidable defense, my Lady. It is not enough, however, and you have barely enough life-force to maintain even your own existence. It is time to submit, my Lady."

Anita responded with a feral snarl that wasn't even human. Shaking all over, she extended her arms and shot a final bolt of energy forwards. The bolt passed through the mist wall only slowly, absorbing the power of the wall. Once the green mist had been completely absorbed, she pushed her arms forward and the bolt rocketed towards Lucifer.

Ren assessed the situation correctly as the mist wall collapsed around the energy bolt. Saving only a tiny reserve, he poured his remaining energy into the image. The angel extended both hands, palms outwards, and blocked Anita's final attack. The energy bolt vaporized as it hit the image, leaving nothing between Lucifer and Anita.

The look in Anita's eyes had turned from being full of arrogance and pride to anger and hatred, and now to those of a hunted animal. Fear had finally taken over her: fear of pain; fear of death. Ren willed the image forward to stand over the exhausted, quivering form that once had been a skilled Adept.

"The temptation to exact revenge is very strong," Ren said, using his own voice rather than speaking through the shadow. "You are responsible for a lot of suffering. It would be so easy to visit some of that pain upon you, but that would be wrong. You have rejected the Light, Anita Delatorre, but the Light has not rejected you. Taste the mercy of the Light as you join with it now."

With those words, Ren willed the image of the Light-bearer to wrap his arms around Anita. As Lucifer's aura completely surrounded her, Ren could sense the breaking of the silver cord which bound her body to her soul. Her body collapsed, now totally lifeless. The energy field that had been Anita's soul merged with the image of the Light-bearer and shot skywards, bursting through the protective dome above. The dome exploded in a soundless flash of intense color and light, leaving Ren standing, shivering, in the evening air. The body of Anita Delatorre lay on the other side of the monument, finally at rest.

"You don't need to check her. She is gone. You saw the departure of her spirit," the female voice spoke in Ren's mind.

"Where did she go?"

"To the Light. Let's hope that her next walk upon Earth will be better for all than her last one."

"I don't understand."

"You will in time, dear Ren. Do not worry. This is merely the beginning of your journey. You will learn much along the way. Now, you need to get out of here, Renard. You don't want to have to explain this dead woman, and you have a friend waiting for you."

“I do indeed, don’t I? And I could sure use a drink,” he said aloud, with a grin.

Epilogue

Ren sighed, and looked around. He felt as if he should “clean up” the scene, but there were no Magickal resonances left behind. When Anita’s spirit left, it broke the circle, and the magic dissipated into the earth. He gave silent thanks to the Light before descending the southern steps of the monument without looking back. Ren made his way back to the old main entrance of the cemetery, where he exited and re-locked the gate.

He carefully crossed the street, walked beneath the highway overpass, and headed for the main gate of Greenwood Cemetery. A familiar figure was sitting at the foot of the clock tower there.

"You know, this is one of the ugliest structures in any cemetery in this city, the figure said as it pointed up at the clock tower. I'm glad to see you, Ren, but you look like shit. Come sit down and rest."

"I feel like shit. I've never killed anyone before. I feel like there's blood on my hands."

"There is, my friend." Mike O'Donnell reached into his pocket and pulled out a small silver flask. He unscrewed the top and handed it to Ren. "Drink."

Ren took a healthy slug at the contents and color rapidly returned to his face. "Ah, the port you mentioned earlier. This truly wonderful. You may drink with me anytime, good Father," he said, now laughing.

“OK, that should boost you enough to give me your memories of what happened,” Mike said.

Ren reached out with his mind, sending his memories of the cemetery experience to his mentor. Less than a minute later,

Mike opened his eyes.

“Gabriel’s feminine aspect? Brilliant! Not sure where that came from for you, but it was a good choice. Keep your opponent confused and all that,” Mike said, nodding.

“Yeah, I’m not sure where that came from at all. I’m sure there’s a Brother of the Sacred Heart or two now, wondering where they went wrong.” Ren smiled.

Chuckling, Mike reached down and grabbed a can of NOLA Brown beer and handed it to Ren. "Have a chaser.”

Ren quickly guzzled half of the beer, and immediately became lightheaded.

“It’ll be days before I get my new friend from tonight out of my mind, Mike,” Ren said, reaching for another beer.

“I can’t be sure what to make of her ‘former boss’ comments. There’s more than one thread throughout angelology that postulates Lucifer was never evil, but who the fuck knows?”

“She’s just so beautiful,” Ren sighed.

“And no wonder, for even Satan disguises himself as an angel of light,” Mike admonished.

“I’m Catholic, remember? Bible study? No bueno!” Ren laughed.

“Yeah, yeah. Second Corinthians, eleven to fourteen. We’ll have to keep an eye on this. She’s gorgeous, but, careful what you wish for and all that,” Mike replied.

“OK, but I’m going to savor the memory for now. Beats incredibly powerful angels and soldiers with swords any day.” He downed the rest of his second beer, and then looked up at the sky. "Jeez, I shouldn't have drunk that on an empty stomach."

"I got a bacon donut here."

Ren smiled. "With good Port? That sounds wonderful."

***

“I cannot begin to tell you how sorry I am, Mrs. Delatorre. Anita was one of our finest young executives. She and her dedication to the company will be sorely missed. Yes, ma’am, I will be at the funeral tomorrow. Is there anything else I can do? Well, please know our hearts and thoughts are with you and the family. We are all just so sad here. Yes, thank you. I will see you tomorrow, then. Good-bye, ma'am."

The man hung up the phone on his desk and turned back to the file in front of him. The top-floor office in the Marcus-Kayson headquarters in suburban Dallas was dark, with just a lamp illuminating the desk.

The police report, coroner's report, and the new story from the New Orleans paper all concluded that the death of Anita Delatorre was a natural one. What remained to be explained was how an apparently healthy young woman simply dropped dead of a massive stroke. He closed the folder and turned to move on to other tasks when the phone rang again.

"Yes? Yes, I'm aware of that. No, I do not want any additional effort spent on Alciatore at the moment...The priest? Proceed as planned there...No, that is another issue altogether... Yes, the two converged this time, but I doubt Alciatore is privy to all of the actions of the priest...As I said, discontinue all activities related to Alciatore directly...Oh, to be sure, we will return our attentions to him at some point. We owe him a debt I fully intend for him to pay." He smiled grimly as he hung up the phone.

About the Author

Edward Branley is a writer, teacher, historian, and computer nerd. He graduated from Brother Martin High School, and received a degree in Secondary Education from the University of New Orleans. Branley is the author of five Arcadia books on New Orleans history, as well as the YA novels, *Dragon's Danger*, and *Dragon's Discovery*. He lives in New Orleans, with his wife.

Connect with Edward!

Follow me on Twitter: http://twitter.com/EdwardBranley
Join the "Bayou Talents" Facebook Group: http://facebook.com/group/BayouTalents
Subscribe to my blog: http://ebranley.com

Acknowledgments

Dear Reader: I want to welcome you as we journey into the world of the Talented. I've lived in this universe for some time, and I thank you for joining me. Naturally, some folks merit special commendation:

Brava! to Wendy Warrelmann, whose cover illustration brings Renard Alciatore to life so wonderfully. She's brilliant. Thanks to Stephen James Smith, for taking on the challenge of editing a novice writer's madness.

Special thanks to the incredibly skilled Dara Rochlin, Lady Editor of dragon's fame, who tolerated my thought processes and insanity as we updated the technology and continuity of sections of the manuscript that were written over the span of several years. She's been everything a writer could want in an editor, and even more so as a friend.

Thanks to the many beta-readers who have given me feedback on the Talented through the years this has been percolating in my brain. Thanks again to my teachers at Brother Martin High School and the University of New Orleans, who taught me how to think critically, and my students way back when at Redeemer High, who called my critical thinking out regularly.

All my love to my wife Helen, and my sons, Kevin and Justin, for everything, especially tolerating me taking weird routes to various places, as I tried to discern where Teleport Gateways are in other towns and cities. Thanks to Jenifer Hill, for so much insipiration and motivation, along with demonstrating the proper attitude for strong female characters. Love you, Maria Stambaugh and Christine Stephens for inspiration and ideas. Special thanks to Lisa Graves (The History Witch), and The History Chicks, Beckett Graham and Susan Vollenweider. Their art, research, and crazy notions make me stop and wonder if the folks they're drawing/explaining were Talented. A tip of the Yat hat to everyone who supports me on social media, and many, many thanks to the folks at PJ's Coffee in Clearview Mall and Wakin' Bakin' on Banks Street in Mid City, for the wonderful places to write and contemplate Teleport Gateways, Angels, and Talents.

Are you ready for more of the Talented? Here's a preview of Trusted Talents, scheduled for release in April, 2017.

Trusted Talents

Prologue

The sight of a man in his late-thirties stepping out of a janitorial closet in a bespoke suit might draw attention in many places, but nobody gave him a second glance in Boston's Park Street subway station. Park Street is one of the busiest stops on the "T." Working his way through the crowd, he emerged into the sunlight onto Boston Common, close to the corner of Park and Tremont. He turned into the Common, walking briskly past the Frog Pond, which was quiet. The cold winter had frozen the pond over, but there were not more than half a dozen people skating, since it wasn't a half-price weekday evening. Just past the Frong Pond was his destination, the Soldiers and Sailors Monument. Even in the cold weather of Boston in early February, tourists and locals alike took advantage of the sunny Saturday morning to get out for a walk.

He spotted the man he was meeting first, and walked around the monument so he approached the older man in the Burberry coat from the front. They stood side-by-side for a moment, then the older man turned to walk towards the park exit at Charles and Beacon Streets.

"Thank you for using the public Gateway, I've proposed you for membership in the club, but I don't want to draw attention to our activity in Dallas just yet," the older man said.

"No problem, sir. Teleporting into a public setting was good for me. My focus and discipline needed the extra motivation," the younger man replied.

"Hmmm, right. I trust you are not allowing last fall's ... setback ... to affect your plans for our current project?"

"No, sir, not at all. We are prepared and ready to move forward."

"Have you ascertained the location of the other two artifacts yet?" The older man asked.

"Not yet. Once we have the two whose locations we know, we will be able to use them to track the locations of others. Additionally, when we move on the first two, we'll know the characteristics of the wards surrounding them. That will make it easier to sense similar wards in other locations." The younger man's tone was very confident.

"I'm still a bit surprised we've missed this information for so long. Objects of power such as these usually project enough energy that they tend to be more-easily found."

"Sir, these churches are in New Orleans. I haven't felt anything like this shielding outside of Rome. The Assembly clearly has been active in the city for much longer than our records indicate."

"We will have to give this notion much more attention, Daniel. If these artifacts to indeed turn out to be of a power level we anticipate, our plans for a full Lodge in Dallas will be approved. That will give you the resources to further extend your operations into Louisiana.

Daniel James McCain maintained his composure. "Thank you for that vote of confidence, sir."

The older man slowed his brisk stride, paused, and turned to his companion. "And what of our opposition?"

"They are quite inactive, sir. We dropped regular surveillance on Renard Alciatore after Samhain. The priest appears to have a gateway in his residence, making it difficult to easily track his whereabouts outside the city. Externally, however, his movements have been consistent with his mundane responsibilities as a teacher and priest. We have active surveillance on the bar they use as a gathering point, and again, nothing out of the ordinary there."

"Are you sure? That place mentioned in your report, what is it, the 'Triple-7'? It's fairly close to your objective."

"Yes, sir, but I am satisfied we haven't tipped our hand to them."

"Very well, then, Daniel. You have my permission to proceed. I look forward to your report on the artifacts. They will be very useful in future endeavors." The older man extended his hand to seal his approval.

"Thank you again, sir," the younger man replied as he

took his superior's hand.

"We'll want to see these things once you obtain them. After both operations are complete, meet me at the Temple Club, Wednesday evening. We'll toast your success and do some preliminary analysis. Use the Gateway in the Club; your membership will be finalized Monday."

Daniel nodded. The older man turned to step up onto Beacon Street, making his way back to the Temple Club. Daniel turned to walk back to the "T" station. As he reversed direction, a young man in jeans and a Red Sox jacket walked straight into him.

"Dude, watch where you're going! You can't just around like that!"

Daniel's eyes smoldered as he examined the young man. The encounter broke his reverie, angering him.

"Ah but what I will is the Whole of the Law," McCain replied. He raised his right hand, open-palmed, so it was chest high, then balled it into a fist.

The young man was at first confused by Daniel's movements, but then looked panicked, as he grabbed his own chest with two hands. He collapsed and died.

McCain continued to walk to Park Street Station, but paused before entering. He looked across the street, at the Dunkin Donuts, and decided he was in the mood for a muffin.

Once back on the top floor of his company's headquarters in suburban Dallas, Daniel made his way from the meditation chamber housing the building's Gateway to his office. A man dressed in black paramilitary gear waited for him. He raised an eyebrow as McCain entered the room.

"Go," Daniel said.

The man nodded, reached for the smartphone in his pocket, and texted directions to his team.

"The plane is ready, and I'm heading there now. Care to join us?"

Daniel shook his head. "No, I don't want to go down there yet. And I don't want you within a kilometer of that church until the op. Low visibility, get in, get out, for now."

"Yes, sir," the man replied, as he consulted his phone. "The operatives are staged in separate hotels. The Endymion parade begins at sixteen-thirty. The parade will serve to draw attention away from our survey of the target. At twenty-thirty the team will conduct their final pre-check, then return to their hotel. The operation will commence at twenty-one hundred tomorrow night. Exit strategy will be as planned."

"Very well," said McCain.

The other man nodded and left the office. McCain sat his desk, picking up a gold ring and squeezed his fingers around it. The psychic imprint of its former owner, Anita Delatorre, was still present to an Adept such as Daniel.

"I won't be able to avenge you this time, dear Anita," he thought. "But the clouds are gathering, as we begin our strike."

Trusted Talents

Chapter One
Endymion Saturday

"Carnival will be a good time for you to practice control of your shields. Parades are crowded. People forget their worries and cares for a while. Some drink too much, and lower their inhibitions, which are a major foundation for our shields. Go out and walk around on Endymion Saturday. Walk a few blocks with your shields up, then lower them a bit. Notice the difference in how people treat you..."

Renard Alciatore thought back to his mentor's guidance from a few weeks earlier, as he turned onto Orleans Avenue from City Park Avenue.

He smiled and stepped onto the beginning of the route that the Krewe of Endymion would take in just a few hours. It was 1pm, but the area was already packed solid with people. Bands played from a stage across from City Park. The smell of grills cooking up burgers, hot dogs, and sausages of all kinds all came together. Ren raised his shields to a complete defensive position, so that he bottled up every bit of psychic energy he had. It's the closest thing someone with Talents can do to become "invisible".

Walking down Orleans Avenue meant walking through walls of people. Families, fraternity groups, work colleagues, some of whom had been out on the street's neutral ground—the grassy area in the center of the street that the rest of the world called a "median"--for over 24 hours, were all now enjoying the company of their friends and loved ones. Food and drink were everywhere. There was also the occasional dispute, sometimes from folks trying to provoke those who staked out spots for the parade, sometimes just a spat between a couple.

The vibe on the street side was slightly different, as people sat on the curb, walked back and forth on the sidewalk, and in and out of the homes along the route. The sense of belonging was tighter on this side. These folks would be here after the parade passed. People on the neutral ground were transients; the sidewalk side were the neighborhood.

Ren walked three blocks, taking in the sights, sounds, and smells. Beads, burgers, beer. Classical, Cajun, and Country, blaring from homes and portable sound systems. The purple and gold of Louisiana State University blending in with the purple-green-gold of Carnival. High school shirts and caps, worn by teens currently attending those schools, as well as their parents and grandparents. Police barricades kept the street relatively clear and open. Ren stood in the middle of the street, not noticed by anyone.

He walked down another block, passing at least three groups of people he either went to high school with, or he knew from his time at Loyola. After walking by a couple whose wedding he shot last year, without either of them "seeing" him, he paused, in the middle of the intersection of Orleans Avenue and N. Alexander Street.

"This really works!" He thought.

Ren took a deep breath and lowered his shields as he exhaled. They were now at what his mentor would call a "daily" level. His defenses were still high enough to keep out distractions, and to blunt the force of any outright attack he might experience. He heard his mentor's explanation again, in his mind.

"It's like the 'opacity' setting you use in Photoshop. Put up an image. Overlay a second image on top of the first. With 'opacity' set at one hundred percent, you can't see the image underneath. That's how your shields work when you have them fully raised. Now, think about reducing the opacity of that overlay image. Bring it to eighty percent, you start seeing something underneath. Go to fifty percent, and you very much see what's behind the shield.

"On a daily basis, you'll want to keep your shields at about the twenty percent level. Maybe raise them to fifty percent when you walk into a party or a big gathering, then gradually lower them as you relax. Just remember, alcohol and pot accelerate how much you relax, and that means they accelerate the lowering of your shields."

"OK, no worries on those two right now," Ren thought.

He had his shields raised as much as he could, focusing on the opacity concept. Stopped now, in the middle of the street, he visualized sliding that opacity counter down...ninety percent...sixty percent...forty percent...down to twenty percent. His vision and perception of his surroundings was unchanged. Others' perception of him, however...

"Ren! Ren Alciatore! Hey, Ren!"

The voice came from the other side of the intersection, on the neutral ground side. A man about his age called to him, waving at Ren when he saw where the speaker was. Ren smiled, waved, and walked over to that part of the barricade.

"Tommy Gandolfi, how the hell are you?" Ren said, shaking the other man's hand.

"Doing great, doing great! Haven't seen you in a while. You still doing photography?" The other man was about 5'8", and wore a red polo shirt that said "Brother Martin Band".

"Sure am! How 'bout you, still doing the law thing?"

"Yup! Working for myself, for a while, though, now that my boy's in high school. It makes me more flexible to help out with carpool and to see him play at games and such," Tommy said.

"Fantastic! Well, y'all have fun today, I'm walking around to see who I haven't seen in ages. Take care, Tommy!"

The two men shook hands again, and Ren continued his walk.

"Wow!"

Ren encountered several other folks he knew on Orleans Avenue, before even getting to N. Carrollton Avenue. Turning onto that street, he raised his shields again. His regular neighborhood coffee shop was just a block away, so there would be a number of people who would recognize him. He made it past the coffee shop and all the way to the train tracks at St. Louis Street, with nobody noticing him!

Four blocks to Canal Street ... he lowered his shields there, waving to the occasional acquaintance who called out to him, then seven blocks down Canal, to Jefferson Davis Parkway, where he suddenly felt lightheaded. Knowing he'd extended his Talents during the walk, Ren decided it was time to get out of the crowd. He turned off the parade route at Jeff Davis, heading down that street, back to the head of Bayou St. John.

Walking along the bayou would allow him to use the water's energy to re-charge. The waterway was once very important to the city, connecting Lake Pontchartrain to the early neighborhoods by the river. The bayou always ended here, where Ren stood, in Mid City. The Spanish government, financed by Creole merchants, built a navigation canal that ran from just north of the French Quarter, up to the beginning of the Bayou. Small boats, oyster luggers, barges, and other craft could then move from Faubourg Treme, and the turning basin on Basin Street, up to the end of the canal, then north to the lake via the bayou.

The canal was closed in 1927. Other, larger canals handled shipping traffic. The bayou became a sleepy place, whose water flowed up and out of the city. Its banks were the scenes of Voodoo rituals, some led by the famous "Voodoo Queen", Marie Laveau. The area became a place of power. Ren took a deep breath, pulling that power in, feeling it rejuvenate him. The sounds from the parade, even though they were some blocks away, grounded Ren once again, and he made his way up the bayou, and home.

Come over here to this party for a bit, if you can. Some people you should meet.

The invitation came from Michael Aloysius O'Donnell. A Google Maps link appeared next, showing a house on Bungalow Court, not even half a mile from his house. He checked his phone. It was just past 10pm; the parade crowds would be long gone by now.

Sure, I'll be there in a few minutes. I'm going to walk.

A thumbs-up followed as a reply.

Renard Alciatore locked up his house on Moss Street, along Bayou St. John, and headed around the corner to N. Carrollton Avenue. He usually walked at a brisk pace, so he made it over to the party in about ten minutes. After pausing for a moment to collect his thoughts and raise his psychic shields, he rang the doorbell. A woman in her late thirties opened the door.

"Hi, I'm ... "

"You're Mike's friend Ren, no doubt. Unless you're a cop. Or, you're Mike's friend, Ren the Cop. I'm Tara, nice to meet you!" She welcomed Ren in with a smile.

As soon as Ren crossed the threshold he felt a psychic bump against his shields. He paused just after entering the house and closing the door.

"You're among friends, Ren," Tara said softly.

Ren smiled, and then followed her through the house to the den. There were five people sitting around, watching and listening to a short, dark-haired woman pace around as she spoke.

"Mind you, I don't dislike 'char-grilled oysters', I just find them a bit lacking. It's just an excuse to sop up butter on the french bread they give you with them at Katie's."

"Oh, but the garlic makes them wonderful!" One of the men added.

"Try the Oysters Foch at Antoine's sometime. They even do them as a po-boy at the Hermes Bar, also. Less ceremony. Fried in a cornmeal batter, and the sauce is to die for," Ren said, as he stood on the edge of the room.

The woman in the middle of the room paused for a moment, taking in Ren from head to toe.

"That sounds absolutely wonderful!" She exclaimed.

"Ren! I'm glad you could come over. Everyone, this is Renard Alciatore. Call him Ren, and please make him feel at home!" Mike O'Donnell made the introductions as others waved or saluted with their beer cans or glasses. Mike stood to greet him properly.

"Ren, this woman who talks too much is Mary Margaret FitzRyan, 'Meg' to her friends, and I'm sure you'll be counted in that number soon. I'm actually surprised she doesn't know about Oysters Foch, since she lives, what, three blocks from your family's restaurant," Mike chuckled.

"Bite me, your Excellency!" Meg retorted.

"I'm merely a Monsignor, so I'm a 'Right Reverend', not an 'Excellency'. But I am excellent in many ways," Mike said, blowing her a kiss.

"The man is incorrigible!" Meg laughed.

"Speak for yourself, La Strega!" Mike replied, with a bow.

"In case you don't follow that reference, Ren, I'm part of a Wiccan coven that gathers at my shop in the Quarter. You'll have to come over and hang out sometime. In the meantime, beer on the patio, whiskey in the kitchen!" Meg said, smiling in such a way as to disarm any concerns Ren may have had with Wicca.

Ren smiled, gave Meg a half bow, and made his way into the kitchen. On one side of the counter were a number of bottles of top-shelf vodka, tequila, a couple of rums, Jameson, and The MacAllan. On the opposite side's counter was a Bushmills 21, The MacAllan 18, Chinaco Anejo tequila, and a bottle of The Balvenie he'd never seen before, "Caribbean Cask". Clearly, these came out after most of the guests of the day's parade party departed.

"Try some of The Balvenie that's out there on the counter, Ren. It's aged in rum barrels...interesting!" Mike called from the den.

Ren agreed, and poured two fingers from that bottle. He took a sip, sighed, and lowered his shields to a more "friendly" level as he returned to the den. One of the men who had been seated on the couch was standing to greet him.

"Leave it to the priest to suggest somebody else's good booze to others! I'm Fabian Rodrigue. You met my wife, Tara, at the door. Mike's told us a bit about you, Ren. The story of last Samhain ... incredible! We'd all love to hear about it," his host said.

"Wow, let me finish two of these, and I'll tell you anything you want to know!" Ren laughed, returning Fabian's firm handshake.

Another sip of the whiskey helped settle his anxiety. Ren had spent the day in relative anonymity, walking along the route of the Krewe of Endymion, before the 4pm start of the parade. Ren didn't expect the level of personal scrutiny he now faced, surrounded by Mike's friends. Clearly they were more than just passing acquaintances, given Fabian's reference to his duel in Metairie Cemetery last Halloween. Even though he trusted Mike totally, he didn't quite know how to react to this situation. Whiskey was the perfect prescription for inhibitions.

"Y'all are overwhelming the man! Let him sit down and he can talk dirty to me about oysters some more," Meg said.

Ren did just that, explaining his connection to the restaurant to the group, which included additional couple, McCoy Donaldson, a librarian and local writer, and his husband, Chuck Riley, a computer specialist. The conversation turned into a general one about old-line New Orleans restaurants in general. Fabian poured another two fingers of The Balvenie into Ren's glass as they chatted. Tara caught his eye as her husband poured the whiskey, winking at Ren, and then waving her right hand above her head, casually.

Ren blinked twice, as the room's occupants each appeared to emit a slight glow.

"Lower your shields a bit more, Ren," Tara encouraged.

He did as she suggested, and was startled by just how much more he could "see" of the others in the room!

Tara's lavender aura surrounded her, as she sat down next to Chuck on the couch. Only now did Ren notice her brown hair, with a touch of blonde highlighting. She wore a green t-shirt that said "Sidewalk Side", a reference to watching Carnival parades, over black leggings. Chuck, the man next to her, wore loose-fitting cargo pants and a New Orleans Pelicans shirt. His aura was royal blue, slightly muted. McCoy, also casually dressed for a day of parade-drinking, had a muted red aura. Fabian's aura was the same shade of blue as his jeans, and Meg was surrounded by a golden glow. The white aura of a Teacher engulfed Mike, when Ren looked his way, using his inner Sight.

Those still sitting began to stand. Tara helped him up, leading him into the dining room, where she sat him down in between Meg and McCoy.

"OK, Ren, the plan is for everyone to join hands and set up a common link. This is something you've done with Mike many times, but now we're going to extend it to include all seven of us. Just relax, pick up on what McCoy passes to you, then pass it on to me," Meg instructed.

Ren nodded.

"Just breathe deeply ... lower your shields even more ...

don't worry, Tara raised the house wards, and you're among friends ... that's it, just relax ... " Meg encouraged Ren as she nodded to the others to join the link. They did so, easily slipping into a rapport with Meg and Ren. When she was content with Ren's position in the link, she nudged Mike with her elbow, indicating to him to send a thought or visual around the link to test it. Mike stared at her breasts, then sent the image to Fabian, sitting on his left. He chuckled, passing the image to Chuck, who sent it to Tara. She passed it to McCoy, who also giggled, passing it to Ren, who sent it to Meg without a word.

"Asshole," Meg sent across the link, while looking pointedly at Mike, then continued.

"OK, now that we're all in, Ren, please show us what happened on Samhain..."

An hour later, Ren was back on the couch in the den, with another glass of The Balvenie in hand. Showing the group the events of last Samhain took about fifteen minutes. They all stayed at the table, but closed from the psychic link, for about ten minutes, absorbing the impressions Ren sent. Meg then gave everyone a "nudge", and they all shared some of their reactions. After going around the table, they released the link, each person raising their shields back to a relaxed by aware level.

Ren wasn't the only one who went for more booze when they returned to the den.

"I have to admit, Ren, I'm a bit jealous that you've had contact with an angel. That power rush must have been incredible!" McCoy said, wistfully.

"Yeah, it was. I wish the circumstances would've been a little less hostile, though," Ren replied, with a grin.

"Me too. To this day, I'm still not quite sure what to make of that being. I know she pretty much saved Ren's ass during the duel, but I don't even want to begin to speculate on the motives of an angelic being. This shit's going to bug me for a while," Mike stated.

"Well, what we do know is that Ren was on the winning side of someone's agenda on that one. I'm good with that. We all should be cautious, though, if we've become the interest of beings with that much power," Meg warned.

Ren started to say something, but was overtaken by a huge yawn before the words came out.

"OK, that's all for me," he chuckled, as he stood up.

Meg stood as well, looking him in the eye.

"I don't think it's a good idea for you to walk home alone, even if it's a few blocks. Mind if I crash at your place? I was going to spend the night here with Fabian and Tara, but someone should walk you home," she suggested.

Before coming over to Fabian and Tara's home, such a proposal from a woman would seem incredibly forward to Ren. After an hour linked to the minds of the other six in the room, he felt like they were old friends, and this was no big deal at all. He yawned a second time, nodding to Meg that this should be the plan.

They said their goodbyes and walked back up N. Carrollton Avenue to the bayou.

"It's difficult for me to buy into the notion of Christianity as a 'goddess religion'", Ren said.

"Stop and think for a minute. Our Lady of Prompt Succor. Our Lady of Perpetual Help. Multiple churches, here in New Orleans alone, named St. Mary's. There's as many places to worship the woman as there are for the man!" Meg countered.

They were sitting in the corner of 'Wakin' Bakin', in Mid City. After an uneventful night at Ren's house, the two woke up surprisingly early. Ren had expected this, one of his favorite restaurants for breakfast, to be crowded on Sunday morning, but the aftermath of the Endymion celebration clearly kept the neighborhood in bed.

"OK, but look at St. Mary's Assumption. The altar is all about the 'Crowning of Mary', but look who is above her, God the Father, and God the Son."

Meg snorted and sipped her coffee.

"Yeah, but nobody cares! Consider the size of the statue of Mary, she's a goddess!"

"Still not really buying it. After all, Christianity is a patriarchal religion. Why go through so much trouble to include women?" Ren asked.

"That's simple. Christianity wasn't ever a 'native' religion. Wherever it took root, it had to supplant something before it. In the Middle East, Judaism was there first. In Greece, then Rome itself, you had extensive pantheons of gods and goddesses. Concessions had to be made to Christian theology so they could fit in. Sure, there came a time when rulers would issue proclamations demanding everyone follow their Christ, but underneath that, the people had their goddesses, along with their gods. It was easy to replace the god-forms with the White Christ, but what about the goddesses? They couldn't just be tossed out into the street. These grits are good, by the way," Meg said, digging into her breakfast bowl.

"But Christianity, like Judaism, all but makes women into second class citizens. Why the need for a goddess?" Ren was still skeptical.

"That's where the 'virgin birth' comes in. Women bad, Mary special. As if no experience with sex is a good thing," Meg chuckled.

"Ah, OK, the Mother of Christ versus the Magdalene. I get that. Personally, I'm OK with the deity being female. I used to like how Father Greeley would refer to God as 'her' in his novels," Ren replied.

“You’ve read the Blackie Ryan stories? I LOVE THOSE!” Meg exclaimed, almost louder than Lady Gaga singing “Poker Face” in the coffee shop.

“Yes! I’ve read them all. It broke my heart when he passed away. I wanted to see Bishop Blackie take over Chicago,” he said, smiling.

“Pfft, he already had by the last story. Greeley was a master of the ‘locked room’ mystery. And he was quite a reasonable guy, for a Catholic priest,” she grinned.

“Ha, we know at least one other ‘reasonable’ priest,” Ren pointed out.

“That annoyance! He’s a pain in my ass, sometimes.”

They both laughed at that.

“Seriously, though, there are more common elements between Christianity and Wicca than either group would care to admit. And I do mean both groups on that. There are traditionalists in Pagan/neo-Pagan groups who are just as adamant about not want to have anything to do with Christianity as there are Christians who reject any connection to other religions," Meg stated.

"I want to understand this more, but it's as if I have a mental block," Ren said.

"I call that the 'Catholic box'. It's not hard to open. We'll work on that as we go along. In the meantime, I need more of this wonderful coffee!" Meg said, standing to walk over to the coffee pots.

www.ingramcontent.com/pod-product-compliance
Lightning Source LLC
Chambersburg PA
CBHW061314170626
46817CB00001B/176